IN THE LAND OF
THE YELLOWSTONE

Mac took off for the mountains. He'd always loved the fields and the forests, and the crafted beauty of his gun. Mountain men came into his father and uncle's store on Fourth Street, full of stories, looking wild as Injuns, and smelling that way, too. As a lad, Mac had even seen painted Indians on the streets of St. Louis.

To him, like his dad, the mercantile business was tedium—the mountains were romance. Now, he would do mountain mercantile as a trader.

Of course, Mac had no money to start a trading post. No wherewithal to buy blankets, knives, kettles, beads, tobacco, coffee, lead, guns, and whiskey to trade for hides. He would need five thousand dollars, or more likely ten thousand, for a modest outfit.

On the sentinel rock above the Yellowstone he swung his legs exuberantly. The mere lack of money didn't matter to him now—he had an idea, an answer. He could stay in the mountains.

The image of Annemarie rose in his mind. Stay in the mountains, he was saying to himself, and have Annemarie. . . .

The Yellowstone

Winfred Blevins

BANTAM BOOKS

NEW YORK • TORONTO • LONDON • SYDNEY • AUCKLAND

THE YELLOWSTONE

A Bantam Domain Book / September 1988

DOMAIN *and the portrayal of a boxed "d" are trademarks of Bantam Books,
a division of Bantam Doubleday Dell Publishing Group, Inc.*

ISBN 0-553-27401-5

Published simultaneously in the United States and Canada

---

*Bantam Books are published by Bantam Books, a division of Bantam Doub
day Dell Publishing Group, Inc. Its trademark, consisting of the words "Bant
Books" and the portrayal of a rooster, is Registered in U.S. Patent and Tradem
Office and in other countries. Marca Registrada. Bantam Books, 666 Fi
Avenue, New York, New York 10103.*

PRINTED IN THE UNITED STATES OF AMERICA

OPM   14   13   12   11   10   9   8   7   6   5

In thanks for the love she has given me for a lifetime, this book is dedicated to my mother, Hazel Dickson Blevins.

Lots of hands go into the writing of a book, particularly a book about other times and other cultures. I thank four colleagues and friends especially for their guidance in writing this one: Richard S. Wheeler of Big Timber, Montana; Murphy Fox of Helena, Montana; Linda Hasselstrom of Hermosa, South Dakota; and Judge Clyde M. Hall of the Shoshone-Bannock Reservation at Fort Hall, Idaho.

≈ PROLOGUE: THE RIVER ≈

The man knew little about the river, but he knew he loved it.

He stood deep in the yellow-walled canyon, the river at his feet. From the rim it looked like a silver-green ribbon, remote, a fantasy. Down here the river flowed up to the lip of rock and, in seamless grace and faith, bolted out into the empty air. Here it was roaring, churning, raw power.

Where it collided with the earth, several hundred feet below, the water chameleoned into spray and leapt back up the canyon, making the yellow walls glisten.

The man, a beaver trapper named Mac, looked at the river, and heard its roar, and felt its foam on his face. He bent a knee to drink its sweetness. Then he felt a temptation: Lie down upon the earth—you're alone—no one will think you a fool. Sheepishly, he did. And there, through dirt and rock, he felt the elemental force of the cascade, he quivered to the surging of the earth's blood.

He sat all afternoon by the great waterfall, staring, taking it in. It was a foolish thing to do, for he ought to have been hunting.

He was hungry. More than a week ago this very young man and his companions came through Two Ocean Pass, a place where one stream actually divided toward the Atlantic and Pacific oceans. Then they descended into the land of boiling waters. Cursed country, their leader called it. Yet it was the most beautiful country the young man had ever seen.

Soon they camped east of the great lake formed by the great river, the Yellowstone. There the young man, a beginner at the craft of trapping beaver, a pilgrim in the mountains, rode out alone exploring. And got lost.

Lost! A pilgrim a thousand miles from civilization, and lost!

The next day he spent riding in circles on the high ridges, looking for camp. But he could not even see the great lake. The day after that the clouds dumped a foot of snow—it was September—and turned land and sky into a trackless sea. That was when he began to think that he was going to die.

Yet he was not so discontent to die in this fairyland. He went exploring, half hunting hopelessly for his companions, half sight-seeing in this amazing place. He chewed what jerked meat he had. He kept an eye out for elk— might as well die on a full stomach—and with mystic awe he beheld the wonders about him. Not cursed, he thought—enchanted.

Perhaps it was enchantment that came to him on the third night after the snowstorm. The young man was building a fire by a hot spring, where the ground was bare of snow. He looked up from his labor with flint and steel and saw an Indian at the edge of the clearing. The Indian was simply standing there, unmoving, evidently at ease, the carcass of a bighorn sheep slung over his shoulder.

It seemed a fairy tale. Or maybe the Indian was an apparition. The young man beckoned him to the fire. The Indian came. He stayed. They cooked and ate. The young man, hungry, ate greedily.

The Indian apparently had no horses. The young man supposed he was a member of the wild tribe that lived in these high mountains, called Sheep Eaters by the other Indians. Sheep Eaters were so poor they lived without horses and without guns, and kept to inaccessible mountains. The Indian said nothing. He acted neither friendly nor unfriendly. He did not respond to the young man's attempts at sign language. When both men were satisfied, they slept. The young man felt trusting of the Indian as a child in an innocent dream. The next morning the Indian was gone, with the sheep.

Since he was young, scarcely more than a boy, the trapper did not know what in this country was mundane and what was miraculous. So he accepted the appearance and disappearance of the Indian equably, and set out looking for other wonders. The notion of death was strangely unreal to him. But if he was to die, he wanted to die full of miracles.

It seemed to him that the greatest of the miracles was the river, the Yellowstone, because it was exceedingly beautiful.

He had seen it further down, in the big valley it cut on the plains north of this mountainous plateau. There the Frenchmen, the first white men to see it, named it Roche Jaune, Yellow Stone, for its ocher rimrock. There lived the Indian tribes to whom it was now home, Crows, Blackfeet, Cheyennes, Sioux, and Assiniboin. They called it Elk River.

He had also seen the Yellowstone above its lake, where rivulets and creeks formed a slow-moving stream that coiled its way through marshy meadows surrounded by high ethereal peaks.

He had seen the lake, huge, cold-watered, unimaginably blue, home to gulls, bald eagles, ospreys, and even to pelicans. It was a marvelous lake, full of cutthroat trout, and bordered by the strange hot springs. The young man had heard old Gabe Bridger boast that in Yellowstone Lake you could catch a trout in one cast, and cook it in a hot spring on the way out. As with the other miracles, the young man believed.

Now the young man saw the river's huge canyon. He stood by its majestic lower waterfall, and the lovely upper one. He saw the elfin sprays of water that joined the great river in the canyon. He saw the rapids and in imagination felt their furious force. He was consumed by the desire to follow the river forever, to see all that he could, to come to know it as a lover.

He did not know its past. Did not know about the hunting people who lived along it twelve thousand years ago, feeding on the mammoth and the giant bison. He did not know about the millennia this verdant country spent as an arid plain, a veldt, when the game and the hunters left, and gathering peoples replaced them.

He was barely aware of its present. He had seen the

people who lived along the river now, both the shy Sheep Eaters of the high mountains and the tribes of the buffalo plains. He knew that the river was a throbbing artery that moved these peoples up and down in their boats, and an artery as well for the trappers, who used it to float their furs down the Yellowstone to the Missouri, and down the Missouri to St. Louis, a world away.

He imagined that one day steamboats would work their way up the Yellowstone, along its many miles as a majestic plains river. But they would never ply the river after it neared the mountains, after it became unpredictable and turbulent. They would never come here.

Standing by the great lower fall, the young man mused that to see the entire river, he must stay alive. And to stay alive he must hunt and eat—hunting was easy in this blessed Yellowstone country. He gave thought to rejoining his companions eventually—they would be at winter camp, at the mouth of Clarks Fork, two months from now. He decided to take the long way to the Clarks Fork, to follow the great river along its twisty, mountainous route. If he lived. And now he knew he would live.

He wanted to see all the creeks and rivers that braided together to make the single, mighty stream. He wanted to know all the personalities of the river, its places swift and slow, clear and murky, trickling and thundering; its many colors, the blue of the sky, the greens, the subtly varied browns, the reds over certain bottoms or in certain lights, the white in its rapids and falls; its bottoms of rock, gravel, weed, muck, and sand. He wanted to walk along its banks and step to the river at many spots and put a hand in, or a foot, and feel the river's energy, its downhill movement, its suction, its electric, restless, irresistible current.

The young man got to his feet and looked back up the wall of the canyon where he had climbed down. A long, hard way, and harder going back up. He told himself it was time to stop being a romantic for a while, and become a hunter. And survive.

≈ **BOOK ONE** ≈

≈ 1 ≈

June, 1843, Moon when the horses get fat

"Boys," cried Skinhead, "I say the beaver that acts drunk, is drunk." The fat man swigged deep from the water jug and pranced around the fire. Bald skull gleaming in the twilight, he leaned back and kicked his legs high in a strut. Then he started adding his own music to dance to. He flapped his elbows against his ribs and bawled an unmusical drone—Skinhead's imitation of bagpipes, intended to be funny.

Well, what the hell. Mac Maclean did have reason to get drunk. It was his twenty-fourth birthday. The outfit was plumb out of whiskey. It was nearly out of powder, lead, and the other necessities of life, not to mention beads, cloth, and tobacco. Besides, this bagpiping sounded like a goosed mule wailing.

So Mac grabbed the jug of unblended, twelve-minute-old crick water. "To twenty-four," he hollered, and swigged deep.

He imagined a gigue tune over Skinhead's awful drone and stepped it out. The Indians didn't call him Dancer for nothing. Mac loved to dance, and he had the knack for it. The girls in St. Louis used to flirt with him boldly because he had a reputation as a dancer. What would they think of him now, a civilization away from St. Louis, broke, dirty, smelly, and pretending to be drunk on crick water?

He did feel a little giddy. It was true—if you pretended to be drunk, you felt drunk. "Twenty-*four*," Mac roared, "and an aimless wanderer on the empty, barren plains of the West, among the benighted savages."

Til, Skinhead's nephew, took the jug, drank, and echoed, "Twenty-four!"

Jim Sykes, the Indian, made his usual mocking sign for talking too much, fingers tapping thumb rapidly, and joined Mac in the dance. Jim was agile and could pick up a step with casual ease that Mac had worked to learn. "Here dances Robert Burns Maclean, a Scot," Mac cried out. A Scot all right, red-haired, fair-skinned, slight of frame, and boyishly appealing. The two of them jigged to Skinhead's ridiculous music. "A thousand miles from civilization," hollered Mac. "Dressed in rags. Indifferently mounted. Partnered up with three villains." This last was sort of true. "Far from the succor of white women." Indian women aplenty, and for any purpose, but no white women. "Devoted to a dying craft, the pursuit of the wily beaver." Poetically put, but factual. "Afflicted equally with lice and mad fantasies of freedom. And broke—thoroughly, disgustingly, heartbreakingly broke."

"Give us a song," urged Jim, still sticking with Mac's steps. A Delaware, Jim had a strange, soft, singsong voice, like a saw blade fiddled. Mac obbligatoed a song over Skinhead's drone. And he noticed Til had his Jew's harp out, twanging away.

Skinhead looked out toward the horses—a mountaineer's habit. They were picketed not ten yards away, beside the single bale of furs.

A raggle-taggle band of trappers, beaten-down, worn-out. Mac was thin and hard as outhouse boards. Scraggly sons of bitches, too, everything but Skinhead's bald pate needing a shave. Their buckskins were holey and black with dirt—they wouldn't last another season.

Might as well dance, thought Mac. In fact, in the last of the pale twilight of a soft June day in the north country, he felt melancholy. Well and good to roam. Well and good to be free, owe no one, promise no one. Well and good to follow the beaver and the buffalo. But these men were on the spot, worried about getting to Fort Mackenzie without powder and lead. "If the Blackfeet attack," Skinhead said, "we'll have to beat the niggers off with wiping sticks." Might as well dance.

Skinhead handed Mac the jug. "Drink up, coon. On your birthday you gotta have some fun, whether you want to or not." Skinhead raised his own cup. "To crazy good times. Act drunk and you'll feel drunk."

Mac cut loose. His body swayed like grass in the wind. He was dancing till the moon shone high, dancing till the sun came up, dancing until the end of time. It was idiotic, but it was fun.

"This child loves whiskey," cried Skinhead. Maybe this was the best way to get drunk, thought Mac. No hangover.

Skinhead suddenly switched to a boatman's ditty. He knew plenty of those, and they suited his style better. Mac and Jim went right along.

Mac noticed the horses stirring—all the noise sure didn't calm them—but he didn't care. That's what picket pins were for.

Skinhead switched songs again, motioning that he wanted to strut alone. It was a drinking song this time. He thumped his cup into his hand and danced a drunken stomp.

"Whiskey-y-y-y," he roared, head thrown back, face to the sky. He reached down, picked up his rawhide rope, and began to march, bellowing out the beat and swirling that rope out in front. Skinhead had put in some time out among the Californios and could make a rope do tricks. He marched straight away, toward the horses. Mac was afraid he might scare them.

Skinhead, getting fancy, lowered the whirling loop to knee-high and kicked his feet through by turns. Then he sent the loop straight into the sky.

Suddenly—what the hell?—the rope snaked out ten yards into the dark. Mac heard nasty words in the Blackfoot language.

"Hey, beavers," called Skinhead, "look what I got."

Something dragged on the end of Skinhead's rope, bouncing roughly toward the fire. A human shape. A Blackfoot. A very mortified Blackfoot.

"Boys," crowed Skinhead, "I done roped us a Magpie. Magpie is an old friend, and he loves horses. Particular this child's horses."

2

Every man stood hangdog still, looking disagreeable.

Mac and Jim were irked at Skinhead for his stunt—if he heard someone out by the horses, why didn't he let everyone know, instead of going off solo?

Til was miffed because he had to hold the wiping stick through the thongs that bound Magpie's hands and twist them if Skinhead felt ornery.

Magpie looked disagreeable because Til was hurting him.

Skinhead was mad because his partners wouldn't shoot at the damned Blackfoot.

It seemed that Magpie was an old enemy of Skinhead's. A Blood, which was a kind of Blackfoot. Seemed the Indian once got drunk and traded Skinhead his wife for the night. When the whiskey ran out early, Magpie sought out the two of them and kicked Skinhead right out of the saddle and took back the woman, and Skinhead's pants and moccasins and knife and pistol besides.

Mac gathered that there had been a couple of other episodes of enmity since then. A friendly, edgy, show-the-other-bastard-up enmity.

"This child don't want to kill the nigger," said Skinhead. "Just torment him for his insolence."

Trying to run off the horses in the twilight was pretty insolent, thought Mac. And the bastard nearly pulled it off, which would have left the four trappers really gut-busted.

So Skinhead proposed that they let Magpie run and shoot at his feet. Just to teach him.

"Nix," said Jim.

"We ain't gonna waste ammunition on this," said Mac. Even Til shook his head. The outfit was low on powder and low on lead balls—Skinhead was completely out of balls for his .39-caliber. "And no way we can let him go now that he knows we're short on shooting materials."

"Bastard's got no English," answered Skinhead.

"Use your Green River," said Jim.

"No sport in killing him," snapped Skinhead, going into a sulk. Then a wicked smile curled the corners of his mouth. He began to chuckle. "I'll shoot the son of a bitch with that." He grabbed for the wiping stick.

Til let go and jumped back. The wiping stick was pushed through the whangs binding Magpie's hands. Til was half afraid of his uncle Skinhead when he got crazy like this.

Mac and Jim looked exasperatedly at each other. Skinhead gave the stick a little twist out of meanness and pushed the Blood to the ground backward. The Indian's face was frozen in stony indifference. Mac admired that.

"Not your wiping stick!" Mac exclaimed, sort of tickled. A good hickory wiping stick would cost plenty at the fort, and Skinhead didn't have enough to trade for powder and lead. But the fat man would do anything in one of his tirades.

Skinhead had the stick out.

"Just shoot a patch," said Jim softly. "Scare him to death." Jim has clever ideas, thought Mac. The wadding that went behind the ball would shoot all right, but it wouldn't penetrate.

But Skinhead was having a good old time now. He measured powder into his flintlock and jammed some patches down on top of it, then the wiping stick. It jutted out like a finger.

"Magpie, you son of a whore, you wiper of babies' bottoms, this child is going to let you run for your life."

Skinhead cut Magpie's bonds with his patch knife and backed off.

Mac had to admit it was an ingenious solution: sport without cruelty.

Magpie finished rubbing his hands and reached for his knife, tomahawk, and musket on the ground.

"A-a-a," Skinhead said nasally, like scolding a cat.

The Indian stood up and waited.

"Start running, you son of a bitch," Skinhead ordered.

Magpie didn't move. Mac thought his eyes were glinting

a little—maybe the Blackfoot knew what Skinhead had said.

"Run!" Skinhead thundered. He did a little pantomime of running and lost his broad-brimmed hat. His scalp gleamed in the twilight.

Magpie didn't move.

Skinhead set the butt of his flinter on the ground and made signs. Magpie nodded. He made signs back, smiling a little. Mac read something about Skinhead's father and an unnatural act with a horse. Skinhead glared and motioned him off, fast.

The Indian started trotting. Twenty yards off he turned it into a skip, then he put in a crazy sideways jump. Fifty yards out he did a cartwheel and some gyrating dance steps.

"Show-off bastard, ain't he?" said Mac.

"This child has changed his mind," said Skinhead. "I'm gonna shoot him center."

"Wagh!" grunted Jim in approval.

Skinhead held on Magpie. Now the Indian was swooping, arms out, floating to the ground. Magpie's signature dance, a magpie. Skinhead's muzzle followed him back and forth, steady.

Flint struck, spark jumped, and white smoke belched. Mac caught a glimpse of something far beyond Magpie, sailing up like a spear, glinting in the last of the light.

"Keep your head down, Lord," bellowed Skinhead.

Magpie turned and made some signs. Too far to read. Mac raised his own rifle to his shoulder and leveled.

"Shoot him," said Skinhead. "He's my birthday present to you."

Mac shook his head. The Indian started trotting off.

"Even the damn Blackfeet ain't worth killing anymore," Skinhead muttered.

Moon when the horses get fat

"You got any ideas," Mac asked Jim in the morning as they were loading the pack horses, "about how to get supplies with nothing to trade?"

Jim shook his head. "Wise Delaware saying," Jim singsonged. "Sufficient unto the day are the troubles thereof." Jim had been raised by a missionary family named Sykes. People saw his skin color and got expectations. He liked to play with that.

Mac knew Skinhead didn't have any ideas, not any serious ones.

So how were they going to get outfitted for next season? Mac didn't even have the beaver pelts (they called them plews) to pay for last year's stake. The clerk of the fort surely wouldn't extend them more credit. Snobby Mr. Horne, with his plummy accent and his "mistering" and his amused eyes and curling mouth. What Mr. Horne is going to advance me, thought Mac, is a pound of mockery and a plug of humiliation.

Not that Mr. Horne had anything to be snooty about. Fort Mackenzie was no Fort Union, where Assiniboin concubines dressed in the latest St. Louis fashions. Much less Fort Laramie, rich from the trade of the Sioux. Or Bent's Fort on the Arkansas, where William Bent had a cellar of wines that would make old Chouteau proud. Mr. Horne's place of business, Fort Mackenzie, six miles up the Marias from the Missouri, was miserable, out of the way, cramped, and had little to trade, now that the Blackfeet were poor.

Mac Maclean was twenty-four years old and new to the

Shining Mountains. Here he'd lived the time of his life,
and he was afraid it was over.

2

That was Skinhead's theme those days—the Indians
have gone to hell, the country has gone to hell, the life has
gone to hell. But none of that seemed to keep Skinhead
from having a high old time.

The Indians were gone to hell—the Blackfeet were
decimated by smallpox six years ago. Lucky for these four
trappers. Now you had a reasonable chance of getting
across Blackfoot country alive.

Mac tugged his hat down against the glare of the sun.
They were riding slowly in a string across the plains of the
basin of the Judith River, leading the pack horses. The
animals' heads were down, they were nose to tail, their
tails swishing—it was hot and dry and fly season.

Skinhead irked Mac, though, when he sounded off
about how miserable everything was. Skinhead had been
in the mountains twenty years—he was once an Ashley
man. Mac had been riding and trapping the Rockies for
only three years and was crazy about the life. He thought
Skinhead, properly George Gant, was in love with the
sound of his own grumble.

Mac kept his eyes moving, gazing across the rolling
hills, the slopes deep in green grass. The life was shining,
but dangerous.

Til started humming behind Mac—some hymn. When
Til was supposed to be watchful, like now, he was off in a
dream world or half dozing. Maybe tetched. Sure did
weird things. All Mac liked about Til was his talk. This
morning he had described Skinhead's shooting the wiping
stick as "profligate," a word Mac had never heard outside
of church. But if Til weren't Skinhead's nephew. . .

It was true, though, that Mac felt protective of Til.
Everyone did. The village slow-wit, maybe, but *our* vil-

lage slow-wit. Bucktoothed, boyish, likable Til. If only he
would trap with someone else.

Mac rode into deeper, greener grass, and it brushed his
stirrups. He loved the smell of the grass. Grass fed the
buffalo, and the buffalo were the wealth of the Indians.

The wealth of the fur trappers was beaver. Mac snorted.
The price of beaver had hit the bottom of the well and
busted. Besides that, the trappers had no plews to sell.
Funny as getting both your ears clapped at once.

Mac could hear Skinhead's wail again: "This country is
trapped out."

Maybe so. In March these four men trapped the cold,
swift creeks running into the Yellowstone River from the
great plateau to the south, the land of hot springs and
geysers. The take was poor. Now they'd worked the small,
nameless creeks of the Snowy Mountains and the Little
Belts that came into the Judith basin. Poor again.

Mac looked at his own two pack horses plodding along,
thought of the others, and heard Skinhead's dirge. Pitiful
beasts, bearing few possessions and few peltries.

"This child knows when he's at the end of his string,"
the fat man liked to say. "In '33, just ten year ago, we
marched this country in fur brigades fifty and a hundred
strong, too mighty even for the Blackfeet." The Blackfeet
liked to kill mountain men, and all the neighboring Indians
and anyone else they could find—everybody in the mountains, red and white, hated the Blackfeet, which meant
the whole Blackfeet confederation; Piegans, Bloods, Blackfeet
proper, and Gros Ventres.

"We filled the mountains with men. Now look at this
beaver," Skinhead would go on, "riding with two boys,"
meaning Mac and Til, "and an Injun." Though Skinhead
knew Jim was one sly, subtle Delaware.

Mac had heard it all a hundred times. Ten years ago
they would have gone to a rendezvous, a gaudy trade fair
with hundreds of trappers and thousands of Indians, a
rowdy, rip-roaring carnival of tests of skill, tomahawk-
throwing, shooting, card playing, and trick riding, spiced
with drinking, brawling, fornicating, and storytelling. Those
were shinin' times, beaver aplenty, and six dollars a pelt. A

beaver man was rich—he could afford whiskey, plenty of traps, powder and ball, horses, dalliances, even wives, if he had a mind.

In those days, if you didn't have plews to trade, why, the companies would give you all the credit you needed. Mountain men were rich, or would be next rendezvous.

These days, thought Mac, we're ruined and don't have sense enough to know it.

3

They camped in the bottoms along the Teton River, among the cottonwoods. Plenty of water, no fire. Til piped in his high, cracking voice to nobody in particular, "Sure wish we had some coffee." He was addicted to it, with heaps of sugar. Which cost two dollars a pint. They were all perched on deadfall, chewing pemmican.

Skinhead struggled up, pulled his breechcloth aside, and unceremoniously pissed in the dust. "This child is gonna quit," he declared. "He's gonna go to telling stories of wild Injuns in the St. Louis taverns for whiskey."

"All you're good for," Jim put in softly. "Tellin' stories." The small, slender man always talked as if he had meal in his mouth. Needling Skinhead was his favorite pastime.

Mac got up and started off into the twilight. He wanted to smoke his pipe and look about and do he knew not what. Alone. Skinhead would bluster a little at Jim, and Jim would needle gently, and Skinhead would end up telling stories again. Skinhead could seem a fool. Could play the fool. But he was mountain-wise and beaver-canny. Skinhead, who looked fifty, and Jim, who looked thirty, had ridden together twenty years, since the Ashley days.

But Mac had heard all the stories, tales of the cock-o'-the-walk times. Of General Ashley, the man who started it all. Of Jedediah Smith, a captain who wore his Bible leather as hard as his boot leather, but was respected, for all that. Of Hugh Glass, who survived the bear and the treachery of his companions with a griz-sized feat of courage. Of Tom Fitzpatrick, the small, sardonic Irishman with the hair of the bear in him. Of Jim Bridger, Skinhead's old brigade leader, always ready to fight or fornicate, and the savviest of all whites about Indian ways.

Now Smith was dead, killed by Comanches on the Cimarron. Glass got scalped on the frozen Yellowstone. Fitzpatrick was nursemaiding soldiers across the trail to Oregon—"explorers" who couldn't find their way to the outhouse, Skinhead said contemptuously. And Bridger had built a fort and turned trader. Old Gabe, a storekeeper.

Mac climbed a sandstone boulder and perched on top. He packed his pipe slowly, tamped it, lit it with a lucifer, a stick with sulphur on the end. Damned luxury, he thought— lucifers to make fire, but nothing to shoot with. He gave thought to Fort Mackenzie tomorrow. Still no ideas. You couldn't mount a fur hunt without DuPont and Galena, meaning black powder and lead for balls. You needed some tobacco, both to smoke and to trade, and various foofaraw for the Indians. Mac even needed to replace two traps.

This outfit was finished.

For the hundredth time Mac considered doing like other trappers—going back to St. Louis or on to Oregon. Or scouting for the Army. Or guiding wagon trains. But why tease yourself, lad? You're not going anywhere. This place has a hold on you.

He could hunt for Fort Mackenzie probably, or Fort Union. Keep the pork-eaters, people from the settlements, in decent Rocky Mountain meat. Cut and stack wood for the steamboat. But it sounded damned well like a job. And he would have to put up with Mr. Horne or Mr. Kipp, the Fort Union factor.

Maybe he should turn Injun. Live with the Cheyennes, where he had friends. Follow the buffalo. Steal horses. Fight the occasional fight for excitement. Live in a tipi, take a wife or two. Raise kids.

But he wouldn't be able to take a wife. He'd have to go to the Cheyennes poor. They'd make him welcome enough, Strikes Foot, Calling Eagle, and Lame Deer. But without a bride price he'd be a poor relation, living in another man's lodge. And he was not all the way comfortable with the way Calling Eagle was—strange

Mac wanted his own lodge. He could picture it easily in the circle of Cheyenne lodges; buffalo hides stitched together, smoke coming out the flaps, a tripod in front with a medicine bundle. He'd keep his family Bible in the bundle, among other things. He'd have good horses, some to travel on, a buffalo runner, and a war horse, plus pack animals. He'd get a good stud and breed horses—show the Cheyennes how to improve their stock. He'd go with his friends to steal Crow and Blackfoot horses and fight when necessary.

Maybe after a while he would get a scene of coup-striking painted on his lodge, to show how fine he'd done. Maybe after a while the lodge would be filled with children. And their mother, Annemarie.

He drew on his pipe and looked around through the lavender twilight. The cottony down from the cottonwoods floated and shimmered in the still evening air. He watched Jim walk over to check the horses' picket pins. Mac admired the small Indian. He reminded Mac of the way an otter moves, mincing, poised, with elegant control of each footpad. Skinhead called him in Cheyenne, Man Who Doesn't Stir Air in Front When He Walks.

Mac pulled on the pipe again and dreamily let Annemarie play in the pastures of his mind.

He remembered her performing on that pony of hers. She was a sizable girl, broad-shouldered and broad-hipped, and as tall as Mac, who was white-man average. Right now she might outweigh him. She had copper glints in her black hair, along with her name the only legacy of her father, old Charbonneau, the translator for Lewis and Clark on their big trip across to the Pacific. Seemed like Charbonneau left children in every tribe in the West.

On her pony, Annemarie was agile as a squirrel. She and her brothers and sisters and other kids had riding contests, hell for leather. Mac's favorite memory of her was putting those quail eggs of Calling Eagle's on a twist of sweetgrass. Annemarie cantered down on them, leaned

out of her woman's saddle, and picked up the tiny eggs
without breaking them.

Ah, but she was full of herself that evening.

It was that evening she gave him her pet name for him,
Green Eye. Most of the Cheyennes called him Dancer,
because he loved to kick up his heels.

He was staying with Strikes Foot's family for a few
days—Skinhead and Jim and Til were gone off somewhere.
She talked him into playing the hand game with her,
though her mother, Lame Deer, disapproved. The girl had
hardly anything to bet and was teasingly open about what
she meant to win from Mac, a whalebone hairbrush for her
fingertip-length hair.

She told the whole family merrily that she'd get that
brush, and whatever else Mac would put out on the
blanket. She would bet a strip of blue and yellow beadwork, and her porcupine-quill comb if she had to, and the
ermine tails she wrapped her braids in. To get that mirror
she'd even bet her dress, if she had to take it off and play
naked.

This quip shocked the family. Cheyenne girls were not
like Crows— they were chaste. Annemarie was tickled by
everyone's embarrassment, especially Mac's.

Mac felt roped into playing with her, but he had no
intention of letting her lose that dress. At first he did a
sloppy job of concealing the bone in one hand or the other
and let her win.

But she caught on and acted miffed. She felt lucky and
wanted really to win, she said. She claimed that when she
wanted to know which hand the bone was in, she only had
to look at his eyes. The blue eye was unreadable. But
when she started to touch either hand, the green eye told
her whether it was the one.

"Which hand, Green Eye?" she'd say teasingly, and
then choose—usually right.

Finally she egged him into putting the brush on the
blanket. She matched it with an awl. The first bet she lost
the awl. But then she won the brush and retired delighted. And never had to take off the dress.

That night, after they all bedded down in the lodge—his

feet were to Annemarie's—the smell of her seemed to fill
his nostrils. He thought of her young body under the
blankets and imagined how it would feel to touch it.

Lord, Mac told himself, hadn't he acted like the lovesick
boy that night! And him a grown man, experienced with
women.

He thought of speaking to Strikes Foot about her then.
He still thought of it, every day. But Mac didn't have the
necessary. He was worse than busted—he owed. The
damn company owned even the shirt he was wearing.

4

"Goddamn Br-ritishers," railed Skinhead, his voice echoing
through the Marias River valley. He might as well holler
here—there could be no danger this close to the fort.
"Goddamn John Bull. This nigger says they should use the
Union Jack to wipe their r-r-ruddy ar-r-rses. John Bull
oughta be outa this country, north to Hudson's Bay. They
take our plews and don't even know what way the stick
floats."

He was sounding off, Mac knew, because they were
getting close to the confrontation with Mackenzie's factor.
But Mac didn't rail like Skinhead. For one thing, Fort
Mackenzie was owned by the American Fur Company, not
the Hudson's Bay Company. For another, Mr. Horne was
Mac's countryman, and the accent Skinhead was mocking
was a Scots burr like Mac's. The fur trade was full of Scots.

Maybe Mr. Horne would give them enough to fend off
starvation. Surely he wouldn't turn white men out on the
plains to starve. Jim had spoken of simply taking what
they needed but it was idle talk.

What Mac wondered was, if Mr. Horne rebuffed them,
how were they to go on without powder and lead? Without
a loaded gun in the Rocky Mountains, if you didn't get
scalped, you'd starve.

Mac also wondered why there were no lodges here,
downriver from the fort. These bottoms were good camping—

plenty of water, handsome meadows. Usually there were
Blackfeet here, come to trade. Horse herds. Yelping dogs.
Raucous children. Now there wasn't even any sign.

They rounded a bend and saw the cultivated plots. Here
the fort provided its staff with a little corn, some parsnips,
beans, and even potatoes. The plots were overgrown with
weeds, the fences down, the vegetables trampled.

Skinhead glowered at Mac, as though it were his fault,
and kicked his horse to a lope. The four trappers clattered
along the river bottom and then up onto the bench above
the river.

Charred logs. Ashes. A blockhouse tilted onto its side.
Most of the palisade lying flat.

Down at the landing the boats were gone.

The trappers rode into the yard of the outpost of the
powerful American Fur Company. The fur press was taken
away. The rooms—council room, trading room, dining
room, quarters, lockup—were all destroyed. The smith's
gear was gone, water barrels gone, trade goods gone.

Skinhead, Mac, Jim, and Til, short of powder and ball,
were in a hell of a fix. A mockery more insidious than Mac
had imagined.

On the hot, dry breeze Mac heard a weird laugh.
Skinhead, cackling. And Til's high-pitched squeak, a parody of amusement. Even Jim was quietly shaking with
laughter.

Mac considered it—the great Pierre Chouteau and the
American Fur Company, their asses kicked back downriver.
That was worth being in a fix for. Mac joined in the
hooting and hollering.

It was an eerie, haunting sound, crazy. Jim opened his
dark, Indian arms, taking in all the destruction, the deso-
lation. He issued a mock-plummy cry, "Courtesy of the
Blackfoot nation."

"'At's right," said a grainy voice in English.

Magpie, from beside the tilted blockhouse. His musket
was steady on them. So the bugger did speak English.

The trappers said not a word. Seven Blackfeet stood
behind the fallen palisades, surrounding the trappers,

with guns on them. From this distance even muskets were deadly.

"You had no enough powder and balls shoot Magpie," the Blood said. "We have plenty. Off horses!"

The trappers looked at each other.

"Not worry—you don't shoot Magpie, we don't shoot you."

They swung slowly out of their saddles. Mac made up his mind to make a move. Dying by Blackfoot torture was unacceptable.

"Back away!" Magpie barked. Mac stayed within grabbing distance of his mount's reins, on the ground.

Magpie made a sharp gesture. One Blackfoot, a teenage boy, came forward and took the reins and lead ropes of Skinhead's horses and led them outside.

"Put down rifles!"

They all did. That left only their pistols. When the boy came to get his horses, Mac would grab the kid and use him as a shield. It wouldn't work, but he had to do something.

The Blackfeet were easing closer with their muskets, to twenty feet.

"Not be afraid, Skinhead and friends,"Magpie said unctuously, gloating. "We not kill you now."

Mac glanced sideways at Jim. The Delaware was still— too still. He was about to try something. Mac would be ready. He stepped sideways and put one moccasin on his mount's rein.

"Magpie know you come to Mackenzie. And know what happen to fort. White men cannot live without powder and ball," he sang sarcastically. "White men not Blackfoot hunters."

He drew himself up. "Today we leave you on prairie like Magpie yesterday. No food, no knife, no tomahawk, no gun." Now he barked, "Put down pistols!"

The trappers didn't make a move. Magpie nodded curtly at one of his companions.

Suddenly Mac heard the ugly *whuh!-whuh!* of a tomahawk spinning through the air. Til cried, *"Hunh!"* and jerked forward onto his face. The hawk was buried in his back to the handle.

"Put down pistols," repeated Magpie, "and you live! We leave you here!"

A short, ugly Blackfoot grabbed Til's hair, made a quick, circular cut around the crown, put his foot on Til's neck, and popped off the scalp with a *plock* sound. He turned the body over and started collecting Til's belongings.

Sick, Mac played along with Magpie. He set his gun in the dirt. Skinhead and Jim did the same. The boy led Mac's horses away.

From behind, an Indian kicked Jim down. Jim started to jump up and fight, but a muzzle on his belly kept him still. One Blackfoot stripped off Jim's hunting pouch, his hawk, and his knife while the other held the muzzle in his navel.

Mac put his own possessions on the ground. Skinhead did the same. In a moment everything they owned was gone.

Magpie glared at them, sneering, over the barrel of his musket. He cackled, "Is fair, huh, leave you like you left Magpie? One thing. Magpie Blackfoot hunter, live. You white men, die."

≈ 3 ≈

Moon when the horses get fat

They buried Til first. Having no shovel, they hefted him down to the river and piled rocks on him. Keep the scavengers off some.

Then they squatted in the shade a few minutes, waiting. Magpie and his gang didn't come back.

"They buzzarded us," said Jim at last.

"Picked clean as a buffler carcass," agreed Mac.

Skinhead was too glum to talk.

They put Til out of their minds and took inventory: Each man had his slouch hat, one pair of moccasins, a cloth shirt, a wide leather belt, and an empty scabbard. Skinhead and Jim had leggings made of skin, and cotton breechcloths. Since Mac wore dropfront pants of deerskin, he had more hide, which Jim said they'd need. Jim and Skinhead had hidden knives, Jim an extra patch knife and Skinhead a small dagger. Mac was embarrassed about not having a secret knife. Jim had some line for snares. All three men had extra flint and fire steel—you didn't get caught in the mountains without a way to make fire. Mac had the lucifers he kept in his *gage d'amour,* the bag for his pipe.

They talked it over. Probably five hundred miles to Fort Union, down the Missouri, all the way through Blackfoot country. Similar distance to friendly Indians like the Cheyennes, with a chance of coming on Crows sooner, and less than half the route through Blackfoot territory. Long chance either way. Not a man wanted to try for Fort Union.

They rummaged through the ruined rooms of the fort

24

and found some empty flour sacks, even some without holes. Skinhead took a couple and headed for the vegetable patch to scavenge. Jim said he had something to do and would be back in a minute to help Mac finish searching the wreckage of the fort.

Mac started hunting. It was hard, at first, to think what might be useful. In the smithy he found some headless nails and picked them up, unable to think how they might help, but... The scrap iron he left.

Jim reappeared looking sweaty, Til's clothes over one arm. He gave Mac a crooked smile and said, "Too bad his pants are cloth. We need the hide."

They checked the kitchen and were disappointed. One sack of flour, with a couple of pounds in the bottom. Jim thought flour useless, period. Mac grabbed it. In the storeroom off the kitchen Jim came up with a tin of something—smelled to Mac like a paste of meat.

"Let's feast, niggers," Skinhead called.

They hurried outside to see a sack and a half of fresh vegetables. More than fresh—underripe. The beans were embryos. But the potatoes and parsnips were ripe, some even half-rotten.

"This here beaver thinks they left these in the ground since last fall," said Skinhead, chomping on a potato. Mac and Jim hastily helped themselves. Mac set the tin of meat paste in the middle.

"What's that?" Skinhead said eagerly, reaching with his knife. "Mmmm. First time I ever ate the booshway's fancy doin's."

"Booshway" was the way they said bourgeois, fort boss.

They ate hungrily, greedily. A feast of meat paste, crunchy potatoes, and tart, green tomatoes.

Mac, realizing it first, dried his juicy hands on his buckskin pants. "Maybe we should back off."

Skinhead looked at him offended, ready to be outraged. Jim wiped off his own hands.

"Long way to go on not enough fuel," said Mac gently.

Skinhead opened his mouth to protest but then stopped. "That child's right," he told Jim. "Let's stretch it out."

They packed up the garden stuff and kept the emptied

tin to use as a cup. Jim stuffed a bunch of flour sacks into one sack, saying they'd come in handy. Mac made a thorough search of all the half-destroyed rooms and found one item of value, a tin kettle. It was half-crushed and had a hole on one side, but maybe it would work if, well . . . He would think of something.

2

They set out back across the basin of the Judith River, walking the hot dry plains of midsummer. They meant to strike for the Judith Gap, between the Big Snowy Mountains and the Little Belts, hit the headwaters of the Musselshell, and then head south along the Crazy Mountains for the Yellowstone. Not only would they find friendly Cheyennes downstream in Powder River country, they'd have a good chance with the Crows and Sioux. Anybody but the Blackfeet.

This was bizarre. None of the men knew whether he could make it. No one talked about failure, death by starvation. Skinhead said one hungry evening that they should have fattened up on Til. Mac didn't know whether he meant it. Couldn't have done it, Mac thought, but Skinhead was probably right.

Mac wondered whether, if one of his companions died, he would be able to eat the meat. He didn't think he could keep it down.

They soon consumed all the vegetables, even the ones far underripe. Mixing the dough with ash and water, they wrapped it around sticks and roasted bread. Then everything was gone.

Their days fell into clear divisions. At night they traveled, making miles in the safety of darkness. In those cool mountain nights, Mac suspected, he wouldn't be able to sleep anyway, not without blankets. He wore a couple of flour sacks for warmth while walking. In the middle of the day they slept. Early and late in the day they sought food. Some nights they made twenty miles, but as they got weaker, and their moccasins wore out, they covered half that. Skinhead judged it was a couple of hundred miles to the Yellowstone, and that was less than halfway.

Mac Maclean learned fast, looking to find Jerusalem artichokes and eating them gratefully. Likewise rose hips, breadroot, cattail root, red turnips, wild onions, and skunk cabbage. He came to regard serviceberries and chokecherries as manna from heaven.

He acquired new skills. He and Jim prowled through areas of giant sagebrush with long sticks, rousted out rattlesnakes, and smashed their heads with clubs. Mac came to think of the flesh of the rattlesnake as delicate and pleasing, like chicken. Mac even learned to snare prairie dogs. Sometimes they were able to bash sage hens on the head.

It was possible, even easy, to get food, but impossible to get enough.

At first he did not mind the hunger, that constant tug, a nag. He played with tolerating hunger, a game of the mind, and found it bearable. He was pleased by his self-control.

But it got worse. In the foothills of the Little Belts they could find almost no food at all. Sleep became a parade of visions of banquets, kings' feasts once seen in pictures, imagined from books. After such dreams, waking was a torment.

One dawn they saw magpies feeding on the carcass of a buffalo calf, well stripped. Mac hoped for some edible meat. Skinhead and Jim insisted that the flesh would make him ill, and to get sick now was to die. There wasn't a thimbleful of meat anyway.

Jim said they should, however, cut off the hooves. With their tiny knives it was hard getting through the joints. As he hacked, Mac nearly gagged on the smell—he knew he couldn't have eaten any flesh.

Before they slept, Jim rigged a tripod over a small fire, hung the dented kettle with the holey side up, and boiled the hooves. Later, they drank the hoof soup. Then they cut off some thick hide, some sinew, and splintered a bone for an awl. Wearing out moccasin soles frequently, they had been tying new ones on uncomfortably. Now they could sew them on.

Mac's days were desperation. His pants cut up, he was wearing flour sacks around his legs, to keep the sun off his fair skin, and a sack breechcloth. He felt like a beggar, or a leper, in rags. He no longer thought he would survive. He plodded onward merely from a sense of destiny, a destiny of infinite repetition, then final weakness, then madness, and then merciful death.

On one occasion he sat on an anthill, let the insects run all over him, and licked them off his arms and ate them. And cackled.

Sometimes Jim found eggshells, but here in June they were always cracked and empty, which was maddening.

Skinhead grew more and more silent, monstrously silent. That scared Mac. Jim said Skinhead was only brooding on the vengeance he would bring down on Magpie's head.

Days passed in a trance. Mac put one foot in front of the other like a machine, his mind wandering to scenes of childhood, especially dinners his mother made in St. Louis. He yearned most for ham and eggs, which he hadn't eaten since leaving civilization. Memory was more powerful than mountain, and he scarcely saw where he tread. He knew he was walking to his death, one step after the other, endlessly, pointlessly.

One morning Jim spotted a small, shallow pool with a downstream entrance. He planted Skinhead in midstream opposite the pool. Then he and Mac stomped upstream toward the pool, and the three chased a fat female cutthroat trout in. Quick as a flash Jim blocked the exit. Then he flipped her onto the bank, and then farther into the grass.

They boiled her in the squashed kettle and devoured her. Suddenly Mac felt new vigor and knew he could make it to Cheyenne country. Sleeping during the afternoon, Mac dreamt of the taste of that fish, and of trays of salmon, a fish he had never tasted, tendered by formally attired waiters in Scotland.

That evening they caught and ate another cutthroat, but they had to move on. They couldn't spend much time hunting, fishing, and gathering—time was against them. All three men had lost too many pounds. Skinhead's fat flesh was now slack, and Mac was gaunt beyond gaunt.

On the plains east of the Crazies they were bedding down for the day beneath some cottonwoods. A buffalo herd was grazing out on the flats. They all looked at it longingly, but that meat was as unattainable as a mirage.

Then Jim said quietly, "We've got to try it."

"Crazy," said Skinhead.

"What's your idea?" said Mac.

"Not much. Hoping you'll have a better one. Tackle a calf, see if we can cut its throat with these little knives."

"We're too weak," said Skinhead impatiently. "We'd get kicked or stomped or gored."

Jim and Mac ignored him.

Mac had no better idea. Jim said they'd best wait until the heat of the afternoon, when the beasts would be sluggish.

Mac couldn't really sleep. He dozed and woke, dozed and woke, tormented by incredibly vivid sensations of the taste of fresh meat, of raw liver, of blood—sensations without pictures, ripe in his mouth and nose. Before midday he couldn't stand it any longer and nudged Jim awake.

Miffed at Skinhead's skepticism, they left him there, sleeping, and took his dagger.

The worst time of Mac's life was spent in trying to approach the animals. They spotted several cow-calf pairs on the edge of the big herd. Jim insisted that they move stealthily from downwind, walking down a wash, slipping from depression to depression, and slithering through the short grass to get close. It took a couple of hours. Jim was patient, relaxed, even looked content. Mac was raging with anxiety.

They got a bit of luck. Two cows and their calves, a bull calf and a heifer, were grazing near a sandy wash no more than a foot deep. Jim and Mac eased down the wash as close as they could get. Still, the beasts were twenty feet away, and there was only grass for cover. They lay in the sand, thinking. Mac finally whispered, "Maybe they'll come this way." Jim shrugged. They waited.

Suddenly Skinhead came scurrying toward them, crouching, but in clear sight of the animals. Mac glanced at the buffalo, hoping their backs were turned. They weren't, but the heads were down, and neither cows nor calves seemed to take notice.

When Skinhead got close enough, Mac whispered, "You stupid son of a bitch!"

"We may as well all get stomped together," Skinhead replied equably.

Jim and Mac talked it over, leaving Skinhead out. Mac was utterly, insanely angry at Skinhead.

They decided not to wait—Mac couldn't wait. They would watch until all four animals had their backs turned and then step quietly but quickly toward the closest calf. Mac would grab it by a hind leg. He had to make the attempt himself, hold his fate literally in his own hands.

Jim would hamstring the critter.

Since both of Mac's hands would be occupied, Skinhead took his little dagger back. He would come up after and cut the jugular, he said.

Minutes passed. Mac's hands were sweaty and he kept wiping them on his flour-sack clothes. He could feel his heart raging in his chest.

Without warning Jim stood up and padded softly forward. The bull calf was nursing, the cow gazing the other way. Mac caught up to Jim, fixing his attention on the hind hock of that bull calf.

Closer. Closer.

Mac dove and grabbed the leg.

The calf kicked. Mac lost his grip.

He lunged and got it again and bellowed for Jim to hamstring it.

The calf kicked hard. Mac felt his fingers pried off the leg and the hoof clipped him in the head. The calf dashed off.

Mac sat up dizzily in the dust. He shook his head, then wiped blood out of his eye. He turned and looked at the bull calf. It was standing fifty feet off, head turned toward them. Its mother caught up, and the two of them trotted away.

There goes my life, Mac said to himself.

In grief, he looked around for Jim. He was running toward Skinhead.

Skinhead had one big paw around the heifer's leg. She was already hamstrung and on the ground. The mother bawled at Skinhead, hesitated, then lowered her head.

On the ground, Skinhead observed, "She'll stomp us or she won't."

Jim ran toward the cow, shouting and stomping. She dodged. He ran at her again. She sidled away gracefully.

"She won't," said Skinhead.

Jim circled, drawing alongside her. Maybe his wonderful agility would save him, Mac thought. Suddenly Jim bolted forward and kicked the cow in the muzzle.

She shook her monstrous, shaggy head, looking confused, and trotted off. Twenty yards away she stopped and bawled. Then she loped away to the other cow and calf. Some animals in the herd were looking toward the commotion. None seemed disturbed.

"That's why they call them buffler-witted," Jim said to Mac.

Skinhead was just lying beside the heifer calf with a huge, dumb grin on his face.

"By God, you did both jobs," exclaimed Mac. Skinhead nodded happily.

Jim knelt beside the calf and opened the jugular with his patch knife. Bright blood pulsated onto the neck, matting the tawny hair. He watched it for a moment. Then he put his mouth to the wound and sucked.

≈ 4 ≈

Moon when the horses get fat

Mac thought this bite, this particular slice, was the best piece of food he'd ever tasted. He held it up and studied the dangling morsel. A slice of buffalo liver, raw, dipped in bile.

He held it over his open mouth and let it slither in. He chewed briefly, not as deliberately as he would have liked, and swallowed. Satisfaction. He reached for more.

Each man had eaten liver, each had drunk blood, each had taken that slight edge off his appetite. Mac could not believe that he drank blood and that it tasted ambrosial.

Jim and Skinhead were cutting the carcass into quarters with their ridiculous little knives. Oddly, Mac felt weak, even giddy, after eating a little.

"You coons grateful to this child, ain't ye?" Skinhead said.

"You saved my life," Mac said seriously, beginning to feel better. He got to his feet and held a hind quarter while Skinhead cut. When it came loose, he started for the creek.

Mac had to rest several times before he made it. Jim and Skinhead brought the rest of the animal, Skinhead hefting the ribs.

Jim started in with flint and steel to make a small fire. Still dizzy sometimes, Mac stretched out against a piece of deadfall. He meant to eat until he couldn't rise.

And he did. All of them did. They roasted meat on sticks and let the fat drip into their open mouths and stuffed themselves with half-cooked flesh. "Damn heathens we be," said Mac

32

"We so strive," said Skinhead. The fat man was so gloatingly proud he didn't need to boast any more.

In an hour not one of them could get to his feet readily. They were keeping no watch. Mac looked around the plains, with their slant sunlight and stippled with shadow. Would Indians come up on them, silent? To hell with it, thought Mac. We are at the mercy of the land, and the winds that blow thereon.

2

"Damn your hide, Maclean," Skinhead said softly, casually. Maybe that was why it seemed so threatening. The hairs on Mac's forearms stood up.

All Mac had said was, "Don't you think we'd better dry some meat?" That is, all he'd said again, and again whimperingly. He'd badgered them about drying meat last night, and now he was starting in again first thing this morning. He knew it wouldn't work—he knew a crazy mood had hold of him—but he couldn't stop.

Sure, he could give reasons for drying a bunch of meat. They still had to cross from the Musselshell to the Yellowstone, several days travel, go a long way down the Yellowstone, and then go overland to Powder River. Then it could still be a while before they found the Cheyennes. But the reasons weren't why Mac was pestering his comrades.

"Don't you think we'd better dry some meat?" he repeated weakly.

They ignored him.

He ate, desperately.

At length he got up and walked around the creek bottom, trying to get hold of himself. He began to gather sticks, and break off some green ones, for a rack. He erected the upright poles, the supports, and the cross sticks for the strips of meat at head height. He got a small fire going underneath.

Once in a while he cooked a little meat to munch on as

he worked. Skinhead and Jim ignored him. The task took most of the morning.

He went and got the front quarters of the calf and enough hide to lay them on. Jim was napping now. Mac picked up Jim's patch knife without a word to Skinhead.

The front quarter of a buffalo is the meaty chunk. Mac started cutting it into long, thin strips, laying them flat atop the rack. He didn't even look at Skinhead, who was still eating.

About noon, finished, Mac lay down with the others and slept. For the first time in days he dreamed not of food but of water.

In the dream Mac and his did go swimming in the Mississippi above town. Sometimes his mom and Uncle Hugh are there, his uncle making witty, bookish fun. They picnic on blood sausage. After lunch Mac swims in a big eddy. His dad, sandy-haired, bearded, severe, sits on a huge log and watches moodily. The two men share a pint. Mac dives to the bottom, flailing his hands about in boyish exuberance to feel a catfish. He grasps something cold, and slimy. Inert. With his fingers getting sticky, he suddenly knows that it's his father floating on the bottom, drowned.

The boy surfaces in terror and looks for his father. The beach is empty. Empty of family, empty even of log, of brush, of leaves. A blank beach, like an incomplete painting. Panicky, the boy looks up for the sun. It is a magenta eye, dripping a purple tear down the face of the sky.

Mac Maclean, twenty-four years old, itinerant and half-starved on the plains of what would become Montana Territory, awoke uneasily. Jim and Skinhead were eating again. The sun was low in the sky. The fire under Mac's rack was out. He was ravenous.

3

Mac was awake first in the predawn light, working at his fire. He had lots of pounds of meat spread here on the rack, drying. He wondered what was going to happen now that all the meat was being dried. Jim was sleeping his light woodsman's sleep by the other fire. Skinhead was belly up, back down, wheezing.

Or had been. Skinhead sat up, rubbed his face vigorously, got to his knees, then his feet, and shook his body like a dog. He glanced at Mac, eyed the rack, strode over, and lifted off half-dried strips of meat with a big paw. He went back to the other fire without a word.

Mac had thought about it. He was desperate to save some meat for their travel, but he couldn't force his partners.

Skinhead started chewing, loudly.

Jim woke up, looked at Skinhead, looked across at Mac, rose, and padded his graceful way to the drying rack. He also helped himself, generously, eyes averted from Mac.

Mac helped himself, too. Might as well. He sat with his partners and started gorging. A parody of gorging—stuffing meat down his gullet. He looked at the two of them balefully, made a nasty face, and stuffed more without swallowing until he couldn't move his jaws.

"Maclean," Skinhead snarled, chewing, "you ain't gonna tell me when to eat."

Mac didn't know what to do. He got to his feet, feeling idiotic. His feet started moving, moving in a kind of gigue. He started humming through his mouthful of meat—"Hnnnnh," rising and falling clumsily in pitch.

Skinhead began to belt out the bagpipe march "Bonnie Dundee"—almost unrecognizably. He was pushing with his elbows on his gargantuan rib cage, bellowing the bagpipe.

Jim Sykes began to chuckle.

Mac was dancing more wildly than he'd ever danced, by turns hopping, strutting, larking, spinning, whatever fancy led him to. He felt utter abandon. If he danced hard enough, long enough, fast enough, crazily enough, he would stop being a man and become a dance. Which would be wonderful.

Jim and Skinhead got up and began to dance, Jim stylish, Skinhead clumsy as a bear. Skinhead sang louder and more wretchedly than ever. Mac hummed as fiercely as he could. They all started laughing, except that Mac's mouth was too full. The others laughed at Mac. Skinhead threw his huge arms around both of them and they all fell to the ground in a pile. Each man had the giggles. Each man was crying.

Mac sat up. He fingered some meat out of his mouth, then the rest of it. He set in determinedly to eat the wad. The other two helped themselves off the rack, as greedily as though these were their first bites. They feasted until food seemed disgusting.

≈ 5 ≈

Moon when the horses get fat

"Bloods," whispered Skinhead, and ducked back down.

They were crouched in a dry wash, out of sight under a cutbank.

From the Judith Gap they'd been paralleling the old Indian trail, thinking to spot some Blackfeet. Now they'd done it. The idea of killing a dog had sounded good, but it looked dangerous.

Jim had seen the dust that meant a village traveling along the trail. He woke Skinhead and Mac, and they moved here from the creek.

"Bloods sure," repeated Skinhead. "Do we dare chance it?"

If Magpie was among them, thought Mac, the bastard would want to finish what he started.

The idea was to slip along behind the parade of man and animal, and when the Indians camped, creep close and kill a dog. But with Magpie's Bloods?

Yet the Indians had plenty to eat, and lots of horses.

"Maybe we could steal some mounts," put in Mac.

He was looking at the Indians greedily. Men to the front and on the flanks, mounted and on the watch. Women and children alongside the travois, horseback and afoot. The travois heavy with belongings, and sometimes with small children. Dogs walking beside them or cavorting or dashing away and trotting back.

Skinhead shook his head. "They'd track us. We're in no shape to stay ahead of them on horses."

True. Mac could feel himself slipping into starvation again. They had eaten the last of the dried buffalo yesterday.

"I can do it," said Jim. "It's worth it."

Skinhead looked hard at him. Hell, thought Mac, maybe Man Who Doesn't Stir Air can do it. And otherwise we starve.

"I'm going alone," Jim said. "Safer for me." He fixed them one by one with his piercing look. "May have to wait most of the night. I'll be back before noon. Right here. After noon go on without me."

2

Mac had just spent the coldest night of his life, shivering in his flour-sack rags. He had enjoyed maybe an hour of sun, and was longing for more, when he heard soft, running steps.

Jim jumped into the dry wash, breathing heavily. "Let's move!" he shouted in a whisper.

Skinhead jumped up and out of the wash without a question. What the hell was going on? Skinhead set a trot for the creek. Mac supposed the Bloods were hard after Jim. "Go!" Jim whispered hoarsely at Mac. Mac did.

Where was the dog? Jim had no dog carcass. Mac looked back. Jim pointed forward urgently. Jim did have a bow, arrows, and a hawk and man-sized knife. Plus Indians on his tail. Not worth it.

They had about two miles to go to Sweet Grass Creek.

The miles went by hard. Ordinarily Mac could trot this way comfortably. Today his chest was threatening to blow up. He was surprised he could run at all, weakened as he was. But Jim stayed on his heels, and Mac kept moving.

He wished to hell he knew what was happening. Or maybe wondering was just a way to get his mind off his hurting.

The creek was running high, full of riffles and deep pools. Maybe they could splash along a ways and leave the creek on rock. But it would slow them down.

They tramped through the water sometimes, and along the creek-washed bank rock other times, always hurrying, never relaxing. Mac felt desperate. His breath was coming in heaves. He thought he was going to die.

After a mile or two Skinhead held his arm level, pointing. A huge pile of driftwood at the top of an island. Skinhead looked back, and Jim nodded.

They ran toward it, splashing along knee deep, then going waist deep, then swimming into a hole. Skinhead ducked underwater above the logjam. His feet disappeared. And nothing reappeared.

"Come on, Dancer," came his grating voice from the darkness.

Mac took a huge breath and dove. Under the logs he groped for a way up. Wood everywhere. He didn't have enough air. He thought of turning around and swimming back out. The current had him pushed against the logs. He was going to drown. He began to see lovely colors, rainbows like oil on still water.

A strong hand grabbed his arm and yanked. He banged his head on a log, opened his eyes into sweet, breathable air, and saw Skinhead's rough face.

Jim popped up in the next log hole over. They couldn't get to him. He was smiling slyly.

"How far back are they?" asked Skinhead.

"Not far enough," answered Jim.

Skinhead nodded his huge head a couple of times. "Wagh! lad, you done right. Weapons is better than a dog.

"Quiet!" Skinhead pointed upstream. Mounted Indians came to the creek, split up, and rode down both banks.

3

Mac woke to the smell of smoke and burning flesh.

Dreaming again. He had crawled up out of the water, mostly onto a drift log. In the creek he was freezing, colder than he'd ever been in his life.

When he lay on the log, he could doze. But when he dozed, he dreamt. And in the dream Magpie burned the logjam, with the three trappers in it. Mac's last sensation was not even the agony of the fire—it was the stench of his own flesh, burning.

So he was glad to be awake. But exhausted.

He wished they could move out. But not until dark.

He whispered. No whisper could carry over the shoosh of the creek. "Magpie's Bloods?"

Skinhead nodded.

Mac started to speak again, but Skinhead's big hand gripped him roughly. Down, Skinhead gestured. Mac slipped into the water up to his eyes.

A moment later the Bloods rode by quietly on both banks going the other way, upstream. Not so many of them now. The others must be searching the banks downstream for signs of where the trappers came out of the water.

Skinhead winked a huge eyelid at Mac.

4

In the full dark they slipped out of the logjam. They had to climb out upward. It was impossible to push upstream underwater against the current.

Then they walked downstream in the water, swimming when necessary, Jim always holding the precious bow high.

The going was slow, perhaps a mile an hour. But Skinhead stuck doggedly to the creek.

Shortly after first light they came into the broad, crosswise valley of the Yellowstone River. Slowly they worked their way to the confluence. To Mac the north bank of the Yellowstone represented the far edge of Blackfoot Territory, and the south bank felt like safety. He wondered if the Bloods would be waiting at this spot. The great river rolled by, deep and strong.

"Just let it take you," said Skinhead, "and stay near me."

They floated along in the big river, sometimes touching bottom, sometimes not. The river seemed benevolent, but beneath the surface Mac could feel its strength. He thought of the great waterfalls upstream, in the geyser and hot-spring country, and their awesome force. That force was here, subtle and sinewy.

The sky brightened steadily. The sun rose behind gray clouds far to the east. Mac couldn't help thinking what good targets the three swimmers made from the north bank.

After about a mile Skinhead turned onto his side and started kicking for the south bank, Mac and Jim close behind. Soon they were hard against some sandstone bluffs, floating in deep, strong water. Skinhead kicked hard toward a crevice. When he got there, he muscled out quickly, leaving room for Mac and Jim. The two friends followed Skinhead up the six-foot chimney and out onto bare rock. No tracks.

Skinhead slapped Mac's shoulders and grinned. They were maybe halfway to the Cheyennes. Mac wanted to whoop and holler, but he didn't dare. Right behind him he heard—a coyote cry.

It was Jim. Jim was yipping a full-blooded coyote song, a primal call.

The song rose shrilly on the cool dawn air, complete with warbles, trills, and ululations, punctuated by yips and screeches, a coyote aria.

Skinhead and Mac were laughing wildly but silently. If the Bloods heard it, what would they think? Some coyote must be spectacularly happy. Or hungry. Or desperate for a female.

Mac decided to join in. He lifted his own voice in coyote cry, a lugubrious and mournful voice. Eyes closed, thinking of elaborations to add, Mac felt a big, rough hand clap over his mouth.

Skinhead was laughing uncontrollably, but he wasn't damn well going to let Mac howl. "Sounds like a bowel-blocked buffalo moaning," grated Skinhead.

Skinhead let go of Mac, and Mac held up a finger for attention. "Announcement," he said confidently. "Good-bye Blackfoot country. This here is home."

≈ 6 ≈

July, 1843, Moon when the buffalo bulls are rutting

Mac Maclean had an idea. That was about all he had, being shorn of gun, horse, and meat, yet it was enough to make him happy.

The sun was up. Mac, Skinhead, and Jim had scattered to look for food. Mac had found nothing. It would probably be a hungry day. Ten days ago, before the calf, he would have been panicky. But now they had bow and arrows and would find buffalo, or elk, or deer. He wasn't starving. He was simply hungry, and content with that.

Because he had an idea. An idea how to stay in the Yellowstone country.

He was sitting on a sentinel rock projected out from the ocher sandstone that rimrocked the Yellowstone, dangling his legs, looking down on a bench above the river about three miles below the mouth of the Big Horn River. Below him was a fine, grassy bottom shaded by big, old cottonwood trees.

In the bottom sat the fountain of Mac's happiness, the remains of old, abandoned Fort Cass. Tulloch's Fort, some called it. The American Fur Company had Sam Tulloch build it here back in '32. Went off and left it in '35—the Company started pulling back from the mountains then.

Sublime accident, Mac thought, that he had stumbled on it. The Yellowstone River was the southern edge of Blackfoot country. The Big Horn was Crow country. A little east, the Yellowstone along the Rosebud and the Tongue and the Powder was Cheyenne and Sioux country. This spot, the mouth of the big Horn, was a crossroads.

Three hundred miles to the east, Fort Union had the

Indian trade. Fort Union, far out on the plains, huge, impregnable, once the castle of Kenneth Mackenzie of the American Fur Company, the king of the Missouri. Fort Union of booshway James Kipp, the vain. Of illegal whiskey stills. Of monopoly prices. Hated Fort Union.

But it wasn't as invulnerable as it used to be. American Fur had pulled out and left it to Pierre Chouteau of St. Louis, who did not have untold wealth and could not afford to ruin competitors by buying high and selling low.

American Fur (everyone still used that name, though it was now Chouteau's outfit) had just lost Fort Mackenzie, its mountain post. It had no trading post close to the Crows. No post for the Sioux and Cheyenne short of Fort Laramie, to hell and gone south on the Platte. No post in the middle of the West's best buffalo country.

Skinhead had decided to go back to St. Louis. Gonna trade his mountain yarns for the sweet flow of whiskey in the taverns, he said. Jim didn't know what he was going to do, as usual, and didn't seem to care. Now Mac had seen his personal light on the road to Damascus. He chuckled at his vision: He would be a trader. A merchant. Restorer and owner of Fort Cass, crossroads of the northern plains. And proud resident of the Rocky Mountains.

Perched on the sentinel rock, looking over his new domain, he was giddy with delight. Or is it hunger you're giddy with, Mac Maclean? he teased himself.

Mac was amused at the irony. Scots had always been traders—Hudson's Bay Company had been spearheaded by Scots in Canada. Northwest Company, too. King Mackenzie was a Scot. Yes, Scots were always traders, Mac's Uncle Hugh said. Scots liked to go to exotic places and bring back exotic coins.

But Mac had never wanted to be a trader. His father and uncle set up in mercantile trade in St. Louis—they spent their patrimony on it. Hugh liked the business and thrived in it. Alexander, Mac's dad, loathed it. The only loves for Alexander were Mac, the verses of Bobby Burns, and whiskey. He died when he passed out on the levee in St. Louis, drunk, and fell into the river.

Mac took off for the mountains. He'd always loved the

fields and the forests, and the crafted beauty of his gun.
Mountain men came into his father and uncle's store on
Fourth Street, full of stories, looking wild as Injuns, and
smelling that way, too. As a lad, Mac had even seen
painted Indians on the streets of St. Louis.

To him, like his dad, the mercantile business was tedium—
the mountains were romance. Now he would do mountain
mercantile.

Of course, Mac had no money to start a trading post. No
wherewithal to buy blankets, knives, kettles, beads, tobacco, coffee, lead, guns, and whiskey to trade for hides. He
would need five thousand dollars, or more likely ten thousand, for a modest outfit.

On the sentinel rock above the Yellowstone he swung
his legs exuberantly. The mere lack of ten thousand dollars
didn't matter to him now—he had an idea, an answer. He
could stay in the mountains.

The image of Annemarie rose in his mind. Stay in the
mountains, he was saying to himself, and have Annemarie.

2

Perhaps Mac Maclean was in love with a woman, or
rather a girl. Certainly he was in love with a place.

He had come to the Shining Mountains three summers
ago, 1840. He rode out with the annual far caravan—up
the Platte, rising from prairies to high plains, past Laramie,
on to the Sweetwater, across the top of the continent at
South Pass, and up the west side of the Wind River
Mountains to rendezvous.

It was a glum affair, the 1840 rendezvous on Green
River. A small Company caravan. The fur boss, Drips,
couldn't say whether the Company would be sending any
more wagon trains to meet the beaver men in the wilds.
The price of plews made it a bad proposition.

Camp talk was of what men would do now. Go to
Oregon and set up farming. Head for Californy and sport
among the Mexicans. Go to sea and visit the Sandwich

Islands. Go back to Westport or Springfield or Chillicothe or Williamsburg and live like a white man.

Some of the plans sounded good, but Mac didn't think they would work. The problem was, not many of the fur trappers seemed like white men anymore. None of them was accustomed, any longer, to white ways—to the labor of the plow, the commerce of the store, the commands of the boss, the will of the community, the sway of church, the rule of law.

Mac thought all American frontiersmen were enamored of adventure, danger, and wild-hair freedom, but these men were addicted.

Besides, it didn't matter to Mac what they decided to do. During rendezvous he explored the valley of the upper Green River with the Delaware Jim Sykes and a Shoshone named Black Circle. Mac shot a mountain lion and saw Bighorn sheep on the high ridges. He camped by Stewart Lake, the most gorgeous spot he'd ever seen. He fell wildly and romantically in love, in the way only a very young man can. He cared nothing about whether he could make a living here—spending his days in these mountains was all that mattered.

So Mac Maclean partnered up with Jim and Til and Skinhead. They trapped the Uintas and spent the winter at the little post Bridger was building to trade with the trappers, a substitute for rendezvous.

In the spring Mac again rode with Skinhead and some other scalawag trappers hunting beaver. Across the Green River they went, and north along the Wind River. Over the divide and into Jackson Hole. Across the high, rolling geyser country to the Yellowstone.

All the way the other men groused. When they found beaver, they crabbed about the low price. When they didn't, they groused about the country's being trapped out. Mac didn't care. The place—the high, sun-struck summits of the Tetons, the cold cricks, the alpine meadows rich with elk, the mountain buffalo, the majestic waterfalls, the delicious hot springs—these meant everything. Mac learned the country, learned the Indians, learned the ways to

survive. He ceased to be a pork-eater, the term for a
greenhorn, and became an honest pilgrim.

Then by luck he took the step that made him a mountain man.

That second autumn in the mountains, Skinhead, Jim,
Til, Mac, and the bunch took the old Indian trail from
Togwotee Pass north into the Yellowstone high country,
one of Mac's favorite places. Out exploring late one afternoon, Mac simply got lost. He never did figure out how he
did it. Didn't know where camp was. Rode around in big
circles for a couple of days through the complicated high
country and never did see it. So he swallowed his fear and
set out on his own to get to winter camp at the mouth of
Clarks Fork.

He struck out north across some of the continent's most
rugged and most beautiful country. Keeping the valley of
the Yellowstone in sight far to his left, he followed the
ridges. When he saw the big canyon of the Yellowstone,
with what seemed like the two biggest waterfalls in the
world, he knew where he was. From last autumn he knew
the Indian trail crossed the river near another falls not far
downstream. He followed parallel to that trail toward
Clarks Fork.

During those sunlit days he unconsciously changed from
afraid to at home. He became aware of the benevolence of
the earth. The nights frosted, but the days were pleasant.
He saw game galore. Twice he stopped at hot springs and
eased his body with the warmth. He felt that this adventure alone was worth coming to the Rocky Mountains for.

At the mouth of Clarks Fork he was in country to live
in, not just travel through. He hunted every day while he
waited for his companions and made plenty of meat. Since
Skinhead and company had wasted a week looking for
Mac, they turned up irritable. But Mac had grown from
pilgrim to mountain man, and found his home country in
the mountains, the Yellowstone River.

Yes, he'd found a home, and now he would build a
house. Right here at the mouth of the Big Horn. Wouldn't
be traveling so much—have to stay home to trade. A good
place to call your own.

3

It was nearly dark. The three would be moving out soon, down the Yellowstone, looking for Strikes Foot's Cheyennes. They were gnawing at the bones of two sage hens Jim had killed that morning, pip-squeak bones, Skinhead called them. And Skinhead, prompted by Mac, was telling tales of this spot where the Big Horn flowed into the Yellowstone.

Manuel Lisa built a stockade when he came into this country in '07. Crazy thing happened. Lisa sent a man named John Colter out to spread word of the trading post among the Indians. Colter took off alone and disappeared for months. Walked all this country just for the hell of it, clear to Jackson's Hole, even saw the high Yellowstone country, saw the boilings over on the Stinking Water River, brought back tales no one believed. Exploring new country. Alone. Crazy beaver, Colter.

"What happened to the fort?" Mac asked.

"Wagh!" grunted Skinhead. "Blackfeet kicked Lisa's tail out of the country. Kept kicking everybody else out, too. This nigger helped Major Henry build a fort here in '23, the year Glass got et by Old Ephraim and showed up months later, riz from the dead. Pilcher had made a fort here a couple of years before. Blackfeet burned both of them. Blackfeet was rambunctious in them days."

"What about Fort Cass? Today I saw what's left of it."

"Damn Company. Finally got the Blackfeet peaceable and went off and left the fort. Good spot for it—Company don't know nit from gnat."

Mac stuck to his decision to say nothing of his plans to Skinhead or Jim. Skinhead would blab it all over the mountains. But as Mac traveled that night, one foot after another automatically between his partners, he spun dreams. A substantial building, timber, not adobe, and not as big and gaudy as Fort Union. Comfortable, though not stocked with fancy wines, like some. He could float the furs to Fort

Union, a real advantage, and ship them downstream on the paddlewheelers—that would cut the cost of getting his goods to market.

Imagine, Skinhead would snort, paddlewheelers in the Rocky Mountains. But right here you were protected against the steamboats—forever, Mac thought. They'd never come past Wolf Rapid, at the mouth of the Tongue River, several days away. So you had the use without the nuisance. And Mac dreamed on.

Just like a white man, Jim would have said, to be living high in his head when he was starving afoot, unarmed, and wore out.

≈ 7 ≈

Moon when the buffalo bulls are rutting

Dogs were barking at the strangers. Some children disappeared. Others, recognizing the Frenchmen, ran away laughing and screaming. For a moment Mac thought the girl bringing water from the creek was Annemarie, but she was too slender. When children darted into the lodges, sometimes adult heads popped out to have a look at the odd spectacle.

The three trappers had come onto the Cheyennes all together in one huge camp, all the people who lived between the Big Horn Mountains and the Black Hills, gathered together in their half-moon village for the ceremony of the sacred buffalo hat and then the sun dance.

"Good time to be here," said Skinhead. "Get religion." But Mac was uneasy about Cheyenne religion and wanted to be off for St. Louis. Or he would want that if he could get beyond craving food and get a gun and a horse.

A voice called out their Cheyenne names: Skinhead, Man Who Doesn't Stir Air, and Dancer.

Strikes Foot ducked his huge shoulders through the lodge door and gimped toward them fast, grinning. He shook hands white-man style all around, even with Jim, who didn't like the custom. "Do you have hunger?" he said in Cheyenne.

Mac was acutely embarrassed to be coming into camp this way—dirty, ragged, emaciated, broke, helpless, sore-footed, almost barefooted—hell, almost naked. A beggar in flour-sack rags, and with his face blistered and peeling. But not too embarrassed to use one of his Cheyenne words. "Eat and eat and eat," he told Strikes Foot.

49

"We come to you starving," said Skinhead formally. Strikes Foot would have been too polite to mention it.

"Calling Eagle is making food," he said. They could see her at it in front of the lodge.

Calling Eagle welcomed them chatteringly. She was a tall, husky woman, always cheerful and animated and bristling with talk, yet odd. She added water to the kettle and said she'd kill a young dog to celebrate. The kids were around somewhere. Annemarie, she added to Mac, had gone to see the Assiniboins.

Mac masked his disappointment. It meant she and her mother were visiting the family Lame Deer was born to. He told himself it was just as well—now she wouldn't actually see him in this humiliating state. But he also wouldn't see her before going to St. Louis. Well, that might make it easier to ask Strikes Foot for her.

A pretty girl came out of the lodge, and Calling Eagle introduced her—Strikes Foot's new wife, Yellow Bird. She smiled shyly, eyes down, and set to work peeling cattail roots for the stew. Three wives now, thought Mac. And usually bunches of kids, all except Annemarie, visiting or adopted. A different sort of family.

Strikes Foot was a huge man, six and a half feet, Mac guessed, extra broad, bull strong, full of life. Strange thing was, he had a clubfoot. It made him gimpy. Usually he kept a buffalo hoof strapped onto it—certainly for ceremonial occasions, or hunting or fighting. But he didn't let his foot slow him down—he had a considerable reputation as a man of war and was a leader in the Shield society.

Mac wrestled him once and got thrown, over and over. Strikes Foot couldn't run fast on that hoof in a straight line, but he was quick as a prairie dog on it. And he got his name, Skinhead said, from learning how to kick the hoof into enemies' chests. Skinhead said Strikes Foot was a good friend and a bad enemy. For Skinhead, that was the highest of compliments.

They ate. And ate. Jerked meat, first. Then cakes of cornmeal—Strikes Foot had been trading down at Fort Union. And at last boiled pup. Mac thought again that food was the greatest pleasure of life.

After eating, they lounged in the tipi with the lodge skirts up, the evening breeze making the July heat tolerable. Strikes Foot told about the trip to Fort Union in the moon when the ponies shed their coats, and leaving Annemarie and Lame Deer with her family for the summer. He said nothing about having taken a third wife—its significance was evident. Strikes Foot was a prosperous and respected Cheyenne.

Yellow Bird sat by her blankets, head down, working with her awl, like a proper woman. Calling Eagle, the sits-beside-him wife, joined in the talk just like a man, commenting, giggling, putting in every two-cents' worth she had. She was the only Indian woman Mac had ever seen act like that. He watched her on the sly, trying again to get a feel for her oddness. She carried on as heartily as any man. Yet her gestures were soft, delicate, feminine until they were nearly a mockery of the female. And she gazed at Strikes Foot so meltingly it was embarrassing.

Skinhead told about their spring trapping season— "misuble"—and the trip to Fort Mackenzie. "Hear what happened at Mackenzie?" he asked Strikes Foot.

The warrior spoke two Cheyenne names that meant Francis Chardon and Alexander Harvey. The word was that they killed several Blackfeet near the fort, Strikes Foot said, killings that made no sense. Then they headed out for Fort Union as fast as they could, with all the crew and trade goods. They knew the Blackfeet would take hair for hair. Instead the Indians had to settle for burning the place down.

Mac thought he was hearing satisfaction in Strikes Foot's voice.

"Guess the Blackfeet will trade at Fort Macleod now," said Skinhead. Strikes Foot didn't know.

Fort Macleod—Canada. The British, and their damned Hudson's Bay Company. Mac had other ideas where the Blackfeet could take their trade, ideas he was keeping to himself.

When Skinhead started in on how Magpie robbed them, Mac got some bear grease from Calling Eagle in a cup, excused himself, and went outside. He headed across the village toward Porcupine Creek. He wanted to be alone,

to think, to smoke his pipe. This was his need, his
craving, to be alone for a while each day and be still.
And he needed to think what to say to Strikes Foot about
Annemarie.

2

Mac kept telling himself he was unduly nervous about
getting Annemarie for a wife. The girl was interested in
him, maybe even infatuated—she had flirted with him,
bold behavior among the Cheyenne.

He took his feet out of the little eddy and checked them
over. Four hundred miles of walking had taken their toll.
Now that the blood was gone, he saw they were terribly
chafed and cracked. He'd pushed them hard the last
couple of days to get to the village—he hadn't thought the
feet had more than two days of travel in them without a
long rest.

He spread the bear grease thick on them and rubbed it
in. That would help. He massaged what was left into his
face. In the mountains he always treated his fair Scots skin
with fat as a precaution—until now he had never known
how essential it was. The grease felt wonderful. He imagined Annemarie's fingers massaging it in. And imagined
his hands on Annemarie. He'd been fantasizing about
finding out how far her flirting would go. Cheyenne
mothers encased their teenage daughters in hide chastity
belts. But hide did cut.

Still, Mac knew his fantasizing was idle. You didn't ruin
your chance with your future wife, and future in-laws, by
fooling around. A Cheyenne girl who got seduced got
exposed publicly, and mocked, mocked almost unto death.
No one would marry her—she was an outcast.

Mac heard people coming his way, a couple of female
voices and a man's—no, Calling Eagle's strange, reedy
voice. The women must be coming for water. Embarrassed
for no reason, Mac sat still, hoping they wouldn't see
him.

The women came from the cottonwood shadows into the light by the stream, an old woman, Calling Eagle, and a little girl. The girl straddled some rocks and reached out into some swift water to fill her buffalo-stomach pouch. The old woman dipped her gourd and drank. Calling Eagle had a firkin, another sign of Strikes Foots' prosperity. She hiked up her skirt and waded in knee-deep downstream of the girl to fill it. The little girl was afraid of losing her balance. The old woman stretched a hand out to help the child back. The girl wobbled and pulled the old woman off balance and they both fell in.

Whooping and laughing, soaked, the girl and old woman hurried back toward their lodge. Calling Eagle shooed them along with words. Then she started searching the edges of the creek—probably for small, flat stones, thought Mac. She made lovely bead necklaces accented with bone and such stones.

Evidently finding nothing, she set the firkin on the bank and stretched her arms. She walked to the trees without the firkin, pulled her skirt up, and—what?

She was holding something suspiciously like a penis in one hand. Piss was jetting out of it onto the cottonwood.

3

"Wagh!" grunted Skinhead. "I thought ye knowed, boy."

Mac merely flushed with anger. Jim looked from one to the other with suppressed amusement. Mac was leading a pony around the rope corral, and Jim was sitting it bareback.

"This child told you she's *hemaneh*."

"How was I to know it meant queer?"

"She ain't exactly queer, beaver."

"You mean she and Strikes Foot don't do it?" Mac challenged. He was thinking of the nights he lay in Strikes Foot's lodge and heard sounds of sexual goings-on. He was hoping it had been Strikes Foot and Lame Deer.

"This child wouldn't say that neither," Skinhead proceeded calmly. "He didn't rightly think as you're ready to know about *hemaneh*."

Mac turned back toward Skinhead and pulled the pony's neck awkwardly. "Hey!" said Jim softly. Mac paid attention to his leading.

They were going to have to borrow horses from Strikes Foot to get to Fort Union, so they might as well get them green-broke for him. Now it was almost too dark to work.

"Don't make no never mind to you, anyway," ventured Skinhead.

The hell it doesn't, Mac was thinking—I'm about to marry into this damn bunch.

"She ain't interested in you."

"He," Mac said sharply.

Skinhead shook his head. "She. That's important. She. You call her he and you'll offend everyone. Cancel our welcome, you would."

Jim slid off the pony and took the halter rope to give her some more leading.

Mac walked toward Skinhead. "Don't make sense."

"You don't see the sense of it. *Hemaneh* means would-be woman. It's one way."

"Queer way," muttered Mac.

Skinhead cocked an eye at him. "You worried about being husband to a Cheyenne now?"

Mac just looked at him.

"You got lots to learn," Skinhead went on. "Wait till you see the squaws torturing some poor Blackfoot. And your squaw leading the way, cutting his balls off. They got the taste for torture, indeed they do. Maybe you oughta stay a few weeks, learn something about your new family."

"Seems like being Cheyenne would be hard to take," Mac admitted.

"Don't think so." Skinhead began opening his fold-over hunting shirt. Mac realized he had never seen his friend undressed.

On Skinhead's chest, seeming to glare in the half dark, were pearly white vertical scars. "They put the medicine-lodge sticks in here," Skinhead said. "This child is proud to be a Cheyenne. And sorry to be heading for the settlements to pretend to be a white man."

Looking at the scars from the sun dance ceremony, thinking of the pain and self-deprivation, Mac thought it was past time his friend did become a white man again.

4

Mac had never felt more empty-handed. He came when Strikes Foot was alone in the lodge, the women and other trappers outside. He had been coached in the courtship customs of the Cheyenne by Skinhead. He had made certain of the key words in Cheyenne. He understood the inadequacy of his proposal, but was determined to plunge forward.

"Welcome, Dancer," said Strikes Foot.

Mac suggested they smoke. Strikes Foot nodded and sat down where the center fire would have been if the evening were cool. Mac handed over his clay pipe, a lucifer, and a plug of tobacco. Embarrassingly, it was tobacco he had borrowed from Strikes Foot.

Somberly, the warrior lit the pipe, held it up, blew smoke to the four directions, as was customary, and handed it to Mac. Mac repeated the ritual.

For a few minutes they smoked in silence. Mac was supposed to make small talk, but he could not. At last he blurted it out. "I want Annemarie for my woman."

Strikes Foot just looked at him, probably surprised at his clumsiness. Neither of them knew how to proceed.

"If I were a Cheyenne," Mac lurched on, doubling his Cheyenne words with signs, "I would do this differently. My relatives would come to you with many fine gifts. But I am a Frenchman. I have no relatives here. Besides, we do such things differently. Perhaps the Frenchman's way is not bad—Annemarie's father was a Frenchman, too."

Strikes Foot closed his eyes for a moment, then opened them, perhaps accepting Mac's point. In taking the woman and her son by old Charbonneau into his lodge, he had invited strange behavior.

"Still," Mac forced himself forward, "I do not ask for her now. I simply declare my intentions."

He let it sit a moment and drew on the pipe. The next part was the worst, and Mac lacked the patience to approach it in a measured way.

"Today I am poor. I came to you starving. It is my plan now to go to St. Louis with my friends. I intend to return. They do not. I will return with many blankets, guns, powder, lead, tobacco, beads, and other goods for trade." He didn't mention whiskey. He'd have to have whiskey, but Strikes Foot was against it.

He took a deep breath. "My plan is to live at Fort Cass and trade these goods for hides. I hope Strikes Foot and the Cheyenne people will trade with me there. And I hope Strikes Foot's daughter Annemarie will be my woman there."

Strikes Foot nodded. To Mac it seemed a resounding chorus of assent.

"I have spoken of my plans to live at Fort Cass to no one but you. I hope my secret is safe with you."

Strikes Foot nodded again.

"I do not wait for an answer now," Mac said awkwardly. He was supposed to chat again and simply leave without mentioning an answer, but he couldn't bring that off.

Before Mac could get up, Strikes Foot spoke. "I believe my daughter cares for you."

Mac waited on tenterhooks.

"And she does have Long Knife blood."

Mac waited again, unable to believe his luck.

Strikes Foot shrugged.

Mac rose and restrained himself from sprinting out.

Over at the rope corral, where Jim and Skinhead were green-breaking more horses, Skinhead assured Mac, "It's as good as a promise, coon. You've got his word. Sure," he gave a mock scowl, "you have to get down the river and back with your hair, and some horses, first."

Mac didn't know what to do. Jim and Skinhead were looking at him with stupid smiles. He decided to kick up his heels. He jumped up, whacked his heels together, and cried, "Whoopee!"

≈ 8 ≈

The storeroom reeked with familiar smells, smells that took Mac Maclean back to his childhood—sweet, dark sorghum from Louisiana, musky hemp from Mexico, fragrant Virginia tobacco, Mexican cocoa with cinnamon, and coffee beans roasted New Orleans-style with chicory.

Mac had let himself in the back way because he wanted to remember for a moment before seeing his uncle, to stand here and drink it in. He was taken aback by how sharp these smells seemed, how overwhelming to a nose accustomed to the plains. Standing here in the half light, he felt a little tremulous, a shy eight-year-old again.

He went out into the main store. Uncle Hugh had expanded it—he must have bought the little milliner's shop next door and taken out the wall. The store seemed to Mac a dazzling show of the wealth of the white man—bolts of calico, ticking, wool, kegs of nails, hammers, planes, drills, mirrors, needles, awls, oil lamps, readymade canvas pants, even some with a buttoning fly instead of a drop front. Uncle Hugh didn't miss a step.

Though the display was casual and matter-of-fact to St Louisians, to Mac it was breathtaking opulence. In the mountains these goods would be the gold of Peru. He planned to take such things to Indian country—with his uncle's help.

He walked gingerly through the aisles. A clerk, showing a matronly customer some damask, looked up at Mac in consternation—Who's coming out of the storeroom? Mac strode by toward his uncle's cubicle. The customer said something like, "But Madame Labbadie wants . . ." If the

housekeepers of the old French families were trading
here, Uncle Hugh's business was improving.

Hugh Maclean was working at his rolltop desk, as usual.
He seldom left the desk except to go to the levee to get
shipments. His long body was bent over papers, his half
glasses well down his nose, his reddish hair a little thinner.
His pipe was clamped hard in a corner of his mouth, and
Mac knew it was stem-bitten.

Mac said softly, "Uncle Hugh."

Hugh looked up abruptly, taken by surprise. He looked
blankly at Mac for a moment, and then slowly smiled and
pulled his long frame, bed-slat skinny, out of the chair.

In that smile Mac could see a glimmer of a younger and
more playful man. It was a family joke that people thought
Hugh looked like a leprechaun stretched to double length.
And Hugh would grumble something about how they had
their Celts mixed up, and the leprechaun was his nephew
Bobby anyway.

Mac stepped into the cubicle and shook his uncle's
hand, hard as a walnut, like the rest of him.

"You've come back, Bobby. Are ye ready to give up
roaming to be an honest tradesman? I could use ye, lad."

Just like Hugh. Mac hesitated. "Yes, Uncle. I've come
to borrow money from you to set up my own store." Mac
added a big grin.

Hugh Maclean got a shrewd look in his eye. "Coin from
a Scot, lad, is blood from a stone." He made a little cough
of a laugh.

"Would you care to take dinner with me at Mansion
House? After we get you into some decent clothes?"

2

First they walked to the levee, Mac in ready-made
pants and shirt, which felt strange, and his comfortable old
moccasins.

St. Louis was changing dizzyingly. The streets were
better paved now—you no longer had to choose between

tripping over the cellar doors of the old French houses or walking in the mud. In front of some of these houses gas lanterns stood like sentinels. And now these expensive homes were starting to look old and a little worn. The new houses, built by American businessmen, those were the opulent ones.

The big change was the sense of energy in the streets. When Mac was born, in 1819, St. Louis was a frontier backwater, fundamentally French. When he left for the mountains in 1840, it was floundering deep in the quagmire of economic hard times.

Now all was changed. St. Louis was a bustling American hub of commerce. The levee alone showed the difference. Steamboats were lined up everywhere, bringing products from Cairo, Louisville, Cincinnati, Pittsburgh, New York, and Europe, or from Memphis, Natchez, New Orleans, and South America. The levee couldn't hold them all, so they were moored upstream and downstream, loading and unloading, men scurrying up and down gangplanks, bosses bawling, workers rolling barrels, pulling dollies, lifting bales and boxes into drays.

"It's wonderful," murmured Mac. His uncle looked at him amused. "All these boats, people, animals . . ." Seeing Hugh's look, Mac didn't go on. But he was delighted, inspired. So many objects people wanted to buy, were willing to work for, pay for. Indians, too.

That's what the Indian shared with the white man, Mac was thinking. The desire for material goods. The desire to use applied ingenuity to make life easier, less brutish. To Mac that felt like genuine progress. To bring such goods to the Indians would not be merely a business.

He said to himself, My children will be those Indians.

"Impress you, lad?" asked Hugh.

"Amazing," said Mac.

Hugh nodded and smiled. "It would. Scots like to collect coins."

3

For Mac, Mansion House was a gaped-mouth experience. At the noon hour the dining room was jammed with
humanity consuming huge amounts and varieties of hors
d'oeuvres, soups, viands, vegetables, pastries and cakes,
fine wines, brandies, and for the Americans, whiskeys.
They were served on linen tablecloths by black men in
impeccable white uniforms. Uncle Hugh ate oysters brought
upriver from New Orleans fresh in water-filled barrels,
which amazed Mac. He himself indulged in smoked clams,
creamed asparagus soup, and squab.

Ridiculous for a man who was starving two months ago.
Ridiculous for a man used to making do in the wilds.

They ordered port. Ridiculous for a man used to *aguardiente*,
the crude whiskey made by the fur bosses from pure alcohol
and Green river water, spiced with red chiles, black pepper,
tobacco, ginger, and whatever else was handy.

The owner of the hotel stopped by the table to inquire
about their meal and ask after Mr. Maclean's health. Hugh
introduced Mac. The owner's pleasure was unctuous.

When the owner left, Mac said, "He sure knows how to
bow and scrape."

"I eat here every Friday, lad."

Hugh looked with feigned casualness around the room.
"Are you interested in whom you're breaking bread with?"
Mac nodded. "The round man there by the window, on the
left, is Robert Campbell. Not a bad fellow for an Irishman."

Everybody in the mountains knew Campbell's name.
He and Bill Sublette built Fort William up next to Fort
Union, and then sold it to the Company. Also built the
other Fort William down on the Platte, which the Company
also bought, and now called Fort Laramie. Mac was surprised Campbell was still young, forty or less, and more
surprised that he was so elegantly dressed.

"The silver-haired man with the patrician face"—his
tone made it clear that Hugh had no love for aristocrats—

"in the middle there is Pierre Chouteau, patron of art and science." And owner of the Company. "He's not in St. Louis so much anymore. He prefers New York society. But they don't let him take his damned slaves to New York." Hugh was a firm abolitionist.

"The man with him is Bernard Pratte, the less said the better."

"What is Campbell doing now?" asked Mac.

"President of a bank." Considerable change for a mountaineer. "The touch of Midas, that one."

Mac felt impulsive. "Introduce me to him."

Hugh smiled tolerantly. "Aye, ask Campbell what he thinks of the fur trade now. There's a man made a fortune in it."

Mac flushed.

"He usually stops to say hello. He's seen you and will surely stop today." Hugh signaled the waiter and asked for more water. The waiter poured Mac more port as well, and Mac realized he'd consumed most of a bottle while his uncle's glass was untouched. The sweet wine seemed delicious to Mac. "Now let's hear about what's happening in the mountains, and about your plans."

4

Mac told all. He told more than he realized he knew. Fewer trappers—many fewer. Lower prices for plews. Most traders gone except the Company, and that pulled out of the mountains far onto the plains, clear to Fort Laramie and Fort Union.

He told how they got robbed at Mackenzie. How they nearly starved, and then with the help of the Cheyennes finally made their way to Fort Union. How Mac bucked up wood for the steamboat to earn a few dollars and worked as a deckhand for his passage to St. Louis. He said nothing about Skinhead's being in town, or about Annemarie, waiting in the mountains.

Mac then claimed he brought the future of the trade with him. Strikes Foot and other Cheyennes gave him

hides to bring to St. Louis, to get a better price than the
monopoly would give at Fort Union. There was profit in
the trade, Mac said. The red man wanted the white man's
goods and would pay for them. He was bound to get more
and more dependent on guns. If the beaver market was
down, the whole fur market wasn't. Mac got excellent
prices for the buffalo hides this morning. The market for
salted buffalo tongues was good. Ermine, wolf, muskrat,
and otter were still worth plenty.

"The key is this," Mac asserted. "The white trappers
have mostly pulled out. The Indians are still a market.
They're responding to the traders now—bringing in plews,
and buffalo hides. They're amazed that they could trade
these furs, which are so plentiful, for goods of real value.
Beads—"

His uncle rose from his chair. "Good afternoon, Mr.
Campbell. I don't believe you know my nephew, Robert
Burns Maclean."

"Mr. Maclean," lilted Campbell, gripping Mac's hand.
Ireland still sang in his voice. "You were speaking of the
fur trade."

"Yes, sir, I've been in the mountains three years."

"Stop by my office, then, if you would. I'd like to hear
the news." Campbell handed Mac a card.

"Old times, sir?" Mac felt himself smiling fatuously.

Campbell shook his head. "Tomorrow. I always hope to
find out what's going to happen tomorrow." Campbell put
on his hat—silk, Mac noticed, not beaver—and moved on.

"That gentleman," said Hugh Maclean, "has the capital
to found a string of forts from here to California. But I
don't think he will." Hugh's eyes darkened. "And what do
you want from your uncle?"

Mac took a deep breath. "I want to borrow five thousand dollars at two percent and pay it back in furs, on the
Company steamboat, next summer."

Hugh looked at him hard, rose, and put some pieces of
silver on the table. "I was afraid of that. Let's talk about it
again this evening, shall we?"

5

Mac had to spend the next afternoon watchdogging Skinhead at Jake's Tavern. Skinhead was deep into faro, too deep even to tell fantastical stories about life in the mountains, as he'd sworn to do to cadge drinks. He was deep into his cups as well, and Mac joined him out of duty. Mac enjoyed the sense of unreality that a little inebriation gave him—it matched his sense that every thing about St. Louis was unreal. St. Louis was a dream. The plains and mountains were life.

Skinhead was evidently winning big and losing big, by turns. He'd somehow got more than his steamboat wages for a stake—now he was playing with other people's money. Mac would cover his tail this afternoon, but he was glad he wouldn't be partnering this unpredictable old man much longer.

Mac watched the game for a little while, for safety. There was a farmer from across the river, half-drunk, losing and not giving a damn. He looked as if he'd slept in his clothes for a week. There was a self-conscious, fastidious sort who might be a schoolmaster. He was playing the role of sober citizen, but his eyes gleamed tellingly. The banker was a pleasant, open-faced blond youngster, entirely sober, and less sporting than he acted.

Faro was a simple game. Mac had never seen it played before because it wasn't a mountain game. The players chose any card they liked and named it to win or lose. The banker turned the cards over by twos, into a winner pile and a loser pile. If you named the six of clubs to win, and it turned up in the winner pile, the banker paid. If it appeared in the loser pile, he took. Clearly a fifty-fifty game if the dealer was square.

The open-faced youngster was cheating. He was what they called a palmer, or hold-out man. Amazing how easy it was to spot when you looked. Skinhead had taught Mac how.

Skinhead was doing his I'm-a-beast, I'm-a-wild-mountain-man act. Mac couldn't tell how much of it was genuine. Skinhead liked to act drunker than he was, but this time he really was drinking. Still, he must know the kid was palming. If Skinhead named the jack of diamonds, the kid could palm it and drop it on the wrong pile anytime. Dangerous game.

The kid dropped the schoolmaster's queen of spades on the loser pile.

Mac wandered in and out of the game, talking to people, cultivating the owner and bartender, Jake, catching up with the news. All the talk concerned westward expansion. Men said maybe a thousand people set out from Missouri last spring, headed mostly for Oregon, some for California. A thousand! Mac could hardly credit it. The city was booming because of the emigrants, said Jake. The bartender was glad to talk, but his eyes constantly roamed the room, keeping him aware of the goings-on. Mac wondered if he knew about the hold-out man.

The hot issues, according to Jake, were western: Annex Texas! Kick the British out of Oregon! And gossip about the Indian trade was on every man's lips. Mac picked up more bits of news in St. Louis than out in the western country itself.

The most remarkable news was that Bridger had built another trading post, this time on Blacks Fork, and not to trade with the trappers or Indians—to trade with travelers. Good country, a week or more east of the Salt Lake, right on the main road to Oregon. Meant to take care of the emigrators, Old Gabe did, those thousand.

Think of it—Gabe Bridger gone to minding a store. A child of nature, Skinhead liked to say. And not yet forty years old.

All those Americans bound for Oregon. Too much to absorb right away. A thousand people buying supplies in St. Louis. No wonder Uncle Hugh was prosperous.

Mac's first clue was Skinhead's insinuating voice. It sounded jovial, but Mac knew better. He was going to the outhouse, Skinhead said too casually. Something was up.

Mac asked if he could sit in. Sure. He pushed into a

seat next to the blond banker. Center of the action, Mac judged. Kid with a choirboy face like that, people didn't look twice. But he was off to a good start, heading to be a gambler. Odd, he didn't look more than sixteen.

Mac had been through this with Skinhead before.

Mac placed one bet and won. Good omen.

Skinhead came back. At first he was miffed to see someone taking the space next to the kid, but he gave a slight, faraway smile when he saw it was Mac. The kid offered Mac the deck.

Mac cut, leaving halves for the kid. The feel of the deck didn't mean much to Mac. Skinhead could tell you how many cards he was going to cut and hit it right on, or lift part of a deck and see how many cards were in it. "Reward of a wasted youth," he liked to say.

The cards were picked, the bets were down, and the kid started turning cards over. The schoolmaster lost and looked desperate. Must have lost plenty. And he was mesmerized by the play—trouble. The farmer was barely alert enough to make his bets. The kid seemed to have plenty of marks.

Mac won both his small bets, and the kid started a fresh deal. Skinhead put out a buck instead of two bits. He picked the nine of diamonds to win, and the nine of spades to lose. Mac got his feet flat on the floor and his chair a tad back from the table. He didn't know how Skinhead was going to do it. The fat man relished the rough stuff.

Simplest thing in the world. When the kid palmed a card, Skinhead clubbed the wrist ferociously and the card dropped face down.

Skinhead was sitting there calmly, grinning an immense grin. It was hard to realize he had reached across the table and back that fast. Now he stretched across with his Green river knife and used the blade to turn over the dropped card. The nine of spades.

The kid went for something.

Mac clamped both the kid's wrists hard. Skinhead was all shining head and shining teeth. He stepped onto the table and grabbed the kid's hair. Was Skinhead going to scalp him?

Suddenly Mac whipped backwards, grabbed by the throat. The farmer, perfectly sober.

Damn—he had a pistol in Skinhead's face!

A heavy cane whacked the farmer's gun arm, and the gun fell on the table.

Another whack—the farmer crumpled to the floor, cold-cocked.

Mac rubbed his throat and looked around. A fancy stranger holding the cane. Backing him up, Robert Campbell with a little pepperpot pistol. Behind him, the bartender Jake with a side-by-side.

"Afternoon, Gant," said the stranger.

"A-a-a-agh!" An awful, clotted, tortured-animal sound.

Mac whirled and saw blood pouring down the side of the kid's face and neck. Skinhead threw a big, bleeding wedge of ear onto the table. "He'll wear my mark, by God," said Skinhead. Then the fat man smiled sunnily at the stranger. "Afternoon, Cap."

Mac was staring at the choirboy. He'd have a two-pointed ear for life.

Skinhead scooped up the money the kid had on the table, all of it. He left the pot, and sang to the schoolmaster, "Take that home to your wife." With a jerk of the head in his friends' direction, the fat man headed out.

In the street Skinhead said cheerily, "Good timing, Cap, Mr. Campbell. How'd you find us?"

In a plummy accent the stranger answered, "Who couldn't guess where to find George Gant when he gets back to town?"

The fat man laughed too eagerly.

"Sir William," said Robert Campbell properly, "Robert Maclean. Mr. Maclean, Sir William Drummond Stewart." They shook hands.

"Thanks, Sir William," said Mac. "In the nick of time." Skinhead waved that off.

"That farmer had us fooled with his drunk act," Mac said at Skinhead.

"Had you fooled," said the fat man.

"Mr. Maclean," interjected Campbell, "would you join us in a drink? I spoke to your uncle about your prospects, and to Sir William about you, and he may have a proposition."

"You, too, Gant," added Sir William.

Mac hoped the proposition didn't involve Skinhead. The fat man was getting a little too crazy.

≈ 9 ≈

Plum moon

Mac thought the lord looked like a gargantuan grasshopper. He was perched on the edge of the billiard table in his green waistcoat and tobacco trousers, his long body all jutting elbows and knees.

Four ivory balls, two white and two red, were arrayed on the green felt. The lord's eye was on one of the two white balls, his hand humped to support the cue stick. He stroked smoothly, the ball glided across the green and clicked against the other white ball, into one of the red balls, and then into the other. Meanwhile the white object ball had glided into a corner pocket.

"A three!" exclaimed Hugh Maclean. Mac's uncle seemed a trifle amused at his own enthusiasm.

"And fifty," said Robert Campbell. "Well done."

The lord held out his hand to Skinhead, who shook it too vigorously, his shiny forehead furrowing. "One more game, Cap," rasped Skinhead.

"Sir William," murmured Campbell.

Skinhead and Sir William were old pals from their years in the mountains together, and occasionally broke into reminiscence. Skinhead's familiar way of addressing the baronet evidently disturbed Campbell.

"I think Mr. Maclean may want to try his hand," said Sir William and extended the cue by its butt. Hugh declined, and Sir William offered it to Mac. Mac took it—he was afraid not to. Skinhead would beat him.

"A game to learn by?" Mac asked Skinhead.

"At a wager of two bits, young Mr. Maclean," Stewart

piped up. "You pay for your lessons." The lord gave a dry hiccough of a laugh and a frosty smile. He lit a cigar.

Mac couldn't believe the lord was in a billiard hall, and swilling Matt Murphy's ale. Murphy's was a stalwart local product. As a lad, Mac didn't dare go into such dens of iniquity. Only the river rabble did that.

Skinhead gestured for Mac to go first and showed him how to make a bridge. Mac supposed that making a fool of yourself was part of the price of doing business.

Mac wished they'd get down to whatever business it was—he was wild with waiting.

Skinhead demonstrated the basic shots—the object was to sink the other white ball, and to make your original ball glance off one or both of the red balls. Mac hoped only to sink a white ball, and he couldn't do that. One ear and half his mind were on the conversation behind him between the Scots lord and the American businessmen. The weather, business conditions, the availability of money—maddeningly mundane.

From Jake's Tavern the party had collected Hugh Maclean and adjourned to this nearby billiard parlor, where Skinhead fit in well and the baronet poorly—nobility among the lowlife. Rough sorts of men plied the other tables, and a pall of rank smoke hung in the air. Every sort of uncouth accent and profane language offended the ear.

Sir William cast his eyes about boldly, and seemed inclined to smile at it all. Perhaps he thought it deliciously low. Then he simply shed his brown coat and went to work, cheek to jowl with his inferiors. After thinking it, Mac reprimanded himself for a word such as *inferiors*.

And here, watching this finicky game called four-ball carom and drinking ale, Uncle Hugh whispered to Mac that he should heed the baronet's offer. Which had led to this interminable waiting.

At the billiard table Mac was jumpy. He never knew which direction the struck ball was going to go, and he didn't care. Billiards seemed to him an odd game, cool, too much in the head, played in hushed tones with a lot of softly admiring "Jolly well done"s and such. Skinhead was a hand, and Campbell could make some clever shots, but no one could keep up with the lord.

The baronet was tall, skinny, aloof, perhaps indifferent. Mac caught a glimpse of comradely spirit in Stewart's greeting of Skinhead perhaps, but frostiness otherwise. Mac was informed that traveling the West was a great passion with Sir William, that he had spent six or eight years in the mountains and was a full-fledged *hivervant*, a winterer. But Mac couldn't imagine anything was a passion with this fellow.

Mac was also informed that Sir William and Campbell were great friends, bosom companions of mountain days. But Mac couldn't picture either of them in the mountains, all dusty, often thirsty, sometimes starving, sleeping on the ground, sometimes with Indian companions on the trail and in the blankets. And they didn't demonstrate mountain familiarity. Robert Campbell the baronet called simply Campbell, once "my dear Campbell." Skinhead was "Gant," and everyone else was "Mister." And the group cut its tune to match the baronet's. Mac felt like a wooden doll.

The first game over, Skinhead insisted that Mac put another two bits on the table. Acquiescing, Mac heard Campbell say behind him, "I'd say we have your man in young Mr. Maclean."

Stewart's Scots accent added, "And Gant here." Skinhead nodded vigorously. Whatever was in the offing, he was up for it.

"Do you know what it is Sir William has in mind, Mr. Maclean?"

"Not at all." Mac turned his back to Skinhead's shot.

The baronet smiled, perhaps amused, and took over. "Campbell told me you want to set yourself up as a trader."

"That's so, sir."

"A good Scot, then." Sir William's estates were in Scotland. "Do you know Scots traders are now opening up the China trade?"

"No, sir." He glanced at Uncle Hugh, uncertain.

"The wealth of Cathay, Mr. Maclean, the wealth of Cathay."

"Yes, sir."

"Why the Indian trade, man? It's half dead. You'd be better off trading for this stuff." He held up a glistening white ivory sphere. "Campbell," he declared, "it took one elephant tusk to make a set of these for four-ball carom. They're killing thousands of elephants a year. When I was in Africa, I saw men grow rich in a single season. Truly rich."

Campbell nodded.

"Why an Indian trader, Mr. Maclean? Your uncle here would be the first to tell you it's not sensible."

"I love the West, sir. I love the life." He was desperate to launch into his case—the closing of Fort Mackenzie, his closeness to the Cheyenne people, but he judged it best to wait.

Stewart regarded Mac a moment. "I, too, love the life, Mr. Maclean. But because of my accursed titles and estates, I can't give myself to it any longer. Will you help me, sir? And you, Gant?"

"What do you want, Cap?" Skinhead turned away from his shot and paid attention.

"Buffalo, Gant. Mr. Maclean. And antelope, bighorn sheep, panthers, grizzlies, and a few elk. Plus flora. I want to take the West back to Murthly. With your hardihood and Scots shrewdness, you could do it for me. And, of course, Gant's wilderness wisdom."

"Sir William has spent some money on this enterprise with little effect," put in Campbell.

"Scoundrels," muttered Sir William. "But you have character, young Mr. Maclean. You and Gant both. Gant is perhaps a little chaotic."

Skinhead looked to be getting miffed.

"We've shipped Sir William quite a few animals in the last several years," said Campbell, "but he needs more—problems with injury and death in transit, survival in a new climate, and so on.

"The two of you could take a crew back to, say, Laramie, yet this autumn, and collect animals." It was late September already. "I think you're the men."

"Agreed," said Sir William to Campbell.

Mac felt himself flush.

Campbell held up a finger. "I know you have something else in mind. But this is a step toward it. If you consent, you could end up with some working capital. And good will here in St. Louis."

"And in Scotland," said Sir William.

Hugh was looking at Mac with a twinkle.

"Campbell," said Sir William, looking at his pocket watch, "we do have a dinner engagement."

"What do you say, young Mr. Maclean?" prompted Campbell.

Restraining himself, Mac answered, "Sounds worth exploring."

"Then shall we explore it further in the morning?" concluded the banker.

2

Mac was heated up, but Uncle Hugh wasn't. He insisted quietly on getting home, having some soup from the pot that was always on his woodstove, and getting his pipe lit afterwards. Mac noticed that a book sat on the dinner table—*The Wealth of Nations*, by Adam Smith. So six thousand miles from Scotland and the university he didn't get to attend, Uncle Hugh was still reading philosophy. He was a man of unvarying habits—a frugal meal, a smoke, reading, contemplation. No passions, no whiskey, as far as Mac knew no sex. Not even coffee—the church women claimed coffee was an aphrodisiac. Hugh's only heat was in his pipe.

How unlike Skinhead, Mac thought. How unlike me. And Uncle Hugh, will you please get on with whatever you have to say?

Hugh set some sheets on the table and beckoned Mac to sit beside him. "You see, Mr. Campbell and I have backed a trader in a small way, a man named Primeau. I suspect Campbell does it mostly to annoy the Company, but we earn a few dollars. The figures in this column are wholesale in St. Louis, in this column retail in the mountains."

Mac looked them over. "Mountain prices are about right."

"We're interested in backing other good men. Like you." Uncle Hugh looked at Mac sidelong. "We think it's the time to exploit the Emigrant Road. We think the Indian trade is, well, quiescent. But you're bound to go to that Yellowstone country, aren't you?"

Mac nodded.

Uncle Hugh smiled with satisfaction. "Campbell and I had a good talk about it this afternoon. He knows the Yellowstone country as well as any man—trapped there, and ran Fort William there. A wise man might make a go of it. Campbell even admitted that, long term, it might be the sounder proposition. He respects your judgment on that. But now, and probably for some years, the money is on the Emigrant Road.

"Under the circumstances, I can't advance the big piece of money, lad. Nor will Campbell."

Hugh let it sit a moment. "That's where Sir William comes in. They are friends, and Mr. Campbell would like to do Sir William a service." Hugh put another piece of paper on top. "These are the animals Sir William wants, at these prices. Look them over at your leisure tonight. But Campbell believes you can net in excess of a thousand dollars in this venture. And Gant gets a bonus of five hundred."

Mac wanted to shove the figures away, but he made himself look at them. "If you will help Sir William, you may be able to get a stake out of it. Say you go to Laramie and earn a thousand net from Sir William. Campbell believes you can make a handsome profit with healthy horseflesh on the Emigrant Road next spring—the emigrants destroy their horses on the crossing. He'd be willing to put up a thousand dollars for horses, share and share alike.

"Now, lad, suppose I went in a thousand..."

They talked until nearly midnight, shuffling figures, gauging profits. Mac went to bed feeling unsure.

Maybe it was the horses that made him unsure—horse trading bore sad memories for Mac and Hugh. In '37 Mac's mother died of smallpox, and his father got Hugh to buy him out of the store, which was then poor. With that small bit of capital and Mac, Alexander Maclean hit the road trading horses.

But he was deep into the bottle then, a lifelong failing, and a drunk could ruin any venture. In a year the horse business was gone, and their stake gone. In another six months Alexander was dead, drowned in the Mississippi. Mac ended up with nothing but his knowledge of horses and a taste for adventure.

Mac sat on the bed in his room, mulling. It was the room he'd grown up in, above the store. Now it had a four-poster bed. But it was his room—it even smelled like his room. Stretching out in the clean sheets, drifting off, Mac felt dreams of childhood coming back to him.

≈ 10 ≈

Mac Maclean rolled over in his blankets and smelled something and waited to open his eyes. It was sagebrush— he pulled the smell in deep. Sagebrush made piquant by the dew. He had come home.

He lay there for a moment and enjoyed the feeling. He expected to see Chimney Rock today, and for him that marked the real beginning of the West. Where the land changed. Where the rocks make wild, romantic shapes. Where it got dry, and high. Where the grass was buffalo grass. Where the blue haze on the horizon was mountains. Where he belonged.

Opening his eyes, he saw that the eastern sky wasn't quite black. Time to get up. No wake-up cry yet. Had the entire watch fallen asleep? Who was on watch? Skinhead, Fitzgerald, and Ringman, damn them.

Just then Mac saw movement among the horses.

Indians among the horses. What had happened to the watch?

Mac had been careful. The horses, mules, and oxen were hobbled and picketed, and ringed by tents and charettes and bales of goods and sleeping men. The Indians would have to cut some hobbles and pull at least some picket stakes to stampede the horses.

Mac lifted his new rifle, made by Sam Hawken, and checked the percussion cap. No movement, no sound.

The boom of a gunshot.

"Indians!" Mac hollered.

He saw blue-gray movement on the back of a horse. Men were jumping up all around. Mac fired at the move-

75

ment. The horse bolted. Mac ran after it barefooted. He
heard Skinhead roar at something across the way, and a
yip from someone.

Now it was bedlam. The horses pawed the air, reared,
whinnied, and neighed. Some pulled their picket pins,
some broke their hobbles—some did both, and milled and
kicked and clattered off.

A flood of cussing and bellering. Ringman's voice. The
big man had hold of a horse's picket rope and was trying to
get some footing. But the horse jerked Ringman to the
ground and ran after the others. The men were working
the animals still in the ring, turning their milling into
circling.

Where in hell were the Indians? Run off? At least it was
too dark for any redskin to see clearly to shoot. Mac
slipped to the center of the ring and picked up the
blanket. Blue, with a wide stripe of dark blue at each end.
Made by Witney. Expensive blanket—what kind of Indian
would wear a blanket such as this on a horse-stealing raid?
It had a hole near the center where Mac's ball had passed
through—four holes in fact, through folds. Mac checked in
the faint predawn light for bloodstains, but didn't see any.
Probably he missed.

"Cap, I got both the sons of bitches," crowed Skinhead.

Since Campbell and Sir William named them captain
and lieutenant of the expedition, Skinhead had taken to
calling Mac "Cap." Not even "Cap'n." Mac didn't think it
did anything for discipline.

Mac walked over to Skinhead's rotund silhouette to see
what tribe the raiders were from.

One Indian, a young Sioux, was dead. Lights shot out.
So it was Skinhead who'd fired. The other, small and frail,
looked clubbed behind the ear. Skinhead was cleaning the
blood off the butt of his hawk.

"This child seed 'em creeping up, two of 'em," he said.
"They come past Fitzgerald—he was asleep on watch. One
stayed outside there, and this one sneaked in. Got 'em
both."

"Next time don't play hero. Wake everybody up."

"Ah, Cap, don't spoil the fun."

"Fitzgerald, you're fined ten dollars, and you walk to Laramie," Mac hollered. Ten bucks was a week's pay.

Fitzgerald scowled and looked as if he meant to mope. John Fitzgerald was a bad apple—he even had a poor army record down at Atkinson. Mac intended to sort him out.

Skinhead took out his knife and knelt over the shot Indians. He took a turn of hair around his left hand and popped the scalp deftly. He grabbed the hair of the other downed red man the same way. Mac saw something odd.

"Hold on a minute." Skinhead looked up annoyed, but waited.

Mac checked the hair. It was tied back in a ponytail. He had never seen that on a brave before. He looked at the face. A teenage boy, light-complexioned, and small even for a teenager. The clothes were an odd assortment—Pawnee moccasins, a cloth white-man shirt with a quilled four-winds wheel on the breast that looked Sioux.

Looking at the wheel, Mac noticed something else. And on the other side too. He checked the wound. If the skull wasn't cracked, the wound only looked bad.

The eyes flickered and opened on Mac—large, dark eyes in a tiny face.

Mac couldn't believe it. "Lieutenant Gant," said Mac, "those are breasts. What you tomahawked is a girl. And a half-breed."

2

"Only the two of us," Lisette repeated, sounding desperate now. Her face was tearstained, her hair bloody, she had been grilled hard, and her head felt as if it were busted. She was too used up to lie.

Mac thought it unlikely that one boy and one girl, especially a Sioux and a breed girl, would go out horse stealing. But Skinhead saw only the two and the signs said two, so Mac supposed he believed her.

"It was only a prank," she said defiantly.

"Some prank, girl. A man is dead."

Now she was really pissed off at him, for emphasizing the obvious. She said she was the daughter of Genet, up at Fort Platte, which was just a mile and a half from the big post, Laramie. Maybe Genet had a wayward daughter on his hands and would be grateful to Mac for bringing her back. Unscalped.

But Mac didn't have time to ponder on it now. They were just three weeks out from Westport and a few days from Laramie—Mac and Skinhead had been pushing right along, driving men and animals hard.

"Skinhead, you and Antoine scout. Paul the Blue, ride with us." Paul Ringman had had his shoulder knocked out of place when the horse jerked him down. "Fitzgerald, walk behind." Where the dust will get up your nose and in your teeth, damn you. "Let's move it out."

The men looked a little grumbly. Well, Mac had been hard. For his stake, he could be hard. For his trading post. For Annemarie.

3

"I lost four good American horses. I got back two Indian ponies. I expect to be paid."

Mac had been severe with the girl as they rode, but she acted indifferent. She just rode, listlessly, rocking in the saddle. It was a cool November day, and she had the Witney blanket wrapped tight up to her neck. The four holes Mac's ball had left made an odd decoration on her nice blanket. Why didn't she take a ratty, cheap blanket to steal horses?

She had a beautiful face in a way, thought Mac. Onyx hair and striking dark eyes. But her face was spoiled by scarring, probably smallpox, which had hit the mountains in '37. She was petite, not just short, but tiny all over, and beautifully molded. Unfortunately she had a face that said she could be used hard and might like it.

The way Ringman looked at her, he thought she was

beautiful, too. Poor Paul the Blue hurt when he jostled that arm. He was a big lummox, over six feet, strongly built, with a sweet, placid disposition, like an ox. The men liked him and called him Paul the Blue for Bunyan's ox.

Mac wondered if she was thinking about the Sioux youth who lay back at camp dead. Maybe she loved him. Certainly they were lovers. Mac had seen these soured half-breed women before—wild, angry, promiscuous, abused. Their fathers couldn't get anybody to marry them.

Mac's complaints about his horses meant nothing to her. Of the seven of his that ran off, the men found only three. He confiscated Lisette and her friend's ponies as partial payment.

She didn't care. She also seemed singularly unimpressed with the fact that Mac saved her life. And with everything, including herself.

Mac could use Genet's goodwill. His little post was handy, being close to Laramie, and Mac had merchandise to sell. Campbell and Uncle Hugh had cooked up the idea.

Didn't those thousand emigrants travel last spring along the Oregon Trail, as it was being called? Up the Blue, over to the Platte, upstream past Laramie to the Sweetwater, through South Pass, across the Siskadee, past Fort Bridger, along the Snake, down the Columbia to Oregon. It was the route Mac first took to the mountains, and the one he was on now. Campbell thought the emigration would grow.

Campbell had a superb system of intelligence—most old mountain men stopped to see him when they were in St. Louis. He had a nose for the main chance, and right now it lay in being able to provide fresh, healthy, sound-footed animals along the trail. Horses, mules, and oxen.

Thus his proposition. Mac had to take Sir William's offer. As long as he was going, he should drive livestock west—now, in the fall, with a chance to winter over. By June, when the wagons crossing the continent got to Laramie, half-crippled because of poor draft animals, Mac's horses, mules, and oxen would be fat. And ready to trade,

one for several who were sore of hoof or back. It would be
a seller's market.

At the end of the season, a healthy profit—in addition to
the money from Sir William. Said profit to be split evenly
between the man with the backing, Campbell, and the
man in the field, Mac. Plus another bonus to Skinhead.

And then Uncle Hugh quietly offered to supply a couple
of thousand dollars worth of goods to be traded to the
Indians for furs. "You need something to keep you occupied during the winter," Hugh said wryly. Again the profit
to be split.

So Mac and Skinhead had steamed up to Westport
about the first of October and spent ten days investing in
the best livestock they could find. And putting together a
crew. And buying some wagons to transport Stewart's
show animals back. And buying gear, and seed. On October 21st they set out for Laramie.

Mac had hopes. He could get a good stake out of
this—if he could avoid getting robbed, did some good
trading, kept his animals healthy, kept the redskins away
from them, and if and if and if.

Making a home base of Fort Platte, where this girl's
daddy was boss, would be a good start.

He wondered if he'd have time this winter to journey
north to visit with Annemarie. Strikes Foot said they'd
winter on Clear Creek—a couple of hundred miles. He
doubted it, not in the snow.

Mac Maclean looked forward and saw Skinhead on a hill
a couple of miles ahead. He didn't reach for his Dolland—a
fine telescope, gift of Sir William. No need to look. If
Skinhead was willing to skyline himself, everything was
fine.

≈ 11 ≈

"Oh, that Little One," Genet would say, indicating Lisette, rolling his eyes. And that would be all. "Little One and that One-Dollar," he'd say with an air of exasperation, "they just rutted." Little One was Lisette's nickname, from the Sioux.

One-Dollar was the young Sioux Skinhead had killed. Genet Frenchified his name to "Dollaire." Fortunately for Mac, he was a hang-around-the-forts Sioux and a drinker, not prized by his people.

Genet fascinated Paul the Blue.

The French partisan went around the fort with a long face. It was his conviction that the French explored North America, they created the fur trade, the English did nothing but colonize a little strip along the seacoast, and the whole should belong to France. "Damme," he'd say, making it sound like the French *femme*. "Even the Indian word for white man is 'Frenchman.'"

All this he proclaimed at breakfast, dinner, and supper, and mumbled in between. Aside from that, the trade was going to hell anyway, the Indians were bestial, the whites were worse because they should have known better, his wife was unfaithful and now she was dead, the weather would turn rotten tomorrow, and his daughter was ungrateful, meaning promiscuous.

To Mac and Skinhead the Frenchman was simply a sad sack. To Paul the Blue, an unlettered carpenter, he was a sensitive man, a man of melancholy, in tune with the sad music that was human life.

It was John Baptiste Reshaw that Blue couldn't stand.

81

He was a young French-Canadian trader, sharp, tough, cynical, and the firewater connection. Every summer he went to Mexico and smuggled back Taos lightning. Reshaw was also the brains of the fort, and the reason it gave Laramie good competition.

Blue's problem with him was that he thought Genet contemptible, Lisette beddable, and everything amusing.

Sometimes at supper Genet would tell tales of the beautiful, heartbreaking music his mother used to make on the clavichord back in Montreal. His mother died young, Genet said—the best die young—and she made music like an angel. And after this mournful table conversation he would retire to his quarters and fiddle the evening away, scratching out the sentimental songs of the *voyageurs*, the French boatmen who first explored the forests of North America, in canoes. He never played for other people.

Blue liked to prop his huge frame against an adobe wall outside and listen rapt—the music was soulful, he said. Even Skinhead could be drawn to this solitary music-making. Lisette mocked the fiddling, as she mocked everything about her father.

Blue didn't care what she said. He was in love with her.

All this mattered little to Mac. Genet was cooperative, even ingratiating about practical matters. Mac was welcome to trade livestock here next summer—that would surely draw customers to Genet's humble post. Yes, certainly, Genet was glad for Mac to build corrals. Since the corrals would remain, Genet would be in his debt—might he loan men to help with construction? Since Mac's men would be out collecting animals for Sir William, whom Genet was honored to have met last summer, they could bring in meat for the fort as well. That way they would earn their keep—more than earn it, certainly, and Genet was again obliged. Would Mac like corn for his livestock?

Mac feared Genet would be fired at any time. Fortunately, Reshaw also wanted Mac and his men as winterers. He was tired of Genet's lugubrious company, and seemed to like the Americans, and the money the Americans might lose at cards.

Mac thought Fort Platte might be able to give the older and more established Fort Laramie a run for its money. It was big, important-looking—adobe walls eleven feet high and roughly two hundred paces around—and had plenty of whiskey. If only Genet didn't mess everything up.

Mac divided his forces. Since Skinhead was full of talk about the big bonus he would earn from Cap'n Stewart, he was in charge of the hunting. The Black Hills to the west were a home to every kind of beast, especially mountain lions, bighorn sheep, and the silver-tip bears, the grizzlies. Mac told him, truthfully, that capturing them live would be hard, a job for an old hand like Skinhead. Some would have to be snared, others stunned with neck shots. Skinhead intended to work the rest of the autumn and all winter on this project—bears might be less tricky to catch when they were hibernating. The buffalo and antelope he'd gather up last—they were so easy. And he'd surely be ready to head for Westport early in the spring. Skinhead was all braggadocio.

Mac took on the building projects. Horses, mules, and oxen first—they'd be too vulnerable until he got them penned at night. Sheds to store feed in—Genet wanted these, too. Other corrals for the beasts Skinhead would bring in. Plus cages. Mac had brought Blue and a bunch of log-working tools—double-bitted ax, adze, bow saw, two-man crosscut saw—just for this purpose. Blue was an expert cabin builder.

Mac also set a man to repairing the wagons hauled west, and even making new ones. He thought about making a short trip out to some nearby Sioux to trade the goods he'd brought out. And he teased himself with a bigger idea: Why not do the trading with the Cheyennes, up in front of the Big Horn Mountains, and see Annemarie?

Blue's mooning after Lisette was the joke of the post. Such a big fellow, so mild, so nice. He'd never abuse her. Lisette acted as if she couldn't stand him. She flirted openly with several of the post staff, most provocatively with Reshaw, a small, dark, muscular, and rather dashing fellow. She acted as if she didn't give a damn that he was supposed to marry some Arapahoe woman soon.

One night early in December, Mac, Blue, Skinhead, and Genet were playing whist in the dining room. Genet generally didn't like cards—they were a sign of this degraded prairie life, which he despised—but he acquiesced to whist, which was more civilized.

Tonight's game was not much of a contest. Blue didn't understand it, and impulsive Skinhead was bored because he couldn't win or lose a pile on the single, dramatic turn of a card.

A clatter from next door—Genet's quarters. A body crashing into the common wall, it sounded like. A woman's voice shouting, and a man's.

Poor Genet jumped for the common door. The other three hurried outside.

Reshaw ran out Genet's front door into the courtyard, hauling up his pants. Lisette threw something at him, a candlestick, skittering across the frozen earth. She cursed him. She said something about his manhood. Reshaw scurried off. Little One stepped out into the courtyard and maligned him again. She was entirely naked. She looked across at Blue, Mac, and Skinhead saucily, and cocked her hips. Her father's arm pulled her roughly back inside.

They closed the door and sat back down at the table. Blue looked to Mac sorrowful, not angry.

Skinhead started dealing euchre. "She's a cat, that one," he observed.

Mac watched Blue restrain himself. Skinhead's life and limb were momentarily in jeopardy. He didn't notice.

"She just needs someone," Blue choked out. His face was mottled.

Skinhead shrugged. "Little One has had everyone. She needs a lodgepoling. Ante."

Mac put a hand on Blue's wrist.

Genet's voice came loud through the wall. "Right in my own home," he yelled. The names he hollered included "slut."

Mac took Blue by the arm and led him outside. Skinhead changed to solitaire.

"You can't change a leopard's spots," Mac said softly.

For a moment Blue said nothing. They were walking

toward the outfit's wall tents. "She needs me," Paul answered.

2

Mac regularly moved the livestock to better grass, fattening them for the long winter on the Laramie plains. Genet's corn would get him through the bad months comfortably. At night Mac kept a close guard on the animals. He headed timber trips up the Laramie River. He oversaw Blue's building of the corrals, cages for the captured animals, and more wagons.

And still he had too much time, time to think about his stake, his post on the Yellowstone. He got broody. He started thinking about those bales of trading goods sitting there not turned into furs. Mac was a good brooder—he had a knack for it and could make himself miserable. To recover his spirits, he would fantasize about Annemarie.

One morning he got up, sleepless, and told Blue to get ready—they were going traveling. A long way—to the Cheyennes.

Lisette insisted on making Mac a capote, a heavy, woolen coat. He couldn't go on a winter journey with just blankets, could he? Like a poor Indian? This was December. She would have it ready before dinner, and they'd start out on full stomachs, wouldn't they? Mac saved Little One's life, and she wanted to do something for him.

Mac found it easier to give in than say no. And it was true that since Magpie robbed him, he was a poor man. Even now he didn't have proper winter moccasins. He would have preferred showing up to see Annemarie looking rich.

He spent the morning getting ready. He would take four horses loaded with goods to trade. Blue was going along— Mac wanted to get the fellow away from Lisette. And Reshaw was going with them. The Fort Platte trader wanted to make contact with the Cheyennes, too, to invite them in to trade this spring.

Mac couldn't very well refuse. He went out to look at the horse herd. He had told no one about Annemarie. They wondered why he was going all the way to Powder River country to visit some Cheyennes instead of trading with nearby Sioux. He kept his own counsel.

He eyed the horses thoughtfully. He could take ten extras now, make them a gift to Strikes Foot, and bring Annemarie back as his wife. He wanted to. He wanted to achingly.

But to Mac Maclean it didn't make sense. By midsummer those ten horses would become twenty-five or thirty. And he had no appropriate quarters for her now—he didn't want to start his married life in a tent outside the fort, or in a borrowed room in it. He wanted the master quarters in his own fort.

Mac went back into the fort. He would do what was sensible, and what required self-discipline.

They ate heartily. There was no denying, when starting out on a winter journey, a spirit of eat, drink, and be merry for tomorrow you may die. Yet the young winter was mild—there were just thin patches of snow in spots. Only the incessant wind made men uncomfortable.

Little One stayed in Genet's quarters during the meal, evidently finishing work on Mac's capote.

Finally they were ready. "Lisette," Mac called, holding the reins of his horse. The wind chilled him through his cloth shirt.

She came running with the capote. It was made from a blue Witney blanket, just like the one...

It *was* the one he shot.

Little One held it up, spread for him to see, smiling mischievously. It was sinew sewn, and tightly, a good job. Instead of patching the four holes, she had left them open and actually circled them boldly with vermilion.

"Four's a lucky number, you know," she said. "A *wakan* number." The Sioux word for "sacred."

"Now instead of Dancer, they'll call you Red Shot."

Mac grabbed the capote, put it on, and stepped into the saddle.

"Or maybe Four-Holer," she added.

Reshaw snickered.

Mac applied his spurs.

December, 1843, Big freezing moon

Annemarie could not stop fondling her hair ornament. She rubbed her thumbs over the coral stones, and the oval pieces of onyx. Then she fingertipped the turquoise centerpiece gingerly, giggling foolishly with her mother, Lame Deer. The ornament was a showy work of the jeweler's art and came from Santa Fe. Mac was damnably proud of it.

Even moonstruck, Annemarie was a Cheyenne maiden— eyes averted before a strange man, head down. Mac likewise was subtle in sneaking glances at her square face. He was brimful happy. Now he knew that during his months away he barely realized how much he loved her. She was to be his wife. Even a tough, hard Scots trader could get moony about that.

Right now the warmth in the lodge of the Shield society leader Strikes Foot was not just from the center fire. Everyone was aglow with Mac's generosity. He had brought Strikes Foot a percussion-cap rifle, rare in the tribe. To Yellow Bird he had presented a bright yellow handkerchief of silk. To Lame Deer he had given a wide belt of Mexican hand-tooled leather. He had even provided for the family's newly adopted waifs, a brother and sister about ten, giving them pieces of decorative ribbon.

Mac had been concerned about a gift for Calling Eagle— how do you take thought for a would-be woman? His solution was a wood-framed, brass-studded mirror. It obviously pleased her. Calling Eagle sometimes made herself up elaborately. The mirror satisfied Mac secretly because among Cheyennes mirrors were usually objects for men, and among whites for women.

He was still uncomfortable with Calling Eagle's sexual mix-up. He had talked to Skinhead seriously about it on the boat. Skinhead said that *hemaneh* were revered by the Cheyennes—they were healers, creators of powerful love medicine, vital in the scalp dance and the medicine-lodge ceremony. Nevertheless, Mac would be glad to get Annemarie away from her.

Now Mac dug his last surprise out of his possibles sack and passed it to Strikes Foot.

"What's this?" the warrior exclaimed. He had seen them before, but not up close. A horseshoe.

"For your hoof," said Mac with a little smile. He held it to Strikes Foot's substitute foot. It nearly fit—custom-made for the smaller hoof of the buffalo.

Strikes Foot was half-bewildered, half-delighted.

"Look at this." Mac pointed out the extra touch. The front came to a point, and the edges were sharpened. The shoe was a nasty weapon for kicking.

Strikes Foot started to laugh. He was half out of control. He unstrapped the hoof. Mac got out the small hammer and the horseshoe nails. A few taps and it was done.

Strikes Foot strapped the thing on, stood, and took a kick at the tie-down rope.

Calling Eagle grabbed his arm and pulled him down with a frown, a wifely reprimand. Strikes Foot lay on the ground giggling.

Mac handed him a file. "This will keep the edges sharp." Then he took out four more shoes and handed them over. "If you lose some."

"My name will be Strikes Steel Foot!" the Cheyenne exclaimed, giddily happy. Mac was satisfied; he had done well.

The largesse of these gifts did not count what Mac had brought Strikes Foot in exchange for his five horses and two packs of buffalo robes. Lame Deer was already using the three-legged cooking pot. The blankets, tobacco, powder, lead, and beads sat in a pile at the rear of the lodge, where Strikes Foot slept with his wives. A mound of wealth.

Mac had not even built up the mound overgenerously,

to make a point. He was giving dollar for dollar what he
got for the horses and robes. He had done reasonably well
for the horses at Fort Union, and splendidly for the robes
in St. Louis. Strikes Foot and the family were dazzled. So
the point was made: An alliance with a trader was a great
advantage to the Cheyennes.

Strikes Foot reached for one of his social pipes. Mac
quickly excused himself and stepped outside the lodge.

Matters looked in good order. Reshaw and Blue had the
wall tent up beside Strikes Foot's lodge, and the trade
goods neatly stowed inside. Later this afternoon Mac
would make some presents, and then do his trading. The
trading wouldn't take long—he didn't have that much to
trade.

All seven horses were picketed near the tent, with nose
bags of corn, the last of the sacks Mac had brought. Blue
and Reshaw were gone, evidently gathering the inner and
outer bark of the sweet cottonwood, as Mac had asked.
More feed for the horses.

The trip was not particularly hard on them. Mac allowed
ten days, and it took seven. The ground was almost bare
the whole way, with one light snow of no consequence, so
the horses didn't have to struggle for their feed. The only
hardship for them was covering a lot of ground in a short
time. Mac thought they were in good shape. Which was
fortunate. He intended to trade half of them, or all of
them. In early winter he was lucky to get up here on
horseback—he might have to go back via snowshoe.

He was eager to get alone with Strikes Foot and talk
about his plan. He wanted to persuade these Cheyennes
to come in to Fort Platte early in the summer. Strikes Foot
would transport the hides Mac had traded for. And they
would do more trading. And Mac would find a priest or a
preacher man among the emigrants on the Oregon Trail
and stage a wedding.

He had thought again of using the gifts he had brought
to claim Annemarie now, and of taking her back to Fort
Platte for the winter. His answer was still no. He wanted a
wedding. A real wedding, white-man style. For that mat-

ter, Indian-style, too, at the same time. A real wedding,
ecumenical-style.

Mac ducked back into the lodge. Strikes Foot lifted the
packed pipe and raised one of the lucifers Mac had given
him. Half-wild with amusement, he struck the match on
his new horseshoe. Mac sat beside him and accepted the
friendly pipe.

"So, Dancer," said Strikes Foot, "tell us what happened
since you left."

2

"Reshaw," said Mac low, "get your goddamn eyes off
Yellow Bird."

The little Frenchman didn't answer, or even look back,
but just walked on into the night.

Mac had considered it carefully. Reshaw was flirting
with Strikes Foot's youngest wife, no question. And that
was big trouble. Mac didn't know how to control the
insolent trader, who thought he knew everything, but
didn't know any wild Indians, only hang-around-the-forts
Indians. So Mac got him outside with the excuse of
needing to feed the horses.

Mac hadn't expected the little bastard to refuse even to
answer. Mac took a couple of quick steps in the snow and
grabbed the sleeve of Reshaw's capote.

Reshaw patted Mac's hand. Turning with an easy smile,
as though Mac had not spoken harshly, Reshaw said, "You
want her first, *non*?"

"No." Mac felt flustered.

Reshaw made a loud smacking sound with his lips.
"Then the dusky maiden is mine."

"Back off, Reshaw."

"I slip into the tent with her after supper. A few
minutes." He was leering.

"Blue will be sleeping in the tent. The two of you."

Mac could see Reshaw was taken aback, but he shrugged.
"Then we'll take turns on her. All night."

Mac ignored the big talk. Reshaw was miffed at being put into the tent, which was damn well not as comfortable as a tipi. Strikes Foot had offered the lodge. But taking someone into your lodge was almost like making them family. Mac didn't want Reshaw getting any illusions that he was Strikes Foot's family through Mac's influence.

They got to the rope corral and started throwing sweet cottonwood bark to the horses. Mac felt discombobulated. Reshaw's designs on Yellow Bird were not so crazy, by his lights. She had been friendly to him. And the Sioux who hung around the forts, the ones Reshaw knew, traded the use of their wives and daughters for that Taos firewater. The Crows did it, too—not even for firewater, just for baubles. The Cheyennes did not, ever.

They finished the job in silence and started back to the lodge. "Reshaw, you're going to ruin yourself with the Cheyennes."

"You speak like a child."

"Listen to me." Mac grabbed Reshaw's capote sleeve. This time Reshaw jerked it back and faced Mac pointedly.

"Cheyenne women are chaste," he said hotly.

"Bah! They're Indians! And you're an old maid."

Mac didn't know how to get through to the peppery Frenchman. "Annemarie and I are going to get married," he declared. "Notice how she acts toward me? Shy. That's because I'm not family. I at least could be a suitor. So she doesn't act familiar."

Reshaw turned and stomped off toward the tipi.

Mac grabbed him again. The little man's eyes looked full of fire. "If Annemarie laughed and played with me, she'd be treating me like a brother, or an uncle. Someone she'd never sleep with." Mac felt like an idiot explaining Cheyenne sexual customs, when he himself didn't understand about Calling Eagle. "That's what Yellow Bird was doing with you. If you mistake her, we're all in danger."

Reshaw's lips curled. "You Americans, you drop your disapproval all over the land like buffalo turds." He spit at Mac's feet, whirled, and headed for the lodge.

"Reshaw!" This time Mac didn't grab. The Frenchman turned back, sneering. "You know what Cheyennes do to young girls who are seduced? The seducer mocks them in front of the whole tribe. Then everyone mocks them, almost unto death. They have to run off, or go to another band as nothing, a slave or a fourth wife or. . ." Mac was struggling for control.

"If a wife commits adultery, they shun her, or her husband kicks her out, or even kills her. They are not like the Indians you know."

"Stinking romance," said Reshaw. "They're Indians. They are animals. You take us to live with a queer and you romance about them?"

"Shut up, Reshaw." He advanced on the Frenchman.

"What's the matter, Maclean? You afraid I'll corrupt your Annemarie? Your romantic virgin?" The word seethed mockery. "I'd be the last of a long line of herd bulls, but still in front of you, hah?"

Mac stopped, controlled himself, and spoke low. "If you touch Yellow Bird, Strikes Foot will kill you. If you touch any woman in this camp, the band will have your scalp. And I'll help them take it."

Mac watched Reshaw's face. He saw nothing but defiance.

3

Mac was dreaming of the Sandwich Islands. Though he had never been to the islands, he recognized them. They were familiar in his dreams. He'd read a book with a seaman's account of visiting the islands, and other places in the South Seas. The seaman made clear how compliant the women were. Voluptuous, bare-breasted, raven-haired, and compliant.

Mac's dream was not explicit. In it he was in a reverie. A breeze was lulling him, palm branches were stroking him, and he heard soothing, exotic music. At other times he was being gently washed by the warm surf.

From time to time in the dream he was lying on cushions and sipping, as always, a turquoise liquid from a clear glass. He knew it was the essence of the coconut, a

magical elixir. He did not open his eyes as he drank. He
lowered his head. Dark hands stroked his fair skin softly,
sensually. Desire waxed and waned enticingly.

Suddenly he was alert in the buffalo robes of Strikes
Foot's lodge. The hands were real. Someone was beside
him, next to the center fire. He was momentarily afraid. A
hand was stroking his chest. It teased his navel. It rose and
played with his nipples. Annemarie, surely. He relaxed
and enjoyed it.

But was it really Annemarie?

Mac and the two kids had made a pallet of robes at the
feet of Strikes Foot, Calling Eagle, and Yellow Bird. Lame
Deer and Annemarie were on the far side, at the head.
Evidently Annemarie had made bold to creep around the
fire and lie beside him.

But what if this wasn't Annemarie?

Mac was alien here.

Tension prickled his forearms.

He knew one way to make sure.

Annemarie would be wearing a chastity belt. Pubescent, unmarried Cheyennes girls did. In this lodge only
Annemarie would have one.

Mac slipped his hand to her belly. The hand on his
chest stopped moving, and he heard a small intake of
breath. He moved his hand up and caressed her breasts
softly, both of them. He was relieved—his visitor was
certainly a woman, a real woman. Then, in fear and want,
he moved his hand down. Between her legs he did find
hide, and beyond the hide, mysterious softness and wetness.

The legs squeezed his hand hard. He heard a tiny snort
like a laugh. A hand grabbed his wrist and pulled it away.
And a body slid away from him in the robe. After a
moment he heard a faint slithering sound in the robes
across the dark tipi.

He could feel with his hand on the robe where
her warmth had been. So empty now. And beyond
the robe the frozen ground of the hoop-and-stick game
moon.

His hand out on the cold earth, Mac Maclean thought of
the future. This moon was the first of the new year, 1844.

This was the year he would found his trading post. This was the year he would fill his robes with a good woman. This was the year he would start his family. He was immensely pleased. And aroused.

≈ 13 ≈

January, 1844, Hoop-and-stick-game moon

Everything drifts away. Sounds flicker and glance about, random ricochets. Faces drift by. A cork slides past, not tied to his fishing line, and floating not in a river but in the sky. A cue stick sails along stuck vertical in a cloud, leather tip up.

Mac reaches in slow motion for the cue, but it sails around his grasp. From time to time in this airy dreamland he stretches a hand toward other objects—an uninhabited woman's dress, one of Lord Stewart's ivory balls, a burning candle—but he reaches through them, as though they were clouds, and they drift away.

Mac was afraid. He was aware that he usually loved his dreams of flying, but this time he was afraid of falling. He floated a little toward a cloud, hand out. It rose above him. He looked up at it, more afraid. If he fell, he would be an empty garment shot full of holes, streaking down the sky, tatterdemalion.

The strong odor of the smoke of sweetgrass and cedar rose in his nostrils, thick and pungent, like incense. It was a comfort, something real in this drifting universe.

He could remember someone's touching him, particularly on the belly. He thought the hand belonged to Calling Eagle, but he wondered if that was a trick of his raging brain. The touch felt dangerous. He feared its return—it would make him throw up again.

Spoken words, bits of chant, thumps of drum, tattered pieces of wailed song, floated through his mind. He held on to the earth. He felt nauseated, like once when he was on a raft on the Mississippi with his dad and the wind rose and the waves rocked them and he held on tight and was sick over the side.

The touch came again. He opened his eyes and saw Calling Eagle's face looking into his. He drifted off.

Later he was more lucid. He knew he was in the tent. He had had vomiting and diarrhea—he had no idea how many days. Calling Eagle, yes, was witching over him, speaking, chanting, wailing. Someone occasionally beat a drum. A boy of ten or eleven was helping Calling Eagle. The boy's gestures, movements, way of walking and moving his hands seemed an imitation of Calling Eagle's, an exaggeration of the feminine.

Neither seemed to pay attention to Mac. Calling Eagle chanted, and the boy prepared something, like priest and acolyte.

Mac drew in the rich odor of sweetgrass and cedar bark, one of his favorite smells.

The boy gently opened Mac's mouth and put in something mushy. It tasted bitter beyond bitter. With a finger the boy kept Mac from rejecting it. "Suck on that," he said softly, singsong. "It will help your stomach."

Calling Eagle took no notice. She was entranced in her song, fixed on a world of vision, mystically enraptured.

Mac wondered who the hell Calling Eagle was.

2

Mac leaned off his pallet and threw up into the cooking pot.

It was better now. He had time to aim when he threw up.

He lay back down, exhausted. This was maybe the third day after the healing ceremony, and he was worn-out from vomiting, worn-out from diarrhea, worn-out from fever. And weary, Lord, weary of his own stink.

He supposed that was a sign he was better. Yesterday he was too far gone to care how he reeked.

He smiled to himself. White men were infamous for

bringing illness to the Indians—particularly influenza and smallpox, both devastating to the red man. Yet where did Mac get this malady if not from the Cheyennes?

Annemarie slipped through the tent flap. He remembered her off and on through the last few days. She had evidently appointed herself his nurse, which pleased him. She had broth again now, and water. He waved away the broth and reached for the water. He was desperately thirsty. He sipped it slowly, carefully. He hadn't kept any food down yet.

He lay back down and gazed at Annemarie dazedly, gratefully.

She dipped a cloth in the rest of the water and put it on his forehead. It felt wonderful—so cool. She put her hand on his cheek. He covered her hand with his and closed his eyes. Soon he was slipping back into the warm lagoons of the Sandwich Islands.

3

Strikes Foot and Calling Eagle came through the tent flap. Calling Eagle stooped, and Strikes Foot squatted. Mac was always surprised how easily, as now, he balanced on that buffalo hoof.

"Annemarie tells me you are bored, Dancer," said Calling Eagle. "That's a good sign."

"Calling Eagle has healed you," said Strikes Foot with satisfaction.

Mac looked from one to the other, holding their eyes. "You are my friends," he said.

Blue slipped in now—good, loyal Paul—and Annemarie followed. "How do you feel?" she asked.

Mac sat up and took the soup she offered. "Better," he said thinly, feeling unsteady. Annemarie reached out and held the bowl for him.

"Want come back lodge?" Blue said in broken Cheyenne. The beaver had been working at it. A week and he spoke a bunch.

Annemarie shook her head.

"No," said Mac. The lodge was full of tanned robes and elk hides, wool blankets, willow chairs, parfleche boxes, and other luxuries. Mac wanted to be sick here in the tent, in containers or on the bare ground.

He looked at Calling Eagle. "What did you do for me?"

"I chased off your bad dreams," Calling Eagle said lightly.

"Come back soon," said Strikes Foot, grinning. He stood up easily, poised on his hoof. "Then we can get rid of Reshaw."

Mac had forgotten. "Is he causing trouble?"

"Such a fool could not cause trouble for Strikes Foot," the Cheyenne said. "Maybe I cause trouble for him." Strikes Foot seemed amused.

"He's just sulky," said Paul in English.

Mac nodded.

"I'll stay here this afternoon and tell you some stories," Annemarie said.

"I am the one he needs for stories," said Calling Eagle, teasing.

Annemarie looked a little alarmed.

"Tell him stories for children," said Strikes Foot to Annemarie, chuckling. "For babies. That's all he has the stomach for."

4

Mac came to consciousness gradually, like rising to the surface of water. It was warm, lulling water. He didn't open his eyes, hovering just below the surface. Slowly he became aware of a presence beside him, partly on him.

He enclosed it in his arms. Annemarie. He floated there, eyes closed, nearly awake. He could feel her breath gentle on his ear.

He breathed deeply, in and out. Her arm lay across his chest, her leg over his legs. He raised a hand and wriggled

his fingers through her coppery hair to her head and
rubbed.

She kissed him on the cheek. His experience with
Indian women was that they didn't kiss much. Maybe she
was doing it to please him.

She kissed him on the edges of his lips, teasing.

He kissed her back.

She slid on top of him. She nibbled at his nose, the
corners of his mouth, his upper and lower lips, the whole
of his mouth. At his neck, which made him shiver.

He moved his hands against her back, her neck, her
cheeks. He felt their groins pressed together. She thumped
hers unmistakably.

She sat up, seeming in high glee. She snapped her dress
over her head in one fluid motion. Mac felt as though he
were in a trance. They made a game of the knots of her
chastity belt. The knots weren't *that* clever.

5

Mac Maclean was struggling to think. The woman he
loved was dozing beside him, nude. He felt spent, and not
only physically. He also felt at peace, profoundly at peace.
She would awake soon and touch him again and touch his
heart once more.

He did not know what made it so affecting. Her youth,
yes, her vitality, her playfulness, her enthusiasm. But
more than that. He felt something entirely new.

He grasped one difference. Mac Maclean. His attitude.
Always before he was taking someone. Ravishing someone.
Coming at someone. Always he felt on the attack.

This time he made love *with* someone.

And he felt wonderful.

Annemarie stirred. He rubbed her head. She opened
her eyes, gazed at him blankly for a moment, then mischievously. She licked his ear, slid her hand inside his
shirt, and teased his navel.

He would have to give more thought to his discovery later.

6

"Tie them carefully," Annemarie said. "Lame Deer checks them sometimes." Mac was putting Annemarie's chastity belt back on, finding it absurdly embarrassing. "Put the knots right where they were—that's what she looks at."

Mac could see what she meant. It was clear where the old kinks were. It was not so clear how to wind and pull the thongs so they were intertwined in precisely the same way again.

After an eternity of red-faced fooling with them, he got it done. A chastity belt might be proof against force or haste, but not against patience.

"Feels right," Annemarie said.

Immediately there came a scratching on the tent flap. Mac was frightened—surely whoever scratched had been listening and heard them finish, and knew. Annemarie scrambled into her dress and into a sitting position.

"Come," he called.

Calling Eagle stuck her head in.

"Come in, mother," Annemarie said softly.

Mac had difficulty getting used to usages like *mother*, and not because Calling Eagle had a man's body. Annemarie called Lame Deer, Calling Eagle, even Yellow Bird, who was her own age, "mother" without hesitation.

"You're better, son?"

He nodded.

"You still need rest."

He nodded again, considering her voice, which was made by a man's throat. It was a tinny voice, neither high nor low. If he heard it without knowing who spoke, he might think it the high wheeze of an old man. Yet he had accepted it without second thought as a woman's voice.

"What did you do? I was crazy in the head that night and couldn't tell."

Calling Eagle smiled and said, "I chased the craziness out of your head."

Mac knew she meant it. White people thought of the human body as a mechanism, to be treated mechanically. But the Indians didn't—they thought sickness was a physical manifestation of a psychical problem. When Mac treated Til with camomile, even Jim Sykes told him he was attending to the symptom and forgetting the cause.

But Mac didn't intend to argue with Calling Eagle, now or ever.

"Who was the boy with you?"

"I am training Buffalo Berry as a healer," she said simply. A simple statement masking a complicated reality, Mac thought—maybe a sinister reality. He couldn't help pondering the seduction of boys.

"I make you uneasy, son." It was again a simple statement. Calling Eagle looked at Mac, and he felt she saw through him. "*Hemaneh* makes you uneasy."

Dumbstruck, he nodded his head.

"We do not often speak of *hemaneh* to Frenchmen." She paused sadly. "It is necessary now. Your friend Reshaw insulted me."

She put it out that simply.

"Strikes Foot asked him to leave the camp. And he is gone. Far gone. You must accept this."

Mac was terrified.

≈ 14 ≈

Hoop-and-stick-game moon

Mac felt uneasy in the Cheyenne camp until Calling Eagle herself suggested a sweat-lodge ceremony.

Everything had gone all right. People were friendly. Every day Mac walked awhile around camp, regaining his strength. The third afternoon he and Blue helped move the horse herd, and that left Mac exhausted.

Reshaw was long gone, and well gone, as far as Mac was concerned. The breed took two horses and would probably ride them hard, alternately, until he got to Fort Platte. The Cheyennes told him about some Sioux wintering a couple of days south on Powder River. If he got hit by a big storm, Reshaw could retreat to their camp. He knew better than to come back here.

Mac had failed to find out exactly what sort of insult Reshaw offered. Calling Eagle clearly intended to say no more about it, and Strikes Foot silenced Mac's clumsy hints with glowers. Blue claimed to know nothing about it.

Mac wondered if Blue knew about himself and Annemarie. He wondered if anyone knew, or everyone knew. Every day he took long rests in the tent, and most days Annemarie slipped in to make the second half of his rest glorious.

Mac was wonderstruck at what lovemaking could be in the presence of love.

When he was alone and started thinking, Mac was damned nervous. He was not yet sure the affair of Reshaw wouldn't come back at him. He was also concerned about getting back to the fort. Though too weak to leave and reluctant to be away from Annemarie, he was afraid to stay much longer. His men and enterprises were unsupervised, and Reshaw wouldn't help them—he might cause trouble. Though the winter had been easy, the snow was deepening steadily, and huge storms could come at any time.

Most of all, Mac was uneasy about his liaisons with Annemarie. What would Strikes Foot do if he found out? Denounce her? Run her off? Run the two of them off? Or would he wave it off as the white man's way?

Mac couldn't hope for the last. And he couldn't stop himself from touching Annemarie. Yet he condemned himself for risking his entire trading enterprise and their future for lust.

Lust, yes, that was what he called it in bad moments. But he knew it wasn't lust.

He counted months. If she got pregnant, they could have the wedding in June, which was only five months away, and she wouldn't be showing yet. If he could leave, simply get himself out of her presence, maybe they would survive their desire. Their love.

2

Late one afternoon Calling Eagle came to the tent, again just after Annemarie had left, and announced she would hold a sweat for Mac the next night. Mac thanked her graciously and started to worry.

On the night of the sweat, Mac was acutely apprehensive. He hadn't done a sweat before—he had refused opportunities with ironic remarks about self-punishment. He dared not refuse this one. It was a sign of good faith by Strikes Foot and Calling Eagle, and the last gesture of his healing.

He watched the preparations. The sweat lodge, a little away from camp circle, was a low hut of willow sticks stuck in the ground and lashed into a frame. Calling Eagle and Buffalo Berry got a sizable fire going four or five steps from the entrance, which faced east, and pushed big rocks into the coals. In the middle of the hut was a pit for the stones. Under Calling Eagle's supervision, the boy covered the willow framework with scraped buffalo hides—covered it tightly, to keep the steam in. From the lodge Calling Eagle brought a rattle, a firkin of water, and some sage branches.

At dark the company assembled. Strikes Foot, without his hoof appendage. His brother Three Feathers, a gangly, gap-toothed man given to practical jokes. Buffalo Berry, who would stay outside during the sessions of steaming and provided fresh-heated rocks during the intervals. Calling Eagle, the leader. And Mac, nervous.

Everyone was casual, chatting, at ease, despite the serious nature of the event. When Calling Eagle said it was time, all stripped to a small breechcloth.

As they entered, Mac noticed that a huge moon, as yellow and textured as grapefruit rind, was rising in the east. He had been gone from Fort Platte one moon already.

When the lodge door closed, the blackness inside was absolute. Mac was edgy. By prior instruction he sat erect in the darkness, legs crossed, knees near the hot rocks. Skin brushed his shoulder—Calling Eagle stirring. He was naked in the dark with men of strange customs, and he was afraid.

Mac heard Calling Eagle dip the sage into the water. Hissing erupted. Heat exploded in Mac's face, searing him—he feared he couldn't breathe.

After a moment his panic eased. Perhaps the heat had subsided, too, but it was terrible. He was sure he was gasping out loud. He wondered if the others were chuckling at his agony. He wondered if he'd have to slip out, and so humiliate himself. He wondered if he *could* slip out.

Mac heard a brushing sound, heat flared at him again, and the smell of sage came strong into his nostrils.

Calling Eagle began a chant. Mac ignored the words, but the drone distracted him a little from his pain, took the bitter edge out of the heat. From time to time he heard his name. Mac thought he was going to survive.

Silence. The dip of sage. Mac caught his breath. Again pops and hisses, again the heat erupting in Mac's face, up his nose, and into his lungs. He felt a desperate need to cough, but he couldn't.

After a moment the pain eased. The smell of sage came to him again and Calling Eagle resumed chanting. Too exhausted to follow the Cheyenne words, Mac let them flow over him like water. He imagined the creek, its current ambling over smoothed rocks, and he felt cooler.

After a while, a measureless while, Calling Eagle threw back the lodge cover and cooling air rushed in. Across the rock-filled pit, Strikes Foot lifted the edge of a hide and slid out. Mac did the same. The cold air was delicious.

He lay next to Calling Eagle, a banked fish, panting.

Strikes Foot and Three Feathers, on the other side of the lodge, were murmuring. Mac sensed Calling Eagle waiting and at last the words came.

"Son, you are uncomfortable with *hemaneh*."

Oh, God, not now, Mac cried to himself. Calling Eagle waited. At last Mac nodded. Buffalo Berry was taking new rocks into the sweat lodge.

"It is important that you hear me." Mac nodded again. She raised her voice liturgically. "*Hemaneh* are born so. We are chosen. We are neither man nor woman."

She let it sit a moment. "We discover our calling in dreams." She was speaking seriously, eloquently, joyously. She was a saved soul softly extolling her salvation. "Everything about us is neither man nor woman. Even our dress speaks that." She smiled a little. "I am no secret among Cheyennes—only you did not know me."

Mac remembered touches about her attire that were usually masculine, oddities he had ignored.

She began in singsong again. Her tale—her song—seemed mesmeric. "We *hemaneh* are chosen to do many things for the people that neither man nor woman can do. When a young man needs an irresistible love song, we dream one. When he wants a bride, we make the arrangements. We build the bonfires for the scalp dances. When couples have difficulties, we help them understand each other. We raise other families' children. We heal, and so serve on the warpath. We dedicate the medicine-lodge ceremony."

Mac knew this last alone would make the man-woman central to Cheyenne religion.

Then in a soft, dovelike utterance, Calling Eagle added, "And we have sex like women."

There it was. She was looking at Mac as though with deepest compassion.

"It is time," she said, and reentered the lodge. Powerless, Mac crawled after her into the darkness.

The second session seemed identical to the first, but Mac's experience of it was different. He felt more relaxed. Letting his chest open, he drew in the heat confidently. The pain seemed less—or maybe only his fear was less. He felt a little woozy, a little dreamy. He could nuzzle up to the pain of the steam. Once again he paid no attention to the words of Calling Eagle's song.

In good time she opened the door, and Mac followed her out into the night again. The air was deliciously cold. The moon was risen now, not so bulbous, and chastely white.

Calling Eagle started in matter-of-factly, as though she hadn't stopped. "You Frenchmen misunderstand *hemaneh*. We hear that you shun and despise your own *hemaneh*. You also shun and despise your crazy ones. You might as well hate the trees and the grass.

"Then you make no sense again. Hating *hemaneh*, you then ask us for things we cannot do." She waited, then went on in her matter-of-fact way. "It is not our nature to play the man in the buffalo robes. Only the woman." She seemed to mean particulars Mac did not want to think of. He was amazed she could speak without embarrassment. "And only at the times and places chosen for us."

Mac breathed in the sweet cold, watching the infinite stars. He heard sweetly, without thought.

"There are many ways," Calling Eagle concluded. "Each has something to offer the people. You need not be afraid of my way."

"Thank you for this," Mac murmured.

Calling Eagle got up. "I'm not finished with you, Frenchman. You have lots to learn. But I'll wait till we finish sweating." Said without a hint of smile.

3

Mac and Calling Eagle stood in the snow, bare-footed and almost naked. Annemarie spread elk robes on the ground, and the three sat. Mac was still light-headed from the sweat.

The cold air felt good. He reached down, scooped up a handful of snow, and rubbed it on his arms. Wonderful. Then he rubbed snow on his face and chest. Amazing. Something he'd never have tried. Naked and giddy in the snow under the stars.

Calling Eagle directed him with a hand to sit. Annemarie handed him the four-hole capote, but he didn't put it on yet. The night might be near zero, but Mac felt flushed from the sweat.

"She's with child," Calling Eagle said. For a crazy moment Mac thought Calling Eagle meant herself or Buffalo Berry or. . . Annemarie? Pregnant?

By an act of great self-control he did not put his arm around her. He threw the capote over his shoulders.

"We love each other," he said simply, seriously.

Calling Eagle spoke a little sharply. "The child is not yours. Not so soon."

Right.

"She was carrying a child when she and Lame Deer came back from the Assiniboins in the plum moon. I saw the changes in her body. Her mother saw. No one else knew."

Mac looked at Annemarie. Her eyes were on her knees.

"Lame Deer should have kept her away from the Assiniboins. They live too near the Frenchmen. Besides, they have loose ways of their own."

Calling Eagle glared at Mac. "She will be shamed among the Cheyenne people, Frenchman. Perhaps she is shamed in your eyes. Do you still want her?"

Mac looked at Annemarie. She would not lift her head. By the full moon he could see her cheeks wet and glistening.

"You must decide now, Dancer. Do you want her? And the child? She says the father is a Frenchman."

"Annemarie, do you want me?"

Calling Eagle broke in harshly. "She cannot tell you what is in your heart, Frenchman. Do you want her?"

Mac felt dumbstruck.

"Speak up."

He nodded his head. "I want her."

"Are you sure?"

"I am sure."

"She has told me she wants you. It is settled."

Annemarie was weeping openly.

"She will be in disgrace with her people—the Cheyennes may not trade with you."

"I want her. I want her for my wife."

Calling Eagle nodded. Twice. "You are fortunate, daughter." Then to Mac: "You must go. Tonight. Now. Your gear is packed. The Blue has the horses, your clothes, and the furs. He is waiting in the cottonwoods a mile down the creek. There is no ring around the moon, and you may have good weather."

Calling Eagle stood up, and smiled, perhaps softly. "I wish you well. Sometimes love matches are the best, sometimes not." Mac and Annemarie were on their feet too, murmuring thanks. "Ride hard for two days. Strikes Foot may get angry. I can appease him, but he may insist on following and punishing her. Who knows? He is a man."

Calling Eagle wheeled and crunched off toward the lodge. Mac stopped her with a call. She came back.

"Will you do us a service?"

"If it is quick."

Mac turned to Annemarie. The girl was still struggling against her tears and wouldn't meet his eyes. He wrapped his arms around her and drew her close. He could feel her sobs against his chest.

"I promised her we would be married properly, in the Frenchman style. We will be later. For now, will you say the Frenchman words?"

Calling Eagle smiled crookedly and shrugged.

"In nomine Patris," recited Mac, and he waited for Calling Eagle to repeat the phrase.

"Et Filii, et Spiritus Sancti . . ."

Calling Eagle parroted the syllables.

"Ego conjungo in matrimonio."

When Calling Eagle finished, she held up one hand and made the only Christian gesture she knew, the sign of the cross.

To Mac her hand loomed huge and dark in front of a bland, inscrutable moon. Her smile was ancient, ironic, world-weary.

4

For Mac the long journey toward home was a strange and shifting wandering across a desolate dreamscape.

The days were brief but seamlessly sunny, and cold, as midwinter days in Powder River country could be. The sun turned the vast, broken plains into an empty, rumpled, glistening desert of snow. The dark dots of sagebrush and distant cedars only accented the luminous whiteness. An occasional dark line of willows acted as visual relief. But the plains were ever the same, unendingly flat, monotonous, folding and unfolding, unbroken.

Annemarie, uncomfortable, widened the eye holes in her bandanna without telling Mac or Blue. By the middle of the third day she was snow-blind. At dawn and dusk she could look around gingerly. The rest of the time Mac was obliged to lead her horse and both pack horses, and she rode darkly, miserably, through a landscape of dazzling light.

They had occasional difficulty with drifts and dry washes filled with snow, but for the most part the going was easy. Antelope grazed docilely everywhere, and after two days of swift-moving silence, Blue made fresh meat. Physically, it seemed the trip would be easy enough.

But emotionally troubled. The sameness, the repetitious dreamscape disturbed Mac and sent him into private reverie. Annemarie had withdrawn into some world of her own. She followed passively, unable to see, saying nothing, asking nothing. In camp she simply lay in the blankets, wordless. She barely ate. Mac saw tears on her face often. At night she slept beside him but didn't respond to his touch, a mummy.

Mac was silent as well, and long-faced. He helped Blue with fires and meals and coffee mechanically, not caring to talk. He lay in the blankets next to Annemarie during the long nights, much too long to sleep through, and pondered his fate. He thought maybe he had made the wrong choice—or rather been dragged by the wayward currents of life into a maelstrom.

Enamored of a girl—a girl about to bloom into a woman, innocent, vernal, unsullied—he thought he had her love. But she was off doing the dirty deed with someone else, for sport.

Mac had made his approach circumspectly, politely, through her family. Some other fellow, an anonymous "Frenchman," simply took what Mac wanted, gleefully. Annemarie gave it to him, probably gleefully. How funny Mac's respect for her purity must have seemed. How she must have laughed at her reluctant suitor while she was getting pronged!

Pondering such things, Mac brooded himself into a foul mood.

He had wanted to take a wife for love, and happily to get money as well. Now perhaps she was blighting the opportunity for either. Perhaps her love was merely expedience—she simply wanted a trader, a man of means. Perhaps her people would reject her, and him. They had run away together, they were fornicators, she a fornicator doubly—she would be regarded as no longer worthy of the name Cheyenne. Perhaps if Mac invested his small nest egg in a post on the Yellowstone, the Cheyennes might stubbornly take their trade elsewhere, and all his plans would unravel.

Maybe he should trade on the Oregon Trail, where the money was. Or in Santa Fe, flush with gold and silver from the mines in Chihuahua. Maybe he should forget the Yellowstone country.

He looked at Annemarie's young face. Her eyes were closed, but he suspected she was not asleep. It was a good face—not pale and delicate as a face for drawing rooms, but strong, firm, declarative, a face for real life.

He wondered if she loved him. Was her enthusiastic loving only the natural exuberance of an uninhibited child of nature exploring sex?

He wondered if he loved her. Was he merely enraptured by his fantasy of her, a dream he draped her in, a bejeweled gown that the flesh-and-blood person underneath could simply drop to the ground?

He remembered how he felt quickened by her. Delighted by the way she cavorted with the other teenage girls. Braced by her vigor. Touched by her unconscious grace. Entranced by her playful eyes. Transported, not merely slaked, by the solicitations of her body.

Yes, I do love her, he thought. And that's too damn bad.

He lifted a strand of hair away from her cheek.

She spoke without opening her eyes. "So, Frenchman, will you send me back?"

"No, Annemarie."

He put an arm around her, but she did not respond.

"Will you love the child?"

"I don't know," he answered honestly. "I think maybe so."

She pursed her mouth a little and said no more.

After a while, Mac asked her, "Who is the father?"

Without opening her eyes, Annemarie smiled a little and shook her head. "I came back to you, Green Eye. I wanted you."

She fears I'm rejecting her, thought Mac. He looked at her still face, impassive, Indian. He wondered if that face would always be a mask to him. For now he felt a little less bleak.

Mac remembered meeting Annemarie for the first time, three years ago, when she was still a child. The band had its lodges pitched on Clarks Fork, and the four trappers joined them there in June, before rendezvous.

Mac was just beginning to learn the Cheyenne language then, and she set him up. She told him a story in Cheyenne, a story about the woman who followed coyote, but he didn't understand it all. That night he repeated it as he understood it to Lame Deer. The woman covered her mouth, grabbed a gourd, and took out after Annemarie. The girl ran away shrieking with laughter. Strikes Foot and Skinhead were hooting and slapping each other's back.

It seemed the story was traditional, but Annemarie had made it flamboyantly scatological by the addition of references to male and female body orifices.

Lame Deer didn't really punish Annemarie—the joke was too good. But Mac didn't venture any more Cheyenne sentences for several days.

He pictured the Clarks Fork country in his mind, and Sunlight Creek coming from the Yellowstone plateau above, his home country. A land of big rivers and high mountains, not like these endless, wrinkled plains. A magical land of hot springs, geysers, knife-edge canyons, roaring waterfalls, lovely, solitary peaks. A fertile land of lush grass, thick timber, and abundant game. He longed to be back there. Home.

He traced Annemarie's eyebrows with a finger. If he and this strange girl could plant a love and grow a family, it would be there, in the Yellowstone country.

5

After Mac, Annemarie, and Blue hit the Oregon Trail on the Platte just below the mouth of the Sweetwater, they were in familiar territory, close to home. Yet odd sights appeared. An escritoire abandoned by the side of the trail, its frail legs intact, a drawer pulled out like a tongue and filled with snow. A huge oak bureau on its back, face to the sky. A wagon in a wash, hind end clumped to the earth over a broken axle. Two dead oxen, still in harness. A huge ceramic chamber pot, with a formal design of tea roses with intertwined stems, split in half.

Mac even made one find he wanted to keep. A clavichord, without legs, set tidily beneath a cottonwood, the size of a child's casket. The strings seemed to be intact. Mac liked the idea of a proper musical instrument in his home, for his children.

These objects might have put Mac in mind of the trade the emigrants would bring to him next summer. But they seemed too sad. They were derelicts of civilization come to the Great Plains, small and pathetic in this vastness of landscape, no more than a scum line left by a high tide that came once and receded, perhaps forever.

At noon on a numberless day they rode into the courtyard of Fort Platte. Mac was sick to death of travel, of the plains, of his companions, of himself.

Lisette came out to greet them. "Reshaw is at Laramie," she said, meaning the fort a mile and a half away. "He's quit swearing to shoot you."

Mac started helping the limp and silent Annemarie down off her horse. She had his capote on, and bandannas covering her head completely.

"Who's that?"

"My wife," said Mac. "Turn the horses out," he told Blue.

"Your wife?"

"My wife."

"Why is she in Four-Holer?" Lisette asked. "I made that for you."

"Maybe you'll help her. She's blind."

"Blind!"

"Yes. Snow-blind."

Lisette gave a mock shrug. "Saves me scratching her eyes out." She made a hoot of dumb laughter, but took Annemarie by the hand.

"Where's Genet?"

She jerked her head toward the boss's quarters.

"Tell Reshaw they ran me off, too," said Mac. "Also for fooling with their women."

≈ 15 ≈

June, 1844, Moon when the horses get fat

Mac Maclean opened his eyes without stirring. Carefully not moving, so as not to wake Annemarie, he looked at the candlelight on the ceiling of the little room. She gave a little grunt next to him on the bed, turned halfway over facing him, and rolled again onto her back. She was too big-bellied now to sleep any way but on her back.

It was the middle of the night—no hint yet of the dawn, early as it came in this country in June. Mac hadn't slept well recently. Annemarie, who grew up in unlit lodges, had gotten addicted to a night-light and would not go to sleep without a guttering candle.

He slipped out of the robes and off the slat bed and looked back at her tenderly. Her mouth worked a little, and her face turned anxious for a moment. He wondered what she was dreaming. Or whether the child might be moving within her. He didn't like what he'd been dreaming recently. He pulled on shirt and pants and moccasins and slipped out into the courtyard.

He was in the habit of having a smoke in one of the blockhouses and watching the sun rise over the sea of plains to the east. But he heard music from the trading room.

He cracked the door. Tiny Lisette, sitting at the clavichord. "Come on in," she said. "You can't sleep either?"

He came in, shook his head wearily, and took a chair. He had put the clavichord on a table for fancy decoration until he could get legs made for it. "What are you playing?"

"Nothing," she answered. "Really." She turned back to

the instrument, a kind of miniature piano, and began to doodle. "It's crazy, but I like fooling around on it."

Crazy because some of the strings sounded good and others twanged and clanked. And because she clearly didn't know what she was doing, just sort of picking out patterns that weren't quite melodies, or not good ones.

Little One seemed different tonight, simple and honest. He had seen this side of her sometimes and found her likable. And he knew she had gotten close to Annemarie. A confidante. He got out a clay pipe, loaded it, and lit it with a lucifer.

"How's the trading?" She kept doodling at the clavichord, toying with repeated melodic shapes.

"Good. Excellent." She knew lots of it. Skinhead's crew had done fine gathering Lord Stewart's animals, and Skinhead had not acted his wild-hair self. Mac had avoided losing a single animal to weather or to Indians. His men had repaired a number of wagons left along the trail, built some charettes, and prepared a stack of fresh axles. They were well prepared when the emigrants started arriving three weeks ago.

He'd been trading livestock, at least two broken-down animals for one of his healthy ones, or charging triple the Missouri cash price. Some of the run-down ones had already gotten rested and fattened enough to trade back. He had sold all his axles and had men cutting and shaping more. His repaired wagons disappeared quickly.

"So good I feel guilty about it."

She nodded and smiled. "It feels like taking advantage, doesn't it? But you're giving them fair value. Fair mountain value. A healthy horse or ox is one valuable critter."

"Like Blue." He had noticed Lisette paying some attention to Paul, affectionate attention.

"He's a dear." She stopped playing. "Is Annemarie sleeping okay?" Mac nodded. "Okay" was brand-new slang, carried west by the emigrants. Just like Lisette to pick it up. "How come you couldn't sleep?"

"Dubious dreams," he admitted, not wanting to tell her the whole truth. He had a recurring dream that frightened him.

He is a Scots king, a barbarian in rich, heavy furs, but a king nevertheless. A young woman is brought before him for judgment. She has committed fornication or adultery and brought forth a child.

The circumstances differ. Sometimes her husband has been gone to war, but she has borne a child in the meantime. Sometimes she is a slip of a girl, too young to marry, but a mother. Always she is a lovely creature, shiningly blond, fair, demure, unsullied.

Mac as king refuses to see the child. His counselors tell him, as he knew without looking, that it is a foul thing, dark and ill-favored, half-beast, half-human. He orders it split asunder skull to crotch with a single stroke of the sword. The mother swoons, prostrate and unconscious before him. He feels superbly pitiless. The long sword rises high. . . .

He always woke in an electric start. He hated the dream, but he couldn't cut it off except by staying awake.

"What's got you worried? The kid, huh? Mac, you're going to love that kid."

"She won't say who the father is."

"She shouldn't. It doesn't matter."

"What worries me is her." This was not exactly true. The notion of the child festered in him. It had been an up-and-down time with Annemarie. At first she was withdrawn and weepy. They had several tempestuous quarrels when Mac pressed her to tell him the father's name. Then for a couple of months they were an exuberant young man and young woman together, best friends and lovers enchanted by the vernal months of marriage. In the last weeks, as her time approached, she had gotten weepy again. Mac made a point of being solicitous, but she was unreachable.

"Lucy will get her through it," Lisette assured him. Lucy was Reshaw's new wife, an Arapahoe. She had three children already and said she knew what to do. Reshaw had gone to Santa Fe for whiskey, which was good riddance. The fort was in keen competition with Fort Laramie, so Genet would need all the whiskey he could get. Reshaw was buying some for Mac, too.

"Women die in childbirth," Mac said.

"She's going to be okay. What she is going through is normal. She is tired, drained."

Mac thought Lisette was speaking more than she knew. "I'm edgy."

Racked with anxiety would be more like it. Sometimes he feared the birth—would it kill Annemarie? Or the baby? Sometimes he fretted that he wouldn't give a damn about the kid—it was nothing to do with him, but he was saddled with it. Sometimes he imagined that mother and child would shut him out of their life, bonded with ties alien to him, and he would be an outsider in his own family.

He had no damned idea what to do.

"Come over here." Lisette patted the bench she used for the clavichord.

"Yes, Little One," he said in mock-military style.

"Teach me how to play something."

"I . . ."

"Don't tell me you can't. I heard you play that silly thing."

Mac had fooled with the strings one afternoon, trying to fix them. He hoped some emigrant would have a little skill and be able to re-rig the clavichord enough to make some music. After tinkering with the strings that afternoon, he played "Chopsticks," the only tune he knew.

"Come on," he said, showing her the right-hand part.

She caught on pretty well. They tried it together. "Come on, thump it out," he cried. "It's not dainty."

A rap on the door, loud. They shushed each other, giggling, caught red-handed.

Genet stuck his white-haired head in. "Mr. Maclean, your wife is calling for you. I think it is her time."

2

The damned women put their heads together and made him start a fire under a big kettle of water in the kitchen, and then told him to stay out of the way. So he was working the corrals when his mind and heart were with Annemarie.

"Those oxen are going to live maybe another week," declared Mac, "maybe less. That's a fact. They're never going to mean anything to you, but they might mean a little something to me. And might not. They might die anyway."

The farmer scraped one boot on another, eyes on the ground. "I give twelve dollars for them at Westport, mister. Each."

Mac shrugged. "What will you be able to get for their hides in Oregon?"

The wife spit a brown glob onto the ground. "Ain't no talkin' to him, Em." The inside of her bonnet showed faint, thin, brown streaks from her spitting. Nothing looked so out of place to Mac, clear west to Fort Laramie in the middle of Indian country, as a sunbonnet. But they all had them. Sometimes Mac thought they donned them as an act of defiance.

Full of defiance, these emigrants were. Emigrators, Skinhead called them contemptuously. They marched through the country on a beeline for the promised land of Oregon, despising the great plains they were crossing the people who lived here, red and white. The emigrants didn't like what they saw. They clung tenaciously to their own notions and their old ways. Where the mountain man came and learned from the Indian, the emigrants wouldn't stoop to that. Though they'd starve if the buffalo herds were away from the trail, though they couldn't find water without being told where, though they didn't know where they were going, they considered themselves superior.

Not just superior to the Indians. To the whites who lived here, the squaw men, as they called them. To men such as Mac, married to Indians. Especially to men such as Mac, who according to them should know better.

Mac at first was amused to see how shocked the emigrants were to see him in leggings and breechcloth. The women would stare and mutter. Now he'd quit wearing the breechclout. He had realized the emigrants couldn't bring themselves to trade with such a barbarian.

The Indians were amused at the trespassers, too. They rode down to the trail and watched the big wagons and sometimes collected a small passage fee and were vastly amused at the ineptitude before them. Any one of the minor Sioux leaders could, if he chose, obliterate the westward movement on the Oregon Trail. These people could not defend themselves, take care of themselves, or even care for the livestock decently. The Indians didn't fight because they didn't think these folk worthy opponents.

The farmer moused his feet around and hemmed and hawed and looked at Mac forlornly. Mac gave him no help. The man wanted two good horses for his run-down oxen, and Mac wouldn't go for it. The man would probably take the oxen over to Laramie, where they'd offer even less, and then he'd take the animals up the trail. Within a week they'd die, and he'd have to abandon entirely the wagon they pulled, and leave a lot of his belongings in the sagebrush.

It made no nevermind to Mac. Skinhead was out picking up furniture left on the trail right now. He meant to take it back to Westport and sell it.

"Just can't see my way clear," the farmer said at last. Mac nodded.

"You're not making a Christian offer," the woman added.

Mac heard footsteps and turned. Lisette, running and grinning. "Come on!" she shouted. "You've got a baby girl! She's beautiful!"

Mac grabbed Lisette's hand and started running back inside the fort, giddily. Then they started skipping together.

"Another heathen bastard," muttered the woman, and spit a brown glob into the dust.

3

"Felice," Mac murmured.

Miracles, being miracles, might as well happen instantaneously. Instantaneously, a thing had become a person—a dark, obscure, threatening lump inside Annemarie had become a beautiful, delicate, vulnerable human being in the light of day. Much too vulnerable.

He reached out and took the blanket-wrapped infant. She was perfectly quiet, self-absorbed, at peace. A child of amiable disposition.

Mac looked over at Annemarie. Her eyes were open now, heavy-lidded, barely glimpsing Mac and Felice through her exhaustion. She smiled a little and closed them.

Felice. They had made a deal. If the child was a girl, her name would be Felice, a beautiful French name Annemarie learned from her father. If a boy, a name of Mac's choice—William Clark Maclean. So Felice.

Mac inspected her parts. Each finger was incredibly tiny but a full finger, every part, even shiny nails. Toes likewise. Legs, arms, bottom, chest, each resoundingly human. Broad nose, shapely mouth, lovely blue eyes. Yes, blue. Mac took a tiny finger and articulated it. It worked. He stuck his gargantuan finger into the palm of her hand and she grasped it. He smiled hugely at Lisette.

"You men," said Little One fondly. "You get all dewy-eyed."

The child gave the faintest whimper, and Lucy took it abruptly from Mac and put it to Annemarie's breast.

Lisette put something into Mac's arms. A cradleboard, fully beaded, mostly white with pink and purple geometrical designs, a handsome piece of work. "My gift to her," Lisette murmured. She reached in and showed Mac it was lined with soft, crumbled inner bark of the cedar against the child's soiling.

Mac clasped Little One around the shoulder happily and watched Felice nurse.

"Lucy has something for her, too." Lisette handed Mac a quilled pouch in the shape of a turtle. Mac knew what was in it—the umbilicus. Felice was supposed to wear this pouch until she was five or six—he supposed she would.

What a strange land he had come to. But he found Annemarie and Felice here.

Brusque as usual, Lucy walked out with an armload of bedclothes, heading for the kitchen and hot water. "She asked me to tell you that Yellow Hands would be here soon."

Yellow Hands was an Arapahoe medicine woman, from Lucy's tribe, camped down on Horse Creek. She would give the child a name that would never be used, a private and sacred name. A shock of realization came to Mac: Yellow Hands was a half-man, half-woman, like Calling Eagle. He should have known earlier. All the signs were there. Well, when your eyes are open, suddenly you see.

A strange land indeed. But any land with Felice in it was a land overflowing with milk and honey.

≈ 16 ≈

August, 1844, Time when the cherries are ripe

Something about logs felt good to Mac—he saw in his
head stout cylinders of cottonwood, shaped by Blue's
adze, dovetail joined, well chinked. A stalwart trading
post. Blue had taken one look at the old Fort Cass and
proclaimed, "Forget that one. We build a new one."

True, to the south they built with adobe—Laramie, Fort
Platte, Bent's, all of adobe. Strong, sure, and proof against
fire. But Mac was a northman. He liked a wooded country,
and the feel of building with wood. No matter what you
could say about adobe, it was mud.

But the post was only in his head. The men were just
now trimming off the trunks. Mac was back standing on
the yellow sandstone bluff above the site of the fort, clay
pipe burning, watching the work. He took a shift up here
every day as lookout.

From here he had a fine prospect. To the south, the vast
plains that stretched from the Big Horn Mountains to the
plowed furrows marking civilization. The high plains, land
of the Sioux and the Cheyenne. On the western edge of
the plains, the mountain barrier itself, the crest of the
continent, topped by the strange geyser land John Colter
first wandered through. To the north, in the near distance
the river, wide, deep, swift, and cold, thrumming its way
toward the Missouri. The fine cottonwoods in the bottoms,
giving shade. The bench above the cottonwoods, where
the old fort once was, and where the new one now would
be, within the wide, rock-walled canyon but on high
ground. Beyond all that, more high plains, the country of
the tribes known as the Blackfoot confederation—Blood,

123

Piegan, Blackfoot proper, and Gros Ventre—receding into Canada.

Blue's building was going slowly and it had to go better. Mac was staking everything on this single chance.

In late June, Skinhead headed for St. Louis with Lord Stewart's animals, now bound for a lifetime sinecure as walking-around trophies. Three weeks later Mac brought his little band north, in front of the mountains, to this spot below the mouth of the Big Horn River, burnished and gleaming in Mac's mind.

The band was small and weak—himself, Annemarie and Felice, Blue, and Lisette, who had had a blowup with Genet and left with her best friend, Annemarie. And the two were best friends. Plus three hands kept on wages: Ferry, Dreyfuss, and Valdez. And sixty-two horses, with not enough men to guard them against theft. He would have exchanged some horses for trade goods, but Reshaw was temporarily in charge of Fort Platte, and out of meanness he wouldn't barter.

Mac needed men, but he didn't have the money: twenty-five dollars a month even for a green hand. Or he wouldn't know if he did until Skinhead got back from St. Louis. What if Skinhead got robbed by the damned Pawnees? Or the boat down from Council Bluffs sank? Or the fat bastard gambled it all away in St. Louis—no, Uncle Hugh would prevent that. Or something went wrong on the way back upriver? Plenty could, and often did.

Or if, after all that, the Cheyennes wouldn't come in to trade because Mac ran off with Annemarie.

If the venture soured, the salaries of Ferry, Dreyfuss, and Valdez would go up in smoke. They thought they were wage earners, Mac reflected, but they were river-boat gamblers. Without an edge.

Mac snorted, blowing smoke out his nostrils. He didn't like that. If he got through the season, he'd have to arrange them a bonus.

Those three men were hard workers. With Mac and Blue they'd been getting logs ready. Blue and Dreyfuss felled them with double-bitted axes or a two-man crosscut saw, the only felling tools they had until Skinhead arrived.

Mac, Ferry, and Valdez trimmed them and flattened them on two sides, and the whole crew hauled them to the site and got the foundation started. Blue was a craftsman with that ax, twice as fast as anyone else. Wagh! he had a back, and he drove that ax head beautifully, biting deep. Mac could see that Dreyfuss loved watching Blue wield that weapon. Though he didn't look like a handy fellow, Dreyfuss was getting the hang of the ax himself.

Mac liked Dreyfuss, a round man in his forties with an accent of buzzy sounds, bespectacled, fair with his hands and good with his head, inclined to speak seldom. The other two, Ferry and Valdez, did fine as long as you told them just what to do.

On the long trip, sensing something unusual about Dreyfuss, Mac had drawn him out. He was Viennese and had actually been a college professor, a teacher of philosophy. (How Mac would have liked to introduce him to Hugh.) Something had gone wrong—Mac never found out what—his wife died, and he lost his job. He was a nurse in some war, which was a life-changing experience. And he came to the United States. Dreyfuss told this story reluctantly, and cryptically.

Mac used the Dolland to glass all the plains across the river, methodically, dividing it into areas and searching each one. Big clouds of dust would be meaningless. They were buffalo, or villages of Blackfeet on the move, easy to spot and not out for mischief. On the other hand, the outfits you wouldn't want about, parties hunting scalps, or buffalo, or other people's horses, would be relatively tiny, moving subtly, and hard to spot. Mac didn't see anything suspicious. He doubted the Blackfeet knew about the new fort yet.

He checked the picket pin on his horse and moved up the few steps to the crest, where he could get a view to the south. He hadn't sent word to the Crow, Sioux, or Cheyennes either. He wasn't ready for them. Or anybody. Had nothing to trade. There was no sign to the south.

He damn well needed to keep a lookout. Sixty-two good horses, some heavy with foal. The Crows would steal your horses and then come in for coffee and brag about how they tricked you. If he lost those horses, Mac would be ruined.

He had saved the hopeful part of his search for last. He turned the telescope to the east, along the river, where Skinhead would be bringing in the pack train. The Sioux and Cheyenne used this trail to Powder River and then north to Fort Union or south to Paha Sapa, the Black Hills. Mac held where he knew the trail went, parallel to the south bank of the river, across the rippling sagebrush plains.

Dust. Sure enough. A lot of it.

Too far to make out any figures at all, man or beast. Could be Skinhead. Could be Cheyennes or Sioux in a bunch, coming to trade. Coming openly.

Mac trotted to the edge of the sandstone. He took off his gray, wide-brimmed hat and waved it in half circles over his head. He got the attention of a particular young woman with a cradleboard on her back. Like a good Cheyenne, she took responsibility for keeping an eye on the lookout.

Mac held the hat low over the ground and waggled it back and forth. Friends, it meant. He put it back on his head, then repeated the entire sequence once more.

Annemarie had already turned around and called to Blue. Now Blue was looking up. Do the beaver good to learn the signals. Blue raised an arm in acknowledgment.

Mac looked downriver again. With the naked eye he couldn't pick out the dust. He located it once more through the Dolland. Five or six miles out, probably.

Annemarie was now turned toward someone, and all Mac could see of her was the white beadwork of the cradleboard on her back, catching the sun. Lifting the telescope, Mac focused it on something dark at the top. He couldn't really make it out. Felice's face, though, and her thatch of dark hair.

Lord, Mac Maclean loved that child.

2

Skinhead stood up ceremoniously and glared around the circle. He raised his cup. "This prophet prophesies"—he interrupted his roar with a dramatic pause—"profits!"

Everybody laughed too hard, especially Lisette, perched on the log between Skinhead and Blue. People did laugh too much when they were feeling tired and good and optimistic. And when the boss tapped the kegs

Mac watched in relief. Whiskey didn't appeal to him so much anymore. Certainly there was something to be said for a carefree inebriation on pure alcohol mixed one to four with river water and corrupted with whatever spices were handy. But more to be said for an attentive eye on your wife, your child, your help, your horses, and your trade goods.

Dreyfuss started up a tune on his mouth organ, a boatman's ditty. Blue joined in with a twanging Jew's harp. Voices chimed in one by one, Skinhead's the most vigorous.

> O my love she are handsome, she's not ver-ry tall;
> But her modest demeniour does far surpass all;
> She's slim round the middle, her hair it hangs down;
> She's a bright morning star, oh, she lives in this town.

Lisette got up and stuck her arms out to Annemarie, and the two of them swung to the music. Quickly big Skinhead was up grabbing for Little One, and Blue stopped strumming his Jew's harp to dance with Annemarie. Then a pair of men joined in as partners, and the others began to take turns with the women. It was a song Mac knew from the levee in St. Louis, when he was a kid, and loved to kick up his heels to.

> Pretty Pol-ly, pretty Pol-ly, your daddy are rich,
> But I ain't no fortin' what troubles me much—
> Would you leave your old dad-dy and mam-my, also,
> And all through the wide world with yer darling boy go?

This sort of thing could get out of hand—two women in a camp with sixteen men—but Mac let it go and started dancing with his wife. Blue was dancing with his double-bitted ax as if it were a seductive woman. Annemarie was cutting up like a young girl—hell, she was a young girl—and everyone was having a hell of a good time. They were mumbling the words of the next verse, so Mac belted it out himself.

> *Oh, some call me rak-ish, and some call me wild,*
> *And some say that I pretty maids have beguiled;*
> *But they are all liars by the powers er-bove,*
> *For I'm guil-ty of nothing but innercent love!*

Skinhead was bundling Lisette a bit too enthusiastically there, so Mac moved over and cut in. Skinhead gave way graciously and started dancing around Dreyfuss on his own. Lisette had been an angel since the day they left the Platte, but whiskey and unattached women were a volatile combination, and Skinhead remembered Lisette in her more impulsive days. But Mac was damned glad to have her along. She helped Annemarie with Felice and with all the domestic chores and hadn't flirted or done anything else outrageous. She slept in the lodge with Mac, Annemarie, and Felice, while Blue, Ferry, Dreyfuss, and Valdez kept their own tent. Blue paid court to Lisette in his sweet, awkward way, and she seemed to enjoy it. But she held herself aloof from him and everyone else.

Now Blue was spinning that ax on the palm of his hand, even switching hands and keeping it spinning. He was a wizard with that ax.

Annemarie tapped Mac on the shoulder to dance again. As Lisette spun off, she brushed his cheek with her lips in a sisterly way—well, with maybe a hint of tease.

She had teased Mac one night in the lodge. "When you have one woman in this tipi," she said, "the two of you have a good time. But when you have two, no one has a good time." She capped it off, "You white men are prudish."

Mac paid her no mind. He told himself that a single

woman in camp wouldn't necessarily cause trouble. Even a wild single woman.

3

Tonight he simply watched the drinking. He wondered if he would ever feel like cutting loose again. Certainly not now. And that was fine. He eyed the lookout on the bluff in the last light. The man would be coming down soon and joining the party. Mac would keep just a horse guard.

Skinhead had come in two hours before dark, hollering for vittles. Annemarie and Lisette had several kettles of stew ready, buffalo meat with red turnips and wild onions, plus chokecherry soup—but it wasn't enough for the crowd. Skinhead had hired ten men, eleven counting himself.

Mac was damned glad to see Skinhead, but eleven more salaries! What if things went bad? He made up his mind to pay half of them off and send them back, right away.

Skinhead brought a letter from Uncle Hugh, folded around ledger sheets, and Mac couldn't wait to get into his lodge in private and read it.

The story was in the ledgers—Gant's bonus paid, Mac's profit on the animals, over thirteen hundred dollars, sales on the trade goods less expenses, the split of the take on the horses... Mac's brain swam, looking for the bottom line: He had about five thousand dollars worth of goods and cash, free and clear.

He got up and went outside, feeling weak. He walked toward where the horses were grazing. They were his profit on the horse deal, on the hoof, and in need of being grazed, watered, bred, and guarded.

He leaned against a cottonwood and looked at the herd. Damn, he had gotten away with it. He'd taken an awful chance—now he could admit it to himself—but he'd been lucky.

He read the letter. Good wishes, politenesses, and there it was—Uncle Hugh and Campbell were each venturing another thousand on the same terms, in the form of credit with the Company. With that he could pay salaries and buy more trade goods and—damn! Wagh! Everything had gone right! If he made a good trading season and could get the furs downriver safely, and the peltry market didn't go to hell, and he was able to bring next year's trade goods upriver uneventfully, he should have two or three times that many goods this time next year. If.

It nearly made him dizzy.

Mac tapped out his pipe on the sole of a moccasin. This trading was for men with strong stomachs. Mac didn't necessarily want to be head trader of all the Yellowstone country. He wanted to roam, eat wild asparagus in the spring, hunt buffalo in the fall, and tell stories in the lodge all winter. But he owed his children, present and to come.

He could see a new world for them. Half-breeds, yes— that's why it had to be different for them. Prosperous half-breeds, he hoped. Educated, if he had his way. Savvy of the country and the customs. More equipped, then, than white or red to show the way.

It would be different here in the West. This was not farming country—never would be. Country for the Indians and the buffalo, both roamers. Country to stay unfenced. Country like the vast steppes of Asia, for nomads and herdsmen. It would never change. And so it would give birth to a new kind of civilization, peculiarly its own creature. A civilization built on men like his sons to come, and women like Felice.

"The boys want whiskey, Cap." Skinhead's voice, calling across the sagebrush.

Mac smiled. Sure, time to celebrate. "Okay, let's tap a keg."

4

Mac and Skinhead walked back from checking the horse guard. Four tents of white canvas gleamed in a row in the moonlight. They looked strange next to the buffalo-hide lodge. Odd, thought Mac—a row, a straight line, was the mark of the white man. Indians lived in circles.

Lord, thought Mac, I must own those tents, too. He found it oppressive.

The wind blew chill—September nights could be nippy. Mac put up his hood and tied his four-hole capote. Skinhead sat down by the fire. The fat man wore only a linsey-woolsey shirt—his insulation was under his skin. Mac felt like going to bed, but the two of them had lots to talk about.

"How was it?" Mac opened.

"I wanna be partners," declared Skinhead.

Mac nodded. He'd been afraid of that.

"This nigger has did what you did, full shares. He—"

Mac waved it away. "I know."

"Us two'uns hang out hide and hair together. Same risk—same reward." Skinhead's forehead vein looked popped out.

"I'll think about it." Mac wanted to be somewhere else.

"I taught you what way the stick floats." Skinhead was pushing.

"True."

"You ain't gonna leapfrog over me?"

Mac sighed. "Doesn't seem right."

"So why ain't you saying yes? Straight off?"

Mac drew a line in the dirt with his toe. He wanted to wait. He didn't want Skinhead unhappy right now. But he couldn't go the partners route. And waiting wouldn't help.

"Skinhead, I want you around. I need you around. But running a business isn't your piece of meat. Half the time I damn well don't think it's mine, and I know it isn't yours. You'd get a wild hair up your ass and go hooting and hollering off to seduce some woman, and the business would go to seed.

"I'm not sure I wanna grow up. I'm pretty sure you don't.

"But I want you around. I'll pay you fine. You'll probably make more dollars than I will."

That forehead vein hadn't gone back in at all. "What do you want this beaver around for?" The tone was only half-resentful.

"Right now I want you to take five of these men back to

Union and pay 'em off. I'll give you a letter. There's nobody else here I can ask to do a job like that."

"Mac," Skinhead protested, "don't send 'em back. You're on a roll—let it all ride."

Mac shook his head no. He knew going against Skinhead's judgment would make the fat man mad in the long run, but he saw no choice. "Then I want you to find Strikes Foot and invite them in."

"Cheyennes this child introduced you to!"

Mac ignored it. "Before winter."

Skinhead heaved breath out. "Not so easy, beaver."

Mac nodded. "I know. Take presents." He hesitated. "I'll give you a hundred-dollar bonus now, another hundred if you get Strikes Foot to come in, and another hundred if he comes in this fall. Tell them they can camp here for the winter if they want. There's plenty of feed." The Indian ponies ate the bark of the sweet cottonwood in the winter, and the river bottoms provided plenty.

"Whatever you say, Cap."

Mac couldn't tell if the title was sarcastic or not. He stood up and clapped his friend on the back. "Take a couple of days' rest first."

He headed for his lodge, the lodge with two women in it. He wondered if that bothered Skinhead, too. Skinhead and a baker's dozen other hot-blooded men.

5

Praise Maheo, thought Mac, for Blue. Maheo seemed to be the principal Cheyenne deity, and Mac thought maybe here in the Yellowstone country, for the father of a Cheyenne daughter, the praise was due him.

Blue had the new men up and dragging logs at dawn the next morning. They breakfasted in the half light on jerky and were at work when the sun came up. Blue got a big bay gelding and black mare into the two collars they had and had them pulling untrimmed logs with ropes. Ferry and Dreyfuss were at work as a sawyer team, felling trees with the crosscut saw. The rest of the men were hefting logs more than a foot thick in pairs and carrying them to the site. Blue led by example. He put his big back into dragging logs by himself. The other men were then too ashamed to slack off.

"Pull, you ox," Lisette yelled, grinning. Blue pretended not to hear. Mac noticed she seemed to appreciate Blue more from a distance.

She was working hard, too, helping Skinhead carry water from the river. It was a hot September day, and they could hardly keep up with the demand. Before noon she had Skinhead carrying a branch improvised into a yoke with two firkins of water.

Mac checked the guard and lookout and supervised and helped Annemarie get dinner ready. Laboring men consumed a lot of food.

Skinhead made a show of trying to pinch the bottom of either woman who strayed within reach. Mac took that to mean his heart was all right, which was damned good news.

Mac laid a rope down and checked the length of the foundation for one wall, marked the rope, then checked its opposite. The same. He measured catty-corner distances. The same. Which meant the walls would be square, and the roof and inner walls would fit.

It was coming along well. The new hands were speeding up the work a lot. A solid and worthy structure, built to last for generations. What would he call it? Maybe Yellowstone House. He liked "house" better than "fort"— he was offering friendship, not war.

6

While most of the crew was still at breakfast, Skinhead left with the five men for Fort Union. Three hundred miles each way, just a walk to the barn for an old hand such as Skinhead. Getting the Cheyennes to come in might be trickier.

In half an hour the crew was hard at work, and in less than an hour someone hollered out for water. After five more minutes Blue came trotting up to Mac, who was learning to use the adze.

"Where's Lisette with the water?"

"Don't know. I'll bring the water." Mac took advantage of the trip to the river to splash his face. A nickering sorrel got his attention; something wasn't right.

After delivering the firkins, he went to the horse herd and looked around. Both of Lisette's mounts were missing.

He walked back and asked Annemarie when she had last seen Lisette. At bedtime. He remembered he hadn't been able to lay his hands on his capote this morning at first light. He checked the lodge—Four-Holer was gone.

Damn.

He made his way through the bottom to where Blue was trimming with his double-bitted ax.

"She's gone," he said.

Blue looked at him oddly.

"Lisette is gone. With that damned Skinhead."

Blue just looked at Mac, then stared blankly. And then he drew the long ax back straight over his head and hurled it—*whump-whump*—through the air. Til's outcry rang across time in Mac's head.

The ax stuck in a cottonwood trunk, buried to the handle, quivering.

≈ 17 ≈

It couldn't be Skinhead. He'd be coming alone, or with Lisette in tow, and the column of dust would be a wisp. Or if he was mad, he wouldn't be coming at all.

Mac couldn't figure if Skinhead took Little One off out of spite or lust or just craziness.

This column of dust was wide and dark, like a purple curtain of rain seen at a distance across the plains, but gray, and rising instead of falling. He lowered his telescope and looked at it with the naked eye.

Mac handed Dreyfuss the Dolland. "I better ride out to see who it is." He didn't say he hoped it was the Cheyennes. Skinhead had only been gone two weeks. Maybe he ran into them along the way and got them to come in. It had better be someone friendly. An entire village passing by wouldn't bother the white men, but the young braves might have a little fun on their own, including running off the entire herd of horses.

"Your watch over?"

"Yess," said Dreyfuss, his English littered with thick consonants.

"Want to ride out with me?"

"Sure."

"Saddle up."

Down where the crew was working, Mac told Blue to take watch himself while they were gone. They tripled the guard on the horses.

2

"Skinhead did it!" Mac said to Dreyfuss. Smiling his habitual and enigmatic smile, Dreyfuss put a hand over his ear. Mac hadn't realized he was shouting.

The village on the move was Cheyennes, Leg-in-the-Water's Cheyennes. Which meant Strikes Foot and Lame Deer, and lots of fussing over Felice, and a happy Annemarie. Her family. Hell, his own family. In-laws, at least.

He moved the telescope back along the line, the usual parade of men phalanxed in their warrior societies, women and children behind them dragging travois, dogs everywhere, and riders flanked to both sides for protection.

Something odd was sticking up among the warriors—white, on a long shaft, like a shirt on a clothesline. It bore some emblem. He handed the Dolland to Dreyfuss. "There's something queer near the front, like a flag, white. Can you make out the markings on it?"

Dreyfuss looked a long time, then shook his head. Mac put the telescope away.

Strikes Foot. Calling Eagle. Lame Deer. Wagh!

He kicked his horse to a run, across the low hills, through the sagebrush, across the coulee, breakneck toward the Cheyennes. Dreyfuss kept up, but he was bouncing around, just like a city man.

A hundred yards away Mac shot his rifle into the air, and Dreyfuss did the same. A way of going in unarmed, so a gesture of peace.

Mac brought his mare up short and walked the last twenty paces to Leg-in-the-Water.

"*Hou!*"

"*Hou*, Dancer!"

"Welcome," Mac said in Cheyenne.

The chief inclined his head. Mac noticed Dreyfuss moving his lips silently, repeating the Cheyenne words. Smart beaver.

Where was Strikes Foot? Ordinarily he'd ride up and greet Mac.

But someone was coming up—Jim, Jim Sykes. Beside a man in a cassock. Wagh! A priest! Here in the wilds of Yellowstone country. And the shaft was a cross bearing a white, tasseled rectangle of silk with Our Lady encircled with stars embroidered on it—the banner of the Blessed Virgin.

Strikes Foot was behind the two of them, his face rigidly proper.

"Father De Smet," said Jim formally in his mealy voice, "Robert Maclean."

"Mac," said Mac, stretching out his hand. He introduced Dreyfuss to Jim and De Smet. Mac wanted to clap Jim on the back, but it wouldn't be fitting.

He couldn't stop looking at De Smet. The priest had a powerful aura of vitality. He was a big man, athletic-looking, virile, a commanding presence.

"We're glad to have you here, Father," Mac murmured.

Suddenly a commotion behind Mac, sounds of horses bumping and hubbub . . .

He was halfway turned when it went dark. A damn blanket over his head. He fought the blanket. Someone had his arms around Mac and the blanket. And was giggling. And men were chuckling.

Mac threw himself sideways off his mare and thumped onto the hard ground.

Daylight, rocking back and forth.

Someone shrieked and fell right on him. He threw off the blanket and the person.

Lisette.

Eyes alight, hand over her mouth, spluttering with laughter. "Thought you'd like Four-Holer back."

Yeah, the damn blanket, it was Four-Holer.

"Oh, lighten up, sourpuss." She grabbed his head and kissed him square on the mouth.

Mac pushed her away. De Smet was giggling with laughter. Strikes Foot was grinning and shaking his head. "You Frenchmen are strange."

Mac grabbed Lisette's face. Her scarred face, full of

beautiful, abused, defiant eyes. He dragged her onto his legs and began to whack her petite bottom, hard.

She howled, half laughter and half real hurt.

3

The trading was tricky. The Cheyennes accepted Mac's presents standoffishly, though he gave plenty and did not make the mistake of showing anxiety by giving too much. The men kept the women away from the wares and acted as if they only wanted essentials, such as powder and lead, not foofaraw, such as beads and ribbon and bells. Mac showed them items and talked deals a second day, and a third, before he struck most of his bargains.

Strikes Foot showed no more enthusiasm than the rest, and around the post he took an attitude of indifference toward Annemarie. But Lame Deer ruled out any such foolishness with a whooping welcome for her daughter and granddaughter. From the first moment, Annemarie and Felice were in Strikes Foot's lodge playing and giggling and sewing, the baby fussed over by all three grandmothers. It would be all right. The basic fact was still that Cheyennes adored children.

They gave no indication Mac couldn't be Felice's father and apparently didn't give a damn who was.

Mac still gave a damn. He'd even thought of asking Lame Deer and had made up his mind against it. He was going to *make* himself forget it.

One fine October morning the Cheyennes said they were headed across the river to hunt, to make meat for the winter. It was a splendid autumn day, cool and sunny. Plains stretching in every direction. High, snow-topped mountain barriers to the south and west. Buffalo dark and thick on the prairies on the north bank, thousands of them in sight.

"Let's go, too," Mac said to Annemarie.

The little trading post needed to fill its larder for the long winter. This time they would jerk the meat—in future years they'd have an icehouse to keep it cool.

Mac thought of going off for a few days with Annemarie alone—what else are grandmothers for? But it would be too dangerous, a single pair on the prairie, one riding hither and yon chasing beasts, the other on her knees skinning and butchering. Any passing Blackfoot could count coup on them. So Mac asked Strikes Foot, Dreyfuss, Lame Deer, and Lisette to hunt with him and Annemarie. Mac could have chosen a different woman, but he wanted Lisette within sight. No telling when Skinhead would turn up, or what trouble he and Little One might get into.

She'd made it clear she didn't intend to talk about why she and Skinhead had run off, or why he left her with the Cheyennes instead of taking her on to Fort Union. Frankly, Mac didn't care.

Mac was liking Dreyfuss more and more. He was intelligent, spoke little, and was amiable, with a quirky sense of humor. Mac needed a clerk and thought Dreyfuss was the man. Today the pork-eater was going to learn to run buffalo, and skin and butcher them. Then he would be less of a pork-eater, in more ways than one.

Buffalo were slow thinkers, dumb enough to inspire the expression "buffler-witted." You could get them in a surround and shoot as many as you wanted. You could drive them off a cliff. You could stand downwind and simply pick them off one by one. Today Mac intended to run them. Shooting buffalo at a gallop, alongside, was fun. William Drummond Stewart called it the most exhilarating sport in the world, but then Sir William was a fancy talker.

They sat their horses on a little rise, overlooking the huge herd. It really made no difference where they started. They could ride for days and never be out of sight of buffalo. "We are children of nature," Mac murmured dryly to Dreyfuss, "and take what the Lord provides."

"Wagh!" said Dreyfuss with a little smile. The professor was even learning a mountain man's way of talking, with a German accent.

Mac did wish they had better horses. Strikes Foot was on his buffalo runner, but Mac and the professor rode untried animals. In a buffalo horse you wanted speed to get alongside, agility to stay with the buffalo or avoid it, quick response, nerves that could stand the shooting, and surefootedness on the rough ground. A horse that stumbled would throw its rider into a storm of hooves.

Mac put four lead balls in his mouth and nodded at Strikes Foot. He had told Dreyfuss to watch the warrior carefully at the start. Strikes Foot strung his bow, held it up in one hand, yelled, and kicked his horse toward several cows and calves.

The buffalo started moving, slowly at first. Strikes Foot rode alongside a cow, leaned well out from his saddle, and placed an arrow deliberately, almost leisurely, behind and below the front shoulder. And was immediately ready to shoot again. Strikes Foot had the second cow down before Mac could catch him. A bow was a lot faster than a rifle.

The two of them rode at the great, shaggy beasts, hollered, dashed away a little, and charged again. The herd started to move, slowly at first, the stolid creatures becoming aware of a nuisance. Then more began to trot and more followed, and you could see a great tide beginning to wash across the prairie. Mac and Strikes Foot charged them once more. The leaders were running now, and this part of the herd was moving fast, and faster, and now stampeding blindly across the plains, raging forward like a flash flood.

Mac thrilled to the rumbling thunder of the hooves, the rank, thick smell of beast and dung, his horse at a gallop, the prairie rolling by like waves.

Mac pulled alongside a cow, which veered away at the last moment. He got nearly set on another, but both cow and horse jumped into a wash and upset his aim. He pulled alongside again and finally got a shot. Seemed well-placed.

He kicked the horse for more speed. This was the tricky part. He poured some powder down the barrel, spilling a bit, got some more down, fished a ball out of his mouth, set it in the muzzle, rammed it home, and seated it by whacking the butt on the saddle. These maneuvers were a hell of a stunt on the gallop, but you couldn't leave the chase—you were right in the floodtide of animals.

Mac heard a shot behind him, and no more. Dreyfuss must have got a cow. Mac looked around and saw Strikes Foot in the melee of buffalo, shooting arrows. Another gunshot behind him—now the professor got the cow.

The race went on. Mac brought his horse alongside several cows and dropped two more, but it was hard work. His mare was fearful and would come close and then pull away.

Suddenly the mare grabbed the bit in her teeth and took off. Around sagebrushes, at a breakneck pace past bulls and cows and calves, into a wash and up the other side at a bound. The critter was crazed—Mac couldn't control her.

He chose the least of several evils. He reached out alongside her muzzle and pulled the rein hard straight sideways. Head and neck came around, and Mac quickly eased up on the rein—but too late. The mare pitched sideways. Mac went head over heels through the sage.

Mac scrambled to his feet and roared at a bull that was almost on him. The brute veered off. He jumped for the horse and grabbed a rein. Everything hurt, but getting trampled would hurt a lot worse. He got up close to the mare and gentled her. Now the situation looked scarier than it was. Leading the animal out of the thick of things, he took inventory.

His shoulder hurt like hell where he'd landed on it, his face was scraped and bleeding, and his left hand was gashed. The mare limped on her left front foot. Probably they'd both be all right. Pulling on the saddle horn hurt sharply, but he got into the saddle.

Already the hunting party was strung out over a mile. Mac could see several buffalo down, and there must be a couple more. Human figures stood over three of them far back. Strikes Foot had pulled up.

The mare was calmer now. Mac wanted her to get this experience, to learn what buffalo do and don't do. He mounted and headed her back at a walk.

Mac came up alongside Strikes Foot, and the two of them trotted on to Lisette and the professor. For some reason the skinners were just picketing their horses by a big cow Mac had shot. It made Little One look doll-like.

Lisette showed Dreyfuss how to get the cow's legs arranged, propped out for stability. Buffalo were so big and cumbersome you couldn't put them on their backs—you had to start by splitting the hide down the middle.

Lisette put her knife in at the nape of the neck. "Damn," she cussed, "buffalo skin is so thick you—"

The goddamn critter started getting to its feet. Lisette and Dreyfuss backed off, half-stumbling, unbelieving. The beast charged Little One, horns lowered.

The cow knocked Lisette down, ran right over her, and turned back to do it again.

Before Mac could get a bead, Strikes Foot was in the way. He drove his horse right into the beast from the side. Man, horse, and buffalo went down in a heap, kicking and bellowing. Mac couldn't get a clean shot.

Dreyfuss bolted forward, stuck his pistol in the cow's mouth, and finished it.

Mac jumped off and ran for Lisette.

Dust-in-the-face moon

"For God's sake," bitched Lisette, "don't be shy about showing my tit."

Dreyfuss did. The wound started in the lower outside region of the right breast and ran along the ribs. Plenty of blood, but it was a rake, not a puncture. "She's lucky the horn didn't penetrate and get a lung," he said to the group at large. "And she's so tiny the other horn went outside her. Very fortunate."

"Fortunate! My God, I'm among crazy people," Lisette moaned. In a lot of pain, she'd been just half-conscious coming in from the prairie. Being alert enough to complain was an improvement.

They were in the infirmary tent. Light came through a flap onto an odd assortment of human beings—Lisette and Strikes Foot, there as patients; Dreyfuss, De Smet, and Calling Eagle, there as healers; and Mac and Annemarie, there to fret and wring their hands.

Mac had to take a hand and rule that De Smet and Calling Eagle could help by praying, each to his own powers, but that the professor was in charge of the doctoring. It turned out Dreyfuss's nursing during the war gave him lots of practical knowledge. Mac was continually surprised to find new areas of competence in this roly-poly, middle-aged man.

Calling Eagle and De Smet sat to the side, talking. They were using signs and gesturing too fast and too big, their hands nearly colliding in air. And they kept smiling and laughing like foolish women. Mac was tickled. Two men in dresses, one unknown to the other as a male, both

143

priests, both prayer healers. Though they worshiped different gods, maybe it was logical that they'd get along.

Mac thought De Smet wouldn't be so damn friendly if he knew Calling Eagle had testicles under that skirt.

The professor's opinion was that Lisette was bad off but not in mortal danger. Aside from the big gouge, she had cracked ribs. Her foot had evidently been stepped on, too, and might have broken bones. And Dreyfuss thought she'd hit her head hard on the ground. She would be down awhile, if only to let the ribs heal. "Lucky," he told her again.

She covered her face with her hands, and winced with pain. "Your arms move the ribs," the professor pointed out with a chuckle.

"You're lucky Strikes Foot was close by," said Mac. "He saved your damn life."

Little One opened her eyes at him and smiled as though she'd caught him. "My damn life," she said with a wistful smile.

Mac was embarrassed. "He rode into the cow and knocked it down."

Lisette sniffed a little laugh, and grabbed her ribs in pain, and squeaked at the movement. "Dreyfuss killed it," Mac went on.

Dreyfuss took her hand and felt her pulse. She smiled softly at him. "Thank you," she said, "for my damn life."

"Thank me by being a good patient," he said, and squeezed her hand.

"Thank you, Strikes Foot," she called across the tent in the Sioux language, her head back and eyes on the ceiling. "But it is a foolish warrior who cripples himself for a tiny Frenchwoman."

Strikes Foot replied in the same language, "You are welcome, Little One."

Strikes Foot had wrenched the knee on his clubfooted leg badly and wouldn't be able to bear weight on his hoof for a few days.

The professor started to put something on Lisette's ribs to stop the bleeding, the underbelly fur from a beaver—not something he'd learned in school, Mac would bet.

"Stop that!" Calling Eagle called out in Cheyenne. Mac translated. Dreyfuss raised an eyebrow. "The wound will get sick," Calling Eagle said, coming forward with a horn. She unstoppered the big end, fingered out some sort of salve, and started rubbing it on.

Dreyfuss held the horn for her and sniffed at the salve. He looked at Mac. Mac shook his head. "She won't tell you what it is unless you convert," Mac said with a half smile. "But her poultices generally help."

Dreyfuss just watched Calling Eagle work. Then he put on the fur and a clean dressing.

Relieved, Mac stepped outside the hospital tent and De Smet took his arm.

"I'm going on to see the Crows," De Smet said. "With Jim Sykes."

"Just Jim?"

"The Lord God cares for his children." Seemed the priest went all over the plains and mountains with just one guide, or just another priest. He evidently was convinced the messenger of God was invincible. Well, thought Mac, the Lord God protects drunks, fools, and innocents.

"We'll be gone a couple of weeks. In the meantime, will you speak to the Cheyennes for me?" De Smet wanted Mac to persuade the Cheyenne leaders to let him preach and baptize the children.

Mac felt two ways about it. He'd been baptized himself and raised in the Church. He didn't see that it would hurt anything, but he resented all the white men who came west to teach the Indians the true way. Which only meant their way. What they didn't see, at all, was that the Indians had plenty to teach the whites—if white people weren't too dumb to realize they still had anything to learn.

Hell, the Indians had sense enough to study white ways and pick up what was useful.

Mac supposed he would have to help the priest. And Mac felt guilty—because he himself wanted something from De Smet. "I'll ask them, Father, and I'll have Felice baptized." They both knew that gesture would be the key.

"Thank you, my son."

But Mac wasn't listening. "Mac!" he heard again in a high voice he knew.

Skinhead came striding through the bottoms. "Where's Little One?" he demanded without even a hello or how was Fort Union. "Blue won't tell me."

Blue was trailing agitatedly behind Skinhead. Mac hesitated. "Why do you want to know?"

"I got somep'n to tell her." He looked mad now, as did Blue.

"She's laid up, in the infirmary." He indicated the tent.

Calling Eagle stuck her head out to see what was happening. Skinhead brushed by her. Mac and Blue bumped in the doorway, keeping up.

The fat man squatted beside Lisette at the far end, where she lay on some robes. Lisette's bare breast, which Dreyfuss was working on, embarrassed Mac.

Without hesitation Skinhead said, "Genet's dead."

Mac saw tears well in her eyes. She took Skinhead's hand tenderly. "What happened?"

"They told me at Fort Union. He was coming upriver, to clerk for the Company at Fort Clark and bring you there. He just keeled over. Buried him on the riverbank."

She squeezed his hand for a long time, eyes closed. "Thank you."

"What you done to yourself?"

Blue was hovering nervously, like everyone else. Skinhead seemed too rough a presence.

"I let a buffalo cow run over me."

"You gonna die?"

She gave a sudden, luminous smile. "Not yet." She really looked beautiful sometimes, thought Mac.

"Then let's go to Union and spend the winter. I hired on to hunt."

Blue shot Mac a dark, bloody look. But Mac found Skinhead touching. He'd just given as close to a proposal of marriage as he could.

"Don't be ridiculous," Little One murmured, and giggled a little, then gasped in pain, clutching her ribs.

2

Twilight at the trading post was a time Mac liked, particularly a nippy, salmon-colored twilight such as this one. Annemarie was down in the river, waist deep, holding the hammerheaded bay with a halter. Right now she was rubbing its muzzle, which the horse was holding still for. In a few minutes she would slide onto its back. This was how she started breaking a horse to ride. She did it marvelously well—fast, easily, with excellent results. Since Mac wanted to be a horse trader, he was lucky to be married to a good trainer.

Mac stirred the stew, keeping it from sticking. That was how he freed Annemarie to work with the horses a few minutes each evening.

Some of the hands were hanging targets—scraps of ticking—on the bottom round of a huge cottonwood. The throwers were aiming at the patches with knives or hawks. The stakes were small belongings, hard to come by in the mountains.

Other men were playing euchre. They had confiscated one of the two decks Skinhead brought from St. Louis—those cards weren't going to be used for throwing-knife targets.

Blue was sitting on a stump sharpening his double-bitted ax. He would stick one blade in a crack in the stump while he filed the other. That ax was sharp as a knife. Sharper than some.

Mac wondered, Why do men go for sport with a tinge of risk? Why not do quillwork or some such? Or even break horses patiently? Mac liked that tinge, too, he admitted to himself.

Skinhead stepped off the seven steps from the big cottonwood round once more, to make sure. He took his stance, let the throwing knife drop behind his head, and hurled it hard. It thunked deep into the wood and quivered. Missed by more than a handspan. Truth was, Skinhead wasn't particularly good with knife or hawk, though he'd

never admit to that. He did make them fly fiercely,
though.

Ferry missed, too. And Bass and Paddock. Looked like
nobody would win whatever they had bet. Mac stirred the
stew.

Dreyfuss tossed his knife softly and clumsily and hit
close to the patch, but the knife didn't stick. He laughed
softly at himself. Dreyfuss was way behind on his skills of
war. Despite his sophisticated upbringing, Dreyfuss was a
determined student of woodsmanship. Strikes Foot was
teaching him to track and said he was quick and subtle.
From Strikes Foot, a high compliment.

Finally Skinhead won the wager, whatever it was. He
had a way of coming out better than he looked.

"Hey, Blue, Paul the Blue," called Skinhead. "Come
throw with us."

"You got naught I want," said Blue without looking up.

Mac was looking at Blue's hands and forearms as he
worked. He was a really big man. His wrists seemed as
big around as Mac's knees.

"You bragged on what you can do with that ax. Why not
try against this child?"

"You'll not get your hands on my ax."

Mac saw Annemarie lead the horse out of the river.
She'd be wet and wanting to change. He started down to
take the horse to the corral for her.

"Let him be, Skinhead," said Dreyfuss.

"Let's us think," sang Skinhead. "What does this child
have that Paul the Blue wants? What would he compete
like a man for?"

Blue just worked harder at the blade.

"My rifle from Jake Hawken? Naw, Blue cain't shoot."
He made a show of pondering the problem. "A . . . a sixteen-
hide lodge? Wagh! Big improvement on a tent. But he
don't have nobody to share it with and is too shy to ask."

"Skinhead—" started Dreyfuss, but the fat man squelched
him with an angry look. Dreyfuss was the new man here.

"This child knows," said Skinhead. "A kiss from Little
One! A kiss is all that beaver's ever gonna get from
Lisette." He cackled and looked around for men to join in.

No one did, but Skinhead didn't care. Blue was walking slowly toward him, the ax in one hand.

"You want it?" asked Blue soberly. "You deserve it. How? Bare hands? Knives?"

"Stop it, boze of you!" Dreyfuss shouted, and stepped between them. Blue flung him to the ground with one arm. But Blue stopped.

"Jealous are ye, coon? Jealous of Skinhead's dallying with Little One?" Skinhead was just standing there, eyes fixed on Blue. No one knew what his move might be. "Course, ye be jealous. Blue wants a woman but has no balls."

Skinhead began to circle now, circle to his right with snaky agility. Blue moved with him, opposite. "Skinhead has balls, and what goes with 'em. Skinhead puts it up her till she can feel it in her throat."

They kept moving, each wary. Dreyfuss didn't know if the game might stop in a laugh or move on to something deadly. Dreyfuss saw Mac start away from the river, leading the horse.

"Think on that, coon—up to her throat. She hollers out for it. Makes your balls shrivel up, hearing that, don't it?"

Everyone backed off. Dreyfuss decided to do something. He strode toward Skinhead. "Stop it, damn you!" he yelled.

"Another step, pork-eater," snarled Skinhead, his hand on his pistol, "and I'll shoot you instead of him."

Dreyfuss stopped. Now he was sure it was inevitable. No one could even make out what Mac was hollering through the trees.

Blue and Skinhead watched each other. Skinhead stopped in front of the round of the cottonwood. Blue stood opposite him, looking relaxed. Dreyfuss could feel it grow. He told himself Skinhead would charge, head down, like a bull, and they would grapple.

When Skinhead jerked the gun up, it seemed to happen slowly. The barrel first cleared the wide belt and then rose and then belched white smoke.

At that moment something glinted silver in the slant sunlight.

Blue was still standing, glaring at Skinhead.

Skinhead was standing—impaled on the cottonwood by the ax, his eyes bugged out.

Dreyfuss vomited.

Mac ran up to Skinhead. The forward blade was rammed all the way through his collarbone and throat, stuck deep into wood. The other blade gleamed maliciously under his chin. There was almost no blood. Mac looked across at Blue, and back at the hurled ax. "My God," Mac muttered.

Blue strode up, grabbed the handle, and levered the ax out. Skinhead's body started to pitch forward. Max grabbed it and Dreyfuss helped him. They lowered the fat man to the ground.

Mac turned toward Blue and said, "I don't understand you." Blue just kept walking away. Mac saw then that Blue was limping, and one pants leg was bloody.

3

Blue's leg turned white first. After a few days it started turning black.

Mac knew that was why Dreyfuss called them all together in the infirmary tent. And he observed that Dreyfuss had built a fire in front.

The leg was exposed from the top of the thigh down, the ugly wound just above the knee. Blue was staring at the tent roof. He'd scarcely spoken since it happened, and then sullenly. Lisette attended him constantly, but he seemed not to notice.

"It's gangrene." Dreyfuss pointed at the black leg. The toes looked like bruised and swollen plums. The leg was dark nearly up to where Skinhead's ball tore it up. "It's got to come off."

Mac made signs to Calling Eagle. The Cheyenne healer wanted to see what the Frenchman healer would do.

"Will that work?" asked Mac.

"Maybe, maybe not," said Dreyfuss. "But he dies for sure otherwise."

Little One knelt beside Blue and held his hand. Blue acted oblivious of everything.

"And we may as well get at it now, early in the day, when there's plenty of light." No one objected. "Mac, I want you to help."

"I'll assist you," said Lisette. "I've done it before." Dreyfuss looked at her, uncertain. "I'll do it," she insisted. Dreyfuss nodded. "I'll need both of you."

"I want whiskey," Dreyfuss said to Mac, "and your laudanum. Now. It will take less than an hour to get him liquored up." Mac went to get the medicine.

"I want three knives, very sharp," Dreyfuss said in crude Cheyenne. "And three more—make that four—heated in the fire."

Calling Eagle said she'd take care of that and left.

"To cauterize," Dreyfuss added in English. "Lisette, please get a bunch of horsehairs. Maybe we can tie off the bleeders." He didn't sound confident. "Needle and thread, too."

First she helped him drag Blue outside by the fire and get him stretched out on canvas.

4

Dreyfuss felt so clumsy. He was thankful the patient was in the netherworld of the lotus drug, moaning occasionally but not really aware. He also wished Lisette weren't seeing everything, but she was all business, sitting on the leg ready to hold the flesh back.

"All right, crank it tight," he said to Mac. Mac had a stout strip of canvas for a tourniquet, and an iron tent peg to turn it. He started twisting.

"Tighter," said Dreyfuss "Right down hard." The three of them were crowded around the leg—there was hardly room to work. Calling Eagle was peering around bottoms, arms, and legs.

Finally Dreyfuss could delay no longer. He started his cut on the outside, away from the wound and above it, three or four inches above the knee. That way he would cut away any infected tissue.

He felt as if he were hacking Blue up. He was soon to bone.

Mac handed Dreyfuss Blue's bow saw silently. They figured it was plenty sharp to get through the bone. The other choice seemed to be the two-man crosscut saw, and that was too big and awkward for cutting a leg. The labor of sawing Blue's bone seemed gruesome.

Blue appeared to be passed out.

Calling Eagle was watching the white man's medicine, but Mac had chased the other men back to their construction. He found their desire to look on ghoulish.

Now came the part Dreyfuss was most concerned about. He put it off by cutting a big flap of skin off the calf of the half-severed leg. He would need it to sew on and cover the stump.

Then he went ahead—toward the big artery on the inside he didn't know the name of in English. He cut through the area the ball had smashed, a mangle of tissue. The ball had passed close to the big artery and mashed muscle hard against it.

Dreyfuss looked around and spotted the horsehairs. "Keep that blood cut off, Mac." The artery made an ugly, splotchy blue line under the skin.

Mac took another crank. Dreyfuss took his breath in deep, let it out, and cut. The leg was severed.

The tourniquet worked. An ooze of blood, no more. Dreyfuss pushed the dead two thirds of leg away. Now he would have to do a nice piece of work.

He rooted around a little with the point of his knife and exposed the end of the severed artery, as big around as his little finger. Just maybe enough to tie.

He took a long horsehair and wrapped it around the artery, crisscross. He pulled it tight as he could and tied a knot. Maybe it would hold.

He thought a moment. "Give me the hottest knife," he said to Lisette. She did. The metal was red.

Dreyfuss put the flat of the blade against the raw stump, artery included.

Paul the Blue bucked. His mouth jerked open as though to make a cry, but nothing came out. The sizzle and stench nearly turned Dreyfuss's stomach.

He looked at his handiwork. Maybe he'd just cauterized the end of the artery closed.

He looked Mac in the eye and nodded. "Loosen the tourniquet."

Mac eased the pressure slowly. Nothing seemed to happen. He let the tension off.

Blood squirted everywhere, spraying them all. "Put it back!" Dreyfuss screamed.

Blood was spurting all over with every heartbeat. Dreyfuss wiped his eyes. He couldn't get hold of the edges of the damn artery—it was pulled back into the muscle.

He jammed his little finger in, which made the blood shower, but the artery was a little too small to get his finger up into.

Mac got the flow stopped.

All three of them wiped blood off their faces and hair and looked at each other in desperation. Even Calling Eagle was blood-splattered. She edged closer, to see.

"We got to do it," said Dreyfuss. He fished for the end of the artery.

Lisette could see what was going to happen. The artery was too big to cauterize, too slick to tie. There was nothing to do but keep trying.

They did it all again. They got squirted again and went through the agony of getting it stopped again.

They did it a third time. The spray of blood was less now.

Dreyfuss reached for more horsehair. "I svear I'm going to get zis done." His voice broke as he said it.

"Dreyfuss," Lisette murmured compassionately. He saw something in her eyes, he wasn't sure what, sadness . . .

So, he looked at the face. Eyes fixed. He felt for a pulse—nothing.

Paul the Blue was dead.

Calling Eagle reached out, touched Dreyfuss on the arm sympathetically, and eased away.

Dreyfuss looked at himself. A bloody mess. Bled to death right gottdamn on me.

He looked at Mac and Lisette. Everyone was covered with Blue's blood. Everyone was grief-stricken.

Lisette reached out to both of them. On their knees they all put their arms around one another.

Dreyfuss felt himself sobbing. He thought he could feel the others shaking, too.

≈ 19 ≈

October, 1844, Dust-in-the-face moon

Mac Maclean was fidgety. He expected to be fidgety all afternoon. He had a right—it was his wedding day.

Three United States flags stood in the center of the Cheyenne camp, and the people stood facing them. "The people" meant most of Mac's crew and probably, judged Mac, fifty Cheyennes, acting properly respectful, if you didn't consider the naked children and barking dogs. Respectful of the flags, of the banner of the Blessed Virgin, and of the cassocked priest who stood before them. And even of the priest's acolyte, a Cree half-breed named Gabriel.

"You suppose they're gonna become tithers?" whispered Jim to Mac, smiling ironically. The two of them were watching from the edge of the clearing in their wedding finery.

Mac shrugged. "They might add a little Christianity on."

"Cheyennes ain't Flatheads," observed Jim. That was true enough. The Flatheads had gotten passionate to acquire Christianity, sending a delegation from far west of the mountains to St. Louis to ask for the gift of the holy black book. They were now taking their new religion—second religion, the late Skinhead would have said—very seriously.

The Cheyennes were less impressed with white folks in general. They might be amenable to adding another power to their pantheon, plus a few ceremonies, any that seemed effective. But certainly they weren't about to give up their own god.

It was simple. Your god gave you the sun and moon and water and grass, and in the Cheyennes' case particularly, the buffalo. If the Cheyennes surrendered their renewing of the sacred arrows or their sun dance, they'd starve. But they wouldn't mind finding out about the gods who gave the Frenchmen things—telescopes, guns, books, sugar, and the like. Clearly those were powerful gods, too.

Mac had argued with De Smet that his conversions were a bad joke. De Smet just smiled and said Mac didn't understand how mysterious were the ways God worked.

Mac missed Skinhead. And Blue.

The priest and the acolyte opened the service with a chant. Then De Smet prayed at length and explained the prayers and chanted two more canticles. It went on too long. Mac felt self-conscious in his fancy clothes, a white cloth shirt with pleats and puffed sleeves, and pants of antelope skin as white as Annemarie could make them, marvelously thin and soft, decorated with tiny bells that jingled when he walked, and all his scalps down the right leg. They were real pants with a drop front, too, not leggings. His moccasins were fully quilled, and he sported German silver armbands and handwoven garters. He was putting on a show.

Mac had loaned Jim enough clothes for the best man to look splendiferous, too.

A strange day for Mac, a day of sacraments. Words had been spoken over the graves of Skinhead and Blue, murderers in the eyes of the Church. Words would be spoken over infants and small children, magical words to make them Christians, sort of. Words would be spoken to sanctify Mac's marriage to Annemarie.

De Smet recited the Apostles' Creed and the Ten Commandments and explained each. It seemed to take forever. Mac had no idea what the Cheyennes were making of all of it. They listened patiently, though. Leg-in-the-Water had asked Mac if Black Robe's reading aloud from the sacred book would give the Cheyennes the gift of understanding the talking leaves. Mac told him that reading wasn't a gift, but a skill you could learn. Mac was going to teach Felice and offered to include any children the Cheyennes wanted.

When De Smet started to admonish the Cheyennes for their thieving ways, which meant horse stealing, and their moral corruption, which meant having more than one wife, Mac murmured to Jim, "I can't stand still," and took a walk.

2

Mac could see Strikes Foot holding the horse off at the edge of the trees, ready and handsomely outfitted, a gray gelding with a quilled crupper passed under its tail, the padded saddle ornamented with beadwork at cantle and pommel, brilliant white ermine tails woven into the mane, and the lead rope wrapped with strips of beaver. Strikes Foot was in full regalia, carrying a lance fancied with a row of eagle feathers.

Mac knew Strikes Foot was eager to walk forward to Black Robe to give his daughter away. The Cheyenne liked the literal version of the English in his own language—to give his daughter away. The very definition of a good man, among the Cheyennes, was a generous man. But Strikes Foot was worried. It was important to him not to limp—part of his pride was to walk erect and straight on his hoof. And his knee was still sore.

Annemarie and Lisette were down in front with Felice. At five months, Felice was going to be christened a second time. The first time she got a sacred song and a secret Arapahoe name. This time she would get some ceremonial words, a little water, and a Christian name. De Smet liked to say the innocent get blessed without having to know anything, do anything, or promise anything.

Mac thought of De Smet's counsel. A little talk, he said, was required before he would marry anyone. Annemarie was tremulous before the priest and held on to Mac's elbow.

First, De Smet wanted the couple to understand he

could not give them the sacrament of marriage. They had already given it to themselves, if their hearts and minds were right. They were living together—his glance indicated the lodge they sat in, the home they made in marriage. Did they come together in love both human and divine? Yes, Father. Did they intend to be together so long as ye both shall live? They nodded. Did they plan to bear fruit, to bring forth children in honor of God? They did. Indeed, had they not already done so?

Mac let the reference to Felice pass.

Then, said De Smet, they were already truly married in the eyes of the Church and of God. But the priest could bless their marriage, and he would be glad to, after the baptisms tomorrow. De Smet got up awkwardly. The big man had difficulty with stiffness when he sat cross-legged.

"Father," Mac started in—He couldn't let it lie and deceive the priest. "Felice is Annemarie's daughter but not mine."

The priest sat back down, frowning. He looked long and hard at the girl. That's all she is, thought Mac, a girl—don't be too hard on her. Tears were flowing gently down her broad, flat cheeks, to Mac such beautiful cheeks. Mac saw her lift her face to the priest's and open her eyes, and he admired her.

"Have you been married before?" asked the priest.

"No, Father." She reverted to the Cheyenne language, and Mac translated softly.

"How did the child come?"

"I was a fornicator, Father." Mac supplied the alien, accusing English term.

"You did not make a home with this man?"

"No."

"You did not want to make a home and have children?"

"Only with Mac."

"Fornication is a sin, my child, but it does not rule out marriage." The priest looked at her solemnly. "I want to confess you both. Now."

Mac got up and stepped outside the lodge. Now, he thought, the priest will know the answer to my question—Who corrupted Annemarie? That's how he thought of it.

He no longer put it to himself as, Who is Felice's father? Because he was Felice's father.

3

The priest raised the seashell, bearing its shimmering water from the Yellowstone River. He held it high, ceremonially. Mac saw the waning sun strike the underside, making the white of the shell gleam and the pink-orange turn red. De Smet put his fingers into the water and flung a spray onto the infant's face. He did it once, twice, three times. "John Morning Star," he intoned, *"ego te baptismo, in nomine Patris et Filii et Spiritus Sancti."*

De Smet was adding Christian names to the kids' Cheyenne names, names of the twelve apostles. Mac wondered how, after hundreds or thousands of baptisms, the ceremony still had meaning to De Smet. Yet from the priest's face, it seemed to. The way he sang the words and the solemn joy of his countenance spoke holiness. As the drops of water flew from the priest's fingers to the face of the child, they were invisible, and Mac could almost believe the water was transformed in that moment from substance to spirit. The water power, the Cheyennes called this ceremony. And De Smet was using Yellowstone River water—Mac thought of the enchanted high country it came from, full of geysers, hot springs, fumeroles, and other wonders. Maybe such water was a little bit divine.

Another child was brought forward. De Smet looked at it lovingly, and heard the name. "Peter Green Fire," he chanted, *"ego te baptismo, in nomine Patris, et Filii, et Spiritus Sancti."*

Jim nudged Mac and whispered, "Look!"

A dog was standing by the firkin that held the river water De Smet dipped from. As the priest shook the holy water onto the child's head, the dog raised a leg and watered the outside of the firkin.

Jim coughed to pretend he wasn't laughing. "Good thing it didn't piss *in* the water," he spluttered.

Today Mac could even accept the peeing of a dog as the outward sign of the miracle of water power.

Time to go up with Felice. Annemarie stood beside Mac with Felice wrapped in a blanket, asleep. De Smet smiled at all three of them, a beatific smile. Annemarie held Felice toward him. "Felice Red Hair Maclean," he said, *ego te baptismo, in nomine Patris, et Filii, et Spiritus Sancti.*" The priest shook his hand, and drops sailed through the air and dotted Felice's face.

She scrunched up, but she didn't cry.

4

Mac stood up before Father Pierre-Jean De Smet and tried to look at him. Mac was sure he was going to throw up or pass out or something.

He tapped Jim's arm again. Jim opened his hand and showed it to Mac once more—a garnet ring, his only memento of his mother.

Lisette smiled at Mac reassuringly. Maid of honor Lisette. The petite girl looked wonderful, her dark eyes gleaming— even her smallpox scars making her look vulnerable and appealing.

Dreyfuss had stayed away from the holy services, but he was ready now. At a nod from the priest, Dreyfuss started up a stately march on his mouth organ. Mac turned and looked back. Here came Annemarie on the handsome gray, Strikes Foot leading. The warrior was walking smoothly, though carefully, on his hoof, and he was grinning like a kid at the circus.

Annemarie looked glorious. She had slipped off to change her clothes for the wedding. Her hair gleamed black with copper highlights in the late-afternoon sun. It was loosely braided into a single long strand that came over her shoulder and rested on her lap. It was tied at intervals with long strips of green trade cloth edged with buckskin.

Mac couldn't help knowing something about what her dress would be like—she'd worked on it in front of him for weeks. He wondered how it would turn out, because some materials she had asked for were unusual. She wanted various items that were medicine, including a sample of the white man's writing. Now he saw the final product, and it was beautiful.

She wore a light-blue wool dress and calf-length moccasins. The dress was ornamented on the bosom with shiny elk's teeth. When Annemarie turned to dismount, Mac saw that she had sewn brilliant gold and purple quillwork onto the back, the largest wheel of the four winds he'd ever seen. And on the skirt in front she'd trimmed some white cotton in red trade cloth and displayed the great symbol of her husband's culture, writing. The piece of sack read STRODE & SONS FLOUR, TEANECK, N.J.

Mac grinned hugely and looked at the priest, whose face was full of kindness and mirth. Mac would have to teach his wife to read.

Annemarie and Strikes Foot drew beside Mac and Jim. Dreyfuss honked out a little fanfare.

De Smet cocked an eyebrow at Mac, and Mac nodded.

"Robert Burns Maclean," asked the priest in a conversational tone, "do you take this woman to be your wife?"

"I do," said Mac.

"Annemarie Charbonneau," De Smet went on, "do you take this man to be your husband?" A simple and happy deed, De Smet made it seem.

"I do."

De Smet waited. Finally Jim and Mac remembered, and Mac took the ring.

Mac turned to Annemarie, and she looked level at her husband. Her eyes gleamed in that splendid Cheyenne face. God, how he loved her.

Mac held up the ring. The sunlight fragmented on the red garnet. Annemarie extended her left ring finger, as she'd been coached. Mac slipped the ring on.

"Robert Burns Maclean and Annemarie Charbonneau," intoned the priest, "*ego conjungo vos in matrimonio.*"

5

Mac stood with one arm around Annemarie and the other holding Felice, watching pandemonium.

You don't get married every day, Mac said to himself uncertainly. He had broken the kegs out, all of the St. Louis kegs, every bit of legal alcohol he had left. There were only two Taos kegs held back for the winter. It meant he'd have to make a winter trip to Taos. Or send Jim. If the Delaware would hire on.

Mac had expected the pandemonium. Dreyfuss played and people danced. Even the Cheyennes were learning to do a jig, *voyageur*-style.

Some of the young men would get drunk, crazy drunk. Mac wanted to see if any of the leaders would. He hoped these Cheyennes would show better sense than the hang-around-the-forts Sioux.

Lisette put her arm around Mac from the side away from Annemarie. Her ribs were still a little sore for dancing, or no telling what mischief she'd get into. She laid her head against his shoulder. Annemarie smiled at her across Mac.

"Don't you two think it's time to go to bed?" Lisette asked.

"I do," said Mac.

"I do," said Annemarie, laughing.

"I moved my robes into Dreyfuss's tent for a while." Mac looked at Lisette in surprise. One woman with Dreyfuss, Ferry, and Valdez in a tent? "Just for a few days," she assured him. "Newlyweds need privacy."

Annemarie squeezed Lisette's hand.

"I'm taking Felice, too," Lisette said. "Come on."

Mac and Annemarie followed Lisette into the tent and put Felice on the floor. She was awake and might want to crawl around. Lisette sat down on her robes.

"Bye," she said, waving. "Have a good time."

Annemarie got down on her knees and hugged Lisette

around the shoulders. Mac squatted and did the same. Lisette kissed him softly and warmly on the cheek.

"It was a beautiful ceremony," she said, lying back, tired, and smiling lazily at the two of them. "Annemarie and I agree. De Smet won't perform my wedding."

"Why not?" asked Mac.

"Because he's against bigamy." Mac just looked at her, puzzled. "Annemarie and I agree. I'm going to marry you. When you're man enough for two wives."

Annemarie was covering her mouth, laughing.

≈ INTERLUDE ≈

In 1844 Robert Burns Maclean built Yellowstone House, and for the next twenty years he lived outside the pageant of history. The so-called great events of the time—war and peace, booms and busts, the deeds of presidents, the comings and goings of famous people—these left him untouched. He took only casual notice of the principal events in the West—the Mexican War, the migration of the Mormons to Utah, the discovery of gold in California and Colorado. Even the War Between the States did not affect him.

His story, unlike history, was measured in simple, personal experiences—the births of children, the deaths of friends, the moments of intimacy between wives and husbands, the rise of the river, the stories old men tell in winter, a room added to a house, a book read, a good garden or a bad one, the time spent riding over the prairie with wives and sons and daughters.

His life was seasonal. Spring marked the year's first hunt. He made fresh meat, a cause for celebration after a winter of jerky and pemmican. He took buffalo robes still thick from winter. Mac did his hunting with Strikes Foot's band of Cheyennes, to let his children understand what it meant to be an Indian, and a nomad.

Summer was spent on the move. In June, known to the Cheyennes as the time when the horses get fat, he made a trip to the mouth of the Yellowstone. There he met the steamboat and exchanged bales of fur, packets of accounts, and letters addressed to his Uncle Hugh in St. Louis, for letters and bales and kegs of trade goods in return. In July, the moon when the buffalo bulls are rutting, he and his family visited the Cheyennes for the annual renewal of the

sacred arrows, their homage to the beneficence of the
earth.

In autumn he shipped his bales of fur downstream
again, this time by bullboat, then keelboat, and finally
steamer, all the way to St. Louis. And he conducted
another buffalo hunt. He set the robes and dried buffalo
tongues aside to ship to St. Louis—they were now far
more valuable than beaver pelts—and put up meat for the
coming months of cold and snow.

In the winter he worked at projects in the trading post,
brought his books up to date, and wrote long letters to
Hugh. Among the Cheyennes, winter was the time to tell
stories, and with Mac and his family it was the time to
read the histories and novels of the white man, which
seemed as fairy-tale fantastic as the legends of the Indians.
Mac read to his wife and children and taught them to
read. Books were scarce and precious.

And every winter, in the hoop-and-stick-game moon,
which white men know as January, Mac took a trip into the
high country where the Yellowstone River sprang up, the
land of geysers, waterfalls, and hot springs. It was a
difficult trip in the snow, but the plains were almost always
passable enough for him to ride as far as the mountains.
Then he would snowshoe to the hot spring where the
younger Mac had found solace when he was lost. The trip
always felt like a pilgrimage to him, and he always went
alone.

In every season he smoked the pipe, raised the cup,
and traded with the Cheyennes, Sioux, Crow, and Blackfeet
who journeyed to the fort, exchanging the products of
manufacture for the products of nature.

He became a kind of Indian, his lodge and his family as
welcome as any in the Cheyenne circle of lodges. But he
knew he was not truly a Cheyenne. He did not forget, or
regret, that he was a white man. He did not suffer through
thirst and hunger to seek a medicine dream. He did not
dance before the sun and mortify his flesh until he dropped,
exhausted. Instead Mac chose to be a civilized man in a
savage land. To him, wonderfully savage.

He did develop his own place of meditation, the small

summit of that chimney rock overlooking his beloved
river, where he first had the idea of Yellowstone House, in
1843, when he was half-starved. He called it a place to
think. A Cheyenne would have called it a place to envision.

Mac also developed a place for spiritual cleansing. Below the sentinel rock the river widened, got shallow, and
left a small island just a few yards off the bank. There Mac
built his own sweat lodge with his own hands. At irregular
intervals he went there to sweat alone, naked, contem-
plative. Sometimes he stayed all night, alternating between the intense heat of the sweat lodge and the sweet
cold of the river. His ceremony was his own, adapted from
the Cheyennes and every other tribe. He found renewal
in it.

From time to time the outside world, the so-called
civilized world, imposed itself on Mac. In June of 1846, at
Fort Union, he heard that the United States was warring
with Mexico. In September of that year, when Jim Sykes
made the run to Taos to trade for *aguardiente,* he found
the entire province of New Mexico in the hands of American armed forces. What's more, Jim reported to Mac, an
immense herd of religious fanatics had crossed the Oregon
Trail that year and settled in the valley of the Great Salt
Lake. Mormons, they called themselves. Short on sense,
according to Jim, but hardscrabble and then some.

None of that mattered to Mac, Annemarie, and Lisette.
It was too far away. The birth of their first son did matter,
borne by Annemarie that winter. To please Uncle Hugh
they called him Adam Smith Maclean.

Lisette and Annemarie persuaded Mac to expand his
family by one wife before Felice was even a year old. In
the autumn of '46 Little One was brought to bed with twin
girls, but they were stillborn, and she was barren from
that day.

Mac heard from the factor at Fort William, the next
June, that the United States had laid hold of all of the
Southwest, Texas to California, via the Mexican War, and
had also settled its boundary dispute with Great Britain
and taken the Oregon country into the Union, from the
Rockies to the sea. The nation, once a north-south strip

from Maine to Florida, now swept majestically west to the Pacific Ocean.

Hurrah! said Mac pleasantly, and lifted his glass. Practically speaking, it didn't make a hell of a lot of difference to him what the government of the United States did. It seldom ventured within a thousand miles of him, never helped solve his troubles with Indians or white men, or deep snows or raging rivers. It didn't protect his life or property or give him a court to seek justice in—it asked him for nothing and gave him nothing. Which was fine with Mac. Yet he loved his country for its ideals: It was the first country to say no man is born higher than another.

That same summer Dreyfuss left Yellowstone House. He didn't know why, he said. He was a Jew, he said, a minor revelation, but not one that mattered in any way Mac could see. Dreyfuss didn't know what he wanted to do with the rest of his years. He said that he felt like some benign Wandering Jew, destined to roam the earth until he understood . . . something. He speculated that he should simply walk about and observe humankind. That was hard for Mac to understand. Yet it was Dreyfuss. Mac gave Valdez the clerking job, but he missed Dreyfuss sorely.

After the Mexican War the country turned its energies to quarreling about slavery, but that had no direct effect on the Macleans, except for the abolitionist declamations Uncle Hugh started adding to his letters. As an abolitionist, Hugh was in the minority in St. Louis.

Those same letters showed that Mac was doing well as a trader—he was prosperous, if not rich. The prosperity was theoretical. Money in some St. Louis bank changed nothing in the way the Macleans lived.

The business was tricky. Mere trading was relatively easy. The reliable patronage of the Cheyennes was invaluable to Mac. Getting other Indians to come in and keeping them peaceable if enemy bunches showed up, that took some subtlety. It was even trickier getting goods to and from market. Robert Campbell was financing competition to American Fur Company, no doubt in a spirit of gleeful malice, so he sent a steamboat upriver, on the spring rise. Usually, but not always, it got to the mouth of the

Yellowstone, three hundred miles away. Mac floated his furs down to Fort William, Campbell's post near Fort Union, and picked up his own consignment there.

He was not prosperous enough, though, to do without his partners, Uncle Hugh and Robert Campbell. In 1849 Bloods swooped down on Mac and his men on the way back from Fort Union and stole a year's worth of trade goods. Mac thought he had been betrayed by two of his guards. It was not lost on him that they had worked for American Fur Company for years, or that the Bloods were allies of the Company. American Fur played by hard rules, or none at all.

The next two years were splendidly profitable, but Mac was wary and felt he never knew when he might go broke. When he had enough cash to do without his partners and financiers, he decided to keep them anyway.

In the summer of 1847 Annemarie gave Mac a second son, Thomas Jefferson Maclean.

Three years later she had a difficult birthing, and their second daughter was born with palsy. They named her Christine, Charbonneau's Frenchman name for Lame Deer. Lame Deer said she was a special child, touched by the spirits, and might bring to the people a great dream. Mac doted on that afflicted infant as he had on no other.

The next year an urgent request came from Broken Hand Fitzpatrick—come to Fort Laramie with the Cheyennes for a big talk. Mac knew the Cheyennes, Fitz said, and could help them get what was due them.

What Mac knew about the Cheyennes was that they already had what they needed, and what they wanted. But he went, and immediately saw the problem. The Oregon Trail was a line laid waste through a grand country. The earth was rutted and baked, stripped bare of timber, the game driven away. Yes, the Indians of the plains deserved payment for this devastation. The agreement reached at that big conference gave the whites the right to the Oregon road, and to forts and soldiers. It drew boundaries around the hunting grounds of the various tribes. It elicited promises the Indians couldn't keep. And the payment? About a dollar per person per year for just ten

years. A joke. A treaty that was unfair, unenforceable,
meaningless, and the despair of Fitzpatrick, Bridger, Mac,
and every man who knew the Indians.

Mac felt profoundly grateful he'd built his post in the
Yellowstone country and not on the Oregon Trail. He saw
no reason his country would ever change.

The world of civilization did keep sending emissaries to
the Yellowstone country, and odd ones. The same year,
1843, that Mac nearly starved walking across Judith basin,
Sir William Drummond Stewart conducted an elaborate
hunting trip, and John James Audubon came up on a
Company steamboat to do research for his *Quadrupeds of
North America*. De Smet also came to the Yellowstone
valley that year. In 1851 a young Swiss painter, Rudolph
Friedrich Kurtz, showed up at Fort Union, full of ambi-
tion. He was going to paint the world's most romantic
subject, the Indians of the plains, and display his work in
art galleries, as George Catlin had done. But the Indians
remembered Catlin and connected his paintings with the
smallpox epidemic of 1837, and felt reluctant. And the
booshway insisted on ordering the young man to paint
this but not that. After a winter as a Company clerk, Kurtz
went home disgruntled.

Perhaps the strangest of these visitors was Sir George
Gore, of Sligo, Ireland. Jim Bridger guided Gore to the
Yellowstone country in 1855. Gore wanted adventure,
which to him meant hunting and fishing. He also needed
advice, supplies, and more hands who knew the country.

Gore did things in style. He traveled with six wagons
and twenty-one French carts, painted red. He had forty
employees, 112 horses, twelve yoke of oxen, fourteen
dogs, and three milk cows. He required an entire wagon
to carry his guns—over a hundred of them, made by
celebrated gunsmiths. He brought two wagons of fishing
gear, and a skilled man to tie flies.

Mac and Jim Sykes took turns in the employ of the rich
man, partly just to get to visit with Bridger. Leaving the
Yellowstone country, bound for his home in Ireland and
then on to grand hunting expeditions in Africa, Siberia,
and other far-flung places, Gore showed Mac the list of his

kills on the great plains: 40 grizzlies, 2,500 buffalo, plus too many elk, deer, antelope, and small game to count.

A few prospectors roamed the country as well. Mac told Annemarie that the white people were enamored of great fantasies—country to explore, books to write, pictures to paint, fortunes to find. They liked to use the Rocky Mountains as a stage for their grand romantic gestures and go home with a splendid fund of stories.

None of the excursions of the dream seekers into the Yellowstone country had much impact on Mac or his family, or the crew at the post or the Cheyennes. They lived to the rhythms of the earth and the seasons and noticed little else, except perhaps as a diversion.

In 1860 Mac and Lisette took the boys, Smith and Thomas, to St. Louis to enroll them in a private school. There they found out that a man named Lincoln had been elected President. In April, 1861, when the first shots were fired at Fort Sumter, Mac was back in the remote vastness of the Yellowstone country.

It was not until 1863 that the white world broke into their lives. A white man showed up unannounced and spoke two words . . .

BOOK TWO

"Yellow metal," said John Krier with a tight smile. Mac didn't like the sound of those two words.

"At a place called Alder Gulch, above the Ruby River." Krier let a tick of the clock go by, dramatically. "More than King Solomon's mines."

That news disgusted Mac. He'd been watching about a hundred white people, even a few women and children, troop into the courtyard of Yellowstone House. An incredible hundred white people, nearly as many as had ever been in the Yellowstone country over all the years. Milling around the courtyard wanting things to eat, things to wear, things to get warm in—things Mac didn't have.

They'd arrived on boats, for Christ's sake. Mackinaws. From *up*stream.

He turned back to Krier. More than King Solomon's mines. "Damn," he said softly. "How many prospectors?"

"Not a one," replied Krier drily. He had the soft accent of Southern gentry. From what Mac could see of his face under the broad-brimmed hat, Krier looked like a handsome man, tall, with long brown hair curling to his shoulders. And a hard man. "Nobody has to prospect for it. Two thousand men panning it, rocking it, sluicing it, getting it every which way. If a man drinks that water, he could get dust out of his shit."

A lot of words for a man as unsocial as John Krier seemed. Mac wondered what he was after.

"Two thousand men," murmured Mac.

"And adding a hundred and more a week," said Krier, "up from Salt Lake and Bannack way. Virginia City, they call it. Varina City, really, after Jefferson Davis's wife. But the damn United States federal judge wouldn't write her name down."

So Krier was Secesh. And a federal judge had gotten to Idaho Territory. Mac was having trouble soaking up all the news.

"It's a tent city now, but not for long. Plenty of dust, and nothing to spend it on. For sure no food. Is there somewhere we can talk in private?" Evidently Krier meant to tell Mac why he felt talkative today.

Bannack. Way on the west side of the big divide, where they'd also found some gold, Mac had heard. Country of the Bannocks and Shoshones. Gold rushers going there from the other diggings, from Colorado Territory and all the way from California. Brought their wagons up from Salt Lake City. Brother Brigham and his Mormons must be supplying them. Profitably. Which would please Brother Brigham uncommonly.

The only good part about the gold chasing, to Mac, was that it stayed clear of him, his family, the Sioux and Cheyennes, and the entire Yellowstone country. From above the Platte to the Missouri River was a vast, untouched buffalo pasture. No one had found any gold there. Or looked. Or would—because the Indians wouldn't let them. Mac had put Yellowstone House in the right place, square in the middle of it.

Annemarie motioned to Mac from the door of the trading room. "Just a minute," said Mac. Krier stayed right with him.

Annemarie and Valdez looked confused, amiably confused, not yet flustered. Men were offering them little bags of gold dust. Dust for cloth, thread, and needles. Dust for whiskey and tobacco. Dust for flour, coffee, sugar, bacon, jerky, and beans.

Mac smiled at his wife and his clerk. He could see amusement glint behind Valdez's glasses. These white folks were ragged, dirty, half-sick, and emaciated from hunger. They had nothing, especially not the skills and knowledge to get what they needed. But they had gold.

And they were sure, ragingly sure, that gold was everything there was to have.

They couldn't guess that gold dust was mostly just so much corral grit to Mac. He and his family couldn't eat it, wear it, or trade it to the Indians. It would be worth something later, when he could pay someone to take it to St. Louis and exchange it for useful items. Even the cost of the trip undercut the value of the gold.

Mainly, the MacLeans didn't have any emotional attachment to the stuff. Hell, Yellowstone House didn't even have a way to weigh the little sacks of dust, and Mac, Annemarie, and Valdez didn't know what it was worth, except by somebody else's word. The Cheyennes would have scorned it. Mac wished he could do the same.

The three of them had a look at the ledger. Prices weren't set in dollars—who in this country gave dollars for goods? But the accounts showed what they paid for each item, in dollars, and they knew what they had to get in robes, so you could figure it out. Valdez could—Annemarie didn't do figures much. That Valdez had the brain of a trader.

"The Crows," Annemarie reminded Mac. She meant that of the bands who usually came to trade early in the autumn, Long Hair's Crows still had not appeared.

Mac nodded. He wrote down a way for Valdez to convert prices in robes into prices in dust. Valdez smiled in approval. Yellowstone House's profit would be shining.

"We could trade wagonloads of flour, bacon, and beans," said Valdez.

Mac had to laugh. What would a trading post in the middle of the Yellowstone country be doing carrying food of any kind? With buffalo thick as grass on the plains, who would ask for food?

The pork-eaters stood in front of the counter, gaping.

"Don't run us out of anything," Mac said to them "Anything at all."

"Hell," said Krier, butting in, "these people need you. We're counting on you."

"We have our regular customers to think of," said Mac.

"You can stop at Fort Alexander, at the mouth of the
Rosebud. And Fort Union will have quite a bit."

Krier glared at him. "These are white people. You are a
white man, aren't you?"

Mac didn't answer. He didn't say that the Crows depended
on him and would suffer this winter if he failed them. Or
that he was their friend. Or that he wasn't so damn sure
he felt much like a white man anymore. Krier was putting
Mac into a corner where he had to stand up for red against
white, or the other way. That made him feel guilty, and
that made him mad.

Mac took Krier into his office. He decided not to offer
the man a drink. "No flour!" wailed a voice from the
trading room. Mac closed the door.

Krier's idea turned out to be that Mac and he should go
partners. Krier would transport goods up the Yellowstone
and people down. Mac would put up the supplies both
ways. People were desperate up at Alder Gulch, Krier
said. Desperate for any kind of food but game. Desperate
for amenities—he actually used the word "amenities"—such
as calico, that would make them feel as if they were better
than the wild Indians.

Better than wild Indians. But going hungry in the
middle of the finest buffalo country in the world. Mac
didn't smile.

If they struck it rich, Krier went on, these people were
usually desperate to get back to civilization where they
could spend their money. And if they didn't, they were
desperate to get home.

"Hell, Maclean, this is your chance to get rich. Panning
is chancy, but supplying is a sure thing. You can set
yourself up for life. Those people have the money."

Mac let him run on. He was already set up for life,
unless the gold chasers spoiled it.

Krier had things all worked out. Water transportation
was easier than wagons back to the States—half the time
of going all the way to Salt Lake and across the Oregon
Trail. Not much work—the river provided the power. And
people were willing to pay to float down.

"Use the Missouri," said Mac finally, sounding more

antagonistic than he meant to. "You're almost right on the Missouri."

Krier shook his head. "The Falls." The Great Falls of the Missouri that forced Lewis and Clark to portage. "Plus it's longer. Anyway, feller in your position shouldn't even breathe of the Missouri."

Mac got up, took two tin cups from the sideboard, and poured two whiskeys. He needed a drink. He wanted nothing to do with this man, but had to think how to handle it judiciously.

The implications were immense. Could be a lot of people would be rushing through the Yellowstone country for a few years. With any luck, just a few months. But Krier had said "more than King Solomon's mines." Damn. Fortunately Mac could count on the Blackfeet, Crows, Sioux, and Cheyennes.

"Krier," he said, "it's too damn dangerous. The Laramie treaty gave all this country to the Indians. They accept wagons on the Oregon Trail. They accept steamboats on the Missouri. On the Yellowstone they'll burn every boat they see and scalp the folks."

Krier snickered. "Hell, Maclean, you think Injuns can keep white people out? There's a man named of Bozeman right now making a wagon track from the Oregon Trail. Right along in front of the Big Horns. He started putting it in last spring, when there was just the Bannack diggin's. Alder Gulch makes Bannack look puny. Bozeman ought to be along with a wagon train anytime."

"The Sioux won't let them through," Mac said flatly.

Krier looked a little irate. "I'd say the U.S. government will have something to say about that. That's what soldiers are for, I'd say."

"Government's back east."

"Yeah, got their hands full with Jefferson Davis," Krier snickered.

"You don't know the Sioux, Krier."

"Maclean," Krier said in his soft, upper-class tones, "you don't want to get rich, do you?" Krier sounded disgusted. Mac stood up.

Krier took the hint and got to his feet. "Damn squaw

man," he muttered, and strode out without a backward look.

An hour later, when Krier had his boats loaded, Mac didn't even go to the river to say good-bye. He was up on his sentinel rock, smoking his clay pipe, looking down on his nook in Indian country, thinking what it all might mean. He thought the Sioux and Cheyennes would put a quick end to it. That's what he really thought.

He chuckled to himself. Krier left miffed. Fellow must have thought talking to Mac was like sucking on a thorn.

Squaw man, he called me, thought Mac. For twenty years Mac had been like any other white man he knew. He and his wives had been looked up to. And his children. They were the gentry of the Yellowstone country. If the whites came, he supposed, that would change. He would become a squaw man, a barbarian. Worse than the Indians, people would call him. They'd call Annemarie and Lisette the same. And Felice Maclean, Adam Smith Maclean, Thomas Jefferson Maclean, and Christine Maclean.

He spat into the canyon below.

2

"Coyote must have sucked out his brains for breakfast," Mac said unhappily in their quarters that evening.

"He doesn't see the buffalo," Lisette said. "He thinks Indians go to the store for groceries." Ever since Little One went to St. Louis with Mac and the boys—when they started at the academy—she'd been sarcastic about white people. If her husband and children weren't white, Mac thought, she'd have no tolerance for white people at all. And he wasn't sure her husband mattered.

The children weren't exactly hers. Lisette had borne Mac no children, and that was a sadness. But in her eyes Felice Red Hair, Adam Smith, Thomas Jefferson, and Christine were hers too. And in Mac's eyes, and in the kids'.

"Krier just doesn't know any better," said Annemarie. That woman was understanding of everything and everybody.

"He says people are hungry up there." Mac lay down on the robes in his long johns. The Macleans didn't like a bed. The three of them slept together on a thick stack of robes and blankets on the floor. To Mac, that was luxury. A hell of an improvement on the white man's shuck mattress. For that matter, he wished they spent less time in their post quarters and more in their lodge.

"They won't be ready for winter," suggested Annemarie. She slipped in next to him, naked. He noted with pleasure that though she was nearing forty, her body was still firm.

"Maybe they won't stay the winter," said Mac.

"Huh!" Lisette snorted. "They've got gold fever."

"A strike on the west side of the divide would take them back," said Mac.

"And a strike here would put them in our laps," said Little One. She got her book, *Ivanhoe*. Mac had read all the Walter Scott books to them. Lisette liked to read the ones she knew alone, by candlelight in the dining room, after Mac and Annemarie were asleep. In the marriage Lisette treated Annemarie a little like Mac's wife and herself as his mistress.

"This isn't gold country. That fellow with Raynolds told me so." Lieutenant Raynolds had led a government "exploration" party into the Yellowstone country, four decades after the area was well-known to mountain men.

"Where is Alder Gulch?" asked Annemarie.

"Between the Madison River and the Ruby," said Mac. Annemarie knew that meant over two hundred and fifty miles away.

"Bad to travel in winter," she said.

"I better send Jim down to Union for supplies anyway," said Mac. "Even flour."

"Flour," Lisette sniffed, and started out. Just then Felice came in.

"Did you see the one on the sweep?" she asked Lisette. The mackinaw steered with a sweep at the rear.

Felice these days seemed to expect Lisette to understand her better than her other parents. At nineteen, she

was taller than her mother or father, slender, dark as an
Indian, but auburn-haired and blue-eyed. Tall young men
all over the upper Missouri country wanted to court her.
But she was being kept back—against her will.

"The really tall one? Black-bearded?" said Lisette.

Felice smiled and nodded.

"Zachary Lawrence," said Mac. "An Irishman." He was
really tall. If he hadn't been skinny, people would have
called him a giant.

"Good-looking," said Felice. She was talking such bold
stuff in front of her parents more often, thought Mac. "Is
that what they mean by black Irish?"

"Yes," said Mac.

"I like it."

"A pork-eater," said Annemarie.

Felice deliberately misunderstood her mother. "I wish
we got to eat pork," she said. It was a sore point with
Felice that her brothers had been to St. Louis, even
wintered there a couple of times, and she hadn't. She
loved to hear about the great city, and to page through the
catalogs of merchants and the advertisements in months-
old newspapers. Of Mac's children, she was the most
enamored of white ways.

"Maybe I better strap you into a chastity belt," Mac
said, closing his eyes.

Felice followed Lisette to the door. "It's past time you
can Mistai me, Daddy." The Cheyenne word meant something like "boogeyman."

They shut the door behind. There in the dark, next to
one of his two half-breed wives, Mac reflected that the
trick was in the way she said it. The English word for
"father," and the American way of being a daughter,
combined with one of the Cheyenne spirits. Funny, the
mix. Maybe mix-up.

≈ 2 ≈

Mac had never seen anything like it.

A gulch. Tents everywhere, and in the center of the gulch, streets with buildings of green, raw-looking lumber. Lumpy, broken hills, stripped bare of grass and trees. The cottonwood trees had gone to make the buildings. The grass was tramped out, rutted out, gouged out. The earth itself had been cut away in huge hunks, Mac knew not how.

Virginia City was his idea of what the earth would look like after drought, flood, pestilence, and the plague of locusts. But all that had happened to it was ten thousand human beings.

Weird, open wooden boxes ran downhill on stilts, in every direction, like the appendages of daddy longlegs. Or like long, snaky caskets.

Mac made a small motion to Jim Sykes to take the wagons on down the hill. Mac and John Jacobs rode over to the head of one of the long boxes for a close look. In a minute Mac began to understand. The miners had built a dam and diverted a stream into one of the long boxes. Elsewhere, into a ditch. A gate let the water through.

Jacobs nodded downhill, where men were using the water. Mac trotted his horse along the box. It ran into a big pipe made of galvanized tin and into a huge nozzle. A man was manipulating the nozzle to direct the water against the gouged hillside. "Ka-boom, she hits it," Jacobs said, his vowels melodiously Italian. The water then floated through a sluice box. Men were forking rocks out of the

185

box and letting the dirt run. "Fluming, they call it,"
explained Jacobs. "Very profitable."

Mac had heard plenty about fluming, rocking, panning,
sluicing, drifting, and other such techniques for the last
couple of years. He didn't care how they did it.

"You'd admire to see the way that water tears up a
hillside in an hour or two," Jacobs said ironically. Mac
nodded. "You can move mother earth."

There were other sorts of holes in the earth, too—drifts,
timbered shafts dug into any promising soil. It was like a
giant had come to rummage through the surface of the
earth. The whole of Alder Gulch was going to get turned
up one way or another and sifted through somebody's box.
And then dumped back, minus whatever glinted yellow.

Mac and Jacobs rode back over to the wagons, where
Mac's sons Smith and Thomas were plodding downhill
with Jim and the mule skinners. Mac held an arm out to
the blighted landscape and said, "Welcome to the capital
of Montana Territory." The skinners cracked their whips
and the wagons rolled down the hill toward town a hint
faster.

At least it will be profitable, thought Mac. It had been a
rough trip.

He didn't need to look at the letter again. It was folded
away in a big leather wallet. It offered $20 a sack for 500
hundred-pound sacks of flour, and $15 for 50 sacks each of
coffee, sugar, rice, and beans. Plus a bonus of $500 for
getting it there by April fifteenth, then two weeks away. It
was signed with an X above the name M. J. Hackett,
Hackett Mercantile Co.

John Jacobs had brought the letter and half the money,
in pokes. Six thousand five hundred dollars made about
twenty-five pounds of gold dust, a fat poke. Jacobs was a
red-bearded Italian who had been in the country long
enough, as they said, to know what way the sticks floats.
Mac liked him. Even though the son of a bitch showed
Georgia John Bozeman where to lay what they called the
Bozeman Trail.

"What does it all mean, Mac?" said Jacobs over a
sociable whiskey in Mac's office. It meant Hackett was

willing to pay triple Mac's cost of supplies at Fort Union, and thirty times what he was obliged to pay at St. Louis. It meant Mac would make more than half a year's income on this single trip. It meant Mac would have the cash to send his sons back to that academy in St. Louis.

"Might be we oughta name those pork-eaters flour-eaters," said Mac. Jacobs said the miners were having flour riots in Alder Gulch. Too many people and not enough supplies made it up the trail from Salt Lake before the snows flew. These people were eating nothing but game. They were in a rage for bread. Merchants usually sold flour for twenty-five dollars a sack—now they were asking one hundred dollars a sack.

One day the miners simply ganged up, Jacobs said. Nobody was going to starve them, they declared. They took the flour they wanted and left IOUs for twenty-five dollars a sack.

The Indians and mountain men who heard about this episode shook their heads. Starving because you couldn't bake bread? Some of the old trappers hadn't tasted bread in decades. The Indians didn't want to taste it. The ignorant miners had rose hips growing wild all around them. Serviceberries, chokecherries, camas, cattails everywhere. And they said they were going hungry.

Except for wild game. And if you ate nothing but game, you were no better than a wild Indian, they said. The same Indians who did get enough to eat.

Mac said over and over to his family, "There are none so blind as those who will not see." It had become his motto.

So this Hackett was looking for a quick profit—if Mac could get some wagonloads of supplies there fast enough.

The men and wagons had a hard trip for April. Along the Yellowstone to the big bend in six days, nothing to complain about. Then they tried Bozeman Pass, as the newcomers called it, named for the idiot who tried to force a trail through the center of Sioux country. Two spring snowstorms, a day apart, nearly put an end to the bonus. But the next day brought a warm wind and a quick melt. In three more days they were in Alder Gulch.

As they came down the rough track toward the streets—

four streets already—men started running toward them. Every kind of man. Men in high-topped boots, heels worn to nothing, riveted canvas trousers, and undershirts. Men in waistcoats. Men in clean, pressed dress shirts. Men in loose shirts made of hide. Men in every kind of hat—Mac saw beavers, muleys, Quaker hats, wool caps, the slouch hat of the plainsman, the crudely sewn hide hat, the blanket hat of the *voyageur*, and the simple bandanna.

Mac knew what they wanted. Jacobs had warned him. He could sell his load right there, before he got to town. "No one would blame you," Jacobs said. But his meaning was that the right thing to do would be to take it down the hill to Hackett.

Men were holding up pokes and hollering out prices for flour. Most of the figures were no more than Hackett was willing to pay wholesale. Mac smiled to himself. "There'll be some more wailing about cost," Mac told Jacobs.

The big Italian mountain man shrugged. "Hackett don't mind being unpopular for pay."

Jacob whoaed the wagons at the end of the main street— the crowd was thick now, yelling and milling, and maybe ugly. The mountain man said he'd get Hackett and some hands to move the goods.

Mac nodded. He and Jim and the boys faced their horses out to the crowd and glared at the clamoring miners. Neither Mac nor his crew put a hand on a weapon. Mac didn't think these pork-eaters would stand up to the gaze of a real Montana man for long. Not even if two of them were boys. His boys.

Little men came running from the center of town. Mac glanced sideways at Smith and Thomas. They were smothering their laughter, too. The little men cried out and pushed through the crowd and surrounded the wagons, looking in. They wore blue smocks and funny tasseled caps without bills and they were Chinese.

Jacobs was parading up the street with a woman on his arm. She was plump as a Christmas goose. And yellow.

"Damn," said Thomas, "a heathen Chinee." Mac squelched his son with a look.

She was elaborately decked out. An emerald gown with

a huge, salmon-pink sash. Hair piled high on top of her
head. Gold on her fingers, on her wrists, and in her hair.
She made an impression. From the look on Jacobs's face,
he had a proprietary interest.

The shouts turned to mutters, then to whispers. The
woman barked in a tone of command—she had the voice
of a bullwhacker—and the minders cleared a way. As she
got close, Mac saw that she was alluring, plump or not.
And she had an aura of power. She motioned to her
workers, and they darted back, nimbly as skittering pigeons.

"Mac," said Jacobs formally, "this is M. J. Hackett. Mae
Jhong Hackett." The Italian was grinning like a fool.

"Welcome to Virginia City, Mr Maclean," said Mae
Jhong Hackett. Her speech was slow, stilted, melodious.
"Life here is an adventure."

2

"Her name is Hackett," Jacobs explained across the rim
of his teacup, "because she's a widow. Crotchety old man
Hackett that built this place and that everybody hated.
Call her Mae Jhong." Jacobs made the use of her first two
names—Mac couldn't think of them as Christian names—
sound like a privilege.

Mae Jhong Hackett poured Mac more tea. It felt peculiar to have this woman, certainly an influential woman,
making the artificial gesture of serving him.

"He built the Mercantile," Jacob went on, "but she
built everything else. Two saloons. Whores up above.
Chinese and white and every other color. Laundry. Bath-
house. She owns a piece of the theater. The old man didn't
have enough hair of the bear in him to be a go-getter."

Mae Jhong sat on a cushion at the low, black, lacquered
table, between the men, apparently favoring neither. Mac
supposed her English was such that she undersood the
entire conversation. When she spoke, it was in that stately, melodious way, and only courtesies. She often reached
beneath the lacquered table and brought out a piece of

china the size of a soup bowl, but half-covered. Into it she delicately spat tobacco juice.

"Mae Jhong's some girl, she is," Jacobs went on. From her expressionless face Mac could tell nothing. She was probably forty or forty-five, but striking. Mac didn't blame Jacobs a bit.

A wizened Chinaman brought Mac one of the hide boxes called parfleches. This one was beautifully painted in a complicated geometrical pattern, a handsome example. It was also heavy. Inside were several pokes of gold dust. The parfleche was just a touch of style.

Jacobs was grinning crookedly at Mac. "It'll be right," he said. Mac was sure she wouldn't short him. "Including the bonus for being on time," Jacobs went on.

"I am forever in your debt," Mae Jhong said formally.

Jacobs winked. "She's real pleased, Mac."

Jacobs had had the boys and the crew taken care of—installed in a tent out back, fed, offered a beer. Mac wondered if the boys had tasted beer before. They'd drunk whiskey at Yellowstone House. They were near-enough men, Smith nineteen and Thomas nearly eighteen. Unfortunately, Thomas had the idea that vices were the way you got to be an all-the-way man.

"Let's check things out outside," said Jacobs. He understood. "Might better leave that with Mae Jhong," he added, nodding at the parfleche, "to put in the safe."

Mac asked, and Mae Jhong acquiesced. "You are my guest at any of my establishments," she said. "And your sons as well."

Jacobs led the way. With one hand on the door, Mac glanced back. Mae Jhong Hackett was looking at him boldly. Her face wasn't demure now. It was the face of the general beholding the field of triumph.

3

The tent was in good shape, gear stowed, but it was empty except for a Chinaman standing guard. The boys and the crew must be looking around town, as Jacobs said, so he and Mac set out to do the same.

Bizarre town. Men thronged everywhere—most women and children evidently stayed in their tents and shacks on the outskirts, or by their claims. There was an ominous feel of urgency in the air. Men moved fast, impatiently, bumping and jostling.

Four streets already. A hundred new buildings a month. And Virginia City had a twin, Nevada City, just two miles down the gulch. Incredible.

"Mac," said Jacobs, his voice raised over the crowd noise, "Mae Jhong asked me to warn you particularly to watch your back."

Mac raised an eyebrow.

"We got us a thriving little den of iniquity in Alder Gulch. She figures we've had more'n two hundred murders just in the eighteen months she's been here." Jacobs seemed to find this fact amusing. "Some of them are just rambunctiousness. Some is grievances. A bunch of them is robberies. Man gets his hands on some dust, decides to head for civilization and enjoy his good fortune, and gets robbed on the way. Maybe killed. Much dust as you got makes a tempting target."

"Thought you had a sheriff."

Jacobs shrugged. "Last sheriff, Henry Plummer, give out a lot of advice. Which route is safe. How to outthink the robbers. The ones as took his advice got held up for sure. Hanged him a year back. And twenty-two of his cronies."

Mac nodded. That fit his notion of government well enough.

"New sheriff's probably different. He's an easy man to like. So was Plummer."

A sign further on said HOT BATHS, 25 CENTS—SATURDAY, 75 CENTS, and in small letters, *Shaving and Hairdressing Saloon*. Mac had never given thought to having someone else cut his hair and shave him. He rubbed his light, reddish whiskers and wondered how it would feel.

Jacobs stopped and pointed to a poster advertising a theater. "Opens next week," he said. "Montana Theater, they call it." The playbill boasted of a concoction entitled *Faint Heart Never Won Fair Lady*, along with "comic and sentimental songs and a grand overture by the orchestra," and concluding with a "roaring farce, *The Specter Bridegroom*." Mac shook his head. As far from St. Louis as San Francisco, yet the town had a theater. Unbelievable.

"Mae Jhong keeps track of things. Lots of things, like the robberies," Jacobs went on. They walked. "She has many ears. Hands, too. And knives and guns. She's offering to help you get back to Bozeman Pass. That ought to be far enough."

Mac nodded. "Thanks. I'll think on it."

Mac stopped to look at the front page of the current newspaper, the Montana *Post*, displayed in a glass case. He saw a column headed NEWS FROM AMERICA, an account of a prize fight between Virginia City and Bannack men, a notice of a reward for a lost nugget, and an advertisement for "Dr. H. N. Crepin, Physician and Surgeon, opposite the hay scales on Main St." And there was a notice advertising a medicine for young men who had committed indiscretions or been involved in youthful follies.

"Newspaper's out ever' Friday," said Jacobs with a smile.

Until now, Mac reflected, to get the Montana news you read prints—hoof prints and moccasin prints, not newsprint.

Jacobs looked sideways at Mac, considering. "Maybe we'd best think on how to get your dust home together," said Jacobs. "And then you keep your own counsel."

That was Mac's thought. The two mountain men moved on, stepping around a drunk who was puking into the street.

"Mae Jhong will be straight arrow with you, I believe—she counts the world in two parts, her friends and everybody else. You're her friend now. But anything you tell anybody could get out."

They passed a stone building, an assay office, according to the sign, founded by a man actually named Con Weary. A few steps beyond, Mac stopped for a moment to look through wavy glass at the wonders of the white man's culture displayed by the drugstore. Face powder, curling irons, desk spittoons like Mae Jhong's, gulfweed (for obesi-

ty), and toothpaste of the Clorox and Walrus brands. The
Walrus brand displayed two gleaming tusks.

"Wanna wet your dry?" Mac nodded, and Jacobs went
on, "Let's go to one of Mae's."

"Why do they say 'saloon' instead of 'tavern' these
days?"

"No lodgings. Know why Mae's laundry's profitable?"

"Why?"

"They pan the dirty water for dust. Find plenty."

Mac chuckled.

Jacobs led the way into the Golden Belle. It looked like
a rough club where men sought entertainment. A fiddler
was sawing away in a corner, and two miners were starting
to dance without benefit of female companionship. Men
crowded around round tables, some big enough for card
games, covered with green felt, and manned by a dude in
the traditional gambler's black and white. The floor was
made craftily of the tongue-and-groove boards that came
atop keg lids, except that real boards formed the dance
area. At a small table sat Smith and Jim, with whiskey.
Mac was relieved to find at least one of his sons.

Jacobs and Mac headed that way. Mac wouldn't have
identified the Golden Belle as an Oriental establishment
from the decor, but blue-smocked Chinamen were scurrying about bringing drinks, clearing tables, and sweeping.

Smith and Jim smiled up at Mac kind of funny, he
noticed. Then something caught his eye. The second story
was surrounded by a rail and open hallway, with many
doors opening onto the hall. Women leaned over the
railing, some dangling braceletted wrists. Some of the
women were white, some black, some Mexican, some
Chinese. They wore shirts of gold silk.

Three of them were coming down the stairs now, and
Mac could see them better. Gold shirts on top, scarlet
paper flowers in their hair, silk stockings below, fastened
by elaborate garters. In between garter and jacket, they
were bare.

Mac sat down. "Where's Thomas?" he asked Smith.

"Upstairs," Smith said simply.

Mac took a breath. "He would."

"So did I," said Smith. Typical of Mac's elder son to say that easily.

"Me, too," said Jim.

The fiddler was belting out "The Arkansas Traveler," everybody's favorite dance tune, and two gartered ladies partnered the dancing miners.

Well, what the hell, thought Mac. "Where'd you get the money?"

"We're on the house here," said Smith with an enigmatic smile. "Convenient."

"All you Macleans," Jacobs reminded Mac, "and Jim."

Jacobs ordered whiskey from a Chinaman. Mac noticed people staring at their group, in half-open hostility. He ignored it, as he had taught his sons to do.

But it made no sense. His sons were somewhat dark and Indian-featured. They accented their Indian blood, maybe three-eighths, with feathers and quillwork. Jim Sykes, dressed as a white man, had a much more distinctively Indian face. Mostly people automatically treated all three either like servants or like scum.

Yet all three could read and write, which was more than most of these miners could say. Smith could do it really well. His sons knew more of the ways of polite society than most frontier ruffians. Jim Sykes could travel safely alone from here to St. Louis without benefit of roads. Smith and Thomas could find their way through the wilderness, and comfortably. These white people would get lost and perish, even on a road, without a guide such as Jim or Smith or Thomas. They couldn't find water or wood or the easy route or game—they were helpless in the face of simple realities. Riots because they didn't have flour. Mac snorted.

And the way they were living—crowded, unsanitary, and unhealthy. Killing each other over trifles. Constantly getting drunk and brawling. Madness.

But what was most mad was that they looked down their noses at Mac's sons. Why on earth?

Well, Mac thought, America was a new world, and the West was a new way of living, and such thinking would never shine here. It would die out. He only had to wait.

Mac saw Smith was watching him with bemusement.

"You learn anything upstairs?" Mac asked his elder son.

"Yes," said Smith seriously, "I saw something. While I was getting ready, a huge dust devil came up. It blanketed the town in a cloud of dust. Nothing could be seen. In the murk, though, there passed before my eyes the things the white man loves—hats, blankets, an empty dress, the pages of a newspaper, and a tin sign advertising ASSAYS. I don't know if these things were real, or a vision."

Smith never cracked a smile, but maybe his eyes showed he was having fun.

"Then all grew dark again, and I could see nothing. Slowly came into view something dark, slowly flopping and rolling, over and over. At first I couldn't make it out. At last it came to a stop, right in front of me, unmistakable. A buffalo robe. It lay there, brown and brooding. The wind flicked at it but it wouldn't move. Through the dust storm it held its ground. As the big wind eased, it rose up onto four legs and trotted off."

Jacobs was slack-jawed. He wasn't used to these little improvisations of Smith's yet.

"I was wondering if this meant that the things of the white man will blow away with the wind—'Vanity of vanities, all is vanity,' says the poet—but the buffalo will live forever.

"Just then my new acquaintance came up close behind me at the window, touched me interestingly, and reminded me of the meaning of life."

Mac was shaking his head. "That's what you get for educating them," he said to Jacobs, chuckling. And it was Smith all over.

Thomas pulled up a chair. Thomas was slender, sinewy, attractive. Mac recognized that his younger son resembled him closely—a boyish, dashing quality that appealed to women. Smith, though huskier, was round-bodied and sweet-faced. Smith loved reading, but Thomas hadn't the patience. Mac kind of wished he looked more like Smith and less like Thomas.

"Brother Thomas," said Smith, "what were they this time?"

"Plain flour sacks," Thomas said. "Nothin' fancy."

"The walls between the rooms upstairs," Smith explained to his father, "are cloth."

"Lumber's been mighty scarce," Jacobs put in. "Mills can't keep up."

"I got plain flour sacks the first time," Smith went on, "basted together. And printed flour sacks the second time. AXE FLOUR, in red and blue letters on white. A touch of . . . something extra."

"I had cotton domestic," boasted Jim, "the one time. I'm no young bull like Smith and Thomas."

"The first time," Smith went on, "Thomas had cotton domestic with pictures from *Harper's Weekly* pinned up. A show of taste. We've been trying to figure out if it's a subtle indication of social structure. The classier whores get better rooms. Or the white whores. Or something. But it's not panning out so far."

"Panning out" was new slang, born of the gold diggings.

The whiskeys came. Thomas reached across, took his dad's whiskey, gulped it down, and motioned to the Chinaman for another. Two more. He looked restless. After a moment he got up and started wandering around. He passed a Mexican-looking whore, admiring her bare bottom. Finally he sat down at a card table.

Jim stood up. "Believe I better teach the lad something." Mac often called them "the lads." He nodded to Jim in appreciation.

"The games are square," said Jacobs.

Jim looked hard at the gambler at Thomas's table. After a moment he said, "Three-card monte?"

Jacobs laughed. "No," he admitted, "the monte's not straight."

Jim walked over—Mac noticed again the way his moccasins moved, slick as goose dung—and put his hands on Thomas's shoulders from behind. Three-card monte was a simple variation on the shell game. The dealer turned three cards, all hearts, faceup. One was a queen. Thomas gestured to indicate that he was ready. The dealer turned the cards facedown and, as Thomas watched sharply, moved them around with one finger. And then took his hands away.

A Chinaman brought Thomas a whiskey, and the young man tossed it down, eyes on the uninformative backs of the cards. At last he pointed to the one on his left. The dealer turned it over. The six of hearts. He turned over the middle card—the queen of hearts—and raked away Thomas's money, four bits.

Thomas put another four bits out. The dealer made his show, Thomas made his guess, and the dealer took Thomas's money. Thomas slapped his knee in frustration.

Jim interrupted. "I'll give you five dollars silver to show him how it works."

The dealer looked up offended and started to speak. "Five bucks is enough," said Jim. "You're not taking any more of his money at monte anyway." Jim put five dollars in silver coin from Taos on the table. It occurred to him to wonder whether, in this town, coin was worth more because it was scarce, compared to dust.

The dealer gave an exaggerated shrug. He was a natty man with flourishing chestnut side-whiskers. He laid out the cards, showing the queen in the middle, flipped them, didn't even move them around, and let Thomas take his guess. Then he showed Thomas the queen—in his hand. The dealer then turned over all three facedown cards with the edge of the queen. They were all small hearts.

"How do you palm it?" asked Thomas. "That's clever."

The dealer shook his head, mouth pursed.

"Then do it again," demanded Thomas.

The dealer went through the routine once more, slowly.

"I still didn't see you palm it," exclaimed Thomas.

"I don't palm it," the dealer said with a shrug. He took the cards away and put out two decks. "Faro?" he asked. "It's square."

Jim tugged on Thomas's arm, and the young man got up. "Why didn't you tell me sooner?" Thomas demanded. "Why did you let me lose more?"

"That's how you really learn," murmured Jim.

$\approx$ **3** $\approx$

They walked quietly, the two of them, past the end of the street and into the darkness. Since they were mountain men, they moved softly. Since one of them was Man Who Doesn't Stir Air in Front When He Walks, more than softly.

The road to Nevada City was well worn, but they stepped off it into the darkness. They stood still in the shadow of some boulders for about half an hour, the Delaware Indian and his friend of a quarter century, the Scots trader. Slung onto the Indian's back with rope was a keg, the sort used for water or whiskey. In the keg, toward the bottom, was a paraffin seal. Under the seal, in sacks, lay more than twenty-five pounds of gold dust worth almost seven thousand dollars.

That was as much money as a skilled man could earn in five years. Mac felt fine about sending Jim away with it. That was what real friends were for. And Jim could take care of it. He must be nearly sixty, but not a bit gray or soft. And he still didn't stir air.

Each carried a long gun, Mac a shotgun. Each also carried a cap-and-ball pistol stuck in his belt, at least two knives, and a tomahawk. They were dangerous men.

After the half hour, they began to move slowly down the gulch, walking parallel to the road. They walked in a way that looked casual, standing upright, making no attempt to hide. But they were silent, their eyes and ears alert. And they padded from hill shadow to hill shadow, stopping in each dark place, looking and listening.

It took them two hours easing through the night this

way to get to the outskirts of Nevada City. Jim waited in a shadowed coulee. Mac went into town to get the two horses from the livery stable. Smith had come down and bought them this afternoon. He hadn't known why. No one else had known anything, and Smith was instructed not to say anything to anyone, not even Thomas. Next to Jim, Smith was as reliable a man as Mac knew, whereas Thomas was sometimes the victim of dramatic teenage emotions.

Mac spoke briefly with the liveryman, hoisted the saddle Smith had left onto one of the animals, and hitched a light load of food and bedding onto the other. Then he rode the opposite way out of town, down the gulch, and waited there in the blackness. No one followed. He tied the horses to a burned tree and went to get Jim. The two of them checked out the area carefully before Jim went to the horses and mounted.

They slipped together down to the creek and filled the gold-bearing keg with water. Mac had joked earlier today that Jim should check the paraffin seal from time to time and look at the color of the water, lest he drink the profits.

The two of them had worked out the plan alone. Jim would now slip off with the gold and head for Fort Benton. There he would make American Fur Mac's depositor and bring back a load of trade goods. The keg ruse should work. A mountain man could travel alone safely. By pushing hard the first night, Jim could get well clear of the gold diggings before anyone knew he was gone.

Tomorrow morning Mac would pay a visit to Sheriff Hospers and ask for advice on getting the gold back to Yellowstone House. If Hospers was crooked, that would lead his outfit astray.

Jim would keep off the traveled routes for a few days, far enough to get clear of anyone following him, and then take the new Mullan Road, which used the old Indian trail, on to Benton. Openness would keep suspicion away. Besides, who would expect a dirty Indian to be carrying nearly seven thousand dollars?

They did not shake hands, a white-man custom. A nod and Jim was off.

Mac wasn't worried about Jim. Jim was sneaky and mean and smart. Also courageous and true. If Mac spread the word after several days that the gold was gone, he could feel okay about his and the boys' going home.

He walked away from the creek a little way and sat on a head-high rock. He filled his clay pipe and lit it with a match. After about ten minutes he felt a touch on his shoulder.

He turned. Strikes Foot, and behind him his son Red Hand. "Well done, Father," said Mac in Cheyenne. "Good to see you."

"We would say it's good to see you," said Strikes Foot, grinning. "But we have seen plenty of you. It was you who didn't see us." It was a statement.

"Sure didn't." And wasn't supposed to. "Thanks."

≈ 4 ≈

Mac was enjoying himself hugely. Smith and Thomas were hiding their grins. The waitress watched while Strikes Foot ignored the spoon and dumped sugar into his coffee directly from the bowl. He managed this one-handed, because the other hand was resolutely atop the cane Mac had bought him yesterday. The cane was a piece of straightened horn from a bighorn sheep, topped with brass. When he first saw the cane, Strikes Foot was delighted. Then he got miffed because he thought Mac was suggesting his limp showed. Then Mac demonstrated what a tremendous cudgel the cane made, and he said Strikes Foot was only supposed to fake being a cripple until he started clubbing with the cane and kicking with his shod hoof. Strikes Foot was thrilled.

The aging warrior took a big swig of coffee—he loved brew because he had a sweet tooth. Red Hand waited until his father was finished with the sugar and did the same. The lad was only fifteen, and shy. Strikes Foot was scooching around on his bentwood chair—Mac wondered if the chairs would prove too much and the Cheyennes would sit on the floor at the restaurant table. They eyed each other over the rims of their cups, their first experience of china. At more than sixty, Strikes Foot looked like a kid in a toy store.

The waitress was waiting for their orders, but the Cheyennes didn't realize it. Mac studied the menu and ordered for everyone: steak, fried eggs, potatoes, and toast with butter and jelly, followed by apple pie. Neither Indian had tasted any of those items. Mac guessed they

201

would scorn the steak and bread, and love the butter and jelly and pie. Potatoes and eggs he had no idea about.

This was fun, but expensive fun at ten dollars a head. Mac was surprised at himself, squandering fifty dollars away like this. Very un-Scots. But Strikes Foot and Red Hand had done him yeoman service on the way over. They'd been his scouts, coming in to the wagons only at night. The reason so many wagon trains had trouble was that they didn't keep scouts a mile or two ahead, checking.

As Mac was stirring his own coffee, he heard boots behind him. Krier. Mac stood up, shook hands, introduced his sons, and smoothly introduced the Cheyennes as well. Strikes Foot and Red Hand stood and waited politely for Krier to stick out his hand. He didn't. Like some other patrons, he just looked at the Indians funny.

Krier introduced the man with him, Owen Mackenzie, the son of King Kenneth Mackenzie of Fort Union. The old man had been gone from the mountains twenty years, but the half-breed son had stayed. Mac wondered fleetingly why Mackenzie hadn't taken Owen to the settlements. Shame? Or had the young man made the choice?

Owen Mackenzie was a big, strong-looking man, Mac's age or a little younger, handsome enough to run for political office. Except, of course, for his dark skin. "You're the one married Annemarie Charbonneau," said Mackenzie. There was a faint air of menace about him, Mac thought, which didn't hurt any man with women. Neither did his gleaming black hair and beard, or his aura of vitality. But Mac didn't want to talk about one of his wives. He just nodded.

"Did you hear the news?" asked Krier. "About the war?"

"No."

"Wagons come in from Salt Lake today." Which meant they came with a lot of news after a long, shut-off winter. "Something for everybody on the telegraph," Krier said with a kind of sneer. "The War Between the States is over. Lee surrendered in Virginia. Appomattox. The damn Yankees will be rejoicing tonight." Krier paused, eyeing Mac. "And a Southern gentlemen assassinated that damn Lincoln."

Mac grimaced.

"So I suppose both sides will be celebrating tonight," Krier went on. "Which one are you with?"

"Neither," Mac said evenly.

"I hear you do take sides, after all, though," said Krier in his soft, Southern-gentry accent.

Mac just looked at him.

"Decided to partner the Chinawoman to supply the diggin's."

Mac shook his head. "I'm on my own. She only bought from me."

"You got more," said Krier, "I'll buy from you. I'll go get it right now."

Mac shook his head. "I'm stripped bare."

"Or maybe you don't side with white people," said Krier. Mac got a whiff of booze on Krier's breath.

Mac glanced quickly at Mackenzie. The breed looked amused. So racial slurs didn't bother him. "I don't deal with drunks, for sure," Mac said quietly.

Then Mac turned his back on Krier and sat down. That ought to be enough to drive the man away. Mac's sons and the Cheyennes didn't sit. Strikes Foot held the cane by the middle. Maybe he thought there was going to be some action. But there wasn't. Mac could feel that in a white man. Krier was nasty but no more.

Krier and Mackenzie moved off and found their own table. From beyond them came the click of the ivory balls on the billiard tables, and the noise, like that of any mining-town bar. But the evening was young, and the din was minor.

The waitress brought five plates of steak and eggs balanced on two arms, a neat trick. Strikes Foot picked up his steak with his free hand—round steak, thin and curled from frying. Strikes Foot took a big bite and frowned. He looked at Mac in shock. No one moved for a moment. Strikes Foot took the meat out of his mouth with the one hand and set it on his plate. "Poor bull," he said in Cheyenne.

"These white men truly don't know fat cow from poor bull, Father," said Mac. Mac picked up knife and fork and indicated that Strikes Foot should use them. He'd seen that at Yellowstone House.

Strikes Foot didn't want to set his cane down. He scooped up a fried egg with the fingers of one hand, and it slithered onto his lap. Strikes Foot looked around with perfect composure, to see if anyone had noticed. One other diner had—she was scowling and telling her husband.

With a touch soft enough to gentle a meadowlark, Strikes Foot put the egg back on his plate. A string of orange yolk trailed behind. He nodded briefly at Mac and started cutting his eggs up one-handed with the fork. He kept hold of that cane.

A startlingly tall, lanky young man came to the table. Mac recognized Zachariah Lawrence, the sweep man from Krier's boat, Felice's "good-looking" fellow. "Don't get up, Mr. Maclean," said Lawrence softly. "Just wanted to say hello. I'll be seeing you in a month, I guess."

"Krier's boats?" asked Mac.

"Yes, we're building more." Mac had seen four mackinaws in various stages of construction below the big bend of the Yellowstone.

"We'll be glad to see you, Lawrence." Maybe Mae Jhong Hackett's money will have our shelves full of goods for your passengers, Mac thought. Jim Sykes should get the supply wagons there in about a month.

"Thank you, sir." Lawrence went to Krier's table, stood talking for a moment, and headed into the bar area alone. He wasn't just tall, Mac noticed, he was stalwart. Mac wondred if Lawrence had noticed Felice as well. Felice, already twenty, was ready to be married, but Mac fended the young men off. He didn't want her to live as a squaw—he wanted her to use the education he'd given her. Maybe he'd send her to St. Louis by the summer steamboat with her brothers and let her learn how to act in society. Yet he didn't want her to end up a thousand miles away from home either, married to someone who would despise her mothers and brothers. And in a different way, her father.

Finished with his eggs and potatoes, Mac turned to his steak. Agghh! Overcooked, tough, gristly. Strikes Foot looked at him sympathetically. The Cheyenne was having Red Hand spread butter and jelly on thick slice after thick slice of bread, gobbling them up, and tapping his shod hoof with pleasure. His first bite of steak sat mangled on the rim of his plate.

Thomas said, smiling at his father, "That beef's something, ain't it?"

That's how it started, innocently enough.

"What does the Injun know about beef?" It came loud and slurred from the bar, from a stocky, flabby man perched high on a stool. In drunken jest.

The man beside him took it up. "Yuh-yuh-yeah, Injun, what do you know about b-b-beef?"

Mac looked a warning around the table. Smith and Thomas had seen enough of this sort of thing in St. Louis.

"Injun's been feeding on dawg," the stocky man said. "What can he tell?" The other was skinny and scraggle-bearded.

Thomas was looking angrily at his father. He didn't take baiting as well as Smith. "Let it go," Mac murmured in Cheyenne, mostly to tip off Strikes Foot and Red Hand.

There was no reason to react. These men were just frontier trash. Mac had seen plenty of them.

The scraggle-bearded man raised a forefinger commandingly. He got off his stool slowly. He levelled the finger at Thomas theatrically. Even the men at the billiard tables had stopped to watch.

"What do you know about beef, Injun?" Scraggle said, his stutter gone.

"I was only going to say—" Thomas started.

"You—you was only going to *say*. *You* was," said the scraggle trash. The stocky trash had a bowie knife stuck into his boot, Mac noticed. Scraggle would have similar. "You was only going to s-say—*what* was you goin' to s-say? That's what *I* want to know."

Mac shook his head at Thomas. Strikes Foot was looking at Mac with the damnedest expression of curiosity, and rubbing the brass head of his cane. Mac had the feeling everyone at his table had scooted his chair back from the table a little.

"He was going to say he's the only thing sucks hind tit to a Chinee," bellowed Stocky Trash, and let out a rip-roaring laugh. He laughed alone. But everyone else was leaning forward, or inching forward. They smelled a little fun.

Mac saw that long Zach Lawrence had moved to the bar, near the two trashes. Evidently Lawrence would help out. Krier and Mackenzie were tilted back on their chairs. No telling what side they'd be on.

"What was it you said?"

Thomas just glowered, silent.

"Don't you raise your v-voice against me. Or the South. Or the C-Confederacy. Cause *I* won't *s-stand* it." Scraggle was leaning over the table now, spraying spittle in Thomas's face.

Mac slowly slipped his pistol out of his belt and laid it next to his plate. He deliberately started taking off the caps, so it couldn't be fired. Smith and Thomas did likewise. Strikes Foot and Red Hand had no guns. "*I* won't *stand* it," Scraggle repeated.

Mac looked around to judge what was coming. He saw rabble. And he felt it, something sinister, something ugly. He set the feeling aside and thought to take concern for knives, and billiard cues, which made nasty weapons.

Mac got to his feet. "I appeal to men of decency to help me put a stop to this trouble," Mac said loudly and slowly.

"So says the Injun lover," called someone sarcastically.

"He's a Injun lover okay," said someone else. "He bangs Injun. Them boys is his sons."

Everyone at Mac's table was on his feet now. Stocky Trash was up. Everyone was ready.

Mac stepped forward to Stocky Trash, hand out. "Let's shake and forget what's been said."

"Maybe I want to say some things you won't ever forget," said Stocky Trash, his hand behind his back.

Mac stepped forward again, past Scraggle, close to Stocky Trash, hand out. "Peace," he said, and with that word he started it.

He blindsided Scraggle hard, backhand, and kicked a chair into Stocky. The knife from behind Stocky's back got tangled in the chair. Instantly Mac was on Stocky and riding him to the ground with the chair. Stocky's head hit the stool support, and he looked out of the fight. Mac tossed the scum's knives behind the bar.

Mac bellowed in Cheyenne over the hubbub, "Don't kill anybody!" And then he got lost in the jangly satisfaction of fighting.

He seemed to see the fight only in ragged bits and pieces. He saw Strikes Foot pretending to limp on his hoof. Then a slack-jawed man rushed Mac hard. He stepped aside, grabbed the man's arm, and flung him headfirst into a post.

Someone kicked Mac in the back, and for a couple of minutes he was on the floor, people falling over him, unable to get up. While he was down, Mac heard a shotgun blast. Probably the bartender, a warning shot into the floor. But no one stopped fighting. Mac saw Strikes Foot whomp someone in the kidneys with the cane. The victim screamed.

Smith grabbed a wild-eyed man from behind and clubbed the knife out of his hand. Thomas kicked the man in the balls. Smith scooped up the knife and hurled it hard into the wall, handle aquiver.

"Don't use your weapons," Mac hollered in Cheyenne.

As Scraggle went for Thomas, Zach Lawrence rabbit-punched him with an arm long as a rake, and Scraggle went down.

Red Hand was pussyfooting, Mac saw. "Fight, Brother!" he bellowed.

A fat, mustachioed fellow squared off with Strikes Foot across a table, billiard cue against cane. Strikes Foot met the cue in midair and shattered it. Now it was more dangerous. Suddenly Strikes Foot kicked the table underneath in the center with his sharpened hoof. The table bucked into the air, split down the middle, and plates and silverware flew everywhere. A dramatic warning. The mustachioed fellow backed off.

A warrior is a warrior at any age, thought Mac.

It occurred to Mac that no one had guns out, and he was glad.

Someone jumped on Smith's back. Owen Mackenzie jerked the fellow's head backward until he let go, hoisted him straight overhead, and heaved him face first into the ceiling. An incredible feet of strength. The man fell flat on his back and lay crumpled on the floor. Mackenzie was evidently enjoying himself. And helping out, praise be.

Something came down on Mac's head, and he blacked out for a moment. He came to on the floor and saw Krier had Red Hand down and was stomping him—Red Hand's face was a bloody mess.

Strikes Foot came from nowhere and kicked Krier in the gut with his hoof. Krier coughed air hard and fell down, bleeding under the rib cage. Strikes Foot cocked the hoof with its sharpened shoe again, his eye fixed on Krier's face. But Smith grabbed the Cheyenne.

Suddenly everyone was backing off, stopping. Two men had dropped cues and were holding what looked to be broken arms. Three or four more were on the floor, holding the backs of their heads. The bartender was tapping a crowbar into his palm, ready to crack more heads. But it wasn't necessarily over—Mac could feel the bloodlust pulsing in the air. While everyone was stopped, Mac picked up his pistol off the floor and started capping the cartridges. Smith and Thomas did the same.

Just then Sheriff Hospers banged in, followed by a deputy, both bearing side-by-side shotguns.

Hospers discharged his ten-gauge into the floor, blowing puncheons to smithereens. He leveled the gun. "Who wants the other barrel?" he roared. The deputy was ready as well.

Men backed off. Mac and Smith lowered their pistols. Now it was over.

"I'll pinch the pokes right now," said the barman sharply.

"Every man sit down!" bellowed the sheriff. He reloaded the shotgun.

They did. Mac helped Strikes Foot lift Red Hand onto a table. The boy was moaning softly. His face was all chopped up.

"Pokes on the table!" the sheriff shouted.

Krier didn't get to his feet. He was curled up holding his belly. Mac wondered if he was hurt bad.

The barman got a beam scale and started making his rounds. He dipped his fingers into every man's poke, except a few in back who had kept their seats, and came out with dust. He had to tap his fingers on the tin scoop to get it out from beneath his long fingernails. And probably didn't get it all out, thought Mac. Handy.

"How much you figure, Amos?" called the sheriff, his shotgun thrown down on everyone, grinning big.

"Five hundred," said the barman, still pinching dust.

"Fifty ounces, then," said the sheriff. Gold was sixteen dollars an ounce. "Any man doesn't want to pay a little extra to run the jail, he can spend a couple of days there."

Sheriff, judge, and jury, thought Mac.

The waitress came in with a man carrying a medical bag. Maybe this was Dr. Crepin, who advertised his office across from the hay scales. He started examining Krier. The injured man was sitting up now, propped against the bar.

Amos the barman faced Mac. "Let's have your pokes too."

"We didn't start it. They did." Mac tipped his head at Stocky and Scraggle. Stocky was sitting up by the stool, holding his head. Scraggle was tippling from a bottle.

"Makes no difference," said the bartender. "And your Injun busted that table."

Mac stacked coins on the table. "Take for all of us," he said. The barman helped himself.

"What in hell made this wound?" demanded the doctor in a bass voice.

Mac pointed to Strikes Foot's shod hoof and spoke in Cheyenne. Strikes Foot held up the hoof and let the doctor check out the filed shoe. "My holy Jesus Christ!" he boomed.

"Some of you brawlers carry this man to my office." The doctor sounded disgusted. "He'll live, if his liver isn't bleeding."

The doctor started checking out Red Hand, clucking as he did. Red Hand was up, but looked out on his feet.

"Someone show this boy over to my office," said the doctor. "He needs stitching up." No one but Zach Lawrence stepped forward.

"How much you got?" the sheriff asked the barman.

"Forty-six," he answered, adding an ounce weight to the beam scale.

"Take the rest from them as started it," ordered the sheriff.

Amos reached into the pokes of Stocky and Scraggly again. He dropped the dust into the scoop, but didn't tap his fingernails. He'd clean his fingernails in his own poke, Mac supposed.

"You!" Sheriff Hospers barked at Strikes Foot. "Come on, you're under arrest."

"What for?" Mac said sharply.

"Could be murder," said the sheriff pointedly. "Depends on whether Krier lives."

"You know it was self-defense," growled Mac.

"What I know is an Injun attacked a white man," snapped Hospers, glaring.

Mac looked around. "He gonna be safe?" The mob was watching, maybe hostile, maybe dully indifferent.

"That's my job, Maclean."

"How long you gonna hold him?"

"We can talk to Judge Bissell in the morning. If Krier's dead or out of danger."

Mac thought of the little jail, freestanding, one room of wood with barred windows the size of a man's hand. He spoke softly to Strikes Foot in Cheyenne. "Father, I suggest you go along with this impolite man. He's going to lock you in a small room. I think we can solve this without trouble in the morning."

Strikes Foot nodded. Mac was glad his father-in-law had patience. He didn't resist when Hospers took his arm and led him toward the door.

At that moment came the shot.

Strikes Foot lurched violently forward and crashed to the floor.

The pistol was in Krier's hand. The man showed a sick

smile, lying slumped there, and his gun was still moving, seeking.

Neither Mac nor Smith nor Thomas got a shot off before the sheriff emptied one barrel of his ten-gauge into Krier's head.

Mac bent over Strikes Foot. Blood of brilliant scarlet was pulsating out his back.

Mac turned him over. The life was already dimming in his eyes.

"No man lifts a gun!" the sheriff hollered.

Mac held the Cheyenne's head in his hands and put his cheek down against Strikes Foot's. Mac's tears wet both their cheeks. He murmured softly, "Good-bye, Father."

"Goddamn Injun lover," Mac heard someone grouse.

He looked up at his sons. Both of them were bent over their grandfather, their faces awash in grief. And in Thomas's face, something else. Hatred.

≈ 5 ≈

Fat moon

When you're in trouble, some people turn against you, like a herd cutting out a cripple. Others come to help, like human beings. That's why Zach Lawrence's long frame sat folded against a wall, and maybe why Owen Mackenzie paced the floor. And why everyone was in Mae Jhong's parlor.

Mac looked across at his sons and his brother-in-law. Red Hand's face was puffed up like a pumpkin, and stitches made ugly tracks all over it. Thomas was playing solitaire on the table next to Mac. Smith was on the sofa with Red Hand, staring out the window. Mac reached for the tea and sipped some. It was cold and he didn't give a damn.

Mac had spent the night adrift in sorrow and guilt. He had brought Strikes Foot and Red Hand to Virginia City to learn about white men and be amused. Now Mac was responsible for his father-in-law's death.

But he had to cope. He had to get the rest of his family home to Yellowstone House, to the big circle of Cheyenne lodges. It might not be easy. Some of Krier's friends might want revenge. They didn't give a damn who actually pulled the trigger. Krier was dead, wasn't he? The Injuns and the Injun lover was to blame, wasn't they?

Others might believe Mac still had the gold on him, whatever story he gave out. So it would be an edgy journey home.

Mac stood up. "We'll go tomorrow at dawn." No one responded. "Whether Jacobs gets back or not. We have no drivers." The mule skinners who had driven Mac's wagons

212

over wanted to stay and try their luck at gold in Alder Gulch. "Red Hand will drive.

"We'll be taking Strikes Foot home," Mac said needlessly. Home to be buried in the traditional manner, and where his relatives could come to pay their respects.

"The word for that is *dangerous*," said Smith with a smile.

Mac smiled back, bitterly. It was a sort of family game, The Word for That Is. . . . It started a decade ago when nine-year-old Smith sniffed some sage grouse Anniemarie had cooked. She had almost no sense of smell. Smith said, "The word for that is *putrid*," showing off his new English term. Thomas smelled the birds, and with a seven-year-old's vocabulary, took up the game with, "The word for that is *sti-i-inky*." That night Little One applied it to a way Mac rubbed her back. "The word for that is *luscious*." It got to be family play. Mac encouraged it because it improved everyone's English. Anniemarie's was the weakest, Smith's the best.

Mac said quietly to Smith, "The word for life is 'dangerous.'" But Smith was already back to his staring. Mac was concerned about him. About Thomas, too, masking the hatred Mac had seen by playing cards indifferently. And Red Hand, completely numb and passive.

Mac couldn't help mulling about how awful this death would be for the family. Strikes Foot's three wives would each hack off a joint of a finger, or more than one, and maybe scarify themselves as well. Then they would be split up—the family would die, too. Strikes Foot had no brother to take them in as wives, and three were too many anyway. Perhaps Mac could get them to come and live at Yellowstone House for a little while, but that would be awkward. It was forbidden among the Cheyennes for a man to speak to his mother-in-law.

What would happen to them? Calling Eagle was aged, and a would-be woman. Yellow Bird, Red Hand's mother, might be past the age of bearing children, and so of marginal use. Corn, the youngest, had two little kids. Mac supposed the wives would go to the lodges of their brothers, or of their sisters' men. Even Calling Eagle would.

Strikes Foot's other sons and daughters—Mac never knew
how many adopted children he would find in the lodge—
would go with one of their mothers and lose the other
mothers.

Strikes Foot's married children would grieve as well.
Since Lame Deer was long dead, Anniemarie had neither
father nor mother. She lived away from the tribe, and her
sons and husband were only Cheyennes in part, so she
might feel the Cheyennes' most terrible affliction: I have
no relatives.

A gentle tap on the door. Smith stood up and opened it.
A stout, elderly white man stood there. Skullcapped, a
black-bordered newspaper in his hand, and a white terrier
of some kind perched on his shoulder.

"Young Mr. Maclean," said the man in a guttural accent,
"I am Peddler. May I see your father?"

The voice took hold of Mac, but for a moment the
picture of the stout old Jew in a skullcap didn't add up.
Then Mac saw. Dreyfuss.

He reached past his son and embraced his old friend by
the shoulders.

"I'm sorry to come to you, Mac, in this time of trouble."

"You couldn't be more welcome." Mac discovered he
was a little choked up. He put his arm around Dreyfuss
and ushered him in. While once Dreyfuss had said nothing about being a Jew, he now wore a yarmulke centered
on a shiny pate. He had only a thin fringe of gray hair. But
that wasn't what was really different. In his old age Dreyfuss
seemed to have a glowing benevolence, an aura of robust
spirituality. Had Mac not known him, he would have taken
Dreyfuss for a priest, at once beatific and jovial. A priest
with a little white dog for a mascot.

Mac introduced Dreyfuss to everyone—his sons, Red
Hand, Zach, Owen. It felt awful that with Jim gone and
Strikes Foot dead, not a single one of Mac's companions
knew as good a friend as Dreyfuss.

But the old man corrected Mac gently. "My name has
not been Dreyfuss for many years. People call me Peddler.
I want you all to meet Punch, too."

Peddler set the little dog down and spoke to it in a

strange, guttural language. The dog approached Mac, sat up, and put its paw out to be shaken. And then shook the hand of every man there.

"Dreyfuss—Peddler—tell us everything," Mac urged.

"There is little to tell. I have wandered the earth and passed among its human beings, joined them in their travails, and felt their joys and sorrows. These years have been a great gift."

"You don't work for a living?"

Peddler smiled gently. "I pull a cart and sell a few sewing items." His shrug added, It's not important.

"My friend," Peddler said to Mac, "do you know about Sand Creek?"

Mac shook his head.

"Then I'm obliged to bring you sad and important news. Start with this."

The peddler handed Mac the newspaper, folded open to an inside page. The peddler pointed Mac past the head-lines about Lincoln.

SLAUGHTERER OF CHEYENNES UNPUNISHED.

Mac looked at the newspaper—all the way from St. Louis. He read about the slaughter of hundreds of inno-cent Cheyennes at Sand Creek, and about why their murderers could not be brought to justice.

Mac looked up. "Zach, would you go get the body and bring it here?" The young man nodded, a puzzled look on his face, and went out. Strikes Foot was in a pine casket at the doctor's office.

"Are we leaving now?" Smith asked.

Mac spoke instead to the Chinaman. "Mac Jhong, please." The old gentleman bowed and scurried out.

Mac read how women and children were killed under a take-no-prisoners policy, and how the soldiers showed off parts of Cheyenne bodies on a stage in Denver.

Mae Jhong appeared immediately in one of her elabo-rate gowns. Mac asked her please to send his wagon for a load of ice.

"Immediately," she said.

Had she heard anything from Jacobs?

"I'm sorry, no," she said demurely.

The demure part was an act, but Mae Jhong was a friend, to help when it could be held against her.

Mac read that retaliation, terrible retaliation, was expected from the Cheyennes, and their allies the Sioux and the Arapahoes.

"What happened?" insisted Thomas. Mackenzie was watching Mac with hard eyes.

Mac took a deep breath and said, "There's been a massacre. Cheyennes." The boys look gut-punched. Red Hand looked too numb to know what was happening. "As soon as I tell this," Mac said, looking everyone in the eyes, "we're getting out of here."

The boys nodded. Mackenzie nodded too.

"Denver was having some trouble back in the fall." That was the site of the rich Cherry Creek gold diggings, where fifty thousand white people lived a thousand miles from civilization. "Indian raids along the Oregon Trail."

Mac used the English word "Indian," a family irony meaning some redskin, any redskin, who knows which one or what tribe, let's just kill 'em all.

"The telegraph connection with the East got severed. The stage lines cut. Some supplies didn't get through.

"The soldiers decided to punish the bad Indians. They told the good ones to camp on Sand Creek. Black Kettle's circle. So they couldn't mistake them for the bad ones.

"Then they made a surprise attack on Black Kettle's lodges. Killed four or five hundred, including lots of women and children. Killed the horses, burned the lodges. The people fled miles and miles on foot to other circles, Arapahoe, Lakota, whoever they could find.

"There's gonna be hell to pay. And since we're Cheyennes, we better get out of here."

The boys, Red Hand, Owen, Peddler—all accepted this necessity immediately. That's what it meant to have red blood, or mixed blood.

Zach Lawrence and a teenager from the doctor's office came in with the closed casket.

"Mackenzie," said Mac, "will you go with us as far as

the Madison?" That was fifteen miles away, at the site of a mill.

"This child is with you all the way to Yellowstone House," said Mackenzie. Funny how everything the man said and did had a kind of mockery to it.

"Fine. Take the north side of the road."

The damn road would provide rocks and cedars and gullies enough to hide a dozen highwaymen.

"Smith and Thomas, take the south side. Use your own judgment. But if you find anyone, probably the best thing is to wait till we get there and they start their move. Then take them from behind. We'll wait two hours to leave. It's enough. Whatever you do, take your time and don't let them see you."

Mac didn't like having to use his sons for serious work, but they should know how to do it, and he had no one else.

Smith and Thomas left with Mackenzie.

"Zach, you're with us?"

The tall man nodded.

"Then bring the wagon around and load it right here in front. Let everyone see we don't have any gold. I'll ask Mae to send some boys to help you. I'll be above at the second-story window with a rifle.

"Red Hand, you go with Zach." The boy didn't respond. Mac touched his arm and repeated the instruction. Red Hand shrugged. Zach hustled him out.

Mac sent the Chinaman for Mac Jhong and then took a moment to think. His chores were in the present, but his mind was on the future. For sure the Cheyennes, his wife's people, his children's people, really his own people, would rise against the whites to get even for the horror of the destruction of Black Kettle's circle. Their friends the Sioux and Arapahoe would join them. Together they would close the gate tight on John Bozeman's road to Montana. Might close the Oregon Trail itself. Would kill plenty of whites, most of them not in the goddamn U.S. Army. And then would draw the full wrath of the U.S. government. It was going to get bloody.

Mac and his family would be right in the middle.

"Mac."

Mac jumped. He had forgotten about Dreyfuss—Peddler—standing over the casket. In fact Peddler had opened the lid and was looking down at Strikes Foot.

Mac went to him and touched his shoulder. Strikes Foot did not look serene in death. His features spoke pain. Mac could not see how that death could be paid for.

"Thank you for your help," Mac said to Dreyfuss. "What a terrible day to see you again, after twenty years."

Peddler inclined his head. He put the dog on the other shoulder. "I want to go with you," he said softly.

"You want what?"

"May I travel to Yellowstone House with you?"

"Of course. Anniemarie and Little One will be thrilled."

The dog opened its mouth and closed it. Twice. "Thank you," said the dog in a guttural accent.

$$\approx \ 6 \ \approx$$

Mac had never felt such a fool. He felt a fool on the wagon bench, holding a shotgun across his lap next to Red Hand, instead of on his horse. Felt a fool surrounded by a crowd of funny-smocked, funny-hatted Chinamen milling around him. They carried a comical variety of out-of-the-bottom-drawer pistols and knives. They looked like laundrymen dressed up as pirates. Which is exactly what they were.

Maclean's army, Mac thought mockingly.

On one side Zach sat astride an extra saddle horse, and from the look of him he hadn't ridden much and wouldn't be much good at shooting from horseback. Mac didn't know if the black Irishman had ever pointed a gun with deadly intent anyway.

On the other side stood Peddler, ready to go. Mac was getting used to calling him Peddler. He had a two-wheel cart strapped around his ample waist. His items for peddling, light sewing stuff, had been transferred to the wagon. Mac had never before seen a human being hitched up as an ox. He felt for Peddler, but the Jew seemed cheerful about it.

And atop the cart sat the fool dog, Punch, doing tricks that tickled the Chinamen and the bystanders. Peddler would speak, and the little terrier would jump straight up in the air. Or chase its tail savagely, barking at itself. Or Peddler would hold up two fingers, and the dog would bark twice. Or Peddler would toss a ball of vulcanized rubber and the dog would leap off the cart, catch it in the air, bring Peddler the ball, and bound back onto the cart. That little dog was a whirling dervish.

It was an appealing little dog, a West Highland terrier, according to Peddler. Mac's people were originally West Highlanders, but he had never seen one. A blocky little fellow, with perky ears, and smart as some people.

Now the peddler held up his other hand and slowly stuck up one, two, three fingers. Instead of barking twice, the dog sat up, opened its mouth, and called out loudly, "Three." With a guttural accent, of course. It got a roar from the crowd.

Ventriloquism, Peddler said. Mac would be damned curious about that, some other time.

The dog jumped from the cart onto the peddler's shoulder, agile as a cat. Then Peddler removed his skullcap, Punch stepped onto his bald head, sat up, held its paws out, and bowed its head. The crowd burst into applause.

Mac nodded to Red Hand, and the boy clucked the horses up the road, away from the damned town of Virginia City. Mac was taking nothing home but Strikes Foot, packed with ice in a pine box.

Mac looked over the Chinese marching raggedly along. Two were giggling, like boys off on an adventure. The leader scowled at them. Mac didn't know a single man of the Chinese and had no idea what they could do. Nothing, he guessed. He'd had Mae Jhong tell them they were just for show, unless fired on.

Mac felt bilious himself. He didn't like being surrounded with a bunch of amateurs. That applied even to his sons, to Zach, maybe to Peddler, to everyone except a mountain man like Mackenzie. Mac would have given a lot to be backed by Jim Sykes. Or Jacobs. Or his old partner Skinhead, dead twenty years.

Where would the trouble come? Mac wondered. Probably in the fifteen-mile stretch between Virginia City and the sawmill on the Madison River. No point in speculating about it. It was coming—he felt it. He half hoped for it. He felt bloody-minded.

2

Easing down the long hill toward the sawmill, the horses well under control with Red Hand at the reins, Mac felt disappointed. And ashamed of himself for being disappointed.

Nothing had happened. No highwaymen, no lynchers, no dry-gulchers. He and his foolish army of Chinamen had gotten out of Alder Gulch okay.

Smith and Thomas were coming in from behind on the south side at a lope. Mackenzie would be along soon, Mac supposed. He looked over the little mill community. A main cabin, a bunkhouse, a cookhouse, some wall tents, the big mill building on the diversion ditch, a couple of sheds, and an icehouse on the bank of the river.

The sun was low in the west. Mac hadn't decided whether to camp at the mill or push on a little. The miller, Caseen, would be glad of company, Mac was sure. His crew was mostly upstream now, getting timber cut and floating it down to the mill to start the cutting season. The man would be home minding his fine sawblade. The first time through he had wanted to talk Mac to death about that wonderful blade.

Mac was inclined to go beyond the mill and camp, even though it meant giving the Chinese further to walk back.

Smith and Thomas rode up alongside, their horses blowing. "Nothing," said Thomas.

"No fresh tracks, not a thing that looks questionable," said Smith.

Mac was pleased. His sons were good trackers. If anything was there, they'd have spotted it. "We could still get into something tonight or tomorrow," said Mac. He didn't think so, but wariness was his way, a way of long years' standing. He'd be glad when Mackenzie came in with the same report.

On top of Alder Gulch, where the country opened up, Mac had gotten down to walk a spell. The country was greening up nicely, the hills covered with new grass, and it was a good day to be on the move. Mac listened idly to Zach and Peddler talking.

"Often travel alone?" queried Zach from high in the saddle.

"Usually," said the peddler.

"How do you keep your scalp?" Zach asked with a skewed smile.

"How would they take it?" answered the peddler, lifting the skull cap to show his shiny pate.

"Tell me, really."

"Indians don't bother me. Maybe I'm too old and pitiful to matter."

"How long you been traveling?"

"Since I left Yellowstone House twenty years ago. I've walked to San Francisco, and back to St. Louis, to Mexico, to Salt Lake, and back here. Selling my few notions along the way. Mostly walking with just Punch for company." He indicated the dog behind him on the cart.

Peculiar enough to fit, thought Mac.

"Never any trouble?" Zach went on.

"A little sometimes. Some Pawnee boys rode up fast once like they were about to puncture my old hide. But they stopped to issue threats first, and Punch diverted them, and I gave them a rubber ball and sent them along happy."

Mac would bet the peddler could do that.

The high-pitched scream of the sawblade came to Mac across the rolling, baby-green hills. That meant the miller had got some logs downstream and was at least a little bit back in business.

Mac climbed back into the wagon and bumped to the edge of the mill settlement. When Mac got beyond it, he'd get back on his horse, tied to the rear. A saddle was damn well more comfortable than a board seat.

The blade screech stopped.

Was that the miller running out toward them from the raw, stacked boards?

Then Mac saw a figure stand out alongside the sawdust below the millhouse, holding up a rifle.

Mackenzie. He was making the lookout's long-distance sign that said, "Enemies."

Mac took off his tattered beaver hat and waved it up to the right, as if he were shaking it, then put it back on. That was the sign confirming, "Enemies," usually made with a blanket.

Mackenzie moved back out of sight. Whoever it was, and however many, they must be this way of Mackenzie.

"Here's our trouble," murmured Mac. "Follow my lead. We don't suspect anything." Smith and Thomas looked away, casual, not letting on. Red Hand blanched but made no gesture.

The miller arrived out of breath. Really out, thought Mac—he's panicked.

"Come quick, Mr. Maclean, my man has cut his arm off on the blade."

The sight and coppery smell of Paul the Blue's leg spurting blood clanged through Mac's brain. He pushed away the fear and nausea.

"I'm not a doctor, Caseen. None of us is." So they wanted him to follow the wagon ruts between the bunkhouse and the cookhouse toward the millhouse and the stacks of lumber.

"But couldn't you just try to help him, Mr. Maclean, just comfort him? It's so awful."

Mac was setting the layout in his mind. Millhouse way across by the diversion ditch, bunkhouse and cookhouse just ahead, tents, main cabin.

Whoever it was, and however many, they didn't know Mackenzie was behind them.

Why didn't they think he might take the back side of the bunkhouse if he caught on? Because a man-high pile of sawdust stood in the way, where they'd bucked timber into lengths.

Mac's style was aggression. He let the muzzle of his shotgun drift toward Caseen. Then he said softly to Red Hand, "Back of the bunkhouse. Right through the sawdust." He gave Caseen a crooked smile. "Now!"

The driver cracked his whip over the team and the horses took off, nearly bowling Caseen over. Smith and

Thomas galloped alongside, Zach lagging a little. Mac wished like hell he could keep his sons out of it, but there was no way.

The Chinese trotted along behind in a gang, their leader barking orders.

"Go hard!" Mac hollered as the lead horses approached the sawdust. Red Hand made the whip explode.

Someone jumped out from behind the bunkhouse with a rifle leveled. Mac let fly from the bouncing wagon with the shotgun. He missed but scared the fellow back.

The wagon tilted up on the two right wheels—it hung at a rakish angle for a long moment—and Mac jumped. He rolled in behind the bunkhouse.

The wagon went over with a splintering crash. Dragging, it brought the horses to a screaming halt. The casket slammed against the bunkhouse and bounced away. Chunks of ice flew everywhere. Strikes Foot rolled out and turned ceremoniously onto one side. His eyes seemed to open slightly.

Red Hand was crumpled against the bunkhouse wall, but he got up and grabbed for his rifle.

Mac heard some shots. The Chinese were herding in behind the bunkhouse, overexcited. Mac wondered whether any had been hit.

Smith and Zach were already standing on their saddles by the eaves, climbing onto the roof with their rifles. Mac followed them fast.

Red Hand and the Chinese pushed the wagon back onto its side and used it for cover.

Looking around the settlement, Mac saw the bastards were all out of sight. He felt exultant. Now who had the high ground?

A figure poked out by the corner of the cookhouse and Mac emptied his second barrel at it. Couldn't tell the result. Started reloading. "Keep 'em pinned own," he shouted at Smith and Zach. His elder son had a sober, satisfied look on his face. His .50–.70 Springfield boomed.

"That's enough, Maclean!" screamed a voice. From the end of this bunkhouse. Mac set his loads and crawled toward that end of the building.

Stocky Trash had Thomas seated on the ground, dragged away from the building, clamped by one wrist and his arm sharply twisted, a pistol hard in his ear. Thomas looked dazed. He must have been jerked off his horse and kicked or clubbed. He'd gone too near the other end of the building—maybe didn't see the man jump out from behind there. From the look of him, Thomas was dizzy with panic.

Peddler came strolling up with his cart and his fool dog.

Scraggle was prancing around Thomas and Stocky, overcome with his good luck, calling out gibberish orders. Mac would barely have to take Scraggle into consideration, though he did hold a pistol and had even remembered to load it.

Two other men came out from behind the cookhouse and into the wagon road. One stood up on the roof. Outlaws, they'd call themselves. Mac called them frontier scum without enough sense to stay behind something.

The peddler was walking up close, looking curiously, like the guns were props in a show.

Mac thought of blowing Stocky Trash away. Too risky, with that barrel halfway into Thomas's ear. Mac's bowels ran cold. He hoped Mackenzie would see it the same way. Even a killing shot could make that trigger-finger jerk.

"The other boy stands up in the open!" barked Stocky. "Everybody in the open." Mac looked at Thomas, who was trying to twist to ease the pain in his shoulder, and turned white. Mac nodded at Smith, and Smith stood up but didn't drop his rifle. Red Hand and Zach did likewise. Scraggle held his pistol on them two-handed.

The Chinese stood there like spectators. Well, Mac had told them not to make any plays.

"Drop your guns!" snapped Stocky.

The fool dog started barking at Stocky, idiotically.

Mac shook his head no. "Seems to me we got a standoff here," he said. "You got Thomas. But we're not stupid. If we give up our guns, you'll kill us all. If we don't, someone gets hurt, but mostly you."

Stocky's eyes shifted. "All I want is the gold, Maclean."

That damn dog was close to Stocky now, making an

awful racket. The peddler spoke to it gently in some foreign language, but it didn't back off. Stocky was getting irked. Mac too.

Mac stepped to the edge of the roof, near Stocky. "I'll give you my coins," he said simply. "That's all we're carrying. They're in here." He touched the pouch that held his flint and steel and tinder, plus half his coins.

Stocky gave a coarse laugh. "The Chinese bitch's gold, Maclean. We want all of it."

Mac wondered what would happen if he jumped for Stocky from here. Would the bastard's hands jerk up by reflex? Mac was going to have to force something. Which would get someone hurt. But Mac couldn't bear for it to be Thomas. Looking at his son there on the ground, wrenched with pain and fear, froze Mac.

"I sent the dust with Jim Sykes, the Delaware, to Fort Benton three days ago."

Stocky eyed Mac, keeping the contemptuous sneer on his face. He couldn't tell if it was true. Even Scraggle stood still for a moment.

Peddler spoke a single word. The dog bounded in two jumps into Stocky, straight at his groin, jaws wide.

By reflex, Stocky grabbed with both hands to deflect the vicious little animal.

Mac gave him a full load of buckshot square in the chest.

From the millhouse Mackenzie's big rifle roared, and Scraggle went down.

Mac was already flat on the sod roof. He loosed the other barrel at the man on the other roof. Smith and Zach were firing. Mackenzie spoke again from the millhouse.

Peddler dragged Thomas to safety.

"Enough?" boomed Mac.

All guns were silent.

"Put down your weapons and you live!"

The man on the roof opposite threw his rifle onto the ground. He was unhit. Mac got up and looked at the men in the ruts. One was crumpled up. One was standing, quailing, miraculously untouched. Mac looked everywhere for more.

Scraggle lay on the ground, alternately holding his hip and staring at his hands covered with his own blood. Mackenzie had shot a little low. Scraggle was mewling self-pityingly and weeping.

Thomas was getting up. He looked dazed.

Zach started putting Strikes Foot back in the casket.

Mackenzie came on the run. "There's one down behind the bunkhouse," he said. "Makes six. They killed the miller's man."

Caseen had wandered down close and was standing there in a stupor. Mac supposed he wasn't part of it. Plenty of greed, Mac guessed, but not enough guts.

Mac looked down at Peddler. "Thank you for my son."

The Peddler inclined his head. "You are welcome, my friend."

"I owe you," Mac said to Mackenzie. "Without the signal we're dead."

"It was a pleasure to kill them," said the big man. Mac wondered if he was one who enjoyed killing. "I picked up their tracks. Time I saw what was happenin', you was here."

"No, no, God, no," wailed Scraggle's voice.

Mac ran down the roof to the end of the bunkhouse.

Thomas knelt in front of Scraggle, holding the muzzle of his pistol where Scraggle's whiskers met his nose.

"Thomas, no!" yelled Mac.

Thomas blew the back of Scraggle's head out.

Mac screamed, "No-o-o!" For a long moment the world reverberated with the agony of his own scream.

Smith was cradling his head in his hands.

Thomas was taking what was left of Scraggle's scalp. Mac supposed it was his first one. He wondered if the breath-grabbing fear of that muzzle in his ear had done something to Thomas. He told himself it would do something to anybody.

Mac set to cleaning up. He asked Zach to hammer the casket back together tightly. After a little thought he had Mackenzie take the blunt back of an ax to Caseen's fine sawblade, tall as a tall man, and shipped all the way from St. Louis or San Francisco. Caseen looked at Mac pathetically. Mac wanted the weakling to hurt, and remember.

At last Mac went to face Thomas. The boy was sitting against the end of the bunkhouse, the bodies of Stocky and Scraggle in front of him, sloppily scalped. Smith was sitting next to him, silent, merely there. Thomas had the scalps hung through his belt, blood running into the hair and onto his pants.

Mac knelt in front of Thomas and looked into his eyes. He saw bewilderment, panic, and crazy glee.

He wanted to slap Thomas's damned face, hard. He also wanted to put his arms around his son and hold him.

In the end all he did was murmur, "What the hell," and walk away.

≈ 7 ≈

Mac could hear them through the door, squabbling like fishwives. No doubt over the usual.

Lisette, the Little One, was a fastidious person. Where she was permitted—the office where she worked and their personal quarters—she kept everything clean as a martinet's boots, and everything in its place. But Annemarie was amiably sloppy. Not only was she content to live in comfortable disorder, she seemed to feel resentful of order.

Once every season or so, regular as the solstice and the equinox, Mac's two wives held a pitched battle. They not only shouted, they threw things. Once Annemarie, nearly a foot taller and fifty pounds heavier, rode Little One to the ground and sat on her until her fury turned to tears. Mac had seen Valdez picking up broken crockery behind them as they quarreled. Aside from this ritual, they were best friends.

Standing outside the door of his parlor, Mac looked at Owen Mackenzie. The big breed was grinning above his luxuriant black beard, his eyes electric, his animal vitality palpable.

Mac wished he'd come alone. He'd ridden ahead of Smith, Thomas, and the others to break the news of her father's death to Annemarie. Owen had said simply, "I need to ride," and set his horse at a lope alongside Mac's Appaloosa mare.

Mac opened the door. Annemarie and Lisette paused in mid-shout and mid-gesture.

Annemarie came running. Then she stopped short. "Dancer," she said softly, and took his hand and put her head on his shoulder. Lisette stayed by the horsehair-stuffed sofa. After Mac was away on trips, Lisette often kept distance between them for a few days.

Mac heard Owen open the door the rest of the way and step into the doorway. Annemarie went rigid beside him. Did seeing the stranger give her a clue that all had gone wrong?

"Strikes Foot is dead," Mac said gently in her ear.

For a moment she was still. Mac said across the room to Lisette, "Strikes Foot is dead."

Annemarie let out a cry, a great welling, plaintive wail, the voice of the women of the world when their men leave their life's blood on the ground. Lisette came to her moaning. They gave forth a Greek chorus of grief.

Mac glanced at Owen. What he saw seemed the most bizarre sight of his life. Owen Mackenzie was amused.

The idiot.

2

The music of the ocarina floated over the purpling, twilit prairie, emanating from the pubescent girl Mac beheld in love and awe, his daughter Christine. He watched her backlit against the western sky, her body rocking gently with the motion of the horse, her head tilted to the instrument, her face shadowed—and her soul flowing out through the ocarina into the lovely May evening, plaintive and wistful.

White people looked upon her cerebral palsy, spoken in her spastic gestures, as a repulsive physical affliction. At times like this, though, Mac thought the Cheyennes were right, that she was some kind of spiritual essence sent to live among mere mortals for a time.

He loved to look at her riding. On horseback she looked for once fluid and graceful, her hair waving clear to her waist, her reedy arms held close against her bosom, her fingers moving slowly on the ocarina. Now he could see

radiantly beyond her body, and its spasms, to her soul.
And she was exquisite.

The ocarina had turned out to be the best treat she'd
ever had. Smith had found it in a pawn shop in St. Louis
and wanted it for his sister. Mac bought it reluctantly. He
and Annemarie and Lisette had tried so many things for
Christine, had held so many bright, fragile hopes of
finding something she could do well and please herself.
And been so often disappointed.

But she had the musical gift, Mac had no doubt of that.
She could not speak plainly and made those crazed-
looking movements when she talked. But when Little One
played the clavichord, the small keyboard instrument Mac
had found on the Oregon Trail so many years before,
Christine sang. Tunefully. And if you allowed for certain
lapses, artfully. She loved singing.

So Mac had bought the ocarina. It was a clay pipe
shaped sort of like a sweet potato. That was its common
name, the pawnbroker said, and that's what it looked like,
a sweet potato with small finger holes.

Christine took to it wholeheartedly, and from the first
she seemed to spend her time on nothing else. She had
some difficulty maneuvering her fingers in rhythm, but
managed by playing slowly and sometimes covering the
holes with the first joints instead of the tips. Soon she was
playing songs she made up herself, slow tunes, sustained
and mournful. But she didn't look mournful when she
played a new one for the family. She looked exultant. And
the sight of her face, delicate and pretty, intensely focused
on making the lovely sounds, brought tears to her father's
eyes.

They came to the edge of camp, and Owen came out
and helped Christine down. He was always solicitous of
her, but Mac had a feeling he thought her affliction
amusing. Still, Mac was indulgent of anyone who was kind
to her. Owen had volunteered to take her over to see the
ancient Indian paintings on the rocks this evening, one of
her favorite treats, but Mac had done it himself. Now
Owen let her lean on his arm and get a seat by the fire,
with everyone else.

Mac crossed near the group and went to his blankets. He knew he should sit up and talk, but he wanted to preserve for a little while the special feeling Christine's music gave him. He heard Lisette laughing and knew Owen and Christine had sat next to her, and that Owen was flirting with his wife.

He stretched out on the blankets and tarpaulin and looked up at the first stars of the evening.

Christine let fly a peal of laughter, and Mac heard the terrier Punch talking to her in his bark-words. That dog delighted her.

Peddler took her into his confidence about Punch. He taught her the Yiddish words to say and let Christine give commands to make the dog stand on its hind legs, shake hands, or nod its head. The girl was thrilled and begged Mac for a terrier of her own to train.

Mac would have been thrilled for her had he not felt remote and withdrawn this entire trip. He knew he shouldn't be, but he couldn't help it. He was carrying the news of Strikes Foot's death to the Cheyenne people—Strikes Foot's people, and his own. He felt the burden.

The Cheyennes would be in a time of grief and anger anyway—so many had been killed at Sand Creek. And the young men would be off seeking victims among the whites. A time of bitterness.

So May, usually Mac's favorite month on the high plains of Montana Territory, was wasted on him. The grass was turning color, as usual, the cottonwoods were leafing, the willows were making their annual change from red to green—the whole world was becoming verdant. The wild-flowers were contributing their vivid colors. Even the prickly pear was getting into the show, speckling the prairie with its fuchsia blooms. And Mac didn't give a damn.

It was not only the burden of his duty. It was this odd company. Yes, his family, both wives, both sons, daughters. (Zach and Valdez were at home minding the fort.) Plus Peddler and that crazy dog. Plus Red Hand, still numb from what had happened. Plus Owen, who was strange in a way Mac sometimes thought insidious.

Mac would have said no to Owen—No, you can't go with me to visit my family's people, like one of us. But Mac owed him. When a man saves your life, and even more your sons' lives, and you're Mac Maclean, you don't act indifferent.

He rolled over in his blankets and wondered again why Owen really wanted to visit the Cheyennes. He'd been around the Cheyennes his entire life. Now he seemed just to want to hang out with the Maclean women. And he was a damned nuisance—all that flirting with Lisette.

Twice in the two decades of their marriage Little One had disappeared with another man for a few weeks, and then reappeared unrepentant, carrying on as though nothing had happened.

Mac admitted to himself that he was afraid Little One was now going to run off again, with Owen Mackenzie. Why not? he asked himself bitterly. Owen was attractive and virile.

Mac was still good-looking, he knew—slender, hard, with a nicely weathered face. And his boyish good looks had always attracted women. Yet Annemarie had borne a child by another man, and Lisette had run away twice. It galled him.

Annemarie clumped down next to him. He could feel her anger even through the earth, it seemed.

Mac knew what was bothering her. She had come to him last night beyond the firelight, where Owen was entertaining Christine and Felice and Lisette and had them all enthralled. She whispered harshly, "You've got to get rid of him."

Mac had been taken aback by his wife, as congenial a person as he'd ever known. He looked into her eyes, looking for a reason, but saw only anger and frustration. Well, she was always mysterious to him in some ways.

Besides, Annemarie sometimes seemed to look at Owen speculatively. He never seemed to pay her any mind.

I would do something about Owen, Mac told himself, except that decency, honor, and pride say I can't.

Annemarie was turned with her back to him. Mac

spooned up close behind her. Even through the blankets she felt good.

At bottom, he thought, I can't run Owen off because I'm jealous, and too proud to admit it openly.

The last sound he heard was Lisette giggling like a schoolgirl.

3

Peddler liked to talk as he walked. The miles of the Great Plains were yawning, were seemingly infinite. Since he mostly walked alone, he talked to Punch. Out of loneliness he even taught Punch to talk back, a simple act of ventriloquism. On command Punch would open and close his mouth and turn his head from side to side, as Peddler did the voice-throwing trick.

You might think that a man spending his years walking about a vast country alone—almost alone—would yearn for company. But as Peddler walked toward the Powder River country with the Maclean family, he often drifted back, or off to one side, and simply put one foot in front of the other ceaselessly, or talked with Punch. He was doing his mechanical walk when Smith rode over.

Peddler spoke to Punch in Yiddish. The little terrier immediately bounded from the cart to the rump of Smith's horse. The horse skittered a step or two, but was somewhat accustomed to the dog. Punch sometimes preferred the rhythmic motion of a horse to the bumping of the cart.

"What have you done these twenty years?"

"I have walked and looked."

"What have you seen that was beautiful?"

"Human beings walking in love."

"And terrible?"

"I was at Sand Creek. I saw children shot down, men and women hacked apart for souvenirs."

Smith rode in silence for a moment.

"Have you always peddled?"

"No, I traveled with a roving puppeteer once, and

another time with an animal trainer. They were enjoyable, but I prefer being alone."

Smith switched. "I know about the road of war, and about the good road of peace." Smith glanced sideways at Peddler shyly. "De Smet tells us about the Jesus road." Smith waited; Peddler let it sit. "We don't hear anything about the road of the Jews."

"The road of the Torah," said Peddler, nodding.

"Tell me about it," Smith said amiably.

Peddler knew Smith brought more to the question than idleness and boredom on a long ride—Smith had a good mind. He was an appealing young man with a sly way of pretending to be a country bumpkin, or ignorant redskin. But Peddler had given up such discussions.

"It is an ancient wisdom."

"Like the Jesus road."

"More ancient." Punch jumped down and trotted out in front of Peddler.

"Like the wisdom of my people, the Cheyennes."

"Yes." Peddler had noticed that Smith identified most readily with his mother's people, perhaps in defense.

"What would you say is good about the road of the Torah?"

Peddler gave it thought. "It speaks of men's responsibility to each other."

"And bad?"

Peddler glanced up at Smith with a quick smile. "Perhaps nothing."

Smith shrugged.

Peddler spoke to Punch. The terrier turned, walked on its hind legs, and said, "It's a superstition."

"Who doesn't see the world through superstition?" asked Smith rhetorically.

Men and animals walked in silence for a moment. Peddler was thinking Smith was a young man to be valued, valued highly.

"What do you like about the Cheyenne road?" asked Peddler.

"They live . . . beautifully. At peace with themselves."

"And you don't like?"

Smith didn't speak for a moment. "They don't understand. They think angels or some such make watches and
guns and cooking pots."

Peddler adjusted the thick cart strap around his middle.
"And you don't like what about the white road?"

"I can't believe how they cheat and fight and murder
each other. They live ugly." He sounded sure of that.

"And you like?"

Smith waited a long while and spoke as though reluctantly.
"They're becoming masters of the world. Because they
figure out how it works. Steamboats and trains. Talking
over the telegraph. Three-story buildings. Telescopes. Who
knows what next?"

On cue, Punch turned toward Smith and said, "*Wis-
senschaft.*"

"What?"

"Science," Peddler translated.

Smith considered. "And what does that mean, really?"

Here Peddler was at ease. "To abandon supernatural
ways of looking at the world. To put experience of the
world above all beliefs. To seek natural explanations of
what you see, not supernatural."

Smith looked interested but stumped. "What does all
that mean?"

"Give up 'The gods make water flow downhill.' Change
to 'It is the nature of water to flow downhill—why?' "

At length Smith nodded.

"I hate philosophy," growled Punch, and hopped back
on the cart.

"Thank you," said Smith, looking at Peddler thoughtfully. He touched his spurs and loped back toward his father.

Peddler thought a seed had been planted. Whether for a
noxious weed or a lovely flower he didn't know. But a
seed, still.

≈ 8 ≈

Shiny moon

The Powder River camp was in an uproar. Some Lakotas were camped just upstream, and the Lakotas and Cheyennes were on a rampage. The Lakota leader Red Cloud had declared the Powder River road absolutely closed—no white people could come up the route John Bozeman was promoting to Montana Territory, none at all. Red Cloud even declared open season on parties on the old emigrant road, the Oregon Trail. Small trading posts, haying operations, telegraph stations were being burned out, and the people killed. The Indians liked to fight the bluecoats, but they would take on any whites available.

This was the reply of the Cheyennes, Lakotas, and Arapahoes to the treachery and slaughter at Sand Creek.

It was a time of endless war councils. The Cheyenne people held councils with each other, all the northern peoples with the Lakotas and Arapahoes. Mac sat in on these talks, as he was expected to. Though Smith and Thomas could come and go, Mac was an older man, respected, something of an adviser. He heard the leaders of the warrior societies speak their hostility, and individual warriors dedicate themselves to vengeance. He grew numb hearing how justified was their anger. He could not naysay them. The Sand Creek action was inexcusable.

Peddler turned out to have lots to contribute to the talks. The Cheyennes wanted to hear first hand what Peddler had seen at Sand Creek. He had been asleep in the lodge of Black Kettle, the chief. The firing started at first light, when the people were just arising. Black Kettle

had hung an American flag in front of his lodge to show
the band's loyalty.

Peddler told the story simply, in a child-like Cheyenne
vocabulary, and more in sorrow than in anger. The soldiers
shot at women and children as much as at men from the
start, he said. Later the soldiers told him the order had
been, Take no prisoners. And some soldiers drove off the
horse herd right away. There was no time to defend the
village, really, only time for some people to scurry into the
slight cover of the creek and run away, while others gave
them a little protection with bows and arrows and guns.

Peddler himself was shot in the leg and could not flee.
He lay in the middle of the village and watched the
carnage. He estimated that seven or eight hundred slept
in that village, Cheyennes, Arapahoes, a few visiting
Lakotas, and a white trader and his family. Of those,
Peddler said sadly, about half died. Then the soldiers
burned the lodges and all the people's belongings, and
destroyed the horses that remained. For the rest of the
day the soldiers, who were not soldiers at all but short-
term volunteers from Denver City, prowled the grounds of
the camp like scavengers, mutilating bodies, even cutting
the breasts and genitals off women. But Peddler and two
other whites escaped with their lives. At the time Peddler
was sorry to live.

An investigation by the great white father condemned
the leader of the soldiers, John Chivington, but the U. S.
Army could not court-martial him because he had resigned
his commission.

As Peddler sat down, the Cheyennes burst into a murmur of hot anger. They would be glad to punish Chivington
themselves.

Chivington was said to be a king-sized preacher of fire
and brimstone. Mac tried to imagine a man of God, even a
warped one, who would create such an eruption of bloodlust.
He couldn't, but knew it was so.

So now it would be war. Blood and death, the fever-
madness of the human species.

At least the tribes were saying in thunder that the
Yellowstone country would still belong to the Indians, the

great river and all the rivers that fed it, the land given
them by the Laramie Treaty of 1851 for as long as the grass
shall grow. That meant Mac's life would stay the way he
wanted it, the way he loved it, for yet a while.

Mac was forty-six years old. He might get to be an old
man before things changed. His grandchildren might get
to see the Yellowstone region as it was when he first saw it
in '40, the loveliest, most pristine land in the world, its
high country magical with parks, geysers, hot springs, and
stupendous waterfalls, its plains the best buffalo country in
the world, and its lifeblood the river Mac loved.

Ninety-six are ye, lad, to be talking so memory-heavy?
Mac had gotten into the habit of teasing himself in Skinhead's
voice. You don't even got no grandkids yet.

If Zach succeeded with Felice, Mac might have some
soon. He was wishing Zach luck, and thought the young
giant would succeed when Owen left. Felice was a little
distracted by Owen, and his flirting.

But love was not the order of the day. War was.

Late that afternoon Mac stood with Peddler as a half
dozen young men came riding through camp, back from
the war. They rode ceremonially, at a stately pace, their
lances held forward, draped with scalps. Scalps not of a
uniform black, but of the varied yellows, reds, duns, and
mouse browns of the white race. The men stood and
watched admiringly, and the women raised ululations of
joy to the sacred sky that blessed those bloody deeds.

"Hatred," murmured Peddler, "rampant upon a field of
blood."

2

Mac was back in the talks, wearied and bored. It was
the third straight full day of talks he'd sat through. His
body was stale with sitting.

So he was pleased to see Felice come in and sit among
the women listeners. At first she'd wanted to hear a
council, which she'd never done. She said she didn't care

if it droned on endlessly. She understood the Cheyennes
let every man speak his piece, however long a piece it
was. She wanted to hear a full-bore war council. But
Felice was restless as a creek, and she lasted just an hour.

Now Mac watched her sit. Watching his daughter was a
lot more fun than listening to the speech. She was a
beautiful woman, no question, beautiful in the way her
mother was—sizable, robust, and bristling with energy.
She wasn't willowy, wan, and delicate in the way of many
white women, but vibrant, strong, primal.

Every night the taller young men stood outside the
lodge that used to belong to Strikes Foot, where Mac and
his women were living with Strikes Foot's women, and
waited in silence in their blankets for a word with her.
Every night Felice appeared not to notice.

Of course, they showed no interest in Christine. Not
because they found her palsy disgusting. Rather they
thought it a sign she was mysterious and holy, a woman set
apart by the gods. The band's men of vision came to speak
with her and listen carefully. Calling Eagle had now taken
Christine as her own special responsibility.

Calling Eagle. Mac should have known how it would
come out. Calling Eagle was coming to live at Yellowstone
House. Strikes Foot's other wives, Yellow Bird and Corn,
were going to the lodges of their sisters to be wives again.
But Calling Eagle was aged and went to the lodge of her
daughter—her daughter truly enough in the Cheyenne
way.

Mac regretted that having a would-be woman in his
home still wasn't comfortable for him.

Across the big council lodge Felice was staring at him.
No doubt about it, staring. That would be rude, unless . . .

Mac nodded.

Felice got up and went out. Now he realized she had
the long face that meant she was scared.

A moment later Mac followed.

Outside all she said was "Mother wants you."

3

"He said," Annemarie blubbered, "he said . . ."

She stopped and cried on her husband's shoulder. He waited, patient on the outside, on the inside jittery.

"He said," she went on, "Owen said, 'I'm going to disappear soon, and take something of yours with me.' With that goddamn wolf grin of his."

Mac couldn't remember the last time his first wife had cussed. He looked into her eyes and spoke hard, "Tell me what's going on."

She bawled.

After a moment she said, "I feel so awful." And bawled harder.

"Tell me," Mac insisted.

Between heaves of sobs, she said, "He's ignoring me, completely ignoring me. He's flirting with Lisette so much. He's . . ."

Mac waited.

"Even Felice," murmured Annemarie. "Even Felice."

Mac grabbed Annemarie by the shoulders and shook her. Even shaking her, he loved her. That's why he was scared. "Say it!" he barked.

Annemarie waited a little and composed herself. She waved Felice out of the lodge and waited until the footpads grew faint. Annemarie looked at her husband with what seemed dignity. "Owen Mackenzie is Felice's father. And he's laughing at all of us."

Then Mac knew that he had known all along. He sounded out Owen's threat in his head: "I'm going to disappear soon, and take something of yours with me."

"Where's Lisette?" he snapped at Annemarie.

"Out teaching Red Hand to fish," she said evenly. "That's what she said."

Mac headed for the river. Jittery had changed to panicked.

≈ 9 ≈

Mac never felt more of an idiot.

In a rage he had started to ride along the banks. In five minutes he was caught up in the flotsam, cutbanks, and thickets of high willows that tangle any Western river. A man could clamber through and over it, but not a horse. So he decided to ride right out in the river. A mile wide and an inch deep, they said of the Powder—why not?

He surged upstream into the current, once getting in belly-deep to his mare, the water not dampening his rage a bit.

Then he began to ask himself questions. Did he really want to come on them noisily? Maybe Owen Mackenzie would try to kill him. Maybe that was what Owen wanted all along. Who could tell what was on a man's mind after twenty years of waiting? Maybe *he* was jealous.

Or did Mac want to come on them quietly, covered by the swooshing sound of the river? And risk seeing her topped?

That was a picture he'd had in his mind plenty over the years, Lisette forked. Yes, that was what he wanted, to burn it into his mind. Then maybe he would do the killing.

He picketed the mare and headed upstream on foot. Every sound he made sounded to him like dynamite blasting.

He would give away six inches and more than fifty pounds and whale the damned Mackenzie in front of everyone, send him home to Fort Union on foot and broke, humiliated in the eyes of the Cheyenne nation. He saw himself smashing Mackenzie's beak nose flat against his face, all squishy.

Suddenly Mac felt that he was trapped. He had climbed into a jam of deadfall, left by high water in a big turn. He was spending more time going up and down than forward. He could see nothing.

He was thrashing about pointlessly.

Panic flushed up his gullet. Could he get out of all this jumble?

Sure, he told himself. With patience. Back the way you got into it.

And then you can get the mare and go back to camp and get the Dolland telescope and search from the high ground. Sensibly. Patiently.

2

Lisette was casting off a spit of sand into a little hole. Left-handed, naturally. The fellow with her was Red Hand. After being married to one for two decades, Mac had theories about left-handers. He contended you could pick them out of a group picture, because they were weird.

He lowered the Dolland. She would be saying something like, "You reach-cast *before* it gets to the eddy."

Sir George Gore, the touring Irish sportsman, had taught her this foolishness and given her that bamboo fly rod. Periodically over the last ten years she could be found in the smithy, using the vise to tie feathers on hooks.

Mac felt the harsh twist of anger ease in his belly, like a sigh.

3

"I thought you were gone again," he said to her.
Red Hand had agreed to take the mare back to camp.

The two were walking through the giant sagebrush, holding hands like kids.

"Mmm," she said helpfully.

"Were you tempted?"

She turned her head toward him with a little smile. "No."

"You were tempted twice before."

"That was more than ten years ago."

"It seemed very like you."

She shrugged. "My demons are quiet now."

"I acted like a young idiot," Mac moaned. "Crashing and thrashing about."

"I like that."

He looked sideways at her. She touched her head to the outside of his shoulder. He would never understand this tiny wife.

"I still feel like a pimple-faced idiot," he said.

"Good." Then she turned to him and slipped her arms around his back and tilted her head way back to be kissed. She got what she wanted.

She unbuttoned his shirt deliberately and took it off and spread it on the ground and pulled him down on it with her.

There in the shadow of the giant sagebrush they made love. It was warm and slow and deep and powerful, like equatorial tides.

Mac thought, this is what it feels like to be married. I like it.

4

They were still holding hands, and glowing, when they came into the circle of lodges.

They both saw Annemarie come running toward them through the litter of playing kids and yapping dogs. Then Annemarie stopped and walked, shambling, head down. And then broke into an awkward trot.

Mac and Lisette ran to her. Took her in their arms. She was blubbering again.

"He did it," she wailed. "The bastard did it."

Mac and Little One waited.

Annemarie looked at them and kissed each of them nervously on the cheek.

"Owen's gone. He took Smith and Thomas with him."

5

Hunk, the head of the fox society, explained simply and lightly that it was a war party like any other. Yellow Limb, a fox himself, had gotten it together. Blade—the Cheyennes' name for Owen—and Smith and Thomas had asked to go.

No, of course no one had mentioned it to Mac.

Hunk didn't need to explain that it was customary for young men to run off on their first war parties. Or to add that Smith and Thomas were nearly too old to be starting— they should have been initiated into a warrior society several years ago.

No, Hunk didn't know where they were going. Yellow Limb would never divulge his plans. Probably to the emigrant road, a big place. White people aplenty would be there. Mac's sons would fight, and if they were fortunate, get their first coups.

Hunk shrugged. Mac's questions, and his anxiety, were out of place. He should have been silently proud.

Mac couldn't tell his war comrade Hunk why he was afraid, couldn't say a man with a claim on his daughter had taken his sons. So Mac got up and left. Besides, he was a fool for being jealous after twenty years. Annemarie's fears were silly. Womanish.

But Mac might kill Owen Mackenzie. When he saw him. If he saw him.

My sons are gone, and there's nothing I can do.

He felt as though the anxiety would split him like a dropped melon, its juices and seeds pathetic in the dust.

He heard the mournful tune come across the camp. He

looked toward the lodge—Strikes Foot's lodge, now his own. Christine was sitting cross-legged in front, by the tripod that now held his medicine bundle, playing her ocarina.

The melody was one of her own, and one of his favorites. First she played a phrase in the low register, breathy and plaintive, and then the same bit up high, piping shrilly. Like a moan, and then a wail.

He knew what her notes meant. Come home. I'll help you.

Yes, his palsied daughter could help him, and would. She would sit by the evening fire, ask him to rub her reedlike limbs, and thank him over and over in a throaty voice, and by taking solace, give it.

Felice would help him, too—with her robust good humor she would tease him out of the doldrums. And his wives would help him. So would his mother-in-law Calling Eagle, from her store of ancient wisdom.

Mac crossed toward his tipi. He had a damnable collection of women in his life, intriguing and loving.

≈ 10 ≈

August, 1865, Time when the cherries are ripe

June and July in Powder River country were months of war and rumors of war. Red Cloud and his fighters put a dead halt to traffic on the Bozeman trail. Sometimes they stopped travel on the Oregon Trail as well. They raided. They looted. They remembered Sand Creek and acted as though they were honoring the Biblical injunction "an eye for an eye and a tooth for a tooth."

Westerners raised the eternal cry of people who are in over their heads: "Why doesn't the government do something?"

Now that the Civil War was over, the government did, more or less. It sent soldiers. But the soldiers had just fought a long and discouraging war. They wanted to be at home. They behaved as though they wanted to be at home. They were no match for the Cheyennes, Lakotas, and Arapahoes, who kept doing what they wanted—raiding, looting, burning, and killing.

Mac heard of all these doings at Yellowstone House, but he was far enough away to hear just reports of war and not the din of battle itself.

On the spring rise mackinaws full of gold chasers came downstream from Alder Gulch and Grasshopper Creek, plus the new diggings at Emigrant Gulch and Last Chance Gulch. Fortunately, Jim Sykes had brought supplies in from Benton in time.

Mac decided to stay home while Jim went to Fort Union to meet the June steamboat with the year's take and get more supplies. Mac was needed at home, he said. He needed to be where he could get news of the boys.

Annemarie and Little One told him he needed something more—days on the river. They reminded him of how
he loved that time on the river. They made him think of
mornings of motion, currents, eddies, ducks on the water,
rocking along under a sky as deep and wide and blue as
the mothering sea. They promised to send an express
when Smith and Thomas got back.

Mac went with Jim, a month late, in July.

The two passed up the opportunity to make the trip in a
mackinaw, with plenty of company, and went alone with
the bales of hides in a bullboat, now a craft that reminded
them of old times, buffalo skins stretched over a willow
framework, steered with poles. It would bear up under a
heavy load such as they had, and it would negotiate Wolf
Rapid, at the mouth of the Tongue River, just fine. Mac
remarked to Jim with satisfaction that for all the captains'
daring with steamboats, no captain had ventured far up
the Yellowstone. Wolf Rapid would stop whoever tried.

Floating, the two friends spoke of the future. Or rather
Mac spoke of it and Jim listened. Mac wasn't sure whether
Jim was listening to the words or just the melody of
complaint or only the sound of the wind and the river.
Sometimes, when Jim seemed particularly absorbed, Mac
kidded himself that Jim was listening for the sound of the
earth spinning on its axis.

Mac observed aloud that he could now make all the
money he wanted. What for, he wasn't sure. In three years
the white population of Montana Territory had expanded
from maybe a hundred to eighteen thousand, and they
were hollering for statehood. The governor didn't live in
Montana Territory anymore—he spent his time in Washington City lobbying for that almighty statehood.

Jim just sneered.

The entire Yellowstone country was ceded in perpetuity
to the Indians, Mac repeated. He wondered how perpetuity would stand up to a gold strike.

Jim pointed to two otters playing in the shallows, a rare
and charming sight.

Mac thought but did not speak of Owen Mackenzie and
Smith and Thomas. The subject was too painful.

Jim grabbed the fowling piece whenever he saw a goose. He always said goose flesh was the best taste on earth.

Mac reflected often that his friend did not speak of the future and seemed to give it no thought. But Mac couldn't help talking about it.

2

There was only one letter at Fort Union—from Robert Campbell. It stated simply and formally that Mac's Uncle Hugh had died the previous November, of influenza. It expressed sorrow and sympathy. It stated that Mac was Hugh's only heir, and that Campbell as executor would see to the sale of the house and store and the payment in cash to Mac's account. The extensive library would be shipped upriver unless Mac ordered otherwise. Then Campbell summarized the finances of Yellowstone House and wished Mac well for the coming year.

Mac was taken off guard by how melancholy that news made him.

There was also word of Smith and Thomas at the fort, word from the Cheyennes and Lakotas who drifted in to trade. The Maclean boys were making heroes of themselves. They were dauntless in battle. Smith was clever, Thomas wild and ferocious. They were acquiring reputations among the Cheyennes as soldiers.

That news gave Mac a catch in his throat. He felt half proud, half terrified.

But there was little word of Owen Mackenzie. When Mac asked after him, the Indians merely shrugged—they hadn't seen him. A bullwhacker recollected he was scouting for the Army somewhere. Couldn't think where for sure, though.

Mac made clomps in the dust as he went back into the fort with Jim. "That makes me feel some easier," said Mac. "I been having dreams, sinister dreams, about that Owen."

Jim nodded. "I wish you sounded easy."

Time when the cherries are ripe

Drewyer said, "You wanna get yourself a tobacco pouch?"

Thomas curled a smile toward him and shook his head no. Drewyer meant what the pretend soldiers were reported to have done at Sand Creek—cut off a scrotum here or a breast there and made containers for tobacco.

Drewyer was *too* crazy, but a real friend, the first Thomas had ever had.

Thomas looked down on the little group of pony soldiers, headed south. Probably to Platte Bridge Station, to tell the bosses the Army had gotten its ass kicked again and to ask for horses. They would be obliged to say how Colonel Meyer was bringing his cavalry outfit back to the fort, having sought Indians, seen sign everywhere but no redskins, gotten men picked off, and lost half the horses. So they were walking back, humiliated.

A funny story, pony soldiers afoot.

Thomas meant to see these soldiers didn't live to tell it.

He put the glass on them again. They were sitting around the cook fire. Lambert had gotten meat for them today, fresh antelope. They were eating and Thomas was hungry. Seemed to be always the way it was in life—whites eat and Injuns go hungry.

Thomas stuck his hand out to Drewyer for the flask. Light. A pint didn't stretch far. You had to judge fine to keep just a little edge on, which was the way Thomas liked it. One pint to share during the day, another in the evening. Nice flask. Engraved. German silver. Drewyer took it off a supply officer up at the Rosebud. Thomas wanted one like it. He swigged, deeper than his judgment said.

Oh, well, it wasn't long to dark. Then the two of them would move gently back to the horses, eat some jerked beef, which Thomas hated, and get a refill of the flask. And then move gently toward the soldier bivouac.

Thomas glassed it again. The camp was about half a mile to the east, across the sagebrush plains, on a trickle of a spring.

Glassing was safe. The sun was setting behind them, and Thomas kept the telescope in his shadow. Flat Jack jumped up and made some weird motions. Probably clowning. That was Flat Jack. Thomas wondered again why they called old Jacques Lambert "Flat Jack." The skinny mountain man was a friend of Thomas's father. Maybe Thomas would let him live.

But the bastard was scouting for the soldiers. Except for him, these pony soldiers wouldn't need killing. They'd die of getting lost or starving or going dry. Or better yet they'd drink alkali water and shit themselves to death.

Thomas snickered and handed the telescope back to Drewyer. Drewyer turned over and stared at the evening sky, then stuck his tongue out at it and made a farting noise. Thomas chuckled appreciatively.

They were just waiting for dark.

Drewyer was a breed, like Thomas. Frenchman. Dark. His people had been in the country practically before the Indians. Had a quick wit. He addressed all white men with some Mandan word Thomas didn't know that sounded like *mugrum*. "Mr. Mugrum," Drewyer would say politely to any white man at any fort, and then ask his question in comically broken English. Drewyer spoke not only English but French and Spanish and several Indian languages fluently. When Thomas asked what "mugrum" meant, Drewyer said with a sly smile, "tinkle balls."

And Drewyer had given Thomas his first dance with the mysterious lady, his first journey on the road to Xanadu, laudanum.

It was just opium dissolved in alcohol, commonly used on the frontier to relieve pain. The trick was in the amount. Conservative little sips made you pleasantly sleepy. Neither

Drewyer nor Thomas was a conservative person. Excessive amounts could have results that were, well, intriguing.

Of course, Drewyer explained, different people respond in different ways. Thomas responded like the lady's natural-born bridegroom. He saw things. Different things, always, but always fascinating. Once he saw a world of plants alone, surrounding lovely, gleaming lakes, hovered over by soft, violet clouds. The plants took the most outrageous shapes and sizes and colors and textures, huge bells of lurid green, trumpet flowers soft as silk and yellow as bananas, mushrooms as tall as giraffes and flamingo-pink, turquoise jack-in-the-pulpits, and black, velvety roses floating through the air.

Dancing with the lady was not just a journey of the mind. Sometimes Thomas had intense physical sensations, too. He would get light-headed or even faint. His face would flush hot. He would sweat violently. Or he would simply get incredibly excited, as though heart and lungs and brain and blood were all racing at triple speed. You danced with the lady body and soul.

Drewyer had lifted the first batch from a downed Army medic. Later the two of them cracked a miserable excuse for an Army doctor on the head and took more. This fellow had hypodermic needles. They learned to inject the opium in the form of morphine. Now little would perform like lots.

That was where the two of them left the other raiders behind, Smith included. Black Finger, the leader who imagined himself the boss, got stiff-necked about laudanum, or even booze. Smith himself acted kind of stiff-necked about the lady. Told Thomas and Drewyer they'd have to get crazy on their own time.

Smith didn't understand. Since Thomas started shedding blood—nothing commonplace, like taking a military objective or turning back an enemy, but drenching himself body and soul in human blood—he felt his feet on the path of beauty and understanding. It was not an understanding you could put into words.

Thomas believed that in the sun dance men reached such an understanding. Men pierced their flesh with skewers, blood ran down their backs and chests, they shuffled their feet to the eternal rhythm of the drum, they neither drank nor ate, and they focused their minds on the effigies in the center pole's crotch. And on the other side of those rituals of pain, of self-chastening, Thomas thought, they saw. They grasped the universe of blood, a comprehension beyond words, and moved in time with it.

Likewise Thomas, in the fever pitch of fighting, saw. And raised his voice in praise to the gods of bloodletting, moved into battle in the perfect rhythm of the world.

Those moments of battle were what he lived for. He only drank, or danced with the lady, when he could not sing his song of blood.

Drewyer understood. And felt no need to speak of what was manifest but unexplainable. That's why they were soulmates, and why they stayed clear of earthbound people such as Black Finger and Smith.

But there would be no lady tonight. Tonight was to be a moment of destiny. They would creep up on the camp under the cloak of darkness and commit murder. And take scalps. And Thomas would sever thumbs. He intended to make a necklace of thumbs from men he had killed with his own hands. In fact he already had enough. Thomas smiled to himself.

The sky at last light was a keen, bright turquoise with plush, dark-magenta clouds. Lady colors, Thomas thought. So Flat Jack hadn't moved camp at the last minute, to be tricky. The soldiers lay right there. Old Jack must be slipping.

Thomas touched Drewyer on the shoulder, and his friend nodded. The two dark young men slipped away.

2

Thomas could smell the dead campfire. His father had taught him that—you could smell lots more than you gave thought to. Now it meant to him that they were close, within maybe twenty yards, crouched here in the sage. Still on the rough plain, but within twenty yards of the

soft, verdant vegetation around the spring, and the soft,
vulnerable bellies of the white men.

Thomas heard Drewyer's slow, deep breathing beside
him. On these approaches Drewyer would breathe deep a
little and practically go into a trance. It was wonderful.

They had talked it over as they ate their miserable jerked
beef. They would ease close and take out the sentry. Drewyer's
arrow was the way for that. Then they'd slip all the way into
camp. They'd done it once before. Stood there among
sleeping men—and that time a woman with a small child—
silent and unsuspected, tense, careful, measured; and then
knowing they'd brought it off, relaxing, feeling the blood
flow, looking at each other, and wanting to whoop for joy.

And then they would let that energy explode in murderous deeds. Knife the sleeping bundles until someone,
somehow, made a sound, and then shoot and run if you
have to. They wouldn't spare Flat Jack. That was just a
way to spread your name as a killer and make it harder to
have the silent fun.

Now they stood up tall, behind giant sagebrush. Thomas
liked this, standing full open, utterly still, there for the
sentry to lay eyes on but not to see. Thomas was good at
this making like a tree, and Drewyer was amazing. Even
Thomas couldn't make out Drewyer half the time, though
close by and knowing where he was. Thomas knew that
he'd spot any sentry before the sentry spotted him. He
had a knife in his right hand, hawk handy in his left,
repeating pistol in his belt.

The coals of the fire were glowing but not bright enough
to help. In the light of the half moon, his eyes long
adjusted to the dark, Thomas could make out sleeping
figures, even the rocks they'd sat on to eat. Everything
but the sentry.

"That'll do 'er, boys," came Flat Jack's voice. Behind.
The voice made Thomas think of a reptile tongue, languidly
flicking out and getting the fly.

He heard weapons being cocked. Behind.

3

A smooth, thin layer of clouds lay flat in the east, and the sunrise tinted them the color of dirty syrup.

Flat Jack was eating beans cold. Thomas and Drewyer were tied together, back-to-back, lying on the ground near the fire. Jack was alone. Said he didn't need any help to guard scum. The soldiers, he said, should go out and find the ponies and the belongings. He didn't offer Thomas and Drewyer any beans. No need to feed prisoners, he said, if you were going to kill them.

Thomas was afraid. Abjectly afraid. Drewyer's back and arms seemed brittle and angry behind him. Thomas's body felt slack to himself, like noodles.

Flat Jack was talking while he ate. Flat Jack always talked in his twangy way, like some wheezing machine that worked endlessly and noisily. He'd already spent half an hour hee-hawing about how he'd set Thomas and Drewyer up, sucked them right into the trap. Knew where they was all along, he claimed. Otherwise he would have moved camp at last light. Easy as fooling prairie chickens.

"Boys killed all of them in the Rikers party, heh? Same way. Sneak up in the dark. Redheaded little girl, too. Got that scalp? Bet you do."

Thomas did.

"Tale is, it was you at the telegraph station. The boy described you. Raped his mother, did you?" Flat Jack shook his head, not deliberately like a person, but frenetically like a dog. "Bad business.

"And this child heard it was you over to Platte Bridge Station. Hit that doctor over the head, liked to killed him. You boys are getting yourselves a reputation. We might just put an end to that reputation today. Afore you get legendary.

"Old Mac's a good beaver. You oughtn't to turn out as rotten as you did, Thomas."

"What you plan to do, old man," answered Drewyer, "talk us to death?"

Jack fell silent for a moment, and his features turned somber. Then he drawled it out. "When Sergeant Gray sees what scalps is in your possibles, I imagine he'll see fit to forget the rules about prisoners. And who'd ever know? Except the buzzards and the coyotes."

4

They were still tied back-to-back, but standing now. Three soldiers sat around them, trying to look casual but jumpy as bridegrooms. Sergeant Gray and Flat Jack stood erect next to the two prisoners, handguns at their sides. Sergeant Gray meant to make a proper execution of it, being a man who did things properly. He had an erect military bearing—boots, belt, and weapons shining.

"Who'd have thought it would be a fancy dresser?" snarled Drewyer.

Thomas wanted to yell at Drewyer to shut up, but he said nothing. Thomas didn't give a damn for Drewyer's act of indifference to the muzzle of a gun. But he was right about Gray. The sergeant laid out their scalps, fourteen between them, and their vials of morphine and hypodermic needles. Gray turned mottled above the neck of his uniform shirt, all liver-colored and gray. He actually lectured Thomas and Drewyer about addiction to drugs before standing them up to shoot them.

Thomas had begged for his life. He had appealed to the friendship between his father and Flat Jack. He had cowered. He had cringed. He had blubbered. He had shamed himself. He was silent now, roped up tight against Drewyer, only because he was worn-out with it.

Sergeant Gray said something sharply. Wearing an odd half-smile, two steps off, Flat Jack raised the pistol toward Thomas's head. Without looking, Thomas knew Gray was holding on Drewyer's head. Gray spoke again—words were no longer making sense to Thomas, were only random chirps in the roar inside his head. He saw Flat Jack's thumb cock the pistol.

Sergeant Gray made three sharp sounds in cadence.
Thomas's world ended in an explosion.

5

"He shit his pants," snickered Flat Jack. Meticulous
Sergeant Gray turned away, nose wrinkled.

Thomas felt the next slap sting. As though separately, he
felt his head and neck twist violently. Slowly he swam
upward toward the world.

Flat Jack slapped him again, brutally.

Thomas opened his eyes. Flat Jack was smirking at him.

"Your *compañero* is dead," Jack said. "You've got a little
cut where the wadding hit."

Thomas was swamped in incomprehension. Flat Jack
grabbed his head and turned it sideways.

At first Thomas saw random color and shape. Then color
and shape gathered meaning. Drewyer lay there, his head
half blown away. Thomas rolled to his knees and vomited.

Cut by wadding, Jack said. That meant he put in powder
and patch but no ball. Explosion without missive. He took
his hat off—bloody where the wadding went through.

"We're just gonna leave him on the ground," said Jim.
"He deserves it."

"Why?" asked Thomas. The question sat there between
the men, eternal as the wind, ultimate as the sun. No one
knew what it meant, and everyone knew.

Jack took Thomas's head and pushed it sideways. There
stood Smith, his face set and grim.

"I don't get it," Thomas said to Smith.

"I was tracking you. When they found your horses, they
found me."

"Oh."

"I'm taking you to Yellowstone House."

"I ain't going."

"Yeah," said Smith, "you are."

≈ **12** ≈

On that journey home—at least Smith called it home—
Thomas Jefferson Maclean came to understand that his
brother was a traitor. And his father.

Smith and Thomas first rode to Platte Bridge Station to
meet Peddler. Peddler was heading north into Powder
River country to trade with the Sioux, pulling his cart,
and Smith wanted to escort him. Smith thought Peddler
was mad to be traveling alone. It made no difference to
him that the old Jew never seemed to have a speck of
trouble.

Smith made no pretense of keeping Thomas prisoner. It
felt too ridiculous. He just wanted to get Thomas home,
and to talk about his new infatuation. He'd gotten his head
turned by the white man's science.

Smith spoke of an elementary science demonstration he
and Thomas had seen at school in St. Louis. The teacher
had put an acid and a base together in solution and grown
beautiful blue crystals of copper sulfate. He'd even done
the same thing with spirits of niter—grown crystals as if by
magic, and then ground them into gunpowder.

Traveling north along the Powder River, Smith told
Peddler and Thomas how Doc Lang back at Fort Laramie
amazed him. Smith had always thought of the body kind
of, well, what Doc Lang called mystically. If you got a
pain, you cured it with a prayer or a dance. Doc had
shown him the white man's way of seeing the body. The
first amazer was how smallpox vaccination worked—you
injected a person with cowpox virus and he became immune. Hypodermic needles themselves were a revelation

258

to Smith. How Doc laughed, Smith remembered, when Smith realized the blood goes from the heart all over the body and back. Ether, which put men to sleep for surgeries, seemed a miracle, too, but a sort of natural miracle, unlike the Cheyennes' miracles.

Smith showed a book he'd bought from Doc, a primer called *The Methodology of Natural Science* by Professor Alban Jones. Peddler looked the book over as he walked, expressing surprise that the doctor would give up such a volume. Smith replied that he was, after all, the son of a trader.

Thomas was silently getting mad. The white men wanted the Indian's land. Now, through books, they meant to conquer his mind. They already had Smith's mind, Thomas saw. And then he really saw: Thomas's father, Mac Maclean, was unconsciously the whites' missionary, the advance guard of the invasion.

Smith self-consciously showed Peddler and Thomas his scar from a cutdown Doc had done. Doc evidently was a little crazy. He'd done a dissection on a soldier's corpse for Smith to see—how muscle moved bone, how the heart pumped to the lungs and out through the major arteries, where the major organs were, and their functions. When Smith asked if there was a way to see a living artery working, Doc said, "Sure. Yours."

So Doc did a cutdown. Grinning, he scalpeled back a flap of Smith's skin over the sizable artery on the inside of the elbow. Smith could see the red vessel pulsating, his lifeblood itself. It felt like beholding the inner workings of the universe.

Smith had said to Doc, "This, this whatever it is, science, is the most powerful thing in the world." He touched his own artery gingerly with a forefinger.

Thomas interrupted to ask if Smith was still interested in participating in the sun dance with Thomas next summer. Smith just shrugged.

Exactly, thought Thomas. He saw his brother surrendering, raising the flag of the white man's learning over a mind that should have been Cheyenne. Cheyenne men were first of all warriors.

"You're gonna go back to school in St. Louis, ain't you?" said Thomas.

Smith looked at him and slowly nodded.

This is where it takes us, thought Thomas. Mac Maclean's reading books in the winter. It bleaches our souls white.

2

Three nights later Thomas made his move. It was his watch, Smith and Peddler asleep. First he called the little white terrier over. Punch came from Peddler's blankets willingly—Thomas had established the habit of feeding him scraps. The dog couldn't be allowed to make a noise.

Thomas picked Punch up in one hand and held him in his lap. He dangled a long strip of meat in front of the dog's lips. Punch snapped it up and chomped greedily. Then Thomas gently enclosed his muzzle, held it shut, and wrapped the dog in a blanket. With a warrior's calm he slid the knife into the soft underbelly hard and deep.

The slight squeal was muffled in the wool. Thomas waited three or four full minutes. Neither sleeper stirred.

Then Thomas started walking around camp. That wasn't unusual for the guard—neither Smith nor Peddler would think anything of it. He moved softly out to the picketed horses. Silently Thomas saddled his pony. Silently he saddled Smith's horse. Then Thomas slipped into the saddle and loped off, riding his own gelding and leading Smith's mare.

Both Smith and Peddler woke up to the dull thump of receding hoofbeats.

Smith eased out to where the horses had been picketed. They were gone. The guard was gone.

Peddler immediately missed Punch—the little dog should have been sleeping at Peddler's head. He saw a white blur by the rock where Thomas had sat on lookout. Peddler hurried over, panicky. He picked up Punch and felt the warm, sticky blood. The dog was still warm and quivering slightly. On the underside Punch gaped red.

Peddler looked up at the infinite stars. "That's Thomas, I guess," whispered Peddler. Tears flowed. "That's Thomas."

Smith came walking back. "Now we're both on foot," he said.

Punch gave a quiver, and another, and was still.

≈ **13** ≈

Mac tossed water from the gourd and drew the steam that roiled up from the hot rocks deep into his lungs. It seared him, as always. It brought him peace, as always.

He switched himself lightly with sage branches—arms, shoulders, back, face. And then, instead of raising a prayer, he began to ruminate, to remember, to dream.

Mac treasured his sweat baths here on the little island in his beloved river. This island was his cathedral, his place of solace and renewal, and the sweat bath his sacrament.

He preferred to sweat alone. Sometimes he took Jim Sykes. Occasionally his sons. Last week, when they got back from the Powder River country without Thomas, he brought Smith and Peddler. Never had he brought a woman here, even his wives and daughters. This evening he was bathing entirely alone. He did not want to think, exactly. He wanted to meditate. Perhaps then his worries about Thomas would ease, and the world would again seem bearable.

Mac threw more water onto the rocks and luxuriated in the intense rising heat.

He had long since developed his own ritual for the sweat, adapted from all the tribal customs, or none. During this time of the first and most intense heat, he simply maintained silence, as yet trapped mentally in the pain of the heat. Later he might stay silent, or he might speak or sing, but he would be free of the bodily oppression. If he sang, he would wander among old songs of St. Louis rivermen from his childhood.

Adieu to St. Louis, I bid you adieu;
Likewise to the French and the mersquiters too,
For of all other nations I do you disdain,
I'll go back to Kentucky and try her again.

If he spoke, he might quote from his namesake, Bobby
Burns.

> *To see her is to love her,*
> *And love but her forever;*
> *For nature made her what she is*
> *And ne'er made sic anither!*

Or even one of Burns's ribald verses.

> *Then give the lass a fairin', lad,*
> *O give the lass her fairin',*
> *And she'll give you a hairy thing,*
> *And of it be not sparin'.*
> *But lay her o'er among the creels,*
> *And bar the door with both your heels,*
> *The more she bangs the less she squeals,*
> *And hey for houghmagandie.*

Mac loved the plain Scots word *houghmagandie*. In his
family it was the expression for bedroom doings because it
just sounded like so much fun.

It was good that he took these sweats out of earshot. A
listener might get the impression they weren't sacramental
at all.

Between rounds of the sweat, he would first put more
hot rocks in the lodge. Then he would step naked into the
river and dip his body in cool liquid. Sometimes, in
winter, in very cold liquid. And then return chilled to the
blasting heat of the sweat lodge.

On this evening like the others Mac finished the first
round, did his chores with the rocks, and eased down the
bank at the head of the island into the river. He stood
thigh-deep in the moving water, feet solid in the good
bottom mud of the Yellowstone. He stretched his arms,

leaned his head back to look at the first star, and then on
impulse threw himself backward into the river, to get wet
all over quickly, without thinking.

The bullet thwacked hot past his moving nose.

Mac jerked in breath and nearly got a lungful of river.
He flipped facedown in the shallow water and started
swimming toward the far side of the island.

This time he heard nothing, but he felt a violent slap on
his right buttock. Plunging into deeper water outside the
island, he headed down. The current hit him and nearly
turned him over. He made what he hoped was a half circle
downstream. Then he kicked hard toward the invisible
island. His hands found a dead branch, and he pulled
himself to the surface. The branch broke off, and he was
flailing in the river again. This time he got a willow
bush.

Mac stood up in the shallows and looked toward the
bank, where an assassin waited with a rifle. A repeating
rifle, from the sound of it the cavalry's Henry .44. Bastard.

Mac groped his ass. Plenty of blood. He was damn
well shot. But he wouldn't die from that, at least not
tonight.

He considered. It would be dark in half an hour. But if
Mac waited here, the assassin might come down to finish
the job. Being naked made you feel helpless as a hatched
chick. He did have a choice.

Mac had spent twenty-five years doing what needed to
be done, when it needed to be done, without inner or
outer protest. He did it now. He slipped into the strong
current of the Yellowstone, head low, and started swimming downstream like a porpoise, up and down, snatching
a breath, then gliding under.

Ears underwater, he heard no more shots.

Mother River, he thought, take me home.

Yellowstone House was half a mile downstream.

I can scramble back to my family naked and bleeding in
the dark. Mother River, take me home.

2

Tribes have distinctive styles of cutting and stitching moccasins. Even individual makers do. Sometimes, if you can get a print clear enough, you can pinpoint the woman who made the moccasin.

The print in the dust, a fine, full print, was as familiar to Mac as the buttons on his clothes. The style was Arapahoe, the style of Lucy, who had delivered Felice twenty-one years ago at Fort Platte. The only woman within five hundred miles who cut moccasins like that was Lisette. And Little One made moccasins only for her men—she hated making them and did it only when Annemarie couldn't.

Mac and Smith looked at each other over the print in the dawn light. Jim Sykes eyed Mac. Two of Lisette's men were standing over the print now. The third had made it. Thomas.

Thomas had even turned it into a signature—he'd brushed away all the little marks surrounding the print. And evidently gone to some trouble to leave a nice, unmistakable version, heel to toe.

Thomas's other signature was where they were. Mac, Smith, and Jim were standing on Mac's personal sentinel rock, where he'd come weak and starving twenty-two years ago, then had mounted, meditated, and decided to build a trading post. Where he'd first seen the island. The sentinel rock was a place awkward to climb, and useless. Except to overlook the island and get a clear shot at the man who did his sweat baths there. If you knew the man and his habits.

Mac shifted into a position more comfortable for his tail. He stared out at the river. He couldn't have said what he was thinking. Maybe he wasn't thinking anything—maybe he was just rising and falling on waves of feeling, in the tidal current of half-conscious memory. The child who had taken his first steps holding Mac's finger. Who he'd taught

to swim holding his skinny body in the Yellowstone.
Who'd been jealous of the company of his dad and sometimes barked at his mothers and his brother and sisters to
leave them alone together. His son.

"A warning," said Smith. "Maybe he didn't want to hit
you."

Mac's heart lifted—just a calling card, a declaration of
hostilities? But his head said no. "No," he said softly. "I'm
shot."

"Why didn't he come to the fort?" put in Jim. Mac gave
him an upward look.

Yes. Thomas had chosen a personal place, but it gave
him a long shot and an awkward downward angle. Shooting sharply down, you usually shot high. Thomas could
have done otherwise. Thomas could have come straight
into their home. He could have extended a hand to his
father and let the hand turn out to be full of pistol. At
point-blank range.

"It's the drug talking," said Smith.

Mac nodded. "The drug's been talking way too much."

Three days after Thomas had gotten away from Smith,
the mixed-blood family at the mouth of the Tongue had
been burned out and nearly wiped out. The moccasin
telegraph said Thomas Jefferson Maclean did it.

Nevertheless, Thomas hadn't come in close. That meant
something. He couldn't face Mac. Or at least not face his
family. For some reason he felt murderous toward his
father, but maybe he couldn't quite own up to what he was
doing. Except at a long, impersonal distance.

So in a confrontation, Thomas might hesitate.

Mac coughed, a sound that in other circumstances
might have been a little laugh. He tried to stand up stiffly
but dropped back into a one-legged squat. His ass was
going to hurt like hell in the saddle.

Thomas was probably uncertain and uncommitted. That
was good to know.

A flash flood of fright ran through Mac's body. Are you
thinking, man, of whether you can shoot your son in a
face-off, or whether he'll shoot you?

Self-disgust belched up Mac's throat, burning.

He looked at his other son. "Let's go," said Mac. "We're half a day behind, and we gotta move easy." Because, both of them knew, Thomas would watch his back trail. And maybe dry-gulch his old friend, his brother, or his father.

"I don't think he means it," said Smith.

"When a wasp tries to sting you," said Mac, "you don't ask what it means."

Jim gave Mac a hand, and this time he made it to his feet.

3

But Mac couldn't ride. His wound screamed pain on every step of the horse. It bled like a creek. It got raw and angry-looking. Mac was so determined to go that he stayed in the saddle a couple of hours before he turned around. Then he walked back to Yellowstone House. Leading his horse around back, where the riding horses were kept, he felt old, tired, and defeated.

Before he got past the smithy, Annemarie came running up and grabbed Mac's hand. Good, Mac wanted to sit with her and Lisette and be still and not think about their son. But she was all stiff and agitated.

Then he saw, standing by the big fur press in the center of the courtyard, Owen Mackenzie.

Mac deliberately shot a look of contempt at Mackenzie, but the big breed was immune. Seeing Mac's attitude, he was amused. "Have a look, Maclean," he said with a curling smile. He handed Mac an official-looking piece of paper.

"Read it out loud, Maclean, for those who ain't lettered."

Annemarie was almost breaking Mac's hand. He looked into her face. She'd read it.

It was a bounty on Thomas—also Drewyer and several Cheyennes—issued by the Department of the Army. It cited the assault on the Army doctor for his drugs. It cited the ambush of the Warren brothers and their companions, civilians who grew hay for the Army. It cited the murders of the Rikers. It cited the burning of the telegraph station

at Julesburg, the killing of the stationmaster, and the
cutting of the telegraph line.

The bounty was five hundred dollars each on Thomas
and Drewyer, one hundred on each of the Cheyennes.

"At least Thomas got top dollar," said Owen.

Mac read it again. The Army wanted them dead or
alive. The order was signed by a General Ryan, all the way
to Omaha. The only way Mac could get it undone would
be to get to Ryan.

Owen waited grandly for Mac to finish reading through
a second time. "He's headed for the firing squad, Maclean,"
said Owen. Annemarie felt panicky next to him.

Mac dropped the warrant in the dirt and ground it
under his bootheel.

"He's a real bad un, Maclean. To take a shot at his
father."

So Owen had found out.

"If you're his father."

Mac freed himself from Annemarie. "No," she squeezed
out. He held on carefully, took a breath or two, and
calmed himself. He didn't care that much about giving
away the pounds, but the damn wound would make him
slow, and he needed to be functional right now. He had a
job to do.

Mac heard a spurt and looked sharp at the kid sitting by
the fur press. The kid was lighting a cigar, and the flame
illuminated his misshapen face, flat-nosed and bug-eyed.
A black bowler hat made it look ridiculous.

With a sardonic eye the kid watched Mac looking at
him. He got up and walked over. Now Mac realized: It
was the face of a kid who killed small animals for fun,
grown into a near-man who kills human animals. Annemarie
was twisting Mac's finger.

"Mac Maclean," said Owen, "this here is Lonnie Chapman. My fight-hand man." Owen stopped and laughed at
himself. "Maybe 'fight-hand' is right. The kid can shoot."

Chapman wrinkled his nose. Mac ignored his extended
hand. Owen repeated pointedly, "Lonnie Chapman, my
right-hand man. Him and me and you are gonna get

Thomas and Drewyer." Mac reached and shook the hand.
No sense in provoking a mad dog.

"Drewyer's dead." He told them how and where.

"Let's go get him," said the Chapman kid.

Owen said, "It's been three weeks. He's picked clean."

"I bet they left his clothes and gear. That'll be enough
for the Army."

Owen shrugged. "The other one's more interesting."

"Some profession you two have," put in Mac.

"It's a living," said Owen with a fierce grin. "A good
one. Course it's too wild to be taking women along.
Except on a temporary basis."

He regarded Mac with amusement. "Maclean, we got a
deal for you. You come with us, help us bring him in, and
we'll bring him in alive. Otherwise we bring him in dead.
Makes no difference to us."

"You bastard," said Mac.

4

Mac asked Peddler to go to Virginia City fast on horseback to see Meagher, the acting governor. Maybe if Meagher
would use the influence of the governor's office, the Army
would quash this damned bounty. Whether it would be in
time, Mac had no idea. Peddler would need five days to
get to the territorial capital, punishing Mac's horses all the
way. He'd need some time to talk to Meagher, if the
damned bureaucrat was where he belonged. Then he
could send a message to Salt Lake by stagecoach, just
three days, a day-and-night, hell-for-leather trip. Salt Lake
was the nearest telegraph to Virginia City. Mac might have
word from General Ryan in less than two weeks, damned
good time.

Mac thought he could keep Owen and Chapman away
from Thomas for a while. With luck, Jim and Smith would
find Thomas first anyway. Or if the bounty hunters found
Thomas, Mac could keep him alive till they got to a
fort.

He got Owen to delay one day for the sake of his tail wound—Mac had to endure a close and mocking examination to get the leeway. He spent the evening alone with his wives, in the simple, reassuring ritual of a meal. He spent the night holding them close, Annemarie tense and hard, Little One weeping softly. In the morning he kissed them good-bye and set out with the two bounty hunters to hunt down his son. He went, by necessity, lying on a litter dragged by a horse. It was the most humiliating experience of his life.

≈ **14** ≈

Bumping along on some damned litter, out on the Great Plains but unable to see beyond the backside of a horse, his ass hollering pain at him, accompanying a man who meant to kill his son—all that made things come wonderfully clear to Mac Maclean. Mac hated Owen.

Probably Owen was counting on Mac to act indecisive at the crucial moment. Owen was going to be surprised.

Mac enjoyed mulling on how surprised Owen was going to be. He mulled on it all day, mulled on it in the hours before dawn while he was on watch. He was enjoying it so much he almost didn't pay attention to the coyote calling out in the sagebrush. Yip-yip, yip-yip-yo-o-owl. Yip-yip, yip-yip yo-o-owl.

Mac remembered a summer twenty-two years before, on the Yellowstone River. Three *compadres* in flight from the Blackfeet came splashing down Sweet Grass Creek into the Yellowstone. In the big river they were obliged to swim, held in the grip of the mighty and mysterious current. They swam down the right bank and found a rock chimney where they could pull themselves out. And Jim Sykes raised his marvelous, musical coyote call in celebration— hadn't they escaped the Blackfeet? Mac had answered in coyote talk. And his friends whooped and hollered and begged him not to ever use his coyote call —they said he sounded like a bowel-blocked buffalo.

So now Jim Sykes was checking his back trail. He and Smith knew they were being tracked. And who the trackers were. Very satisfying.

271

It was not long before first light. Mac decided to risk it. He sang out loudly like a coyote.

"What the hell?" snapped Owen, fully awake in an instant. The kid was sitting up with his gun in his hand. The kid was way too quick with that gun. He even practiced how fast he could get it out of the holster.

Mac turned toward Owen and repeated the call once more. After all these years, he still probably sounded bad, but surely not like a bowel-blocked buffalo. Mac kind of liked his coyote call.

"What are you doing?" snapped Owen.

"Time to get up," Mac said.

"What the hell are you doing?" Owen barked again.

"Calling that coyote in for fun," said Mac. "Making him think I'm gonna bang him. And waking you up."

"You ass," said Owen. The kid was still all too ready with the gun.

Mac stirred himself and started making the fire. "Coffee's coming."

Jim called once more, a thank-you note.

2

On the third day Mac was able to ride awhile, and on the fourth all day. He had applied Calling Eagle's poultice each morning and night, the wound looked less angry, and the saddle hurt less. He'd never been so grateful to be astride. The litter bounced uncomfortably. It kept him in the dust of the horses. Worse, he couldn't see.

Owen spotted where Thomas had left the main trail and headed toward the Greasy Grass, or the Little Big Horn, as the whites called it. And Smith and Jim on his trail. The Chapman kid interpreted the signs easily, maybe half a dozen horses headed south in the last day. Where the track crossed a little creek, he read it out thoroughly. Six horses, four of them shod, those moving fast. That fit. Jim and Smith were riding shod horses and leading others. Thomas was moving slowly at night on the Indian ponies, without shoes, and the trackers were moving after him quickly.

Mac wondered what Owen had in mind. Even if they never caught up with Thomas, Mac meant to kill Owen.

Mac was comfortable in his mind about Thomas, or as comfortable as he could be. Jim would not lead Owen up on Thomas. Jim would arrange some sort of deception first.

The question was, where was Thomas headed? To join the Cheyennes on the Greasy Grass, or maybe on the Tongue? That would be good. The Cheyennes would protect Thomas from bounty hunters, and he would have no access to the drug—things should improve.

Or would Thomas circle back to Yellowstone House, for another attempt at patricide? How much laudanum, or even morphine, did he have? What was in his heart?

You raised a lad from child to man, and you didn't know what was in his heart.

3

"The child is headed back to strike his pappy," said Owen, grinning like an ogre.

They were standing over a nameless cut that crossed the trail. It bore a trickle of water now. Most of the summer and fall it would be dry. A rain in the mountains had given it this tiny flow, much of that standing in puddles.

Thomas had done well, but Jim and Smith had spotted it and left their tracks for Owen to behold.

Thomas had ridden past the tiny stream twenty yards, left the trail on some rocky ground, dismounted to lighten his horse's prints, and led his animals along some grass back to the cut. Then he'd ridden in the water back toward the Yellowstone. Maybe the water had been moving better yesterday. Now it was mostly standing, and Thomas's tracks were visible.

What Mac couldn't read from a track was, which way would his tracks go on the main trail by the river?

Downstream, toward Powder River country or Fort Union? Or upstream, toward Yellowstone House? And when he got to Yellowstone House, would he come inside for dinner? Or watch the fort through the V of his sights? Sleep in the room that was his since childhood? Or murder his father?

$\approx$ **15** $\approx$

Thomas Jefferson Maclean lay atop a hogback. He was
watching three men make their camp and their dinner half
a mile to the north, on the right bank of the Yellowstone.
In the old word game the words for them were the Jerk,
the Kid, and the Traitor. He was watching them with the
Traitor's fancy Dolland telescope. Which was satisfying.

He fished the German silver flask out of his shooting
pouch and took a deep swig.

Thomas wondered who the Kid was. In fact there was a
lot here he didn't understand. He'd circled to watch his
back trail and spotted two groups of men and horses
following his tracks toward the river. Smith and Sykes he
could identify just from the way they sat in their saddles.
The three behind he didn't even have an idea about, at
first. Then he identified the Traitor, sitting his saddle
awkwardly, like something was wrong, plus the Jerk and
the Kid. He assumed the two outfits were together, but
then they camped apart. Did they even know about each
other? Were the Jerk, the Kid, and the Traitor following
Smith and Sykes? And Smith and Sykes following himself,
Thomas Jefferson Maclean? Except that he had them
spotted, and they didn't know where he was? The word for
this foolishness was "funny."

It would stop being funny tonight when he took care of
a job. They thought they were the pursuers, but they
were wrong.

The joker in the deck here was the Jerk, Owen goddamn Mackenzie. Thomas and Smith had had some good
times with the Jerk. He liked to ride hard, drink hard, and

275

fight hard. But he didn't care whom he fought for. In fact, he proclaimed grandly that he usually fought for the white man, because the white man paid cash. So after a couple of weeks with the Cheyenne and Lakota raiders, where he had taken Thomas and Smith, the Jerk went off to get a scouting job with the Army. Chuckling, he said, at the grave faces on both sides. Jerk.

Still, the Jerk believed Thomas was his friend, and that would help when it came time to do the job.

Maybe the Jerk was here because the Traitor hired him. Cash is cash, ain't it? The Traitor probably figured Smith and Sykes would be sentimental fools and just warn Thomas to get clear of the country. The Traitor wanted to get his hands on Thomas.

Thomas nursed from the flask again. He was keeping just right, just a little afloat. Later, when the time came, he would lift himself right up on the wave and come crashing down on the Traitor. Probably the Jerk would congratulate Thomas. The Jerk didn't give a damn who lived and who died. He always just chuckled. But you'd have to be careful of the Kid. Probably a spear-carrier for the Jerk, but you never knew.

Thomas had made up his mind to kill the Traitor close up, if possible face-to-face. He'd seen it over and over in his head the last month, to martial music. He'd fronted the bastard and humiliated him. More than a week ago he'd gone ahead in fantasy and struck the ultimate blow—raised his sights and blown the Traitor to kingdom come. He died as easy and ugly as any man. And it had felt fine to Thomas. Grand.

This was the gift of the drug—this ability to perceive the way of the warrior. To imagine great deeds, to envision them clearly, and then make them real. A week ago he'd run out of the drug, but he had its gift in his heart and mind. And he would get more soon and celebrate tonight's achievement.

He would approach from the river. At this point, the inside edge of a big bend, the current was against the far bank, and the near side was slack and shallow. The bank was thick with willows, which would give him protection. The swoosh of the river would cover any sound.

The Traitor so worshiped the Yellowstone, the great brown god, he called it. He so-called renewed himself in the Yellowstone. Wagh! When the sun went down, his death was going to come from the Yellowstone.

≈ **16** ≈

Mac was thinking of Lisette. She would go after this fish
more methodically. She would watch it feed, observe the
little bugs it was sipping from the surface, search her
tackle box for something that looked like those, and match
with her artificial fly. She would also watch the fish's
feeding rhythm, the pattern of its wait, rise, and return to
position, and get her fly there at the time of rise. And she
would probably catch the fish.

Mac didn't have the finickiness for any of that. He'd
borrowed this rig from Owen, to have something to get
out of camp for an hour, the last hour before full dark. He
caught six or eight grasshoppers. He was standing knee-
deep in the shallows and casting the hoppers one by one
upstream of the fish and letting the slight current drift the
bug into range. The fish was ignoring the grasshoppers
completely. Mac probably wouldn't catch the fish. He
would quit when he ran out of hoppers. He didn't care
how dark it got—he would pretend to fish. Anything was
better than having to sit beside Owen and the Chapman
kid.

Fifty yards away the two bounty hunters were sitting by
a big fire, a fine beacon to go home by. They hardly ever
spoke and seemed to communicate with glances. They
seemed always watchful, always alert. Predators. They
were superb trackers, skilled fighters, easy, natural killers.
For them life was killing, and everything else was waiting
to kill.

Mac lifted the line off the water, brought the bamboo
rod back, and nailed it out the way Sir George Gore had

taught him. The hopper floated in a pool of light, a soft reflection of the mother-of-pearl sky to the west. On the edge of the shadow beyond, the trout was feeding. Now it was invisible, and Mac was casting to a feeder he could sense but not see. He was also thinking of Lisette because she had changed recently. She had always been willing at houghmagandie. But when he came back from Virginia City, and again when he got back from Fort Union, she came to him as soon as he got into the courtyard at Yellowstone House and took him to their quarters and made love to him, fast and hard and with a little air of desperation. He found it intriguing, satisfying, and endearing.

He brought back the line, changed hoppers, and flicked the new bug into the current above the fish. He was thinking of his wives because he couldn't think of his son. Where was Thomas? Mac would have bet Thomas had checked his back trail, seen the numbers against him, and cleared out—maybe made tracks for Fort Alexander, maybe even gone home. He couldn't decide: Had Thomas meant to kill him? Why? Or was Thomas drunk, or drugged? Who had turned Thomas against his father? And how?

Mac tried to find it in his heart to harden himself against Thomas, to dispose of Thomas as he would a rabid wolf. Mac was a hard man. He could almost do it. The cold fact of that hot lead roaring past his nose, when he was naked and worshiping, that was nearly enough.

But not quite enough. He was in possession of a thousand pieces of evidence that commanded love instead of vengeance. He could feel in his arms where he had held Thomas the infant. Where he had circled the boy on the horse's back, teaching him to move with the animal. Where he steadied the big Hawken for the boy's first shot. Where he did what a father does. And these memories and a thousand others meant it couldn't be.

So Mac would have to understand better first. He had to know. He had rehearsed a hundred speeches from Thomas, a hundred explanations, but none of them seemed to promise sense. Mac knew that a man divided against himself is a man helpless in action, but he could do nothing about it. He fished instead.

He raised the line into the backcast and shot it forward again. This time he made a lousy cast and got the hopper, line, and thin gut leader in a pile halfway to where they belonged. Before he lifted the line off the water again, he heard a little splash upstream. He looked that way, into gray-lit clouds of the sunset, but didn't see anything. Probably a beaver. Beavers made that sort of splash when they slid down their mud-slick runs into the water. The run must be near that dark stump by the bank.

He cast again. The bait landed in just the right spot this time, where the current would drift it right where the fish was slurping up the bugs. He watched it sharply. The water dimpled right next to the hopper. Mac almost struck, but he waited. Nothing.

"The word for you is *traitor.*"

The whisper came from a little way upstream, the direction of the stump.

The stump had moved closer.

Thomas was clever. He had gotten down into the water to make the stump short and had turned sideways to disguise the dark human silhouette.

Now the stump stood up, turning to show shoulders and head.

"The word for what happens now is *die.*"

Cold rose into Mac from the river, the cold of melted snow, of bottom mud, of humus, of death.

"Thomas," Mac whispered fiercely, "get out of here."

"You aren't giving the orders anymore, old man."

"Get out!" Mac could project authority, even into a whisper.

"Got anything to say before you die?"

He slurred it a little—*anyshing.* Thomas was drunk. Mac eased his hand into his belt for his pistol. He told himself it was because even his whispering might bring the predators. He told himself he had no intention of shooting his son.

"Thomas," Mac practically hollered in a whisper, "there's

an Army bounty on you. Five hundred. They mean to collect it."

"Guess you don't have anything to say," Thomas said full voice, the words echoing over the soft dark of the river, words of doom. The click of his hammer echoed just as loud.

The Chapman kid fired from the bank. Thomas's head snapped back. His body toppled backward into the river. The moment Mac saw the kid's gun blaze, he fired at the shadowed form in the willows. He heard a satisfying gargled outcry.

Owen's rifle sounded almost simultaneously with Mac's pistol. Mac Maclean felt the fire in his chest. He realized he was in the river, on his back. He felt the little waves lap over his mouth and nose. He felt the delicious cool all over his body, soothing the fire inside.

As though from a great distance, he saw once more what had happened. Thomas. His words, the old family game. The predators creeping close, unheard, making out which form was which in the last light.

Mac knew he was sinking. He was drowning. He saw his wives and smiled at them. It crossed his mind to warn them against Owen, but that seemed unimportant. He smiled good-bye at them. He blessed his daughter Felice and her coming marriage to Zach Lawrence. He blessed his daughter Christine, palsied, perhaps the person he loved most unreservedly. He blessed Smith and spoke without words to his elder son of his great future. He blessed Thomas, tortured Thomas, his younger son, and urged him to live if life would let him.

Mac could feel the pleasant motion of the river rocking him gently, softly lifting his body and letting it dip, dancing his arms and legs fluidly to the rhythm of some stately melody—he could feel the music and so did not need to hear it. And in the grace of that last, lovely dance, Mac Maclean gave himself up to the dark, delicious grasp of the Yellowstone River.

≈ 17 ≈

"I'm sorry," Smith said.

Jim Sykes did not repeat those white-man words. He had left such words to white men all his life. He thought the body of his friend Mac Maclean, laid before the eyes of his wives, was enough.

Lisette walked to the body on the litter. She knelt in the dust of the courtyard, touched the place on the right breast where the wound was, and touched the hairline. Then she kissed the forehead lightly.

"Who?" said Annemarie, rigid where she stood, her voice soft and quaking, yet thunderous.

"Owen Mackenzie," said Smith.

Jim saw that Smith's head hung. Because he had gone off with Owen to fight, and that fighting had started this terrible pageant of blood, Smith felt responsible—shamed before his mothers and grandmother. This shame was something else Jim did not accept from white-man ways. A man did what he thought best and did not judge himself by what he couldn't foresee.

Calling Eagle and Peddler came hurrying out of the trading room. Calling Eagle's hand shot up to cover her mouth. Peddler came forward slowly. Jim saw tears flowing down his plump face.

"Tell the rest of it," said Annemarie.

Smith hesitated.

Jim spoke steadily. "They killed Thomas, too, and took away his head. We made a scaffold for the body."

Said flat, just like that. Thomas had turned against his father and should not be buried in the cemetery of

282

Yellowstone House. He was more of a Cheyenne in the end anyway—that was Jim's judgment. Annemarie nodded slightly. She understood and accepted.

"I'm sorry we were too late," Smith said numbly.

Jim and Smith had tracked Thomas, tracked him right to Mackenzie's camp. They had been less than a quarter mile away when they heard the shots, three quick ones, and then no more. They had come on in cautiously. In the dark they couldn't see who was who. Then a rider galloped off into the night. Soon they found the youngster, whoever he was, shot in the throat. And then Thomas, headless. The marks left where Thomas was dragged from the river led them to Mac in the shallow water.

Jim spent twenty minutes pumping water out of Mac's lungs, to no avail.

The next morning Jim put the pieces together from the signs. It was not difficult. Thomas had been shot by a pistol, the caliber too small for Mac. Mac had been shot by a heavy rifle, and only Owen had one. The kid was shot by Mac's pistol, and there could be only one reason to take Thomas's head.

Jim and Smith brought Mac home. There would be plenty of time for Owen Mackenzie.

2

They buried him on the bench above the fort, twenty feet from Skinhead and Blue. The autumn sky was opalescent, the wind still, the people numb. The little group—Annemarie and Lisette, Zach and Felice, Christine, Calling Eagle, and Peddler—all huddled together against the evening chill. No sound scratched the twilight but the crunch of the spade as Jim and Smith took turns digging the grave. Annemarie said words could wait until later—she would get Black Robe, Father De Smet, to speak some when he next passed, the right words.

Jim sniffed. De Smet had insisted for twenty years on saying the wrong words. Though ever cordial to Mac, he had never stopped insisting that Mac give up his second wife. Jim didn't think the priest knew the right words.

Jim and Smith also used the spade to set the little head marker chiseled by one of the workmen, a blank of cottonwood stating simply:

ROBERT BURNS MACLEAN
"Dancer"
1819–1865

Annemarie said she was setting Mac a little away from Skinhead and Blue so his family could surround him later, his two wives, his four children. Coming from a woman of the Cheyennes, who normally formed a new family immediately, that remark touched Jim.

Zach hoisted Christine and carried her down the hill to the fort—she liked to walk, regardless of her palsy, but she was slow, and everyone felt the need to be inside by the big fire. On the way she played her ocarina, the one gift from her father she loved. She stayed in the alto register, where the hollow, fluting notes sounded dark and haunting.

As the burial party wended its way downhill, Jim Sykes dropped back. A pitiful little group it seemed from above, freighted with grief, its frail and pathetic song lifted by a crippled girl. He looked out over the plains of the Yellowstone country. Yes, he thought, it is the best buffalo country in the world, a place of perfection. What is wrong is what white men have brought to it. Themselves.

3

It was the glummest dinner Jim could remember—not just because of their grief for Mac, but because he would normally have sparked the fun at meals. The entire crew of Yellowstone House was at the table—hunters, domestics, blacksmith, and the rest. Ironically, the table was abundant with good food, not only fresh meat and fowl, but corn, beans, and tomatoes. The gardens of Yellowstone House were flourishing.

After dinner they sat in the council room. Annemarie tapped a keg, and everyone sipped at one of Mac's good brandies. Lisette doodled at the clavichord Mac had found years before. Peddler stood up.

"When Mac sent me to Virginia City," he said, "he asked me to see the acting governor and get his help to have the bounty taken off Thomas's head." Peddler let that sit a moment. "And something else. I was to ask the governor to arrange for entrance to Dartmouth College for Smith."

No one knew what to say. Smith looked confused.

"It is done." Peddler stepped across and handed Smith a telegram. "Dartmouth College in New Hampshire is for Indian boys. It is free. Mac deposited plenty of money in the Bank of St. Louis for living expenses for five years."

Crinkling the telegram in his hands, Smith said half-heartedly, "It's too far."

His mother looked hard at him. "This is what he wanted. You will go."

Smith looked at the telegram. It said he was welcome, and that the best time to start would be this autumn.

"You have time to get down before the river freezes over," Annemarie said firmly.

Smith nodded.

"Besides, you love that stuff—science," Annemarie said.

Suddenly Lisette struck a big chord on the keyboard. "I say," she cried out, "let's dance! What would Mac want to do? Dance!"

It seemed to Jim a dumb idea, a levity forced when everyone was miserable. But Lisette started banging out something, one of maybe three tunes she knew, and Annemarie extended her hand to Smith, and they began to dance. In a moment Valdez, his wife, and the two cooks, Crow women married to hunters, joined in. The smith struck up a fiddle. Lisette gave way to him and made Jim dance with her.

He danced. He swigged at the brandy. He danced some more. He flirted with both Mac's wives, and both his daughters. And both the cooks. He lifted Christine clean off the ground and jigged a few steps with her. She giggled uncontrollably.

Jim even danced with Calling Eagle. The old woman, well, would-be woman, was wearing her infinitely knowing look. And before long Jim was happy—not forced happy but really happy, and no little drunk. He felt good. He felt liberated. He felt rip-roaringly ready to have a good time. He even slipped into one of the small rooms and had a quick good time on Valdez's wife, Guadalupe. Valdez didn't seem to notice. What the hell—women were in short supply. So Jim danced with Valdez. He danced over and over with Annemarie. He danced and drank till he couldn't make his legs work and lay on the floor laughing at himself.

And he didn't feel a bit guilty. "Bye, Dancer," he said to himself, and passed out.

≈ 18 ≈

October, 1865, Dust-in-the-face moon

Smith and Jim found the three women, Annemarie, Lisette, and Calling Eagle, where Guadalupe said, in the pantry, putting food into parfleches for the trip to Fort Laramie. Smith asked the foolish question, "What are you going to do?"

"Kill Owen Mackenzie. Ourselves." As she said it, Annemarie gave her son a brook-no-back-talk look.

"My God," Smith said. Even Jim was taken aback. Sometimes these women were white, and sometimes very Indian. Jim thought of a day twenty years past, when Skinhead warned Mac seriously that the women of the tribe he was marrying into were willing torturers.

Calling Eagle smiled a little at her grandson. "I killed a man before you were dreamt of," she said. Jim watched her big, capable hands stuffing the bags with containers of pemmican, like sausages. He believed it.

"You can't," said Smith. "Let us."

"You," Annemarie said pointedly, "are leaving for St. Louis tomorrow." In fact, Smith had built a bullboat today. Peddler would be going with him as far as Fort Union. "And we can. We will send you word. The message will be waiting at the Planter's house in St. Louis: 'Deed done.'"

Smith just shook his head.

"Owen Mackenzie will let me close," Lisette said easily. "Plenty close."

"Jim," asked Annemarie, "will you do us a favor? Take care of Yellowstone House for us."

Jim added it all up quickly. He understood. He nodded.

287

2

In the thinning light of October three squaws walked through the gate of Fort Laramie and went to the trading room. One was big as a sizable man, ageless as the prairie, with a weather-seamed face and work-gnarled hands. She carried herself with a certain pride, and some of the hang-around-the-fort Indians looked at her with deference, but the guard paid no attention.

The two others, one tiny, stood to the rear while the big one traded for sugar and coffee. They kept their faces deep in their blankets, so the clerk did not see their features. Nor did he wonder about them. Trade complete, the big one asked in Cheyenne if the clerk knew Owen Mackenzie.

The clerk sniffed out a laugh. "Everybody knows He Who Leaves His Enemies Headless."

He did not notice the big woman's reaction to that name, a flicker quickly controlled. "Where is he?" she asked evenly.

The clerk looked at the squaw, wondering why an Indian would ask after Mackenzie. Well, he decided, that's what you got when you were half-red nigger yourself. He said the half-breed was a scout guiding patrols, in and out of the fort every day or two.

Annemarie, Lisette, and Calling Eagle walked back to the Lakota encampment where they had pitched their lodge. They talked little, for there was little to say.

Each evening Lisette, Little One, stood outside the fort, wrapped to her eyes in a blue blanket with four vermilion-circled bullet holes. She wet the folded edges of the blanket with whiskey, for she wanted to stink. She looked pitiable, and all too vulnerable. Several times rough-looking young white men approached her with libidinous gleams in their eyes. She simply shook her head firmly—and waited. No one else paid her any mind. Another whore, an unpredictable one. Nor did anyone pay any mind to the tall old woman who sat against the wall of the fort nearby.

On the fourth evening, in the early dark, a big scout wandered near the tiny squaw, slaking his thirst from a tin cup.

"Owen," said Little One.

Mackenzie stopped. He came over to her, looking down from his height to her tininess. He had some difficulty making out her features. When he was sure who she was, he gave his roguish grin.

"I want to be with you," Lisette said.

The big man looked at her curiously. Then he laughed softly. "I don't want to be with you."

Behind him Calling Eagle was ready, but she didn't have to act yet.

Lisette made a lewd suggestion. Owen studied her face. It looked to him drawn, tense, abusable. Something appealed to Mackenzie—who knows what? Perhaps he wanted another triumph over Mac Maclean. Perhaps he merely felt lust. He nodded, once.

Lisette led the way to the willows a hundred yards off, not looking back. Owen watched her, intrigued, anticipating. He did not look behind him.

Little One walked in her measured way a few yards into the willows, turned to Owen, and dropped the blanket. She was wearing moccasins, leggings to her knees, and nothing more.

As Mackenzie eyed her nakedness, he felt heat rise in his loins. He started lowering his woolen trousers.

Annemarie Maclean waited until his trousers were half-way down. Then she stepped up softly behind him, raised her father's heavy sheep-horn cane with both arms, and hammered Owen Mackenzie in the head.

Mackenzie staggered to his knees, lowing like a cow

Calling Eagle grabbed him and jammed an oily rag into his mouth. Another outcry would not have been noticed anyway.

Calling Eagle took a knife out of her blanket and held it up in Owen's face. Mackenzie was conscious, and frightened, eyes wild as a horse's in a barn fire.

Calling Eagle had sharpened the boning knife well.
While Annemarie and Little One held Mackenzie's arms,
Calling Eagle made a careful incision all the way around
his penis and his scrotum. Then slowly and carefully, she
pared them off.

Mackenzie's eyes glazed at the beginning of this surgery
and did not change. He moaned low two or three times.
Calling Eagle held Owen's genitals in front of the castrated
man's eyes, then rubbed the bloody mess in his face.

Mackenzie did not pass out. Good, thought Annemarie.
He's strong—he's showing us he can stand this torture for
hours and hours. Well, we will use his strength to make
him hurt and hurt and hurt before he dies.

Hours later, when Owen Mackenzie was beyond feeling
pain, they severed his head from his neck.

$\approx$ **19** $\approx$

Lisette fooled Jim. Of Mac's women, she seemed to grieve the most passionately, but she also seemed the least forlorn. Annemarie was so listless all fall and winter Jim worried about her. Christine, usually plucky, virtually stopped making the effort to walk and withdrew into morose silence.

Just before Christmas, on a bitter Montana night, Jim finally touched Lisette in a suggestive way. She touched him back, and he thought they were headed to his quarters for a rousing hour. But she took his hands and held them, looked him in the eye, and said, "Later."

The next morning she asked him to make a midwinter trip to Fort Union to get supplies for the spring rise of the Yellowstone. That's when he knew for sure the women did not expect him to play the part of Mac's brother and take the family to his own bosom. Maybe Lisette wanted sex, but no more.

Jim did enjoy watching her get the affairs at Yellowstone House sorted out. It took months. First she got Zach Lawrence to realize Yellowstone House belonged to her and Annemarie, not to him. Before Thanksgiving Zach started building his own post on the Boulder River with Lisette's backing, taking Felice there for good. Lisette also persuaded Annemarie wordlessly that she had a life at Yellowstone House. And instead of trying to haul Christine's mind through the gates of numbness back into the world, Lisette stood aside and let Peddler and Calling Eagle do that slowly. Calling Eagle told her coyote stories, and

Peddler showed her how to train a dog to do crazy tricks, including many of Punch's.

The business part of Yellowstone House was less trouble for Lisette. She let the Company know that she was running the post, and that her credit was as good as Mac's. Deciding the post must be made a major way station for gold-seekers, she invested two decades of savings in expansion. Jim acted as her right-hand man, making the necessary trips to Fort Union and Fort Benton.

Jim came back from Union in early March, during a warm spell. The plains of the Yellowstone country were bare of snow, the cricks were on the rise, and the air felt warm as spring. Some of the hands said this was just a chinook, and in a week the country would be ice-blasted again. Jim said nothing, but he knew it was an early spring. He could smell it—when the grass began to grow again, the country smelled kind of ripe.

Lisette was making a special dinner, splurging nearly the last of the post's tinned vegetables on a go-away feast. Annemarie and Peddler were taking Christine on a trip to St. Louis, the palsied girl's first venture out of her home country. Everyone was thrilled to see how excited she was.

Jim had something special to add, a letter from Smith, written from St. Louis. It was the first word from him since he left.

After dinner, over pie made with canned peaches, Lisette read Smith's letter aloud to everyone. After an account of his downstream journey, Smith ended his letter with good news.

> *Robert Campbell continues to be a great good friend of our family. When I mentioned my interest in science, Campbell introduced me to a naturalist here. This man has gathered specimens of the plant life of the prairies of Missouri and Kansas, and he is classifying them and drawing watercolor pictures of them with a view to publication. I've spent a week with him, assisting in minor ways, and have learned how to classify plants according to genus and species. And*

I can tell you this: I have now come to believe that the white man's science is the most beautiful and powerful medicine in the world. In it rests the power to transform human life. My goal at Dartmouth will be to master science in a small way, and its application to healing as well as I can. And then I shall return to you and minister to our people as a physician. The best thing that has happened to me since I left you is this perception of high purpose. It fills my every day with a special hope and makes me relish the future.

Yet my single great sadness is that I will not see you for several years. It is impossible for me to think of passing so much time without touching you.

2

As Jim was drifting off to sleep, Lisette came slipping onto his pallet naked. At least she said it was Lisette—she wouldn't let him light a candle. They enjoyed each other in the utter darkness. Then she slipped out of bed, lit the candle, and let him see her tip to toe wearing only a crooked little smile. She still had a marvelous body, small but exquisitely shaped. Jim reached out and put an affectionate hand on her hip.

"So you didn't guess," she murmured.

"Guess what?"

"I was afraid you had seen." She moved his hand to her belly. Jim began to count months in his head—yes, it would be more than halfway.

"Mac left me this gift. I'm with child."

≈ **EPILOGUE** ≈

Lisette Genet Maclean sat on the south bank of the Yellowstone river, her skirts gathered between her knees. She bared her arms to the sun. It was May in Montana territory, the moon when the grass comes fully green, the prickly pear blooms, the cottonwoods leaf out thick, and the rivers rise. The moon of fecundity.

Lisette was watching a mayfly hatch. She had lots to be thinking about—such as the new season of trading, one crucial to Yellowstone House. But she was not thinking of her problems. Nor was she dwelling on the people she missed. Mac. Thomas. Smith, gone to Dartmouth College. Felice, married and living upriver. Christine, visiting St. Louis with Annemarie and Peddler. Lisette was just looking at the flies and the moving river.

The child stirred within her. Mac's child, due in June, the moon when the horses get fat. She was heavy with the child now and walked awkwardly.

Though Lisette had lived near the Yellowstone for twenty years, she was seeing mayflies rise off the water as though for the first time. It was a mother, this river, a mother to millions of creatures she had hardly dreamt of.

A week ago a Dr. Addison had come to Yellowstone House, an Englishman and a naturalist. Lisette knew this word "naturalist" only vaguely, from the letters Smith wrote home. She was hospitable to this Addison, though she didn't know what he wanted. When he said he was investigating insects of the Yellowstone country and classifying them by genus, species, and subspecies, she got more interested—this was science, the stuff Smith was learning.

One day Addison took Lisette along the riverbank to show her some of this science. All through the afternoon the naturalist kept exclaiming what a mother the river is, and he demonstrated. He showed her how crayfish put forth live babies in the water. How fish lay eggs in great sacs in the river bottom—Addison scooped some up for her, and they felt slimy. He pointed to the tiny, glistening eggs the water striders laid on plants that stood half in the water, and the shelled eggs the killdeer laid nearby.

Naturally, they spoke of the other creatures the river nurtures. The birds—geese, ducks, mergansers, golden-eyes, kingfishers, great blue herons, ospreys, bald eagles. The turtles and frogs, egg-layers both. The water snakes, who had live births, like mammals. Lisette didn't know what mammals were. Addison mentioned human beings, and river creatures such as the beaver and the otter. Lisette reflected that she dreamt often of otters recently, but she said nothing.

Addison showed her some plants that grew in the river—cattails, bur reeds, lichens, mosses—and mentioned others: wild rice, watercress, plantain, arrowroot.

And then they both spotted the small white insects that were suddenly flying everywhere, and Addison told an amazing story. These, he said, were mayflies. Every year about this time they populated the sky thick as milkweed. They lived just one day in the air, then died.

But what a life they had underwater. There they thrived for about two years. First they were eggs, motionless on the river bottom. Then they were larvae, in the water on plants, restless, feeding ferociously. Then they were pupae, cocoonlike creatures, dormant. And finally they hatched and rose to the water's surface. If a fish didn't eat them there, they flew for one day, and died.

Lisette had seen these flies every spring of her twenty years here and paid them no attention. Yet this was what Smith, her son, was learning in college. And this kind of understanding would in time make him a physician, able to heal the wounded and the sick. She didn't see how, but that's what Smith said, and Addison confirmed.

She put a bare foot in the river. It was cold—the Yellowstone was always cold. Whenever she touched its cold, she felt in the remote reaches of her mind, below the surface of consciousness, Mac's death in these waters.

Later in the summer, though, the river would be warmer, and she would swim. Lisette liked to swim.

She reached down with cupped hands, dipped water from the river, and drank deep. It tasted good, so she did it again.

She felt sleepy. The glare of the afternoon sun on the water made it hard to keep her eyes open. She tucked her feet to her bottom, lay on her side, and pulled a shawl over herself. She closed her eyes. Perhaps she would doze off.

Half-waking, perhaps half-dreaming, Lisette pictured herself swimming in the Yellowstone. This time she did not see herself alone. She saw millions of creatures swimming in the great river—otters, beaver, fish, turtles, frogs, mayflies, and myriad others. She was one of them, another living creature, busily sensing and seeking, feeding and frolicking, struggling, birthing, being.

She smiled in her dream. The child stirred within her.

ABOUT THE AUTHOR

WINFRED BLEVINS was born in Arkansas, attended Hannibal-LaGrange College, and graduated from the University of Missouri, where he spent most of his time playing music and writing bad poetry. He went on to receive graduate degrees from Columbia University and the University of Southern California, and taught at several colleges and universities while devoting his "free time" to more music and (better?) poetry.

The Rockefeller Foundation saved Blevins from life as an academic by making him a fellow in its Project for the Training of Music Critics. Thus trained, he reviewed concerts and plays for *The Los Angeles Times*, and became principal music and drama critic of *The Los Angeles Herald-Examiner*, and later entertainment editor and principal movie critic of that paper.

In 1973 he published his first book, *Give Your Heart to the Hawks*, an anecdotal tribute to the mountain men, which has been in print ever since. Blevins is also the author of innumerable newspaper and magazine articles, four screenplays which producers have been wise enough to buy but not yet to produce, and two previous novels about the mountain men, *Charbenneau: Man of Two Dreams*, and *The Misadventures of Silk and Shakespeare*. He is general editor of the series "Classics of the Fur Trade."

As a young man Blevins fell in love with the West, and has spent as much time as possible climbing its mountains, rafting its rivers, hiking its deserts, and exploring its history. He lives with his wife and the youngest of his three children in Jackson Hole, Wyoming.

≈   RIVERS WEST   ≈

If you enjoyed Winfred Blevins's epic tale, THE YEL-
LOWSTONE, be sure to look for the next installment
in the RIVERS WEST saga at your local bookstore.
Each new volume will take you on a voyage of exploration along one of the great rivers of North America with
the intrepid pioneers who challenged the unknown.

*Here is an exciting preview of the next book in
Bantam's unique new historical series*

≈   RIVERS WEST Volume 2   ≈

The
Smoky Hill

by Don Coldsmith
Author of *The Spanish Bit Saga*

Gabe squatted on his heels and perused the heavy structure that stood in the flat beside the river. Massive in design, it reminded him of a picture he had seen once. It had been a picture in a book, a drawing of a castle. In front of the castle had been ladies with funny-looking dunce caps on their heads, and some knights on horses carrying long lances. He wasn't sure what it was all about, and why the women had to wear dunce caps. Or, for that matter, why the horses all seemed to be work horses. As far as he could remember, there hadn't been a good saddle horse in the bunch.

But what had really intrigued him as a boy was the castle. There was a moat and a drawbridge, and turrets and towers, and a walkway around the top of the wall. There were men standing on the walkway, holding weapons. He had thought a lot about that picture since. With a set-up like that, and enough supplies and water, a few stout men could hold off an army.

Now he had to admit, Bent's Fort wasn't exactly a castle, but it looked like one. The yellow adobe of the walls, several feet thick at the ground, rose impressively to the towers and the catwalk around the top. Part of the wall, not protected by the catwalk, had been planted with cactus along its top. They were in bloom now, reds and pinks and bright yellows. Real pretty, Gabe thought, but a good idea, too. Anybody trying to go over the wall would find it tough going.

His eyes drifted to the main gate. That would have been the drawbridge of his castle. The gate at Bent's was built of thick planks of wood, reinforced with iron fittings. It could be burned, he supposed, if it came to it, but it would be tough. Tough on the one who had to light the fire, because the gate was directly under the catwalk. Men above could shoot down on any attackers.

One thing intrigued him, the massive beam that supported the arch over the gate. It was a single tree trunk, one of the huge cottonwoods that grew up and down the Arkansas. It must be ten, twelve paces long, and nearly as thick as the height of a man. The log was embedded in the yellow adobe and plastered snugly at each supporting end. He wondered how they'd gotten it up there. It would have taken a lot of mules or oxen just to drag it from the river, let alone hoist it into place. Probably ropes and pulleys, he figured, after the walls were at the top of the door opening.

Well, no matter. He knocked the dottle from his pipe and reached to refill it. Damn, no tobacco! He'd forgotten. It was so pleasant to sit or lie around in the summer sun, it made a man forget things like buying more tobacco. There had been a time when he'd doubted if he'd ever be warm again, when they were starving out last winter in the Sierras's snows. He didn't hold it against Captain Fremont. None of the men did. They'd had to eat some things that would gag a maggot, and it had been a close call, but they'd come through. The men would follow the Captain through hell if he said so. Especially if he could get Kit Carson to guide them again. Kit and Tom Fitzpatrick and Joe Walker had brought them out.

He stood and stretched, and sauntered down toward the post to get his tobacco. The sun was warm on the back of his buckskin shirt. But what a day! The sky was clear and blue, and the south breeze fresh and clean. This was a proper way to live.

He wondered sometimes if his brother James, back in Illinois, ever thought about it. His brother was a little older, a lot more set in his ways. James had a wife and three, no, four youngsters. Scratched dirt for a living, and seemed to like it. That was all right, Gabe figured, for them that couldn't help it, but it wasn't for him. He had to see what was over the next hill. Maybe that's what had attracted him to John Fremont. The Captain had the same sort of gift.

He looked across the flat toward the Arkansas. There in

front of the Bent brothers' trading post, called Bent's Fort almost since it was started, was a flat area maybe half a mile in diameter. It was circled by an ox-bow of the river, and the level ground and lush grass made it a favorite camping ground for those who came to trade, both red and white. There were at least 150 lodges, Gabe guessed, in the near meadow and scattered along the stream. He could identify an encampment of Cheyennes, and some lodges that might be Comanche on beyond. A group of Kiowa lodges were separated from the Cheyennes by a small band of Arapahoes, whose red-dyed tassels on their smoke-poles plainly spoke their identity.

Two days, it would be July 4th, Gabe recalled. Independence Day, 1844. There were enough Americans here, they'd likely have a celebration, he figured, with speeches and all. More important, a shooting match, and then everybody'd get a little drunk and disorderly and see if they could find a woman. Some of the girls looked pretty good, after a winter in the mountains, and some of Fremont's party had already paired off. Gabe had his eye on a lanky Cheyenne who had smiled at him yesterday.

He didn't see her. He walked on down to the gate and into the adobe-walled courtyard, where there was a little more hustle and bustle than in the Indian camp. He circled past a half-unloaded wagon, around the frame of the big hide-press, and started toward the store.

"Booth!" someone called.

Gabe turned, identified the speaker, Captain John Fremont.

"Yes, sir?"

He altered his course to move over toward where Fremont stood in a doorway.

"Gabe," the Captain began, "are you busy?"

"No, sir. Just goin' to the store."

"Go ahead, Gabe. But then, start to pass the word. Meeting tonight in front of my tent, at dark."

"All right, Captain. Are we movin' out?"

Fremont smiled.

"Not yet. We'll stay for Independence Day. Just spread the word."

"Yes, sir."

Later, as darkness fell, the party assembled. The breeze across the high prairie grew chill. Gabe sauntered in and squatted next to Shaughnessy. He looked around the loose circle at the men he'd spent nearly a year with. All were burned brown by the sun and wind, except for a couple. Dodson, of course, wasn't going to change color, much. He was a Negro, and a good man. Gabe wondered some why Jake Dodson had wanted to come. He wasn't hired on in St. Louis, like most of the men. He'd come all the way from Washington to follow the Captain. Some kind of a dream in that woolly head.

Preuss was another that the sun wasn't going to change much. His blond German skin never did anything but burn redder. There was a man really hard to figure out. He was the Captain's map-maker, always busy scribbling notes when he wasn't taking compass readings or studying plant specimens. He always seemed uncomfortably out of place, with his thick spectacles and clothes that would look more at home in town. Besides his scribbling at his job, Karl Preuss was always working on a continued letter or diary for his wife. That was written in German. At least, that's what Zindle said. Gabe wouldn't know. He couldn't read English *or* German.

The joke among the men was that Preuss wrote his private journal in German so Fremont wouldn't know how it maligned him. It was no secret that the German often disagreed with the Captain's decisions. He said so, to Fremont's face. Even stranger, maybe, was that the Captain tolerated it. In turn, there was none in the party more loyal than Preuss.

Gabe looked on around the circle. Not as many as they'd started with. They'd only lost one man, it was true. Even that wasn't in the really tough times in the mountains. It had been in a highly improbable ambush in Ute country on the way back. And not even by Utes, but by Diggers.

A couple of the men had left the expedition, with permission, at Captain Sutter's place, Sacramento. They'd wanted to stay there and settle, and Sutter was encouraging that, seemed like. For that matter, Captain Fremont was, too. Then poor Badeau had accidently shot himself crossing the Sevier.

The scouts sat a little aside, as if they were a bit different. Part of the reason the party had survived the mountains, Gabe knew, was because they had the best scouts in the country. Kit Carson, quiet and shy, short and not very impressive. Not in looks, anyhow. He and Fremont seemed exact opposites, yet they were close friends, from the time of the expedition in '42. Carson had come up from Taos to join them last summer after they got to Colorado, and had brought Godey with him.

Tom Fitzpatrick, next to Kit, there, had been with them since St. Louis. One of the old fur trappers, Fitz was said to know the West like the back of his hand. That was an unusual hand to know, too, crippled from an accident with a rifle. Gabe had never heard the details, but old Fitz had taken a rifle ball through the wrist part. As a result, he was known to the Indians as Broken Hand. While they were at Sutter's, one of the settlers had asked Fitz about the hand. The old mountain man had stopped the stupid questioner cold with two terse words: "Got keerless."

Fitz also had the distinction of having guided the first wagon trail to travel clear across the continent to Oregon, two years before.

Next to him sat Joe Walker. What Fitz was to the northern route, Joe was to the southern trail. He'd laid out, a couple of years ago, what folks were already calling the "California Trail." Walker wasn't properly a part of the expedition. He'd just joined them in California, out of interest in the mapping job, and traveled back to Bent's with them. Gabe had been fascinated to watch the three of them, Fitz, Walker, and Carson, as they traveled the way back. A man could learn a right smart, Gabe figured, just followin' those three.

Fremont was counting now, half to himself.

". . . twenty-four, twenty-five, twenty-six. Yes, all here."

He paused, cleared his throat, and the murmur of conversation withered and died.

"Well, men, are you getting rested up?"

There were nods and mutterings of assent.

"Very good. Now, I want to tell you about the rest of the trip."

There were a few intense but very brief murmurs.

"We'll stay here a couple more days, through Independence Day."

A brief cheer quieted as Fremont held up his hand.

"But the next morning at dawn, we move out. Carson and Walker will remain here at Bent's. Fitz goes with us. There will be twenty-six of us, and we'll map one of the rivers of Kansas Territory on the way home.

"Mr. Bent tells me it's almost due north of here. We'll start northeast when we leave the Arkansas, and strike the Kansas in a few days. It's the only stream of any size. Oh, yes, it's not called the Kansas until farther east. Out here it's the Smoky Hill."

≈ 2 ≈

Gabriel had a vicious hangover. Several of the others suffered, too, from self-inflicted headaches and rotten stomachs. Gabe could not have vouched for them, but for himself, he thought he had never been so sick. His stomach churned with the swaying motion of the mule, and with each wave of churning, he vowed never again to touch whiskey. It was a false vow and he knew it, but it seemed like a good idea at the time.

Once he stopped and vomited beside the trail, vomited on an empty stomach, nothing but mucus and green bile. He had vomited all else long ago. Why in God's name, he wondered, would a man do something like this to himself? He had wondered that before, as he had tried to shake off the ravages of a night's revelry.

This, of course, had been a day *and* a night, in celebration of Independence Day. There had been a ceremony and speeches, of which Captain Fremont's had been the best. Lord, how that man could get folks excited with his dream of the United States stretching across the mountains to the western sea.

"He shore talks good," Shaughnessy muttered in Gabe's

ear as they applauded and whooped and hollered when the Captain sat down.

"Yep. He means to do it, too," Gabriel said.

"Do what?"

"Hell, you know, Ike. Map the damn thing so settlers kin come. What'd you think we're doin'?"

They slapped each other's backs and laughed uproariously. Everything was beginning to be funny as the fiery trade whiskey started to make itself felt. Gabe almost forgot the vague feeling he'd had a time or two that maybe he didn't *want* settlers runnin' all over the damn country and spoilin' it.

There were games and races and shooting contests and more shooting, just in the air, to celebrate the patriotism of the day. Gabriel won a tomahawk throw, and collected a little tobacco and a knife from his bets. Then he promptly lost it all in bets on a shooting match. The whiskey was by this time making the target unsteady.

He was urged to bet again, but had nothing left except his rifle. Even in his fuzzy-thinking condition, he could remember some things: survival depended on his rifle, his knife, and his mule. His tomahawk might be handy, too. Very versatile. But, he *could* do without it. The other items were necessities. He could wager his clothes before his rifle. Actually, the rifle and mule were part of the agreement when he signed on with Fremont. Each man was to furnish his own weapon and transportation.

The gun was a big bore .58 caliber made by the Hawken brothers in St. Louis. The ball, as big as his thumb, dwarfed the .30 caliber projectiles of the long-barreled rifles made for the Kentucky frontier. Some of the men in Fremont's party favored the longer barrel as more accurate and compromised on a .40 caliber size. There were many arguments around the campfires. For Gabriel Booth, however, the answer was plain. No matter how accurate, a smaller bullet was simply unsafe in the face of a charging grizzly. The "real-bear," as the Indians said, the bear with the white-tipped fur, the bear-that-walks-like-a-man. This creature, "Old Ephraim," the mountain men sometimes called him, was one to be reckoned with. He was a far cry from the black bear of the eastern woodlands. Yes, when the real-bear was around, Gabe wanted a big enough chunk of lead to stop him in his tracks.

It was handy for buffalo, too. He'd seen a bull with a lung shot that should have killed it stand around a while before it even lay down, when hit by Shaughnessy's .41. Nope, he wanted a load that would tumble a running buffalo when the ball slammed into meat and bone. He liked the balance of the gun, the way it lay across his thighs on the fork of the mule's saddle. The short country cousin of the fine Pennsylvania-made small-bore guns was especially for Western use, for the saddle, for the larger game of the West.

Yes, Gabriel was proud of his Hawken, the costliest single item he had ever bought in his life. It was a part of him, now, along with the bullet mold that turned out the big shiny marbles that the gun hurled. Gabe was pleased with the accuracy, too. He had a hunch that on open prairie the heavy bullet would be less affected by the wind than a lighter ball, hence *more* accurate, even with the short barrel. Usually he shot well enough at least to support his argument. That had made the loss of the contest at Bent's even more disheartening.

To make matters even worse, he had consumed enough more whiskey that he fell asleep and missed part of the revelry. When he did waken, shadows were growing long. He ate some crisp-broiled hump ribs, which did not set too well on his stomach, and went to look for the leggy Cheyenne. He knew where her lodge was located, but instead of the girl he encountered her irate father, who threatened him with a heavy stone war ax and in sign-talk, told him to be gone.

Ah, well, Cheyennes were funny about their women, Gabe told himself as he wandered off into the twilight. Not like some tribes. Mandans, for instance. They'd let you have a go at a wife or daughter and think nothing of it. Or that Pawnee he'd had for a little while, in '42. There was a proper woman. He recalled her warm, yielding softness in the sleeping-robes, and thought again of the long-legged Cheyenne.

Eventually he did find a woman who was willing. He never was sure what her tribe was, but she used sign-talk well, and it didn't matter. It didn't even matter that she was fat and a little ugly. What did matter was that when they wandered off into the dark a little way and she spread her blanket, Gabe was unable to perform. Too much whiskey, he figured. The woman was a little peeved at first, and then decided it was funny. She laughed at him and called him, in sign-talk, "horse-without-stones."

She jumped up, swept the blanket around her shoulders, and strode back toward a group of lodges, loudly talking in her own tongue. Gabe buttoned his pants and followed her, weaving a little as he walked. As he came among the lodges, children began to point and giggle, and adults to chuckle at him. Damn! Did the woman have to tell everything she knew? He wheeled and staggered out into the dark a little way to puke, then managed to collapse, not quite in the vomitus, and fell into a drunken slumber.

He was wakened by someobdy falling over him in the dark. He rolled over and cursed the intruder, who beat a hasty retreat. Finally, Gabe gathered enough strength to get to his feet and lurch unsteadily back to his blankets, where he collapsed in a stupor that would pass for sleep. He had hardly closed his eyes, it seemed, when Shaughnessy shook him awake.

"Come on, Gabe! It'll be daylight afore long. You know the Captain likes to make twenty mile a day!"

So now, here he was, swaying along the back of Rabbit, trying to recover his balance and wishing his stomach would settle down. One thing, Rabbit was a dependable mule. A claybank dun color, of unknown parentage. Some of the men laughed at him for his choice of mounts, but he didn't care much. He knew what was needed, and he favored a mule for the job. Let the others spend all they wanted for their hot-blood Arabians and Thoroughbreds. Their horses were pretty, sure. But, compared to a mule, they were stupid, Gabe figured. Give 'em half a chance, the damn things would founder.

This morning, Rabbit's usually smooth walk seemed to hammer his spine into the base of his skull, and when the Captain moved out in a trot for a little while sometimes, it became sheer torture. He went so far as to wonder if he should try to trade for a day, and maybe ride Ike Shaughnessy's half-thoroughbred chub. No, he couldn't do that, he decided. That would settle the mule-horse argument for all time, and the others would never let him forget it.

So, he suffered. Gradually, he began to feel a little better, and after the noon halt, he was able to raise his head and look around a little. Maybe, even, he was going to make it.

They were following a sort of trail, he noticed, that paralleled the Arkansas. Their general direction was east, with the river on their right, its winding course marked by the thin strip of timber along its banks. To their left was open prairie, the bright green of the gently rolling country unbroken by any vegetation except the grass. Both in that direction and to the south, beyond the river, the grass stretched away to the horizons. Ahead, as far as they could see, and behind, too, Gabe knew that the grass reached to the foothills of the mountains. He had never seen the ocean, but he had an idea that it would look like this. Gentle swells, and the ripple of the grasses in the south breeze, looking at a distance a lot like water. He rather liked the feel of the wide sky and far horizons. Out here, a man could lean back in the saddle and really stretch his eyes. He was feeling better.

The trail moved away from the river for a mile or so. Or rather, the river left the trail. There was a long bend or ox-bow that would have been a long way around, so the trail just cut across. This must be an old, old trail, he figured, used by the Indians for generations. What was it, one of the traders at Bent's had called it? The Southwest Trail? Go south and west out of Bent's, it was said, you could follow it through the mountains to the Mexican settlements beyond. The Santa Fe Trail. It would be interesting to know what was there. Maybe Fremont would try something like that trip next time. There was a lot of trade.

These wandering thoughts were interrupted as Captain Fremont rode up alongside him for a moment. Gabe nodded a greeting, and noted a twinkle in the Captain's eye.

"Well," Fremont said cheerfully, "feeling better, Horse-Without-Balls?"

Jesus, thought Gabriel, does *everybody* know?

≈ 3 ≈

It had been a fairly easy day's travel that first day down the Arkansas. At least, it would have been, if it had not been for recent overindulgence. Still, Gabriel Booth felt progressively better as the afternoon passed. By the time the Captain ordered camp, Gabe was enjoying the easy travel, the cooling south breeze of the high prairie, and the distant vistas of waving grass.

True, he had taken a lot of ribald remarks about his manhood, but there were others who had drunk to excess and had made fools of themselves, too. Since these were among the individuals who would have been Gabe's chief tormentors, they were, for the most part, rather quiet. He recalled something about those who lived in glass houses. He'd never seen a glass house, even in St. Louis. Probably there wasn't any such thing, but it was an interesting idea. How in the hell, he wondered, would the women-folk undress? He assumed that if anyone had a glass house, it would be white folks. Indian lodges never had any glass windows, no glass at all. . . .

Rabbit was moving well, and he was beginning to appreciate the mule's comfortable walk again. He hadn't felt like vomiting since right after the noon halt. Yes, it looked now like he might make it, and live to see another day. Damn, he'd be more careful next time.

Still, he was glad when Captain Fremont called the halt to make camp. It was a good camp site, a grassy meadow to furnish graze for the animals, and the quiet murmur of the Arkansas just to the south. There were trees along the river, mostly big cottonwoods and scraggly willows. Seemed like it should be no trouble to find wood for camp fires, but it proved to be in short supply. One after the other, wood-gatherers came back from the river's timber strip empty-handed, or with only a handful of small twigs.

Well, they'd encountered the same thing on the Platte, Gabe recalled. There were camp sites along the river trails in the prairie that had been camping places for generations. They were favorable because of grass and water and location. Every party of travelers had to have a camp fire, either to cook on, or just for warmth. As fast as the thin strip of timber grew and limbs died and became useful for fuel, they were utilized.

It was no problem. Without even commenting, the men turned from the river and began to forage across the meadow and up the slope, picking up dried buffalo dung. Gabriel soon had an armful. Buffalo chips stacked well. Many were nearly a foot across, an inch thick, and could be stacked in the crook of an arm like a huge stack of pancakes. In a short while, fires were going and the place looked like a regular camp.

There was no cooking to be done, since they carried no fresh meat. The company sat around chewing strips of jerky, or some of the pemmican that they had acquired at Bent's. William Bent, whose Cheyenne wife gave him a good rapport with the Indians, was noted for the quality of the supplies that he traded. Pemmican bought at Bent's would be of good quality, they had been told, and found it true.

Gabe and Ike Shaughnessy sat with several others around the smouldering fire of chips. In actuality, the fire would not have bee. necessary. The night was warm, and the mosquitos not really bad. Not numerous enough to warrant a smoke fire to repel them, at any rate. No, the campfire was a ritual. There was something about a fire that was a declaration to whatever spirits might inhabit the vast wildness of the prairie. A statement in attempt, perhaps to communicate with these spirits. "Here, we intend to camp," it was saying, as if asking permission to do so. Of course, Gabriel Booth and the others did not think these thoughts. It was unnecessary. The ritual, through the centuries, had become so ingrained in the human race that the first thought in establishing any camp was where the lighting of the fire would take place. It was as natural as the dedication of the Indians' first buffalo kill each season.

"We are sorry to kill you, my brother," the medicine man would solemnly intone, "but our life depends on you and your kind."

And life would go on without pause. So it was around the fires in the gathering twilight. Gabriel reached to toss another chip from the pile, and enountered one a little fresher than the rest.

"Jesus!" he complained. "Somebody picked one too green!"

Everybody in the little circle chuckled at his complaint.

"Reckon thet's mine, Gabe," Ike Shaughnessy drawled. "I had to foller thet bull nearly three mile afore he dropped it. I caught it just 'fore it hit the ground."

The others laughed.

Gabe hefted the big disc, slightly damp on the underside, and eyed Shaughnessy speculatively. Ike prepared to defend himself as Gabe rose to his feet.

"Aw, come on, Gabe," he pleaded. "Ain't no harm done. Thet ain't really mine, anyhow. I was jest funnin'!"

Gabriel rose with dignity and took a stance like a discus thrower.

"Well, we can't have one this fresh in camp," he said seriously. "I'll put it back to ripen some."

With a mighty heave, he sent the chip spinning across the meadow. The evening breeze caught the leading edge of the spinning chip and lifted it, to soar majestically, on and on. Finally it began to wabble, lost momentum, and sliced to the right to tumble to the ground, where it disintegrated. The men around the fire howled with delight.

"Hooray!" yelled Ike Shaughnessy.

"Let's see you beat that throw!" challenged Gabe.

"Lemme see a chip."

Ike snatched up a buffalo chip and gave it a toss. It wobbled, broke in two, and fell, a very poor showing.

"Ike, you just don't get the hang of it," said Gabe seriously. "Here, I'll show you."

He selected another chip, balanced it carefully, and let fly in the same southerly direction as the first. This time, the drier, and hence lighter projectile caught the breeze and fluttered a moment, then leveled out in flight, hovering, hanging, soaring on toward the river. The group by the fire cheered it onward.

"Come on, come on!"

"'At's it! A little more!"

"Hooray!"

Ike, a little miffed, watched until the chip crashed to earth.

"Okay!" he conceded. "For distance, anyhow. But what about aim? Kin you hit anything? Gimme a good-balanced chip here."

He dropped to his knees to sort through the pile of dung, pawing the poorer specimens aside, choosing one or two uniform chips to lay tentatively in front of him.

The others were laughing, yelling, and cheering Shaughnessy on. He finally rose, examining an especially fine specimen.

"Yep, this'll do. Now, you see thet willow bush over there?"

He swung an arm to begin his throw, and as he turned, saw a tall slender figure standing near.

"What the hell is going on?" Captain Fremont asked in wonderment.

His stern visage indicated that he had been watching, and understood quite well. Ike Shaughnessy straightened and stood awkwardly, glancing from the Captain to the chip in his hand.

"We was havin' a match, Cap'n, sailin' turds. Want to try?"

He extended the buffalo chip generously.

"No, thank you, Shaughnessy," Fremont answered, tight-lipped. "Another time, maybe. Right now I want to see you and Booth. Follow me."

Without waiting, the Captain turned on his heel and strode off into the twilight. Shaughnessy stood staring at the buffalo chip for a moment as if wondering how it had got into his hand. Then he dropped it on the pile, and the two men followed the retreating form.

Gabriel was puzzled. Why would the Captain care about a little fun? Sometimes he even joined in. Sometimes the captain was a hard man to understand. His head was likely always busy, with all his high-falutin' ideas about opening the West.

Fremont stopped and turned on his heel, to stand waiting as the two approached.

"Well," he began, "now that you've recovered from Independence Day, I wanted to ask you two. Do either of you know the country to the north of here?"

The two looked at each other and back to Fremont.

"No, sir," began Gabe, "not till you get to the Platte."

"Shaughnessy?"

"Nope. I been down the Santa Fee Trail, but just as far as Bent's."

"I see. Apparently we have only Mr. Bent's general directions, then."

"Cap'n," inquired Shaughnessy, puzzled. "This ain't about buffalo turds?"

"*What?* Of course not!" Fremont chuckled.

The others relaxed a little.

"Look, I want one of you to ride point in the morning, a mile or so out, with Mr. Fitzpatrick. We don't know what's out there, exactly. Shouldn't be any trouble, but he'll pick a good way to go, in case there's any rough country."

"What direction, Captain?" Gabe inquired. "North?"

"No, about northeast, according to Bent."

"Are there s'posed to be any Indians in that area?"

"Probably not. Pawnees, maybe, but they'd be farther east, I think. They're on government rations, though. Still, if you see any Indians, you'll come right back to the main party. So, who wants to go?"

"I will, Captain," Gabe said quickly, before Shaughnessy could answer.

There was still just enough kid in him to relish the idea of crossing unexplored country with the great mountain man, Broken Hand Fitzpatrick.